Third Time Lucky

Marie O'Connell

'I do Believe in love, its wonderful -especially love third time around, its even more precious, its kind of amazing.' Robin Williams

'I agree.' Marie O'Connell

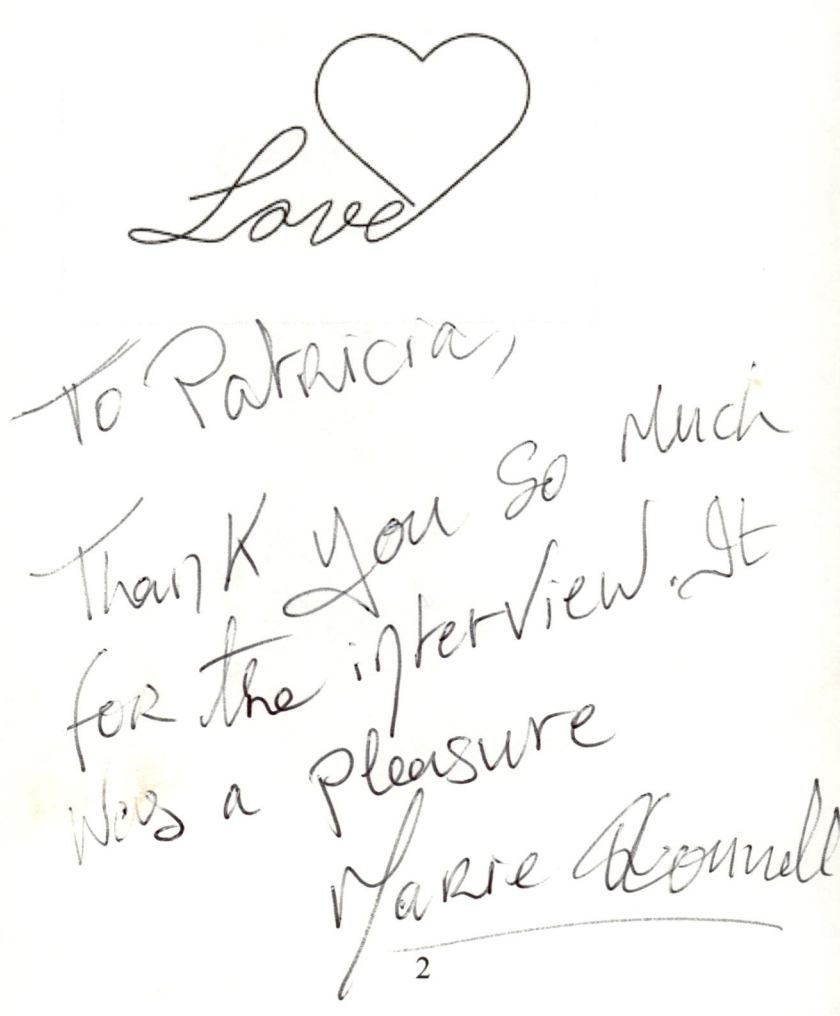

Love ♡

To Patricia,
Thank you so much for the interview. It was a pleasure
Marie O'Connell

Published in 2023 by FeedARead.com Publishing

Copyright © Marie O'Connell.

The author or authors assert their moral right under the Copyright, Designs and Patents Act, 1988, to be identified as the author or authors of this work.

All Rights reserved. No part of this publication may be reproduced, copied, stored in a retrieval system, or transmitted, in any form or by any means, without the prior written consent of the copyright holder, nor be otherwise circulated in any form of binding or cover other than that in which it is published and without a similar condition being imposed on the subsequent purchaser.

A CIP catalogue record for this title is available from the British Library.

'The best time to plan a book is while you're doing the dishes.' **Agatha Christie**

'I did it while dating' **Marie O'Connell**

In Dedication

This book is dedicated to my favourite sister-in-law Caroline. She may read this book, but she will never need it, as she is married to my favourite brother, yes, he may be my only brother, but he is the best. He knows how lucky he is to have Caroline as his wife.

Caroline may have joined our family through marriage, but we always appreciate how she has always been there for our brother, our parents, and us, through the good times and the bad.

Caroline you are a great sister-in-law, wife to our brother, and mother to our beautiful nieces Laura and Rachel. Thank you for the special things you do for our dad.

'We must find time to stop and thank the people who make a difference in our lives.' JFK

'Thank you Caroline' Marie O'Connell

In Thanks

Writing a book is something I always wanted to do. It is harder than I thought but more rewarding than I could ever have imagined. After I wrote my first book, I really wanted to write another one, so I was not a one hit wonder. This my second book would not have been possible without my dating friends. There are too many of you to mention and you would not appreciate if I did. However, you will recognise yourselves in my dating stories section.

I am eternally grateful to all my Pierce uncle's Mike, Pat, Tom, James, John and remembering Simon who I never met and my O'Connell uncle's Michael, Lawrence and Thomas you were all gentlemen. To my Pierce Aunts, Mamie, Kathleen, Ellen, Pauline and Mags, who took me on one of my first dates.

To my O'Connell aunt's Margaret, Kitty and Anna, your beauty and grace astounds me to this day. To the Pierce and O'Connell cousins, you are a great bunch and I love you all. To my lovely nieces and nephews Laura, Rachel, Ciara, Cathal, Eoin, Anna and Bobby you are our future.

'When we give cheerfully and accept gratefully, everyone is blessed.' **Maya Angelou**

'I am Blessed' **Marie O'Connell**

In Thanks

In my first book,' Community at Heart' I thanked my friends, but I will continue to thank you in each book I write as without you I would not be who I am. Each one of you have held me together more than once over the years. To my long-time friends, Ena, Grainne, Geraldine, Maura, Therese, Shirley, Caroline and Jane, you sustained me in ways I never knew I needed. To my newer friends Liz, Roisin, Carmel, Sandra, and Theresa, thank you for the never-ending wine and whine.

To the amazing support of my square table friends Linda, Ania, Marianna, and Dave with whom you can never say the wrong thing.

To my work colleagues in the University of Limerick especially Dee, Mamie, Emily, Eimear, Noreen, Sinead and Cathal, the next book is about you.

To my writers group the Killaloe Hedge School especially to David and Kathleen. To Maggie you are amazing. Your encouragement, support and vision helped me bring my book to being.

Writing this book about the story of internet dating was fun for me. I am forever indebted to those of you who shared your stories. It is because of your honesty and candidness that I have a lot to say, on the subject of dating at a certain age.

'The smallest act of kindness is worth more than the grandest intention.' Oscar Wilde.

'I am surrounded by kind people' Marie O'Connell

In Thanks

Thank you to the men in my life, I am blessed with the best father in the world, Patrick, the best partner in the world, Kerry, the best brother in the world, Patrick and the very best son in the world, Niall.

To the ladies in my life, my sisters, Claire and Clodagh, my sister-in-law, Caroline, you are the best a girl could ask for.

To my daughters Tara and Niamh. It is a miracle you survived me as your mother. To my wonderful designer, Tara, who designed the cover, I love it. To my wonderful editor Niamh, thank you for your constant help.

To all the wonderful staff in 'Brian Boru' you nourish my body and keep me sustained.

To 'The Washerwoman' you nourish my soul and keep me grounded.

To all the Pointe Vecchio crew especially Andrew, Ryan, Eilis, Dan, Holly and Eve you continue to keep me hungry for life. This book would not have been written without you.

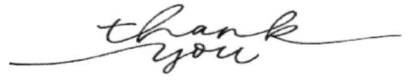

'Keep love in your heart. A life without it is like a sunless garden when the flowers are dead. The consciousness of loving and being loved brings a warmth and a richness to life that nothing else can bring.' Oscar Wilde

'I am so lucky to love and be loved.' Marie O'Connell

In Memory

Always in memory of Brid O'Connell even though you would not have approved of this book.

Remembering my auntie Mags who took me on one of my first dates to the Shannon Rugby Club, Limerick.

"I've learned that people will forget what you said, people will forget what you did, but people will never forget how you made them feel." Maya Angelou

'Mam you always made us feel loved.'
Marie O'Connell

Introduction

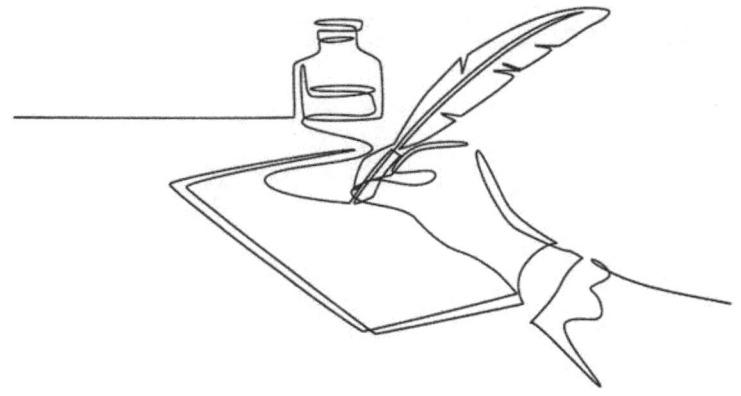

Introduction

Not too long ago I was in the depths of single-dom. I had not had a serious date for some time. I decided it was time to find someone to enjoy and share my life with. I knew this would not be easy. I downloaded dating apps and started swiping. Determined I was going to find the man of my dreams, but all I found was disappointment.

There were some potential profiles, but way too many with bathroom selfies, bad chat up lines, and really questionable bios. I made the decision to keep going, I continued to develop my dating knowledge and researched my best way forward. I am now prepared to share my findings with all of you in the hope it will be helpful. I believe there is always a way, if you are committed. It begins with accepting total responsibility for every aspect of your own life and do not blame anyone else when things go wrong.

I share my story with you to offer you support in your search and to propose evidence of what can be overcome and achieved. Life is too short to be unhappy in your status. This is not to say you are unhappy in your life. Indeed, I was very happy in my life. I just wanted someone to share that happiness with.

Oprah once said the biggest adventure you can take is to live the life of your dreams. I made the decision to live the life of my dreams, and that began with finding genuine love. Why resign our lives to passivity, just accepting what life gives us. You may be very successful in your career so why settle for mediocrity in love.

I dedicated some time each day to find the person I wanted in my life. We all want to be happy, and we know the things that make us happy, but all too often we do not do those things. We are too busy trying to live, we forget to take the time to do the things that bring us joy. I put time aside each evening to concentrate on finding my new love. If we want our life to be different, we must be willing to do different. We tend to believe that who we were, is who we are. This may limit our true potential in the present if we continue to make the mistakes of the past.

I began by reflecting on my past and learning from it. I realised that where I am, is the result of who I was, but where I want to go, depends on who I choose to be, from this moment on. I choose to be the best version of me. To be happy and share that happiness with a nice man. It is all about moving forward.

We all change, so we should provide ourselves with the tools that enable us to live the life we really want.

Perhaps read this book and learn from me, do not procrastinate, start organising your love life, the way you want it to be. In this book you will read some stories about people who took this journey and the lessons they learned. You live your life with change all the time, after-all you learned to walk, you learned an entire language, you learned so much throughout your life without even knowing it, and you continue to learn every day. Despite this, it can be difficult to know what change is.

When we become adults, we get very comfortable in our lives, and we fear any change. You and you alone are responsible for making the change you want in your life.

Some people never live the life they dream of. We are so focused on day-to-day events that very few of us plan ahead. We often use age as an excuse but that is no excuse if you want to find love. Love is available regardless of age, but we need to go out and find it.

Start by forming the belief that what happened in your past does not dictate your future. You are not a victim. You are you, a unique, exceptional individual who can live the life you want, by finding the life you want. All you need to do is believe it now and begin the process.

Reading how other people approach finding love may benefit you, but only you can help yourself. Only you can make your world a better place by living a life full of passion, joy and love. What you used to see as a problem, can be an opportunity to change.

Be open to happiness and love. Don't waste any more time thinking about the past; look to the future. Life is ticking away. My advice is to prepare mentally, physically and aesthetically. Choose your platform and plan your profile. Use this book as a guide and take on the change you want. If my words help you in any way, I will be delighted.

Make the next chapter in your life the most extraordinary you have ever imagined. It is time to wake up and live to your full potential.

Chapter I

'I Blame T.V'

Looking back

Some people look back fondly on dating, from generations ago, with romantic ideas of greater morals and better values. Others think that today's dating is much better with the online apps and matchmaking websites, it has never been easier to meet people. Nonetheless, each generation of dating is not without its pros, its cons, and its own set of silent rules. Romantic relationships have always been a changing and evolving part of culture, just like all other aspects of our lives.

Prior to the late early 1900s, dating or courtship, as it was referred to, was a much more private, unemotional, and impassive affair. Women would meet with numerous men, with their parents present. They would then whittle the options down to the most suitable match for marriage. This heavily relied on many factors, but it mostly revolved around financial and social status. When a young lady decided on the man she wanted to court, their activities as a couple took place at social gatherings and under the gaze of chaperones.

This began to change, however, in the early years of the 20th century, when couples began to go out together in public and heaven forbid, un-supervised. The eventual goal was still that of marriage.In today's dating world, the topic of marriage may not be brought up for several years.

The early 20th century was marked by the figure of the gentleman caller. Back then if a man was attracted to a young woman, he would follow the proper procedure and etiquette of calling upon her.

This meant that he would call to the family's home where he would generally be welcomed into their parlour. If he was suitable, he was invited back for successive visits. This young man would be free to come and call upon the young woman during specified times, laid out by the young lady's parents.

This practice of calling quickly became outdated and unfavourable and dating soon became fashionable. Couples began going out on dates. It was now the man's duty to pay for the date, whereas before it was the woman and her parents who decided the terms of the visit.

The basic difference between courtship and dating was that of freedom. While the traditional courtship had its own set of rules and rituals, dating was less structured. Relationships became less restricted and much more personal, and the purpose of dating was more to have fun and less about finding a marriage partner. It was not until after several dates the couples would decide whether to become exclusive or not.

With the establishment of dating, the focus was now all about falling in love, rather than finding a suitable match. Previously, love was not seen as being of vital importance to a marriage, but with the introduction of dating there came an increased wish for romance and love before committing to marriage.

'Going steady' became the term used for being in an exclusive relationship in the 60's and 70's.

Time has moved rapidly on since then and it appears there are no rules for dating anymore. Young people tend to do what they want, when they want, and our modern-day 'hook up' culture has come to being.

This comes as a surprise to those of us entering the dating game after years of being out of that scene.

The major change in dating started with the introduction of the internet. It took some time before it caught on in Ireland, but it is rare now to find someone without at least one dating app on their phone. Tinder, Plenty of Fish, and Bumble, to name a few. While some people think this move towards dating really works, many despair at the thought of it. Many find it frustrating and complain that it is just too complicated.

The present generation is more focused on themselves than ever before. Technology has played a big role in this, as has the concept of the selfie. The casual culture of hooking up, one-night stands, and friends with benefits, makes finding someone to date seriously complex, and difficult.

There are so many options now that finding someone to 'go steady' can be difficult. We have more freedom to choose how we live our lives than ever before. We tend to make up our own life rules, which makes dating in the present day challenging. We wonder, what does the other person want? We wonder if they are looking for something real or do they just want some fun?

Today's dating world is certainly a maze, it may be confusing but that doesn't mean that love has been taken off the table. We all need that loving feeling. Whether you meet on Tinder, or you meet at a bar, you may end up finding love.

Past dating

My friends and I first dated in the 1970's, it was probably the most exciting decade ever. Many say it's the decade that style forgot, but I strongly dispute that, my friends and I were so fashionable, vibrant and fun. It was a great period in my life.

Living in a small village didn't hold us back. We made life for ourselves. We had disco's, ballad sessions and marquees. We had the 'Bay City Rollers', Blondie, ACDC, Abba and many, many more. We were on the cusp of great change. Born in 1962 the changes I saw in the mid to late seventies was mind blowing. In the early 1970's all tv's were black and white but by the end of the decade colour tv had been introduced. Pac-man was introduced, as were other computer games like space invaders. We played tennis with two dots and a line on the tv screen, and we thought we were amazing.

The changes taking place in life accelerated. There was a major relaxation of dress codes and protocols. My friends and I were lucky to be teenagers in the seventies. It was a fun, innocent time. I know they say that it's the decade that fashion forgot but for us we had fun getting dressed up and going out. We would all meet up at each other's houses to get ready to go out. It took hours of listening to music, trying on clothes, experimenting with makeup. There was no drinking involved. It was all about the energy.

It is well known that everything comes back in fashion eventually, but we were there for round one. We remember being caught up in the style and crazes, wearing some truly memorable fashions.

We were the first to wear high waist skin-tight bell-bottoms. The amazing contrast between the flare at the bottom and the snug fit of the waist made these trousers truly memorable. We would wear our bell bottoms with platform shoes. This was the epitome of seventies style.

Patterns of all types made it on to pants in the seventies, but stripes mostly vertical were particularly unforgettable. Corduroy and velvet were the material of choice. We even dressed from head to toe in velvet or corduroy. I still love velvet to this day. It was also the polyester decade not a choice for me. We loved shopping with the little money we had to prepare for our nights out.

Our night out was Saturday, and we would all meet to get ready. I remember it as if it was yesterday. Hanging out with friends is always fun. Getting ready to go out together was so enjoyable. We were there to help each other get the night started on a fun note before we headed out.
It was important to us to feel cute and confident because that could be the night we met our 'one'. We would head out in our small village to the local pub session, like we stepped off the set of 'Charlie's Angels'. We would spend the night looking for a lift to a nightclub in the hope of finding romance.

We went out in groups, and no one was left behind. It was an understanding that one of us would need to meet a guy with a car so we would have a lift home.
It was a different time, an innocent time, and the young men we met were mostly respectful, although not always, but we were able to spot the cheeky ones.

The conversations after these nights out were hilarious looking back now. We lived in a very different time.

In the 1970s people cherished relationships. When you met someone you liked then you dated, got to know each other over a couple of years, then got engaged and married. My friends and I went out, met young men, dated and married all within the same time frame. We all had the same expectations, hopes and dreams. We didn't have mobile phones and generally didn't meet from one weekend to the next. We didn't live together beforehand as it was frowned upon. When we got married it is fair to say we didn't know each other's foibles.

This is why I feel there are so many break-ups of couples in their fifties and sixties now. These people are now on the dating scene which is significantly different to when they dated in the first instance.

Technology has now overtaken the dating world. Previous generations met face-to-face and spoke on the phone. Long gone are the days when the means of communication was the humble phone. Today there are so many new channels of communication. We can use Facebook, Tinder, WhatsApp and a host of other mediums to find what we need.

In the '70s, relationships were valued. We invested in love. We made a whole-hearted effort to make it work. We got married at an early age. But today, people do not commit to a long-term relationship.
Marriage seems to have taken a backseat as couples want to enjoy life, to travel and date more than one person before committing to marriage.

In the seventies we felt we knew what we wanted but todays daters seem to know what they don't want. There is no urgency in settling down together and couples are having children later in life.

Couples today like to live with their partner before marriage, something we did not do, and something I wholeheartedly recommend. Afterall the old saying 'live with me and you will know who I am' is very true.

Many feel that marriage cuts their independence. They also feel that it is simpler to break the relationship if things go wrong. In the 1970's, divorce was unacceptable and not available in Ireland. For those of us who dated in the 70's and married in the 80's the divorce rate is increasing all the time. There are more people in their later years dating than ever before due to marriage breakups.

It can be challenging for mature people to accept the current scene of dating and relationships, as it is so different now, and more difficult to negotiate. My friends and I all dated in the late seventies and because we were so young and mindlessly followed the expectations of the time, most of us married young, in the eighties. It is not surprising then after raising families, some of us found we grew in different directions from our partners.

It is sad to say that too many of us parted in our forties, and fifties, and found ourselves attempting to heal and launch into the dating game again.
Dating is complex, no matter when in your life you are embarking on the journey. Today's age has brought the complication of technology, and new ways of

communicating, as well as new language. I mean, who heard of ghosting five years ago? No part of internet dating is easy, but it certainly can be fun.

If we really want to meet someone these days, going online is essential. Dating during midlife doesn't have to be so complicated, with that in mind I am writing this book to help keep dating and love fun and light-hearted. Remember nothing is impossible, love is out there.

It is true to say a first date brings expectations and dreams that are not often lived up to. This book is here to bring you stories of disasters, misadventures, triumphs, and laughs with examples of the dating search and the anticipation of that first date. Each story comes with some advice and guidance that can help guide you in the journey of dating in your mid-life.

Online dating is a maze of wonder and hope as well as a muddle of complexity and confusion. I was introduced to it by friends. For women of a certain age, it is next to impossible to meet anyone out and about. I tried all the usual, going to local events, signing up to night courses, and dance classes all to no avail as they were full of women all with the same intentions as myself.

On the upside, however, I learned a lot of new skills. Going online filled me with fear and misgivings but my friends assured me it was definitely the way forward. I would have to give it a go if I wanted to find a love interest.

I Blame T.V.

I blame 'The Little House on the Prairie', 'The Waltons' and love stories like 'An Affair to Remember'. After all, they exposed us to the perfect family, the perfect love life, the perfect woman, the perfect man. They set in motion the picture-perfect couple we all aspire to. I spent my childhood watching mushy TV, and my parents were the perfect couple of love-birds. I had a very flawed view of what love should look like.

I married, had children, and had a very nice life but I was never fulfilled. Real life was not like the movies. I found myself in my forties wanting to meet the love of my life. It is not that I did not love my husband, I did, and I know he loved me, but we wanted very different things from life. We tried but, in the end, we had to face the reality.

After a period of healing, and a festive period spent watching other couples snog their way through to the New Year, I felt my lack of a partner, and I decided, this would be the year I would date again. I would find that perfect someone. I knew I wouldn't meet anyone staying at home. It became clear that I was scuppering my own opportunities to meet someone as I filled my life with so many other commitments. I was constantly socialising but forming no genuine connections. I fell back on the idea that I'd meet someone 'when the time was right', but I wasn't prioritising the looking. This had to change.

I had misgivings about relationships, which could be construed as 'pickiness'. I had been burned more than once along the relationship road. It is not easy to admit that my confidence was knocked. Going back into the fray I needed to proceed with caution. At my age I cannot deny the past, but I felt I could repackage my current status to sell myself and my understandable insecurities to find a lovely partner.

Given that 'The Little House on the Prairie' was not real, I now know that nobody is perfect. I think it is worthwhile writing down some vital qualities when looking for a partner and focusing on those when potentials come into view.

Since the notion of dreamy love took an enamoured embrace of marriage in the Victorian era, the emphasis has been on a monogamous arrangement that lasts the best part of a lifetime. It could be noted that a lifetime in the Victorian era was somewhat shorter. Not an excuse, just an observation. It should be said that married monogamy may not suit everyone. I would love to be married to the love of my life, but I no longer need the piece of paper.

We no longer need to be married to be socially acceptable. This might allow other possibilities to open up for us. Whatever the possibility is, or the commitment we wish to make, it will be what we choose, and not be because society dictates. Perhaps we are single because we haven't yet found that someone who shares our vision for a relationship or perhaps, we are not ready to share our vision. This is the time I opt to change that. I would really like to have someone to share my life and my vision with.

Everywhere I turn, coupledom is praised as a life ideal. I would like to be a part of this, not because it is a societal preference but because I love to love. My life is about giving and about people. I want to be with someone who is giving and would like to share my vision. Of course, we do not need a life partner as there is little to nothing we cannot experience with the right friends. For me I like having that special someone in my life as well as having the right friends.

Companionship is valuable and to be lauded given the loneliness epidemic that people experience today. It is also possible to be lonely in the wrong relationship. That is why I want to get it right this time. Apart from leaving us feeling isolated, loneliness can also make us feel helpless. It is a complex feeling.

When someone says they feel 'lonely' it can mean a variety of things. It might mean you feel unheard or unloved. Or it might be that you are feeling disconnected from your family and friends. The reasons for feeling lonely can be really varied but one of the most common reasons is a change in your life that makes you feel differently about your relationships. You may feel like you need more support.

Feeling your relationships are not giving you what you need can lead to a sense of isolation as you begin to doubt whether you have got your priorities right. It might be that you are not communicating as well as you used to. It can be easy to slip into negative communication habits. You might begin freezing other people out which is never good. It leads to loneliness.

It is not common that someone might admit to being 'lonely', especially in a relationship, but right now people seem to be lonelier than ever before. Being open to meeting others even when it's challenging gives you the best chance of dealing with loneliness. We all need connectedness and a feeling of belonging. That is why I want to make sure I find my close to perfect fit.

I admit singleness in and of itself is not a problem, being single does not equate to being lonely. Being single for a time was good.
It helped me re-evaluate life, and that happiness does not only come from finding a husband.
It is not that I regret my marriage, it brought me three wonderful children, but we made the right decision to separate. This sent me into a dating frenzy until I realised I needed to spend some time alone. My first entry into the dating scene was laughable, scary, and downright complicated.

Taking time alone and single taught me to be more connected with my family and friends and to be self-sufficient and positive. I was always in a relationship, or chasing a relationship, because I felt that constituted happiness. I had the deep-seated belief that I must have a partner in life to be complete. Maybe I felt I wasn't good enough to be alone.

I now believe the constant pursuit of relationships stemmed from my own fear of being with myself. Sometimes I chose a partner just because I wanted to be in a relationship. It took me time to learn that to be happy I didn't need to be dependent on someone else for emotional and financial support. I could support myself.

I figured out I needed to stop focusing on what other people expected of me and start focusing on my own expectations, hopes and dreams.

I piled relationships on top of each other for too long, meaning I never properly mourned what I lost along the way. I reflected on great times with great people and not so good times with not so good people. It was painful to acknowledge all this, but I am happy I took the time to be single, even if it was for a short time. I did indeed find a greater connection to my family and friends, and it was great spending time with people of my own choosing.

Taking time alone I learned to eat in restaurants alone, walk into pubs alone, watch whatever I wanted on tv. Read the books I wanted and go to the movies I wanted. I talked and met with my friends and we laughed a lot.

I don't recommend the single life over the coupled life, or vice versa, as there is no one blueprint for the best life. I believe what matters in life is not what everyone else is doing, or what everyone else thinks we should be doing, it's that we can find the space and the people that allow us to live our best lives.

I enjoyed being single for a time but in taking the time to be me, I came to the conclusion that I would like to remain being me, but I would like to be me, with a significant someone. I would like companionship, fun, stimulating conversation and love with someone who loves me for who I am, and who I can love, for who they are.

Someone once told me that separateness in unity is truly wonderful. I would like to find this. I would like to find companionship, fun, and love. I believe they are all still mine for the taking but I am the one that needs to invite it in. As locking eyes across a crowded room is a thing of the past, how would I invite love into my life again?
When it comes to romantic possibilities in this day and age, nothing competes with technology. This makes it more possible to find someone now, than ever before, particularly if you are older. We no longer need to stand in a bar and wait for the right one to come along. Online dating is the way to go, we just have to learn to navigate and work the system.

Throughout history, dating has never been easy. However, with the dawn of modern technology, dating has become more mystifying than ever before. All it takes now to go on a first date is a few swipes and clicks on your phone. Though please do not be fooled into thinking that every date is going to involve romantic hand holding, gazing into each other's eyes, and drinking hot cocoa in front of an open fire, while the wind swirls outside. Indeed, I found this to be far from the truth. Swiping left or swiping right has made the dating landscape very different and sometimes quite difficult to navigate.

I know many people who had bad experiences, including myself, but I am still here to tell the tale. Fortunately, I have travelled the road and I am here to pave the way for you, should you so desire. I will share my experience so hopefully you will be able to recognise the red flags and you will be able to know what and who to avoid.

Some of the behaviour put on display on dating sites or apps can be overwhelming, and without realising it, we can let it creep into our offline lives. What we accept as suitable behaviour in our lives offline may be different to what we accept online. There is an ongoing discussion about consent and respect between the sexes at the moment, but many of us seem to forget this when we go online. We tend to let our standards slip.

In this book, I am only going to look at the woman's point of view, because it is mine, but men have similar experiences. In my extensive research, it became clear to me that distasteful language, disrespectful insults, and ghosting have all become commonplace on dating sites and apps. Sadly, many users have come to expect, and even accept such treatment as part of the course, when looking for love online. However, as you become more practised you will notice the messages to avoid.

Research regularly confirms that the screen mediates our sense of agency. Because we are behind a screen, we are much braver and bolder. Inviting someone on a date from behind the protection of a screen is much less scary than doing so in person. Also, because people are anonymous, they can be insulting and rude to make themselves feel good. If you don't find them attractive or dance to their tune they can become downright offensive.

Some people expect you to drop everything right now and come to their apartment to play. You will know this is never a good idea, you don't need me to tell you. By making someone else feel bad, some users make themselves feel better.

They are doing this behind the anonymous shield of the internet. You will need to be assertive when entering this arena.

I hate to say it but most people excuse bad online dating experiences as 'to be expected'. We would not expect to have these experiences in the real world, so why do we accept them in the online world? A recent survey pointed out that almost half the women had men pursuing them online long after the woman said no. It also pointed out that one third of women had been called an abusive name.

The bar with online dating has been set very low in my estimation. I feel it is because of the throwaway society we live in. There are hundreds of matches just waiting in the side lines. I agree there are lots of matches, but there are very few suitable ones. We are very open and vulnerable when we are looking for love. We are most likely to accept behaviour we would not normally accept.

If we want to date, we cannot avoid online dating. There are so few options especially for older daters. It's a mistaken belief that harassment and pestering is just a fact of online life, we tend to fob it off as typical. We try to pretend it doesn't affect us, but the fact is it does. Some of the behaviour we receive on dating apps is not only demoralising, it continues to upset us once we log out. It may carry into our day to day and eat into other facets of our life. It may grind us down until we think we deserve this form of treatment. I suggest we stop differentiating between online dating, and real time dating. We should be unswerving in how we expect to be treated in our relationships.

The starting point does not matter. Let us not abandon our standards to indulge potential new loves, who think treating us badly is the norm, just because we met electronically.

I will hold my hands up and say I accepted behaviour I would not normally tolerate when online dating. It was not long before I became accomplished at spotting the bad-mannered uncouth suitors. Whether we admit it or not; many of us are seeking to find our perfect match. The love of our life. Our soulmate. Our life partner. That special someone.

We long to have someone by our side to care for us and love us through our moments of weakness and to make and share memories. We've seen enough movies and read enough books about it, so it must be possible, right?

I can tell you love is no fairy tale; I found that out for myself. I suggest we stop looking for the perfect ten who will fulfil us. Perfection does not exist and even if it did, would we want it? I think it would be exhausting trying to be perfect. It is possible, however, to find someone to take on the messiness of the world with you. To help you experience life and all its ups and downs. I found that 'someone', but I didn't find him easily.

In searching for my significant other, I learned a lot of lessons. I will share them with you here, as well as some stories from my friend's escapades. It is my hope you will learn from our mistakes and believe me there were many. Online dating and dating apps are a quagmire.

Let us start by looking at the basics and some of the lessons I learned. You really need to be truthful and authentic. If you want to find a love that is real, you must be your true self. If you want someone to love you for you, you must be you. Also remember you will want them to be their real and true self. If you are real with yourself, you show readiness for someone else's genuineness.

Before you sign on to a dating site or app explore and ask yourself: what really makes you happy? What do you really want from life? It is very easy to get caught in a pattern of pleasing others and doing what seems cool or fashionable. If you modify your personality to satisfy someone else then you are not being your true self. People are attracted to authenticity. Become self-aware and really get to know and love yourself. Be authentic and you will attract authentically. I know we all stretch the truth a little from time to time but try to be the best you can be. Be your best self.

Though we often hear that opposites attract, we should also understand that like attracts like. You set the standard for the individual you want to spend your life with. You wouldn't look for a lazy, greedy, complainer with gravy stains on their shirt. So, basically it might be a good idea to clean up your own act first.

Be the person you want to attract. If you want to attract a well-dressed gent, then dress well yourself. If you want to attract a hill walker, be a hill walker yourself. If you want to attract a positive person, be positive. Be confident in yourself. I know this can sometimes be hard but as the saying goes 'fake it 'til you make it'. Other people are attracted to a confident person.

If you are your best self, confidence will radiate from you, and you will glow.

It is always good to be open. If you are open with yourself and friends, it is easier to be open to someone new, and if you are willing to bond with the people around you, you will be ready to bond with others. If someone next to you in the café or bar strikes up a conversation, try to engage. That person may not be your type and may not be the love of your life, but it is good practice and a rehearsal for the real thing.

It is always good to be happy because everyone wants to be around happy people. Happy people are magnetic, just think about it when you are out with someone happy you feel better. We all have our difficulties in life but it is never good to go around as if the weight of the world is on our shoulders. Be happy, it makes others feel happy.

Perhaps it would be a good thing to focus your energy on thinking about and doing the things that make you happy. If we know what makes us happy then we will know what we want to look for in those we hope to attract.

Chapter II

'Move from thinking to doing'

Move from thinking to doing

If you picked up this book it is likely you are thinking about online dating. It is time now to move from thinking and talking about it, to doing it. Start preparing your everyday life to get ready for your new adventure. Transform what you do with your day, your week, your time and take control of your love life. Put one foot in front of the other and move on with purpose. There has never been a better time to begin again. We now live in a world of dating opportunities.

Our world is connected more now than ever before. Whatever you want to know, or whatever you are looking for, is at your fingertips. The soaring development of the internet gives you all the expertise you need. It can empower you in creating the change you need in your life. It can help you find your new love interest from your own living room. How exciting is that?

The practices of society that determined the correct way to behave is gone. Those who arched their eyebrows, if rules were not obeyed, have mostly disappeared. These practices may have held people's dreams in check, but thankfully, they are vanishing quickly. Fifty years ago, you had to wait to be introduced to date, now you can go surfing the net to find love.

The world is getting smaller and is totally connected. People care less about conformity than they used to, it is much easier to do something different now. To be someone different. The ideals that used to confine you to a relationship, no matter how bad it was, are no longer imposed by anyone but you.

We are living longer as life expectancy goes up and up. If you are going to be around a long time, you might as well do what you enjoy, and be who you want for as long as possible. Technology has brought the world to our fingertips. It has helped knock down the walls of convention, but it can also suck the life out of you. The remedy for this is to take the initiative and start your search with purpose. Do not confine your dream to waiting, start now, but be careful. Know what you want. We will revisit this again later but for now it is about introducing something or someone new into your life.

There is no one size fits all, there is just the right answer for you. Write down the one thing you want to do most whether it is a casual relationship or a loving relationship. Now that you are serious about dating again, it makes sense to talk it through with your best friends. Do not just talk the talk about what you are going to do, talk with purpose. Be prepared to walk the walk.

Believe what you say you are going to do, say it out loud and in saying it out loud to friends, you really will begin the process. As Muhammad Ali once said, 'if you talk big then you truly are great.' If you suffer from 'poor me' syndrome and think the whole world is against you, it is not, this attitude will hold you back. Thinking that you are important enough to be singled out by the world is not healthy.

Everyone has their own needs but perhaps now is a good time to double check your motives for finding love. Be courageous enough to take risks otherwise you will get nothing done.

As it is said twenty years from now you will regret the things you didn't do rather than the ones you did. Regret weighs much heavier than fear so act now to find your love, or you will regret not following your heart.

I suggest you just start the process, so what if you make a mistake? There is always the opportunity to learn from it and try something different next time. There will always be reasons not to start. Whether it is by reason of location, family situation, financial, mental, or physical. These are most likely excuses so get rid of them. Time is of the essence. The clock does not care about your excuses, it is ticking and it is ticking at the same speed for everyone. Mind you, I sometimes think my clock is faster than everyone else's.

Remember the sands of time may be running out for your hopes and dreams. Recognise your fears for what they are. They are excuses. Be logical now and ask yourself what do they really mean? Are they enough to stop you in your tracks forever? I suggest you do not dwell on them, recognise that we all have excuses, acknowledge them, recognise what they are and let them go.

Another reason you may not want to start is your past. Be mindful, we all have accumulated baggage, this is something we all need to deal with. Try not to dwell on it because the more you dwell the bigger it gets, but your past is something you should deal with because it will not go away otherwise. We all know running away from problems will not make them go away. We cannot change our history, but the future is ours to make.

We should try not to let our past mistakes control our future. Let the past be exactly that, the past.

For the purpose of this book, we will use the past as a learning tool. We will let it inform our future as we choose our next move. You may worry that other people will laugh at you for chasing love. I know when I went online in the beginning, I did not want anyone to know.

I felt it was like ordering love online from a catalogue. I felt my friends and family would think it was smutty and even worse that I was desperate. Those not familiar with online dating think it is a place of ill repute, which it can be, but it can also be an amazing tool to find friendship and love. So let them laugh. Let them ridicule. All in all, the world is not standing around waiting for us to make our move and laugh at us, they are busy getting on with their own lives, so maybe we should get on with ours.

Get smart about how we prioritise our needs. Be true to ourselves while managing our obstacles and excuses. We can always find an excuse but in the same vein we can find inspiration too. Steal the time from wherever you can and commit to your goal. It will give you an extra incentive to achieve your love goal. It is ok to feel apprehensive, this only means it matters to you.

Put yourself in the driving seat and get started. You will make some wrong decisions along the way, I know I did, but you will achieve far more than if you do not get started. No more drifting. The internet has multiplied our possibilities so use it to your advantage. Once you stop talking and start doing, you will feel happy.

Time will fly when you get absorbed in the search and get in the zone.

The decision and will power alone will not get us where we want to be; we need a plan. Make your plan by defining what you want. Keep your feet planted on the ground but dream big. Look at your dreams and goals as coming attractions in your life, and plan for success. Now that you are taking the step to find your new love, prepare yourself. Read on and learn from my experiences.

My advice is to prepare, I did not put in the preparation in the beginning, but preparation is crucial. We should always prepare for events in life, as we set ourselves up for success. If we are prepared, we can help things work out for the best. If we are not prepared and ready, our odds of success are reduced.

I believe that preparation is integral to success in any situation. We need a plan to achieve our goals and dreams. If we are organised in advance, we stand a better chance of succeeding. As the saying goes 'failing to prepare is preparing to fail'. As you prepare for your journey, I suggest you learn from my journey and lay the groundwork first.

Chapter III

'Get Ready'

Prepare

The first thing I did when I decided to date again was to mentally prepare myself. If we want to go chasing a new relationship, it would be great to be in that mental state of readiness. Most of us had our fair share of bad relationships, from 'it's complex,' to 'it's really complex,' to 'manipulation' to 'abuse'. Many of us have gone into each new relationship hoping and wishing it will be different this time.

Like so many women, I have gone through a dating wasteland of nothing happening here. I now want to find someone who will treat me with respect. Of course, I've had my fair share of nice moments, nice partners, and nice relationships. Now I want more than nice, I want wonderful, considerate, and respectful. I want joy. I am serious now, so I am going to put in serious preparation. We should all be with someone who thinks we are the best thing on this planet earth, but we cannot exactly conjure up a partner who thinks we are amazing by snapping our fingers.

I put some serious thought into finding my wonderful relationship. Maybe these thoughts could help you on your journey toward a healthy love. A good place to start is to look at the examples of the healthy relationships you already have in your life.

We tend to prioritise our romantic relationships as the defining intimacies of our lives but is this true? Definitely not. Whatever problems we have in our romantic lives, it is a mistake to think that this somehow means we are bad at relationships.

We have so many other relationships that are genuine and lasting whether they are a family member, friend, or mentor. This shows we are good at relationships. Nonetheless most of us long for that romantic relationship, that special someone in our life.

To find our special love, it is no secret, we first need to love ourselves. After all, how can we expect someone to love us if we do not love ourselves? Self-love, however, is not something we can just turn on like a switch. Also, experiences of bad relationships can make it difficult for us to nurture good relationships with ourselves. This can lead to a vicious cycle, where feeling bad about ourselves, can cause us to expect bad treatment from others. This in turn makes us feel worse about ourselves and on and on it goes.

We are the only ones that can break that cycle. Allowing ourselves to feel positive and optimistic can empower us and help us heal as well as cultivate better and healthier relationships in the future.

I believe there are things we can do to make our relationship with ourselves better. Self-compassion is a good place to start, a gentle acceptance of who we are. Give yourself the kind of lasting and non-judgemental love you give to your siblings or your children. Accept your flaws and accept that we all make mistakes, we even repeat mistakes throughout our life. Remember that is okay, we are all human.

Begin the process by treating yourself with kindness. Look at your mindset, I began by noticing patterns of negative self-talk, so I practised flipping it to positive thoughts. I read a number of self-help books.

I know some people judge these books but honestly, I found some interesting wisdom in them, and I am not ashamed to say I read them, because they helped me to the mindset I have today.

We often think that accomplishment in work and relationships makes us happy. However, research suggests the opposite, it says happy people are more likely to be successful. So, let's get happy. Developing happiness does not need a major transformation. You can start right now. It is very easy for us to blame ourselves and to think that we are simply not good enough or we are not good at relationships. But there is nothing to stop us having healthier experiences going forward.

Therapy can be a great way to work through negative patterns of behaviour and negative thoughts. It can be helpful to foster the skills to build happy, healthy, lasting, relationships. If you want to build healthier relationship patterns for the future, it can be a good idea to talk to a therapist.

I am essentially an optimist so I thought I would retrain myself. It was not easy, but I persevered. It is not all that simple to love ourselves, but we can learn. Loving ourselves is essential to our personal growth and to developing healthy and happy relationships.

It is not good enough to just talk yourself into believing you have self-love, you need to foster compassion for yourself. Try to care as much about yourself as you do for others. Many of us don't do this because we think we are being selfish or that our own needs are not important, but they are.

Treat yourself the way you would treat your family and friends with gentleness, concern and caring. Think of yourself as being your own best friend.

It is good to figure out what makes you feel good and do it as often as you can. Feeling good is all the permission you need, to do what you love to do. The more you do the things you love, the happier you will be. Schedule time regularly to recharge your batteries.

Possibly join a club to meet like-minded people who inspire you. Do what you need to do to be you, and do not let anyone pass judgement or talk you out of it because they think you are being selfish. Pay no attention to them. You need to help yourself to help others. All too often, people scrunch up their nose at the mention of self-love, I understand it sounds a bit self-indulgent. But take it from me, learning to love yourself is very powerful and is one of the most important things you can do for yourself.

Love is your power and when you love yourself it changes everything. Your relationships, your health, your whole life thrives when you start to love yourself. While we all know deep down it's important to love ourselves, doing it is very different. As my mother always said, practise makes perfect. Self-love can be practised and mastered over time, I am evidence of that. When we practise self-love, we foster a loving relationship with ourselves. We become our own best friend. Oscar Wilde, one of my favourites, once said 'to love oneself is the beginning of a lifelong romance' so why not begin a romance with yourself?

Start by focusing on nourishing yourself. By nourishing your body, you show love. Become mindful of what you put in your body, give it what it loves, and sometimes give it what you love. Eat as healthy as you can and enjoy the little treats. I am still working on this. The way we feed ourselves reflects how we love ourselves. By nourishing yourself, you'll lay strong foundations to self-love and future health.

I began a gratitude journal. Another thing some people scrunch their nose up at, but it has been proven if you write down five things that you are grateful for each day, you begin to train your brain to be more positive. This will give you an overall feeling of happiness. In setting up an attitude of gratitude and love, you begin to live a life of self-love. I bought myself a pretty notebook and at the end of each day I write down the things I am grateful for. It really helps.

As well as giving thanks for things that happened that day, and the people in your life that you are thankful for, also include yourself in your gratitude practice. Find at least one thing you can thank yourself for each day, and you will see your relationship with yourself shift into an incredibly loving place. We have much more strength than we realise to generate the feelings we want to experience in life. We just need to learn how to tap into those feelings.

I suggest you remember a time when you were full of joy, perhaps find a photo of yourself at this time, this will help remind you of how joy and happiness feel. Now put that photo somewhere you will see it every day. Perhaps save it as your phone screensaver or put it on your bathroom mirror.

That way whenever you need a boost to your day, look at the picture and immerse yourself, feel the good vibes. Loving yourself allows you to reach a new level of self-happiness. We look outside of ourselves for love, because that is how we found strength, stability and love as children. It is like we never got over this and we still look for love in other people. We are always looking for someone to complete us, but no amount of attention from someone else will make us content. We can only do that for ourselves. The love you are looking for can only come from within yourself. If we work on loving ourselves, we can overcome our restrictive thoughts and live a life that we truly want.

Perhaps throw out the idea of being perfect, perfection is false, remember most photos you see on social media are filtered. There is no point to filters in life. If, like me, you want to live life to the fullest, and find the partner to live it with, give yourself a break.

No one is perfect, but everyone has their own distinctive qualities and personalities. We are all unique on this earth and there is no point in comparing ourselves to others. As Theodore Roosevelt once said, 'comparison is the thief of joy'. Stop searching for perfection in yourself and in others. Recognize all the good that is within you, know how fortunate you are to be a living, breathing, and functioning human being. Living mindfully is living authentically, this will give you higher self-esteem and will help you become more confident in yourself which will attract your best match. Giving up our need for approval from others will help us find our happy place. It may also help us let go of past wounds.

No-one is happy every second of every day. We are all human, just embrace your humanity. We are often very hard on ourselves, so trying to be realistic will help you in your search for self-love. Now that you have devised a plan to love yourself. Get out there and pursue the man you can be happy with. Enjoy who you are and look forward to your wonderful new life.

Being single has plenty of positives. It gives you the space and opportunity to work on yourself in the way that you want and need. It helps you to see if you want a partner and if you do, you can decide what you don't want as well as what you do want. You know you are mentally ready for a relationship when you let go of the need to compare every new man that comes into your life to all the men you loved before.

When you realise true happiness cannot be defined by the people you have in your life, and that true happiness comes from within, you realise that you are ready to be with someone else. Knowing who you are and where you are going shows you are ready for your next chapter.

Whether you have been in a long-term relationship in the past or are interested in looking for one now, it is not a good idea to be with someone that is completely dependent on you, as this can be very unhealthy.

If you have learned to be self-reliant and independent, it is best to meet someone also independent, as a healthy relationship should soon follow. Connecting with someone in a relationship does not mean that they 'complete you', only you can do that, it simply means you are willing to share your full life with them.

You can learn from one another and inspire each other to be our best version. One of the most common reasons that keep people from moving on to a happy and thriving relationship with someone new, is the fact that they're still hung up on their previous relationship. When you are at peace with your past relationships, and you have dealt with any stress because of it, you will be mentally available for a relationship.

Working on skeletons may be an ongoing effort, but most of the work has already been done. I believe once you have fully gotten over your ex, you are mentally and emotionally ready to meet someone new. Why not start your new chapter now and make time for yourself and your new possibilities.

Prepare mentally - love yourself

- Start each day with a self-affirmation.
- Tell yourself 'I love you'.
- Meditate – believe me it really works.
- Read a good book (I enjoy self-help and chick-lit.)
- Sleep in occasionally; you don't have to wake up early every day.
- Put your phone down and let your brain rest. (I love putting it down.)
- Create a vision board, a visualisation list, or a dream list. (I love lists.)
- Try something new, a salsa class, an art class. (I tried yoga and meditation.)
- Take a hike or walk. (I like to walk in beautiful surroundings, close to water.)
- Make plans with friends or family. (I love meeting girlfriends for wine and laughs.)

- Listen to a podcast; finding one you really enjoy will make you feel happy.
- Create a playlist of your favourite songs and listen to it when you feel stressed.
- Take a bubble bath. (I love mine with candles.)
- Do a facial (I love a moisture bomb mask.)
- Declutter your space as it helps to declutter your mind.
- Watch your favourite sitcom; laughter is great medicine.
- Treat yourself; buy yourself something nice. (My favourite thing to do.)
- Plan a trip; give yourself something to look forward to.
- Watch the sunset or sunrise. (I love a good sunset by the sea.)
- Eat more fruit and vegetables as it will make you feel healthier.
- Drink more water. (I find this difficult, but still I endeavour to do better.)
- Take multivitamins; it will boost your immune system.
- Treat yourself to some ice cream. (I love my chocolate.

Example of Self-love affirmations:

- I invite positivity into my life.
- I am allowed to feel good.
- I'm growing and evolving into my best self.
- I do not need to prove my worth as a person. I am enough.
- The world will return what I put into it.
- My ability is limitless and countless opportunities are waiting for me.

- I recognize my worth.
- Everything I need to succeed can be mine.
- My work has a positive impact on me and on the world.
- Saying "no" is just as important as saying "yes."
- I love my body and all it does for me, I am enough.
- I am worthy of love and today, I choose me.
- I am loved and I am deserving of love.
- I am beautiful, inside, and out, and love flows from within me.
- I embrace my unique individuality
- I let go of negative self-talk because I deserve happiness.
- I am whole. Everything I need is within me.
- I am in control of my happiness.
- I will reach my goals.
- I do not let my fears hold me back, I accept myself unconditionally.
- I make time to care for myself and I accept all of me.
- I am strong and resilient, and I am successful.
- I let go of my past and live in the present.
- I allow myself to feel deeply and I am open to receive love.
- I love the body I was born with. I have a warm and caring heart.
- I am exactly who I need to be in this moment.
- I have a lot to offer the world
- I love every part of what makes me who I am.
- I choose to stop apologising for being me.
- I am not my mistakes or my flaws.
- I am wonderful. I am enough.

Prepare to look your best

From the moment we are born we start ageing. I prefer to think we are pro-aging not anti-aging. I did not want to think about getting older. Yes, I celebrate my birthdays, but I do not want anyone to mention numbers. Then my cousin, my little flower girl, Serena, who had a very serious cancer battle, turned forty. She said she was so glad to be getting older. She had beaten the odds to make her fortieth birthday, so in honour of Serena, I should celebrate every one of my birthdays. It is time for me to handle getting older. Am I going to let it happen to me? No. I am going to do what I can to feel and look my best.

I want to embrace every day. I want to be healthy, I want to be vibrant, I want to have energy. I have a lot of living to do. I was very fit at one point in my life, but I lost that fitness over the years. I take care of myself, and I live an authentic life. I never lived my life by the number of candles I blew out, so why start now.

I believe it is all about attitude. I know from speaking to women that dating over forty is not easy and it takes more effort. So why not give ourselves a little makeover, get healthy, get a new hair-do, and discover what clothes really flatter our figure. But also think about an internal transformation. Put yourself first.

Once we look and feel our best it will improve every aspect of our life. I wish I had set the foundations earlier to a healthy older life, but it is never too late to set our lives in a way that we could look forward to the future.

Every day is a new chance to live our healthiest, happiest life and what we do today will pay off in our future.

We women tend to put everyone else's needs before our own, now it is time to change that. It is our time. I am certainly going to make this my time. It is not that I will neglect others but with my family are all grown up, it is time for me. I am going to do my best to be healthy. I am not saying I am going to be perfect because I like my red wine, my chocolate, and my Chinese take-aways, but I will try to keep it to weekends. Giving up the things I love is just not worth it. I suggest having realistic expectations in achieving our healthiest happiest life is best.

There is no such thing as perfect and who wants to be perfect anyway. It is not about changing ourselves completely, after all we inherit our mother's hair, our grandmothers' nose, or in my case my dad's eyes, there is very little we can do to change that. Let us embrace the physical self that we cannot change, stop beating ourselves up, and decide we love these things and move on.

I tell myself every morning that 'today the grass is going to be greener, the sky is going to be bluer, I am going to be healthier and happier, I am going to bring peace, love and joy to those around me.'

I do not take every day for granted any more, I cherish every day and choose to take care of myself. It took me a long time to understand it is not selfish to finally put myself first. It is not about changing everything all at once, just focus on one or two things that concern you and this will motivate you further. It is not for me to tell you what to do but I decided if I was going to be an older woman dating, I wanted to put my best self forward.

I will share with you a few things I did in the hope it may help you, or you may choose other ways of becoming your best self. I didn't have the finance to consult an expert, so I decided to become an expert on myself. I read, researched, and spoke to others, and I was able to have a few sessions with the best life coach I could have found. He was excellent and gave me the permission to be me. I was never body conscious, I never saw skinny or fat, small or tall, I was drawn to people by their aura.

I like people because of their heart. I was blessed with a super-fast metabolism in my twenties and thirties so therefore didn't feel the need to exercise but I didn't know then my metabolism would slow as you get older, so I didn't set the foundations of exercise. Although, I ran a mini marathon a few times, it was more about the camaraderie and the fact that I danced most of my life meant I was fit without really realising it. Now though I need to find something I enjoy.

I haven't battled with my weight and my fitness my whole life so coming to it at an older age means I need to retrain and re-educate myself before inviting someone else into my life. In my fifties, I am at my happiest time, so I would really like to be at my healthiest. I am not going to run marathons, but I am going to be the best I can be and have the best energy I can have.

I want to be productive and active into my future. I also want to look good in a pair of jeans, into my sixties, seventies and beyond. If you feel the same way maybe making exercise a regular part of your life is a plan. It is well documented that regular exercise can reduce your risk of disease and can strengthen your immune system and help maintain good mental health. It increases endorphins and can help lift your mood.

We all need something that helps to de-stress us, for me there is nothing like a good walk. Exercise also increases circulation throughout your body which is good for your overall complexion. It is all about small changes and small efforts, I have no intention of becoming a weekend warrior. I never put my body under too much strain so I am not going to do it now, as it would probably deeply object. I am going to start small and build to a level I am happy with.

Perhaps you could try some new and different activities. Finding something you like to do could make the difference between sticking with the exercise and making excuses not to do it. I like walking so I am going to do more of that. I tried weights last year and I did not hate it, so I am going to do that, and I am going to introduce yoga into my life. I would like to be flexible into my future.

It really is not what you do that counts, it is just about doing something. Making fitness a part of our lives will help us live well for longer. I want to keep well into my golden years as I believe it is never too late. Start now and become the best version of you before you go looking for your new love. There is research that says that adults who did not start eating well, and working out until after sixty-five can still reduce the risk of disease.

It is all about starting to take care of ourselves as soon as possible. I took a day to make a plan. A plan to become the best version of me and a plan to find a compatible partner and lover. Life happens to me every day, so I needed a schedule to plan a daily walk, three times a week weights session, and a weekly yoga session.

I love planning and making lists, even if I don't always stick to them but I like making them. I like having a goal in mind as it gives me something to strive for. My goal at present is to comfortably do a three-kilometre brisk walk and do the bridge pose in yoga. I want to look in the mirror and see the best version of me looking back.

There is only one magic bullet to fitness and that is commitment. Start small and accept what you can do is good enough, you can always build on it if you want. Acknowledge every effort you make and be proud of all your efforts.

On top of exercise, I decided to examine my diet. It did not take long to examine, as I know I do not eat well. I am good with fruit and veg, but I am bad with chocolate and sweets. I read somewhere that sugar is poison and if so, I have been poisoning myself for years. I did not want to diet, but I did want to find balance. Eat for you, for your body and for your complexion. I try to drink extra water on the days I enjoy too many treats.
I feel as if it washes all the toxins out, not true but it makes me feel good.

I am not one for much make-up and I am happy with my face, it is the only one I have, so who-ever I meet will need to like it too. I would like to make the best of it though. I believe we can look our best at any age. Getting a good night's sleep is paramount. My cardinal rule is to remove any make-up I might have on. Make-up as well as a day's worth of fumes and dirt can clog up your pores and suffocate your skin. I moisturise, use a facemask and give myself a hair treatment regularly. It makes me feel very good and mentally rejuvenates me. It sends a message to my brain that I am worth it.

I am not big into make-up but I decided looking my best meant embracing some nice make-up. Wanting to look my best self, I planned a review of my make-up bag and decided to invest a little, not a lot because I believe we can look good on a budget. Play up your best features and play down what you do not like. Recently I got my make-up professionally done, so I could see how to do it properly. My new regime is much the same as my old regime but with more thought. I wear very little during the day but now I will ramp it up when going on a date. The most important part of the make-up look is lipstick. My mother never wore make-up but she never left the house without a dab of pond's cold cream and a touch of her favourite lipstick.

I know they say you should not wear red lipstick as you get older but who are they? We are the experts of our own faces and style so do what you please, and for me I am sticking with my red lipstick for the foreseeable future. Remember you are checking and renewing your regime to feel confident going on that date, so you want your lips to look kiss-able.

I like my hair just below my shoulders and I am not going to give in to the short do, just because I am getting older. I love short hair on other people but not on myself. My hair is too fine and my face too round. Choose a style that makes you feel cute. Age should not dictate how you wear your hair. Wear it in a way that makes you feel happy rather than follow some unwritten rule that says you need to cut it because you are a certain age. My mother and my sister have stunning short hair, but my hair is not as good as theirs, so I am sticking with what I like. The bottom line is that your hair should not have anything to do with what is 'in' at the moment, or how many candles are on your cake, it is about what makes you feel good.

To conclude my project on my best self I thought I would revamp and reform my wardrobe. Most of us now favour leisure clothing to suit our lives. Wearing clothes that are sloppy go beyond your appearance, they can affect your self-esteem and your mindset. A comfortable option is jeans, I was never a lover of jeans but now they have become so flexible I love them. I love fashion and clothes and I like to look hip and modern regardless of my age. No matter how old you are, what you do, or what size you are, you deserve to look good. I like being modern and current, but I do not follow trends.

Whatever you decide to wear, make sure it is comfortable. You want to be able to move easily, and not want to be pulling at it all night. You do not have to spend a fortune to look gorgeous, just invest in items that bring you joy. The clothes you wear affect your confidence and your self-esteem, they make you feel like you are worth taking care of.

You feel comfortable in your skin when you are comfortable in your clothes. Only you can define your own style. If you are not sure what suits you ask a trusted friend. Maybe start by editing your wardrobe. It helped me in my quest plus you can see everything at a glance.

One of the biggest myths about older women is that we are no longer interested in looking stylish. I can assure you this is not true. There is a mistaken belief in our culture that women over fifty are invisible, frumpy, and uninterested in sensuality and beauty. This is not true. We are not all matronly and sexless, we are still very much part of the world of fashion, art, and the creative life force. Women in their forties, fifties, sixties, seventies and beyond are re-inventing the world in many ways. So why not in the ways of feeling good, looking good and dating.

We have checked in with our mental health, given ourselves some self-love, checked our physical health, worked on our appearance, we have revamped our wardrobes, and made every effort to become our best self. We are ready to date.

Ready to take the next step

- You are (mostly) over your last heartbreak.
- You have worked on becoming more independent.
- You know what you want from a relationship.
- You understand your self-worth.
- You feel excited about meeting new people.
- You no longer want to smother your ex.

- You are willing to communicate and compromise.
- You are open and honest and ready for intimate communication.
- You are willing to realistically look at your marketability.
- You are truly open to the possibilities open to you.
- You feel good enough about yourself to go back dating.
- You love yourself more than anyone.
- You believe that you could be a worthwhile partner.
- You trust that people are basically good.
- You treasure the positives in intimate relationships.
- You have learned what you need to know to try dating again.
- You feel renewed confidence in knowing what to do differently.
- You are hopeful things work out the way they are supposed to.
- You want to share your love with someone else.
- You think about falling in love again.
- You recognise your past mistakes.
- You have a handle on your own story.
- You know what you want for yourself.
- You can accept someone for who they are.
- You know it is possible to love again.
- Are you finished playing the field, If not that's ok just date casual.

Chapter IV

'Get Set'

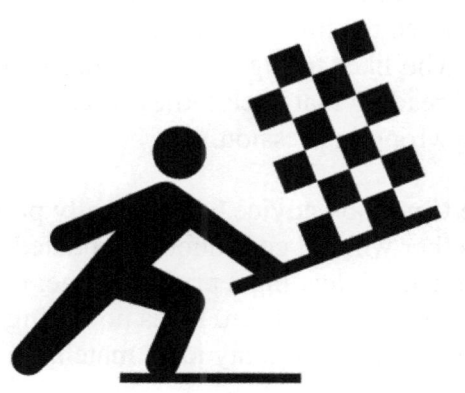

Write your profile

The first time I sat down to explore online dating I was so scared of putting something out on the world wide web that could haunt me forever, that I almost backed down. I signed up but I was a slow starter. I decided to make online dating an exercise. Certainly, it was easier to watch TV or read at the days end and unwind. I started to realise that if I wanted to meet someone before it was too late, I would have to leave the couch.

I realised that this online dating lark would take time and attention. It was like coming home to another job. I was so careful starting out, it took me a week to put my profile together. I wanted it to be truthful, but not boring. I wanted it to be fun, but not that kind of fun. I wanted it to be sexy, but not like I was only looking for sex. It might sound easy, but it is not. It is all about reading between the lines, for instance I wrote 'I am a fun person who likes trying new restaurants and a treat before bed' reading that back I knew it gave the completely wrong impression.

I researched and took advice before finally putting my profile together which I continuously updated.My advice if you are uploading a profile online, is to be honest, light-hearted, and fun. I was not trying to attract everyone, I wanted to find my ideal match.

I began with the headline and decided to make it snappy but to include the type of person I was hoping to meet, 'Family, friends, kindness and laughing are the things I value most' was my tag line. After the headline, I worked on my photo. I wanted to look natural and inviting and I wanted it to be recent.

I personally do not like the mirror selfie as I feel it gives off the air of vanity. I generally do not like photos of myself, so it was difficult to finally choose. I read that the best profile shots feature the three 'c's, colour, context, and character.

For colour, I chose to wear red. For context I included my hobbies with a photo at the beach. For character I chose a photo at a restaurant and one at a theatre because I love eating out, live music and drama. I also included a full body shot, I wanted to avoid first-date surprises. No point connecting with someone online if they do not know what you look like. After all, if their type is skinny blondes, they were not going to find a curvy brunette attractive.

For the main photo, I chose a headshot. I am smiling into the camera. I am not joking when I say I took at least a hundred before choosing one. Even then, I was not happy, but no point in putting up a photo that didn't reflect me because if I met someone, they had to be able to recognise me.

Then comes the challenging part: writing the all-important profile. Eventually, I put a nice profile together, with three-quarters of it about me, and one quarter about what I was looking for in a man.
I feel keeping it short is best, but shorter is not always easier. Highlighting a few attractive traits about yourself, builds up some intrigue and attraction. Perhaps begin by jotting down a list of your hobbies and a list of those you would like to share with your ideal partner as well as features you possess that your perfect match is looking for in a woman.

Write a few thoughts about what you love about your life, your job as well as your hopes, and dreams. Specific details make your profile seem more sincere, that is important. Having a genuine list visible in front of you makes the profile writing process much easier. One of the most important findings in a recent online study is that daters are not interested in seeing edited photos and unrealistic positive self-descriptors. They want more honesty. This leads to more meaningful connections all round.

Your profile is your calling card. It is an opportunity to show who you are, and clearly set out your interests. You can state what you are hoping to find in a relationship and set yourself up for a brilliant first date. As I found out it is nerve-wracking and difficult to write about yourself. It is also very difficult to put a short profile together that can sum up who you are and what you are looking for. Mine read something like this:

'I am easy-going, love to laugh, and am a bit of a romantic at heart, even if practical in life. I love people and try always to see the good in them. I love going for walks, the beach, dining out, or just staying home cuddled up on the couch with a good book and a glass of vino. I am looking for a man who can appreciate the little things in life, who will smile when he sees me and who will love me for who I am. A good friend with similar interests and a lover in my potential partner. If that is you, feel free to message me.'

While it is good to include unique details about yourself, you also want to balance it out and not give everything away.

It never hurts to be clever on a profile, you want to let your potential partner know that you are more than just a pretty face. Keep it catchy, this leaves a lasting impression. Think about your dating profile giving potential matches something that intrigues, amuses, and resonates with them. Try to avoid politics, religion, and past dramas.

To begin with I was very passive about online dating. Most of the men seemed a little traditional for me. The methods of dating had certainly changed since my teens, but it would appear the dynamic had not. Men my age were still looking for someone to take care of them.

I felt it was etiquette to put my profile up and wait for messages to arrive. They arrive fast and furious. I was a newbie, and it would appear newbies are very popular. I soon found out that younger men were by far my greatest interactors. My experience was that men my age and older, were looking for women ten or more years younger, and men younger were looking for older women.

It is funny really, because older men want to find a younger woman, but they still want them to assume the traditional role. Younger women do not accept the behaviour we did in the eighties. These men soon find out it is not as amazing as they thought.

A work colleague of mine met a girl the same age as his daughter, he was a hero to his friends. However, very soon he felt out of place in crowded bars and late-night clubs, as soon as she mentioned having a baby he was out the door in record time.

Younger men want to meet older ladies, because they know there are less expectations. They generally have their own homes, own cars, and own income.
In the mind of the younger man, there is more sex with less drama. This is what some women want, but it was not for me.

I soon decided not to wait for my match to message me, I needed to message the men I found appealing. I made my messages more personal by commenting on something in his profile, followed with a question, as this would invoke a response. Initially I had some interesting chats, but they were not leading anywhere. Some men introduced the saucy chat straight off. Nothing shocks me, but it is not for me.

There are so many married men online looking for the chat, they don't even hide the fact they are married. They are not the worst ones however, the worst are the married men who pretend to be single. The more I chatted to men the more I learned. I began to read between the lines.

After a lengthy back-and-forth with a nice guy who asked, why was I still single? I said, 'that is a story better told over a drink.' He suggested meeting in a car park. I know the car park and its reputation, so I thanked him for his interest but suggested I was not looking for what he was hoping to find. Another one bites-the-dust, I thought.

Then, someone asked me out within three messages. This was more like it. He is into photography, music and cooks and he is very nice looking too.

We have a short phone call to set something up. His voice is smooth, but I am apprehensive. That is online dating. It is a quagmire. They seem too good to be true and they often are.

You read about the freaks, the sex fiends, and the catfish. They are there, but so are hundreds of lovely men. You hear about the cute, funny ones you want to meet, but suddenly they disappear, and you do not know what you did. They just vanish. This is termed 'ghosting'. Ghosting happens to the best of us, I found to keep sane, we need to stop telling ourselves it is because we are not good enough, it is best to let him disappear and make way for that lovely partner we all deserve.

I met this nice man at a restaurant. Usually, I make the first date a quick coffee, one-hour max, but this man suggested dinner and I did not resist. He is just as nice in person, and he looks like his photo. I am impressed. He is sweet, talks about his friends and his family, and we follow dinner with drinks. This is like the date from heaven. It is like finding a magical unicorn. The drinks are flowing, as is the conversation. However, the more the drink flows the more daring my nice man got. Nice turned nasty and my magic unicorn flew out the window. To say I was devastated might be an overstatement, but I was very disappointed. I got myself out of there by calling a friend to come and get me.

I did not think Mr Nice aka Mr Not-so-nice was dangerous, but I made enough mistakes for one night, so I took the precaution of paying the bill and leaving with my friend.

After getting home, I almost deleted my profile, but I took some deep breaths and decided to sleep on it. Next day was Sunday and I put some serious thought into my future dating.

Plenty of my friends do online dating like an Olympic sport. They have disasters as well as some of the most romantic evenings of their lives with men who then promptly vaporise into the earth's atmosphere. Whatever happens, it feels good to be in the game and planning a next date. I love the company of men and I love being with a special someone so sitting back is not an option.

I decided I would meet ten men and on the law of averages, one should be a match.
I read somewhere that our brains are best equipped to handle five to nine options, any more, and we go into cognitive overload. I went one more to increase my chances. I sat down that afternoon to pick ten potentials.

I started by deciding on the age, I was happy going five years younger and five years older than myself. I then settled on three deal breakers, no babies or young children, no young men, no narcissists or 'I' or 'me' men. I opted for three must haves, respect, communication, and consistency.

Of course, I had wants like hot, funny, romantic, but at this point, I decided to focus on needs first, like communication, mutual respect, and intelligent conversation. For me it is not all about feeling initial chemistry. It does not last.

Attraction is important, but I find if someone meets my needs, the attraction follows. I began the search. The abundance of websites and dating apps is not necessarily a good thing but I made a start.

I know quite a few people who have found love through match.com, anotherfriend.com, and tinder. I chose to go with plenty of fish, pof.com. I felt it was a more age-appropriate site. I also know many who have been on two or three dates with nice people from this site. Finding a match is one thing but getting to know them takes effort, but I was ready. There is no rush to meet possible partners instantly. Building trust and a rapport with someone takes time, and there is nothing wrong with taking it slow.

Although you should probably meet before too much time passes, as you need to find out who is at the other end of the keyboard. They are rarely the person you conjured up in your head. They certainly were not in my case, as I am very imaginative. In meeting more than a few you can improve your dating skills and get to know what it is you want.

Patience pays off in the end, which is just as well as I was looking at so many profiles. I was also receiving interesting messages. I did have questions though, like, why does a man have to send a photo of his penis when 'Hello, how are you?' would suffice. Seriously, guys keep the mystery hidden, until after ye meet, at least. I can only believe that men who do this believe the 'gift' will be welcome.

Choosing a match

It would be great if, at the precise moment you decide you are ready to date, your perfect match miraculously appears at your door with a giant smile on his face. Sadly, there is a little work involved in finding a good match. This includes asking yourself some searching questions and being truthful with the answers. You also need to have patience and be prepared to wait for the right person. It is not a straightforward matter to decide if you want to get into a relationship once again but, once you decide it is what you want, you need to be clear about what you want.

Most of us have been in previous relationships but those were different times, and different people. We were different then. Now you are embarking on a new relationship journey, understanding what aspects of a relationship are important to you is key. Ask yourself what personal qualities you value in yourself and in others.

It is time to make another list, an up-to-date list of qualities you are looking for in a man, and in a relationship. It is also important to make a list of things you will not compromise on. Try your best to prevent only listing artificial things, such as designer clothes, nice car, big house. These things will deflect you from what is important. Rather than focusing on the big paycheck, consider how compatible you are. Of course, physical attraction is important, too, but it is incredible how irresistible the right person will become the more you get to know them.

I want to meet someone who is kind, respectful, honest, loyal, and fun. If they have nice eyes and a cute smile that will be a bonus. Once you have made your own personal list, keep it in mind when you are reading profiles and meeting new men or getting to know someone better. If you are still not convinced if someone would be a good match for you, you can always chat it through with some friends and family to see what they think about it. We all know it takes two to have a relationship so try to make sure the person you choose to meet is also looking for a relationship and not just a hookup.

Firstly, try going to places where people with similar interests to you might go. Local clubs and societies produce great communities of like-minded people. There is nothing like a common interest to get you chatting with someone new. Perhaps, put yourself in some new social situations, like going to a gig, a party hosted by a friend or try a new bar. After all, you never know where you might meet someone. They could be anywhere, even in the supermarket.

I met people out and about and even through work, but they were not relationship compatible. If, like me, you want to try online or dating apps, be careful in your choices. Tinder has taken the world by storm. Swiping left and swiping right is all the rage. Think about creating a strategy before you begin swiping. Refer to your list and define what you want.

Once you have thought of all the characteristics you want to find in a mate, prioritise them. This is basically developing an algorithm or process just for yourself.

People who use Tinder tend not to be looking for long-term relationships but sometimes you might meet a nice man. I found that the same people were on more than one website so after some time I stuck to one and worked it.

It is OK to use two or three sites at a time but that is down to your personal choice. Bear in mind you will need to remember who you said what to. I more than once sent the wrong message to the wrong person ending up red faced.

For the most part, dating sites are not anything mysterious but they can be scary places to go initially. They are mostly like a catalogue, and match users based on their responses. I feel it is best to use the site as a giant database for you to explore. I made the decision to click on men I would not have met in the past. I will admit to clicking according to looks before reading the profile, but I am human.

Dating sites attempt to sort through our personalities, our wants, and our desires in order to connect us with our best possible matches. There is no need to put our blind trust in the system, but we can let it do some of the heavy lifting of figuring out what it is we want. This is managed by using the information we entered into our very own phones or laptops. Bad data in equals bad data out. They are as good as we want them to be, as they are calculating our half-truths and aspirational wishes.

Let us be honest, we rarely tell the whole truth. That said you could explore the site and see who is available and start the chats yourself.

It is only by chatting a little that we get a feel for the person before deciding if you want to meet them or not. Start looking now and think about what you will gain from the experience. Your match does not need to be perfect, but they should complement you and help you flourish. They should add to your happiness, not your stress. Ultimately, you should hope to find a man that will support you in your goals and you should be able to support him in his.

It may be simple to over-think things or justify the right or the wrong choice, but sometimes you just need to go for it. In a safe manner of course. I took a simple approach and learned the tools that helped me choose. I have learned a thing or two over the years about what works. It is all about the approach. It is not rocket-science, it is not even calculus, but it may take a little work on your behalf to flip your way of thinking. You may need to change your mind-set as well as your approach.

Sometimes the only person holding you back from the relationship of your dreams is you. I think we are attracted to the same type of person repeatedly. For me it is controlling people, which annoys me, as I like to see myself as independent. When you are choosing a new partner maybe change what you usually go for. It is time to put you first, and to recognise what makes you feel good. Maybe it is time to start inviting singles you like into your life. You will be surprised how much everything can change with just a few fundamental changes in your mind-set. Maybe you will be able to avoid relationship Groundhog Day. When deciding that online dating is up your alley, make sure you are careful in your choices.

Any woman who has tried online dating knows there are dangers. They know there is a lot of deeply weird stuff out there. In this book, we are not dealing with these. My advice is just block anyone weird, or anyone who makes you feel uncomfortable, immediately. It is unsafe to pursue. There are enough nice men out there, we do not need creepy or odd behaviour. Try reading between the lines. It is my opinion that men tell a few more untruths than women do. They say women lie about their age. It is my experience that most men are economical with the numbers because they are more interested in meeting a younger woman.

When I began looking online I believed everything men said until I began to meet them. They all stretched the truth about their height, their age, and their status. Men often say what they think women want to hear. They seem to forget they will meet in time, and their in-discrepancies will shine through. I know women stretch the truth too, but this book is based on women's experiences.

I have learned that when a man says the most influential person in his life is his mother, he is looking for someone to replace her. He sees her as living her life for others, and rarely thinks of her own happiness. Sounds great. We are all told that if a man cares for his mother he is a good man. This seems good on the surface, but I am not so sure, I think this could mean that this is what he wants. This is his definition of a good woman. This is what he is looking for. He classifies women by his mother, and he wants to know what you are willing to sacrifice for him because his mother sacrificed everything.

Maybe he says he is naturally predisposed to undertake a traditional role in a relationship but that he appreciates strong women. Unless you want to be a traditional wife bow out now, he wants to dominate, but he likes a challenge. If he says he is very affectionate and caring, wait until you see the evidence.

Others say I am looking for a woman who is trustworthy, honest, and able to get along with others. That sounds lovely and may be true but maybe he is just looking for a golden retriever. If he says he is looking for a woman who is generous and passionate and there has to be an attraction, it usually means he is looking for sex.

Maybe he says he is looking for an open-minded woman, what does this mean? Perhaps he wants to be with more than one person, or he could be trying to say he is in an open marriage.

He might say he would like to be accepted for who he is. I suggest you find out who he is before you accept it. Some of these characteristics may be fine for you, the idea is not to be judgmental. It is to figure out what is being revealed so you can make the right decisions for yourself.

If he says he was in love once, and this time he wants it for the rest of his life. He wants to be with a woman who gives her heart to him in its entirety. This is music to some women's ears, but you do not want to replace some other woman's shortcomings. Personally, I would avoid this scenario.

If he says, I am looking for a woman who keeps herself slim and fit and is house-proud. Absolutely no. This is a misogynist and so backwards in his way of thinking he has preconceived ideas. He is looking for a Stepford wife. Maybe this is what you would like but it is my firm belief this is a controlling person and a complete jerk. I have always been a giver, and I want someone who knows how to give as well. That was my focus.

By reading profiles as much as possible, we will learn who is sincere and who is not. The more we practise this kind of critical reading and thinking, the better we will become. I know it sounds cold and calculating but the internet can be a cold and calculating place. The more we know about it the better.

It is my experience that by far, most men are online for the same reason you are. Nonetheless, some have alternative motives. It is good to understand the reality of what we are doing. We just need to be smart about how we do it. It is good to avail ourselves of methods that make the most of our chance for success, just as we would with any other technological venture.

It is very valuable to try to figure out who the man is, instead of just concentrating on someone because his picture would look great on your phone. I went for normal looking men with regular pictures. Look for normal bios, not someone who works out non-stop, unless you want to work out with them, or someone who wants to go hiking every weekend, unless you are into hiking. Go into it with an attitude of being open and accepting. Be open to meeting someone outside of your normal type.

Log on to your chosen dating site or app, check out the men in your age bracket and if one jumps out at you, check out his profile. If you feel you are both suited with some things in common, take your courage in your hands and send a message. You do not need to wait patiently for someone to message you. Being new to a site or app, you will get a lot of likes, but many of these will be younger men, much older men and scam merchants but you will quickly learn to pick these out. There is a chapter in this book looking at the dangers and what to look out for when internet dating.

In essence I believe you need to be proactive if you want to meet someone nice and especially if you are looking for a relationship. After all, they are not going to come knocking at your door.

Listening to all the horror stories, you are probably full of scepticism when it comes to any form of online dating. No one could blame you. You may be on Tinder to meet someone special but remember many are on there looking for something casual, and some are looking to scam.

Regrettably, with any online dating site, you are going to come across fake profiles. It is all just part of being online these days. However, try not to worry too much. If you have your wits about you, and you are not the most naïve person in the world, there is absolutely no reason to be too fearful. Just be careful.

How to choose

There are many fake profiles that will try to take advantage of you. We have all heard of catfishing, this is someone pretending to be someone else. There are many reasons and agendas why catfish target people in the first place. They are hoping for financial gain. They want to push a service, product, or business. Sometimes it is to download malware to get your personal details for identity theft. Sometimes they want to mess with you, to make themselves feel better.

Having explored POF and looked at Tinder, I am familiar with most fake profiles. I like to think I can spot them a mile away. If their profile is missing a bio, occupation, or some interests or if it looks empty and lacking the human touch, be cautious. If the profile is hiding their distance, and or age it could be normal, but it could also be a deceit. If the profile pictures look like celebrities, or if you have a feeling, you recognize the person from somewhere, it might be a good idea to swipe left.

If the conversation does not flow normally and their replies do not seem to make sense you are most likely dealing with a bot. Bots are automated, they run according to their instructions, and can often imitate a human user's behaviour.

They do repetitive tasks and are much faster than humans. They may break into your account by scanning the web for opportunities to send spam, or to perform other malicious activities. Usually, they will ask you to join a strange app that no one really uses, like Kik.

Kik has red flags written all over it, in fact, a bot almost fooled me, they are very intelligent. More intelligent than some men. Nonetheless they are easy enough to spot when you are aware of them so do not join any strange app.

I have found if you have a gut feeling that it is too good to be true the chances are it is. For instance if he looks like James Bond and has the photos to prove it, and he wants to whisk you away in his Austin Martin, it is unlikely to be true.

If he immediately invites you into a long-term relationship because he cannot live without you, watch out, it is most likely he will not be able to live without your credit card details either. I know I am stating the obvious here but if he asks you to send money, gift cards, or gifts, no matter how besotted you think this man is with you, do not send money or anything close to it. You do not need me to tell you parting with your private details to anyone is never a good idea.

If you are looking for the reassuring presence of someone by your side or you are looking for a casual acquaintance you will find them through online dating. This book looks mostly at finding that calming presence we long for, we love to love. Love is the bond that connects us all. However, finding love in a life partner can be very challenging. People say it will take time, I say they will not come knocking at your door. Get out there and look because when you meet someone you connect with it is a wonderful feeling. Finding them is not easy.

Deciding what you are looking for is paramount. Finding casual dating is easy but finding a life partner is difficult. Choose someone who you can easily connect with. This way, you can talk about your day and the things you do without getting bored. If you pick someone with similar interests, this will work well in your favour. It is also nice to have some separate interests, it adds to your conversation.

When you decide you want to spend your life with someone, you should look at things the two of you can do together. For instance, if you are a movie buff, you should choose someone who also likes movies. If you like hiking, choose someone who likes to hike, it will make your life more interesting.

Choose someone with similar understanding and emotional intelligence. Think about it if you are a laid-back person but your partner is an overachiever, it could lead to difficulties. When choosing a life partner, you should consider your life hopes and dreams. Choose someone you respect and who will respect you.It goes without saying but I am going to say it anyway, you cannot spend your life with someone who has no respect for you, or your hopes and dreams. So, choose someone who will support you for the rest of your life.

Choose someone who is trustworthy. It is extremely important to choose someone you can trust. You cannot have a happy relationship if you cannot trust each other.

Choose someone who has time to spend with you. Spending time together is just as important as having similar interests.

Choose someone with a similar attitude toward relationships and choose someone with a similar social approach. Ask yourself, do you want someone who has tons of friends around, or someone who is more reserved, with just a few close friends? If you are a social butterfly and your potential partner is more of a wallflower, it could be a problem, or you could bring out their social side. It is a good thing to consider.

Whatever it is you are looking for in a partner it is individual to you. I hope my input gives you some insight. Though you may never know exactly who your ideal partner is, until you lock eyes with them, you can certainly think about the characteristics you are most looking for.

It is also good to consider the qualities you do not want. Especially qualities you consider deal breakers. The characteristics you do not want in a life partner can be just as important as the ones you are looking for. Finding a soul mate is not easy but knowing the things that are absolute deal breakers to you, will help in the search.

I considered the following:

A lack of attraction.
This would be a deal breaker, I believe physical attraction can grow but there needs to be something there to begin with. You may not want to rip off each other's clothes 10 years from now, but you should have a baseline of attraction that keeps things going. Even if the person you choose fits your wish list in all other ways, you cannot just make yourself be attracted to someone.

A lack of agreement on something that really matters to you.
It may be fun to disagree on some things. However, if you are a die-hard leftist and he is a die-hard conservative, there will be trouble in paradise. If there is something that defines you that your partner does not understand, you may have a problem.

Knowing your deal breakers is good, but knowing when to compromise is also good. Having a list of the things you would like, and the things you do not like, can give you a good sense of what will truly make you happy. The reality is that you will never be able to find the one who fits all your criteria.

The right one for you will be the one that makes you the happiest and most content. Turning someone down because they do not meet all your needs will not get you far. Finding that fine balance is the answer. Now it comes time to make your choice. You have all your lists. You are serious about your search. Only you can choose.

Chapter V

'GO!'

Getting started

Online dating may have solved the supply difficulties of romance, but it has not resolved the biggest problem of all, emotional intimacy. This requires hard work. I knew I had a journey ahead. I also knew it would be a roller coaster. I just did not know the direction it would take. I hope my story, my experience and my approach can be helpful to you as you get started.

I made the decision to go back to the beginning and reset the dating-meter. I tried online dating twice before. On each occasion I met a number of men but was unlucky in my encounters. This was my third time; maybe it would be lucky.

Resetting, I would meet for a coffee or a walk in the park, for the first date. That way I would have a chance to get to know my potential significant other and decide whether or not a second date was on the cards.

I would listen to all the advice and keep the focus on the future, not the past, no one likes to hear about an ex on a first date. I know I certainly do not. I was aware I would not find love at first sight but now was the time to get real and stop imagining the perfect dream partner. I would make the most of each experience and learn from it. This time I would be successful.

We all have to kiss a few frogs on the way to finding our prince. The stories contained in this book are based on real dating experiences. Some are mine and some are my friends. I believe, in reading these stories you will learn from them, and be able to draw up your own list of wants, needs, and hopes.

Resetting my online dating was exciting. I was more prepared this time and more confident in what I wanted and needed. I updated my profile with a snappy headline, a short, informative summary and as flattering a photo as possible. It was an honest photo, but I did show myself in my best possible light.

When I began again, it was fantastic in most ways. For the first few weeks, every single man I met was nice, but there was an undercurrent of 'no he is not the one'. The possibilities seemed endless. Seriously, it was like a catalogue of men you could meet if you wanted. Yes, I know you can meet people in bars or supermarkets or wherever else people meet people. With online however, all you have to do is send a message and see what happens, a kind of coward's hello. We have all been warned of the dangers of anonymous keyboard warriors so here we will focus on the positive.

My new profile was noticed. My confidence in myself skyrocketed. I was getting countless messages from Internet strangers, and it was fun. This is proof you are never too old. I felt having a few upcoming dates at once would be a good idea. That way, if one does not work out, it will not seem like the end of the world. I sent some messages, and it seemed to go well for one or two emails, but when they did not give me much to work with I got bored.

There were those who talked to everyone. Those who talked too much trying to initiate cheeky talk. Those who were total time wasters. Those who were most likely in a relationship. I always messaged back and told them if we did not seem to have enough in common, and I wished them luck in their search. I never just disappeared. That is rude.

I spent many dates bored out of my mind, knowing I needed to get out of there as soon as possible, but I tried to make the most of it. It was all experience after all, and would lead me to my 'one.' I did not owe these men anything, but I am not one to be rude. After resetting I knew I needed a get out sentence, and I would say 'I'd love to stay and chat, but I have an appointment, maybe we can chat another time'. Always have your get out sentence ready. In an ideal world, a person's profile is a little bit like getting an insight into who they are. That is if the profile is honest.

Taking time to read profiles will give you practise figuring out who is real, and who is not. I learned to read between the lines, as you will see in the pages to come. If a profile does not excite you, it is best to move on. Their profile should stand out to you. You should be able to see something that appeals to you. You should feel like you could be friends with this man.

I understand the idea is to meet a man you want to be more than friends with, but being friends is a good place to start. This form of dating can be exhausting, but remember it is entirely possible you will meet the man of your dreams. I always said I went online dating, to get off online dating.

It is very difficult to try out dating apps for the first time in our fifties. I began by meeting everyone and anyone and tired myself out. The second time around I tried to be more selective, but I still said yes too many times.

After resetting, I decided not to waste time on anyone, especially to those who did not reach out often enough to me. If they do not communicate when starting out, it would only worsen as time went on. I cannot be with someone who does not communicate.

I love going on dates even if it is terrifying initially but the whole getting dressed up and going out is fun. I recommend you go on a date sooner, rather than later, to find out if you are compatible. I am in favour of a phone call beforehand, as this breaks the ice and gives you a good indication if there is compatibility. The first phone call with someone, is your first real interaction with them, you are going from cyberspace, to exchanging private contact information.

It can be hard to go from messaging to talking on the phone. Use this initial phone call to get to know more about the man you are talking to. This way you can decide if they are worth the time and effort to meet in person. Perhaps approach this call with the mentality that you are screening them and making sure you can have a conversation.

Although you may be nervous, try to be your true self. Once you have messaged forward and back for some time and you feel you might be compatible, suggest a call. Set up a date and time for your call, I would ask for his number, and once you get it send a quick message back saying 'thank you for sharing your number, this is mine. It is that simple. Perhaps follow the text with 'I will text you soon, when we can chat and get to know each other a little better'.

Preparation is key, especially if you are messaging more than one man at a time. Before the call, read his profile again, and list out a few interesting things, that way you will not be dumbstruck on the call. If you reach a point in the conversation where you both go quiet, you can pull one of these topics from your list. It will also safeguard you from mixing him up with a different man. I recommend writing his name down.

Also list out a few interesting things about yourself to keep the conversation going. You want to put forward your best stories here. If the chat is going well, feel free to save them for the first date. Take a few deep breaths before you call and try to have a friendly and nice tone for the entirety of the call. Remember there is no body language to read on the phone, all your communication is verbal.

Try your best to be you and try to project energy and confidence into your voice even if you are not feeling it. Be as fun and playful as you can. Keep things light and get to know each other without getting into controversial topics or without getting into anything too deep. The whole purpose of this chat is to make sure he is worth meeting in person and setting up that very first date.

Fifteen minutes into this call, you will have a good inkling if you want to meet him in person, or not. If you feel you would like to meet, suggest a coffee at the weekend, and see the response you receive. If you decide you do not want to meet him in person because the call does not flow, or you are not getting the vibe, do not worry that is normal, and that is why a phone call is beneficial. It is all a learning experience.

Not every call is going to work out. However, sometimes it is worth giving the benefit of the doubt. Not everyone may be as prepared as you, and let's be honest some people are better in person. If you prefer not to meet, be honest, say he sounds very nice, but you feel you do not have enough in common to meet up.

If you enjoy chatting and you decide you would like to move onward to a first date, you should wind up the call, and get that date set up as soon as possible. You could say something like "it has been lovely chatting to you and getting to know you a little better. Maybe we could chat more over coffee or drinks next week?" Then add, when you are free and ask him what works best for him.

Men do not always want to be the one to ask because they fear rejection. We as women, can actually take the first step. Presuming your conversation went well, moving to a first date will be a natural transition.

Once he tells you what day works best for him, seize the day, and end the call by saying 'I will text you later in the week and we can take it from there'. If you enjoy talking on the phone, you like hearing each other's voice, and you make each other laugh, there is a strong chance you will both get along in person. Having phone interaction before you meet acts as an icebreaker and should help in making you both feel more at ease on a first date. A simple phone conversation will save both you the time and effort of going out on a bad date.

Maybe you should make your first phone conversation your first date, and if that goes well, your second date will be all the better.

Just because you have arranged a date does not mean you sign off the dating site or stop messaging other potential matches but be careful what message you send and to who.

If you start dating, hide your profile, and do not interact with anyone else out of respect. Now that you have spoken and agreed a first date it is time to look forward and prepare.
When preparing for a date, especially a first date, it is important to look forward and do some planning. This was definitely something I was going to do my third time around the dating block.

Getting date night ready involves preparing in advance, that way you can focus on having a good time and putting your best foot forward to impress the man of your dreams. Give your date a text to confirm everything, you want to make sure that you are both on the same page about the time and place of your meeting.

Think about charging your phone and keep it with you. While you should not be fidgeting with it during the date, your phone is helpful to have ready just in case. Always let someone know where you are and have a safety text ready. If either you or your date is running late or has to cancel because of a last-minute emergency, you will need your phone to communicate. You can keep in touch with a friend to let them know you are ok or if you need rescuing. Our phones have become very valuable tools and can be very helpful in this instance.

If you get lost on the way there, or while heading back home, you can use your phone's GPS for help. Make sure you know how to get where you are going. Look up directions if you need to at least a few hours ahead of time. If you are driving, try to avoid rush hour, or use public transport. Give yourself extra time and leave early. I think it is good to be early to prepare yourself, as well as give yourself time to find a good vantage point. Have your purse or wallet ready ahead of time. In addition to money, I suggest some breath mints, lipstick, and a phone charger.

It is important to try to relax. The more prepared you are the less anxious you will be and the better your date will go. Take the last few minutes before you meet up to chill out and relax as much as possible. If you drink, you might enjoy a tipple before your date arrives to help you unwind, but do not go overboard, one is enough. I found this out the hard way. I was once three sheets to the wind before my date arrived and he swung around and ran back out the door.

Stay calm, take slow, deep breaths, try to live in the moment, easier said than done, but it works. Like the first phone call, it might help you feel more self-confident to plan a few things to talk about ahead of time or put together a couple of interesting questions you might bring up during your date, in case the conversation slows down.

Pick out what you are going to wear ahead of time. It is best to do this sooner rather than later, to keep from dashing around at the last minute to find the perfect outfit. Most of all make sure you are comfortable.

I know looking nice is a priority, feeling comfortable will go a very long way to help you feel calm, relaxed, and confident. First impressions are very important. Going home before going out, will give you time to think about how you want to present yourself. It only takes a few seconds for someone to form an opinion about you based on how you look, your demeanour, as well as your manners, and your conduct. Take some time to dress well, but stay true to your style, and dress appropriately for the occasion.

Try not to make things more complicated by planning a whole day out. Keep things short and simple for a first date. You can make a fast exit if it is not going well. However, if things go well, the coffee or drinks could turn into dinner, which could add some spontaneity into the mix.

Some anxiety is natural on a first date and is part of the fun. However, the calmer you feel, the more comfortable your date will be. Texting and messaging can certainly give you a sense of another person, but to really get to know them, you need more than messages, on a screen, even a phone call, you need facial expressions, body language, and tone of voice. I was one for moving from virtual, to real, quickly. I wanted to meet the person behind the words to see if they were who I dreamed them up to be. You will see later in the book how my imagination very often lets me down.

Considering, you would not go to a job interview without preparing in advance, I suggest you put the same preparation into a first date. Think about some good first date questions you might ask, and some nice answers to the questions that may come your way.

However, do not treat the first date like an actual interview. I had those dates, and I heard the alarm bells ringing.

Keep in mind that good first date questions are just as important as the answers. Maybe ask about hobbies, family, what they like to do on holiday. Think about focusing on listening well, and making your date feel comfortable. Avoid sensitive topics and do not ask how much the other person earns, or why their last relationship ended. You might want to know but these are questions best left to another time.

I learned a simple trick of sitting at a right angle to my date rather than facing them directly. This helped take the pressure off trying to fill every pause in the conversation, as you can do a little people-watching instead. Most people love to be around confident, positive people. So do your best to show your confidence, even if you do not feel it, fake it.

Body language is powerful, as this tells your date a lot about how you see yourself. As well as looking confident, hone your listening skills. We all love to talk about ourselves, but no one is as interested in ourselves as we are. If you make your date all about you, you will send out all the wrong signals. However, do not switch off completely, your date will want to hear something about you. The trick is to listen wisely and respond appropriately, nodding and asking follow-up questions.

Now you are prepared, you are dressed well, your hair looks well, your make-up is on, and you feel confident. You have your phone, your charger, money, and some lippy, you are ready for your date.

Set off early to ensure you are not late. This way you will have time to visit the ladies, to make sure you do not need any repairs, before you meet the potential one.

Dating in the present might feel like a struggle, or maybe it has always been that way, but it should not be about winners or losers. It is in fact about finding someone to connect with, someone to care about, someone who will make you happy and someone you can make happy in return. Whether the date works out or not, it is good to be memorable to the other person.

It is good to use their name in conversation, it lets them know you are paying attention and that you care about what they have to say. It is good to put across the best version of yourself. When we hear somebody use our name we instantly think, they like me because they remember my name. For goodness-sake, do not call them by the wrong name. As human beings, we like nothing more than to be appreciated by someone else. When we feel like our opinions matter, we open up and feel secure.

Going out to meet a stranger on a date can be overwhelming, but it can give you permission to ask very personal questions. I learned many fascinating things on first dates. It was all practice, and the more first dates I had the less unnerving it was.

It is so much easier to go out with a stranger, as they are less likely to hurt your feelings, when it feels like there are hundreds of other people in your pocket. Nevertheless, I now wanted to find 'the one' I was no longer interested in the throw away dating scene. As I was resetting my dating brain.

I told myself all the other dates did not count, and really, they did not count but the experience counted. I was back to where I started.

I feel I presented myself in a good light, but this time the goal was not to get the highest number of matches, it was to attract the man who would fit well, with the real me. I was on a mission. My profile demonstrated the real me, I felt it was snappy, interesting and classy. I did not want to be like everyone else. I wanted to be authentic and find that genuine match. I read that educated women were not popular online, but I was not going to hide the fact. I put myself across as smart, confident, silly and quirky.
My photo was the real me. I wanted my profile to lead me to a man who would appreciate me. I tried to limit my time spent on apps, as well as the number of people I corresponded with. As previously, I tied myself in knots chatting to too many men at once. I could not remember what I said to who. It was exhausting.

Online dating is made to be addictive, after all the longer you are on there the more opportunity, they have to eject money from you. Select a good time for you to devote to the process, I decided on once a day in the evening so I could give it my full attention, be fully present and give each new suitor my undivided attention. If you think your online dating matches are slim or you don't click with the men contacting you, try widening your criteria. Conduct your own search. For example, you could extend the age range of potential matches, or you could contact someone you would not consider normally dating.

I received a message from a man, whose photo was him, sitting on a yacht. I checked out his profile and he seemed interesting, but he was younger. I messaged him back and we had a number of communications before I said he seemed very nice, but he was a bit young for me. He suggested meeting for a coffee after all he said, 'he wasn't asking me to marry him'. I decided to say yes.

A lesson I learned previously was that prolonged texting builds up unrealistic, romanticised expectations. In meeting this man as soon as possible, I would know if he was who he said he was, and if the age difference would matter. It is my opinion if the man refuses to meet within a few weeks or keeps postponing a meeting it is best to move on unless you are just looking for a virtual man-friend.

This man's name was Marty, and he liked my dating profile, in addition, I liked his. We saw each other's photos and we exchanged some hopeful messages. It was time to meet for the big first date. I was nervous when I passed on my phone number, but I was serious about dating this time, and if I wanted to meet someone, I would need to trust my instinct. I did my research, I had some previous practice, and now I was ready. I had to start somewhere. Marty said he would be in my area in a week, and he would call me. I told him a venue I felt comfortable in.

I chose 'Pointe Vecchio', my favourite coffee and wine venue. I felt relaxed here, plus I knew the staff, so they would look out for me. I read somewhere that sixty percent of women pick a café as an ideal first date venue.

Meeting someone new, even if you feel you know them through their messages, can still be daunting.

It is not always easy to keep the conversation going with a stranger. It helps if you are somewhere, you feel comfortable. On the day of my first date, I was waiting for Marty to call me. We had arranged our meeting for that afternoon, but we had not arranged a time.

After what felt like an eternity, he called, and you could have knocked me down with a feather. I said hello, then he said hello, it was not the hello I expected, his was not an Irish accent. It never occurred to me that Marty was not Irish as he put himself forward with an Irish username, and he said he was from Co. Clare. He felt my hesitation and asked if everything was ok. I said I was taken aback by his accent, he thought he had mentioned he was German.

Although it threw me, I was delighted to meet someone who might be somewhat exotic. I know German and exotic is not a normal combination, but a different culture would be fun to explore. This added to my nerves. As I crossed the little foot bridge over the canal in Killaloe, I could see Pointe Vecchio, in the distance and the strange man walking up and down outside it.

He was shorter than he said, and his choice of outfit was interesting, just below the knee shorts with red braces a white shirt buttoned to the neck adorned with a red dickie bow. For one moment I was tempted to run but I had come this far and although my heart was going at a rapid pace, I walked towards him with a smile on my face.

He greeted me with a kiss on both cheeks and gave me a rose, a gesture I appreciated. I knew I had done all my preparation, so I began to relax as we sat at table L-2 in the library and sipped our coffee. The chat flowed, the coffee flowed and still I did not feel totally at ease. Maybe it was the accent or the varied topics of conversation. He seemed to be an expert at everything. I felt the need to change the subject. I had some questions ready that I was genuinely interested in, and now it seemed like a good time to introduce them. He was all over the travel questions, this gave me some great insight into his personality, and he seemed flattered by the attention. He loved chatting about himself.

It was not a giddy evening, but the conversation flowed, still I felt it did not feel very natural. Perhaps it was the cultural difference. I was not entirely relaxed. He was a nice man and he seemed happy to see me, but I was not in a flirting mood.

If I fancy someone, I can be flirtatious. I was trying hard to like this date, but it just was not doing it for me. My friend was on stand-by as my emergency contact. I picked up my phone to text her to get me out when he said "what are you doing on your phone, are you on tinder? "I said "no I had to meet a friend and I am letting her know I am going to be late". This is when things took a turn for the worst. He said he had driven from the other side of the county and did I expect him to drive straight home. I was a little taken aback, he muttered something in German, and I said, 'you seem very nice, and I enjoyed meeting you for a coffee, but I felt as we wanted different things in life it would be better if we said goodbye now'.

He was not at all pleased, his face turned puce to match his dickie-bow and he huffed and puffed all the way out the door. I was relieved when he was gone but I learned the lesson to always speak on the phone first. Not to check if the man is Irish or not, but in phone chats you get a better sense of the person you are about to meet.

In this instance, I have to admit the photo of him on a yacht coloured my decision making. It was obvious he had planned the coffee and no doubt he was looking to come back to mine. He certainly had not planned on driving straight home. It was not a dangerous date, but it was uncomfortable.

However, it was onwards from here, I was going to date ten men, and this was just the first and when I looked back at it, it was a learning experience. I want a man to be completely crazy about me, the way I am about him. I know it takes time for feelings to develop but I knew I did not want to charm someone I did not feel totally at ease with. I am big into gut feelings and my gut knew this date was not for me, I forced my gut to be quiet, which is never a good idea. That night I decided to dust myself off and choose Mr Right number two the next evening.

Back to the drawing board

The next evening, I sat down to my laptop to see if I had any messages and to check who was online. I had a message from Mr Germany telling me how I missed out on a good thing, he was not at all happy. After all, I was nothing to write home about, according to him. He was only looking for a washing machine and a dryer. He was not going to put up with a prejudiced women like me. I was so tempted to answer him back but instead I just blocked him and thanked the universe for my gut.

None of us want to be with a man who wants us to feel bad about ourselves, it is not healthy we all deserve much better. It is all about looking and feeling our best. It is not about being fake. We should try to make an effort to look our best at all times. I admit I do not always pull that off, but I will try harder.

Men are visual creatures so looking your best will not only make you feel better, but it may spin the odds in your favour. That can only be a good thing but also when we look our best, we feel our best. Feeling good will let our personality shine through. I am not a big make-up person, but I am the first to admit a little make-up can go a long way. Smiling makes us all become more attractive to others. That is why I love lipstick.

Most of us want to meet someone with a good sense of humour. Try displaying a good sense of humour yourself. It makes everything better. It does not mean we need to be in fits of giggles all the time, or laugh at everything, but we should try not to take ourselves too seriously.

It is good to feel at ease with ourselves and be ready with a laugh, especially on a date. It is nice to be around people who like to laugh. We do not need to be comedians, just light-hearted, and smiley.

I decided to take my time in choosing my next date. I was going to build my self-confidence, it had taken a little bit of a bruising. Every time you go on a date, it takes effort, nerves, and emotion. Becoming confident is not about being loud, boisterous, superior or egotistical. It just means growing into a space where you feel comfortable in your own skin. I wanted to be comfortable in my own skin going on my next date.

I wanted to be secure, sweet, and modest but I also wanted to be ready to come out of my shell. Looking after myself and becoming more poised and self-assured would not only be good for me, but others like confident, interesting people who lead their own lives. We all like to be around interesting people. The only men who like insecure, vulnerable women, are the ones who are insecure themselves.

They may want to dominate. In the cut-throat world of dating we must create interesting and likeable prospects of ourselves. If we meet our long-time partner, they will discover our flaws over time but there is no need to put them out on a plate the first time you meet. As I say, maintain a little mystery. There is no harm in presenting a more polished version of ourselves. I believe it is about being our best self. We all plan what we want from the other person but perhaps we should go into the date thinking about what you want for yourself, how you want to put yourself forward.

Thinking about organising a new date was exciting. This time I would be even more prepared. I started focusing on positive attributes and put my insecurities or perceived imperfections to the back of my mind. I find confidence attractive in other people, so I would concentrate on my own confidence. Remember a time when you felt really good about yourself, visualise that moment, it will boost your confidence before a date. It is always worthwhile tidying up and picking out something nice to wear. It is respectful to showcase the best version of yourself. I am not advocating you completely change yourself to be attractive for the other person, but it is nice to feel attractive to yourself.

Making an effort for your date shows that you are invested in both your own appearance and the date itself. This will make whoever you are sitting across the table from feel special too. Dating is meant to be a fun way to get to know another person, so focus on the fun aspect. Put in your best possible effort and make it an opportunity to become the best version of you.

First date ready

Photo uploaded, profile uploaded, my wish list at the ready, my deal breaker list at the ready, I was ready to find my soul mate, well at least I was ready to meet someone for a first date, once again. Coffee or drink dates offer a lot of flexibility without too much obligation on either part. You are not committing to spending several hours with someone you only know virtually. Nonetheless, you still have the opportunity to get to know each other better.

Imagine going on 100 dates, before stumbling upon the person you want to spend the rest of your life with. This was my third time on the merry-go-round of dating. I have been on just about every date situation imaginable. This third time around, the photo of myself was not one hundred percent representative of me because I did not want to be judged for my looks. However, I realised this may have been a mistake as my date looked me up and down before pulling a face, very clearly surprised by what he saw. This is not what I wanted. I added a full-length photo of me wearing a nice red dress to my profile and prepared for my next date.

The idea of going on yet another first date with yet another man to see if you click can be exhausting. Nevertheless, I was determined. I was only looking for one person to match, but going on past experience this could take some time. The only thing is the online dating ocean is regularly refreshed.

I made dating a profession for me. I approached it in a similar manner and hoped each one would bring me my future love. I approached each date with the best and truthful representation of myself. I have one friend hoping to meet someone nice, and she is very tall and looks for tall guys. She would prefer to meet someone on her eye level at least, but all too often she went on dates with men who added inches to his height. He was the one who ended up more uncomfortable. There is little point in lying.

Keeping things casual is best. Try not to chat about past relationships. I always said we married too young. It is best to focus on what you are good at, and ask him what he is good at, as people show the best version of themselves when they are talking about their passions. If you like what you hear and see, you might get those little butterflies and it may be worth exploring a second date. However, if you know almost immediately this man is not for you, do not suffer through an awful encounter. I used to feel I owed my date something, but I did not. It took me a long time to sum up the courage to say enough is enough. The earlier you learn this lesson the better. After all, if your date shows up looking about 20 years older than the 45 years he'd claimed, he lied, what else will he lie about? It is ok to end a date if you know it is not going to work.

Please learn from me; I sat through too many horrendous encounters. If you know he is not for you and never will be, thank him for meeting you, but you do not want to waste his time, and escape.

It is tiring to keep going, but if you want to meet someone, you have to. Sometimes, it is easier to stay home or simply settle, but it will get better so keep leaving the house. Keep going on dates, when you meet the one for you and you are the one for him, you will know. It will all be worth it. It is best to be upfront about what you want, but you do not need to spell it all out on a first date. Starting with the wedding dress in mind on a first date, with a stranger, is definitely too much.

I am always in a hurry to get what I want, but in this instance, I taught myself to allow things to go at an easy pace. No harm in sharing some of your hopes and dreams as you would like to see if he has similar ones.

No need to go down a negative road with a man who is a stranger for now. I never felt it was necessary to argue about paying the bill. I always offered but I wanted to see if he felt I was worth a coffee and a muffin. I also wanted to see if he was willing to take charge. This is down to you. Many of my friends prefer to pay, as they do not want to feel obligated. This is also a legitimate feeling.

For me, if I was never going to see him again, I did not care, and if I was going to see him again, I would treat him to a coffee next time. Each time I enjoyed a date I sent a message to say thank you for your time and for the coffee and this put the ball in his court. Continue reading through the following stories, they will give you examples of what you might expect, you will realise you are not alone.

Chapter VI

'My Dating Stories'

Table 24

Here we go again, was my first thought as I sat down at table 24. After my Mr Right-now, and my second disastrous stint of online dating, I was online again. Seriously, how do I get myself into these situations? Though I am determined I will get it right this time.

As I sat there I wondered what the next hour would bring. Who would face me across the table this time? The saying 'a martyr for punishment' came to mind as I checked my reflection in the window. I sat there as I have on many previous occasions looking out the arch shaped window, which held some of the most beautiful scenery in the world. For a moment, I got lost in my own thoughts, as I stared at the thirteen arch ancient bridge over the River Shannon that led to Killaloe. I was mesmerised by the flow of the water, which seemed to be in a hurry this evening, I was in a hurry too for my date to arrive.

Staring past the bridge, I could see the Romanesque cathedral built in the 1180s but destroyed soon afterwards when a new gothic style cathedral was completed on the same site. I thought of the impressive Romanesque doorway that I often walked through to feel the peace and restfulness of the ancient walls. I could do with that feeling of restfulness now as I awaited what might be the answer to all my prayers. What am I praying for, you might ask? I am praying for the man of my dreams to walk through the door. So far, I have only met the men of my nightmares, but I live in hope.

Hope is something I only discovered some time ago after coming to terms with the breakdown of my marriage. My optimism and hope is based on the expectation that I will find the right man. I sit here now full of anticipation as I have many times before. On those occasions however my optimism was crushed. My hopes dashed. Nonetheless, I will remain confident and hope that my enthusiasm will not be denied this time.

I wait there sipping a glass of 'Cote de Rhone rouge', as I do, I reminisce about the first time I sat here at 'Table 24'. I was full of expectation, anticipation, and suspense, only to be duped. My would-be Mr Perfect was not as ideal as he made me believe, or as I led myself to believe.

We all have a tendency to build a picture. I always build an optimistic picture, I have a great imagination. The five foot eleven, well dressed, fit man in his early fifties with black hair turned out to be five foot seven, with shirt stretched across his not so fit paunch, and his hair had disappeared. This was not a big problem for me as I am five foot two and I like bald men, but he was definitely ten years older than his most recent photo. I was not looking for older and, more importantly, I was not looking for a liar. I was disappointed. I am no oil painting, but I was, as I described myself, and my photo was only six weeks old. So, needless to say, the man who presented himself to me then bore little or no resemblance to the man I had been messaging online.

I remembered he was not even apologetic about his deceit. I know, telling a little lie here and there will not make you a terrible person, but lying for self-gain, or personal agenda, to manipulate or hide information, is a betrayal. If someone lies about who they are, it is difficult to put your trust in them. A habit of lying is not good for any relationship, and I certainly did not want to begin seeing someone when it was built around lies.

Sitting here reminiscing and staring at the bridge I realised my newest prospect was a no show. The strange thing was I didn't really mind, I was out, and I was spending time with myself. But 'table twenty-four' had not brought me any luck.
So, I thought as well as changing my approach to dating, I would change the venue. I would go for an intimate, familiar, safe setting. A venue I knew well, 'Ponte Vecchio'.

All the Mr's

In writing this book I spoke to both men, and women on their experiences. It is amazing how different yet how similar everyone's story was. My friends have given me permission to write some of their stories as long as I change their names which I did. You can imagine us all sitting around in cosy Ponte Vecchio sipping wine and getting giddy. We recounted our various stories to hysterical, highly amusing and side-splitting laughter. We all need a good laugh and that night we had one.

If you live a politically correct life, I suggest you give this chapter a skip, as it is anything but politically correct.

As a group of ladies, we do not wish to offend but we were in a safe space and there was wine. We said it how we felt. Not everyone on dating sites is looking for their forever love, or their Mr Right. We all know that not everyone who swipes right is going to be the right fit for us.

One of my friends Carrie said she was so shocked, that if someone swiped right on her, they had to be her fit. She felt she got so few swipes she would act on every single one. On one occasion she decided to meet the guy who swiped right on her. She told us the story and we were in tears, we laughed so much.

She went to meet him in a well-known coffee shop in Limerick. She was a nervous wreck, but she had committed to a coffee so she would follow through. She looked around for a table but no sign of a man sitting alone waiting for her. She sat down and just as she tired of waiting, a man approached her table, "please don't let it be him", she thought.

He was wearing glasses like jam jars but all she could concentrate on was his belly that came between him and every table, chair, and person he passed. It was him. He had been waiting outside and apologised profusely for keeping her waiting inside. Carrie wanted to disappear into the wallpaper behind her, as he was nothing like his profile. She did everything she could to stay and talk to this man who was currently telling her about his new car he had just picked up.

At this point Carrie had two large coffees and desperately needed the ladies but this man and his belly lay between her and her escape.

She kept her legs crossed and said she would need to leave as she had to collect her daughter. He took off his glasses and looked at her and said he would love to see her again. Carrie was surprised he could see her at all without his glasses. When he took them off, she didn't know which eye to look at, as they were facing different directions. She told him she would text him as he was like a little puppy, and she could not tell him there and then that she never wanted to see him again.

As Carrie left the car park, she saw a man standing by a car with the bonnet up, it was him and his new car, it really was not his day, but Carrie escaped and putting her foot on the accelerator, she escaped faster. She had not escaped fully, however, as when she got home, he had texted her asking to meet again. She was sure she was not interested in him after that first date, she rang me, and I told her to make sure she told him no right away. Be kind but direct.

There was no point in telling him she was busy, you need to tell men directly, he will not get it if you tell him 'Now is not the right moment to have a romantic relationship with me. I am not in the right space.' Tell him straight, say something like, 'I enjoyed our first date and the conversation. It was nice to meet you, but I do not feel the chemistry. Thank you for your time.' Carrie said this experience put her off for now, but she would try again soon.

The reality of searching dating sites can be isolating and lonely at times. When you do not get a match, it may feel like a personal failure. It is difficult to find connections that you want to hold on to for a long time.

All us ladies chatting that night wanted to find a real connection. You have to be ready to put yourself out there and not beat yourself up when it does not work out. I felt like giving up so many times, but I kept going. Have a laugh with your friends, it really helps. I was very sensitive when I started out, but I copped on very quickly. I went on so many dates, I began to become immune. But I knew I would find 'my one' eventually. He was out there, and I was not going to settle. There were many times I thought I had found the one, and although not as scary as Carrie's date, I also had my unnerving, disconcerting moments.

I was adamant I was not going to meet a farmer, but one man messaged me, and I was intrigued. If I am honest, I was mostly intrigued by the fact his farm was on the West Clare coast, overlooking the sea. I loved this area so much. It is where my soul comes alive. I thought this was meant to be.

He was younger than me, very well built, and had a handsome face plus he seemed nice. We arranged a meeting in the Inn at Dromoland, I was looking forward to it as this really did seem like a genuine dating opportunity.

I arrived at the 'Inn' early so I could go to the ladies and make sure I looked my best me, and I was able to fix my lipstick, a must. I got myself a white wine spritzer and sat back in a lush armchair in the lounge. As I luxuriated into the chair, I saw him walk through the door. The first thing I noticed was the 'farmer' jumper. Yes, there is such a thing. I then noticed how it was hanging off him. The buff man in the picture was now a shell of himself.

He approached me and I stood up to greet him. I immediately got the scent of smoke in my nostrils and I was sure he had non-smoker on his profile. As he sat down, I could tell he was very nervous. It was endearing, but I was not feeling the vibes. However, I could hear the metaphorical waves crashing against his land in West Clare, and that made him somewhat more attractive.

We started chatting and I could tell he was shy. He started to spill his whole life story and it was a tragic one. He said he put up an old photo of himself online, because he knew he was a shadow of his old self. His wife had died tragically. Of course, this had a lasting effect on him, I was amazed he was even out on a date. It transpired he was lonely, and he missed the company of a woman. I was the only one who replied to him. I told him I felt he was too young for me, but I thought it would be nice to meet and see if there was any connection.

I told him his farm by the sea was a great temptation. That is when he took a different direction with the conversation. He was overcoming his shyness, he wanted to know if he could tempt me up to West Clare, I smiled, and said I might be passing by sometime, and he could make me a coffee.

Something had shifted in the conversation, it had been deep and meaningful, but now it was inane and racy. It was off-putting to say the least. I asked him why he chose me from the website. He said he had met younger women, but they were not experienced or mature. His wife had been a younger woman and his friends told him he should look to meet an older woman as she would be more grateful. 'More grateful for what' I asked to which he had the decency to blush. To say I shifted in my plush chair is an understatement. Many older women return the interest younger men show them. But not me. I had been there, and I was not going back.

The attraction that younger men have to older women is one that many people wonder about. To some people age gaps do not matter. Especially if the man is the older one in the relationship. However, couples seem to get strange looks when the woman is the older one.

Many young men look to older women for security, emotional compatibility, social status, and physical experience. Some men reveal they are attracted to the lack of baggage, or excessive demands, that accompany dating older women. Most older women are more established in life, and they are not interested in building a family. They are more focused on growing their careers, bank accounts, and exploring the world than younger women. Younger men find maturity attractive, but I suspect my pal here was more interested in physical experience.

Knowing his recent life experience, I resisted the urge to smack him and leave. I changed tack, and asked him what was he really looking for? He said he wanted a sex life. I wished him luck and told him he should consider being more truthful with the next woman he meets and although older women were a catch, in this instance it would not be me.

I was ready for a real relationship and tough as it may sound, I did not want to babysit.

I am guessing he felt he had nothing left to lose, as he asked me how I felt about men in ladies' underwear? I was quick to say it would not appeal to me, but I am sure it was fun for others.

I thanked him for meeting me and began to say my goodbyes. This is when he got very vocal about how he didn't need me anyway, he had a couple he was meeting for a threesome at the weekend, and I was not invited. I smiled, and although I walked away with most of my dignity intact, I could not wait to get out of there. When I got into my car, I automatically pressed the internal locking system, started the ignition, and raced out of there. On the drive home I began questioning my judgement. I allowed myself to fall into the weird trap more than once. I thought the more men I met the better chance I had of meeting a suitable match, there is logic in there, but I was not taking the time to think about quality. I needed once again to reassess my choices and redefine my search.

As well as the younger man looking to meet an older woman, older men look to meet younger women. It is not a new phenomenon for older men to look to meet younger women. From my perspective, this is irritating. When you go online dating you will notice profiles of men looking for women much younger than themselves.

He might be sixty, but his profile says he is looking for a woman aged thirty to forty. We all know the cliché of women not disclosing their age and pretending to be younger, but I feel men tend to act and appear younger than their chronological age.

I wonder if men are in denial about the after-effects of time on their looks and physique. Men may feel they look younger so being with younger women helps boost their ego.

My friend Lisa met a man twenty-two years her senior but when she met him, she thought he was only five years older than her. After meeting online, she says they did not immediately connect, but he offered financial security. This was important to Lisa, and she hoped she would learn to love him in time. He took care of her every need, he even bought her a car. She was happy out until he wanted to meet her family to formalise their relationship. Lisa was not interested in this.

While he was a good man and provided for her, she was more interested in the financial assistance that he had to offer. Lisa admitted she was neither attracted to him physically, nor did she want to take him to meet her family. She explained to Phil that she was not interested in taking their relationship any further at the moment. This was not the best relationship for Lisa, but she seemed to be happy enough in it. When she found out Phil was twenty years older than her, she lost interest in him as a life partner, but she did not want to let go of the financial support.

Not the type of relationship I would want, but to each their own. Lisa suddenly saw her role as more sedentary into the future. She wants children, she wants to travel, she wants to paint the town red, and she knew Phil had achieved all these things already.

Lisa decided she would have to move on and financially look after herself. Phil did not do himself any favours by lying that much about his age.
I found younger men more exasperating, they were sex-led and saw the older lady as an easy target. My young farmer continued to text me and eventually I had to block him. I certainly had a good escape from him.

Be prepared when you first go online, you will be pounced on, so be ready. Most will be young men looking for a naïve newcomer who will listen to their promises of love. They will be quick to seek out photos or videos of a naughty nature and you may be tempted. If it is something you want and enjoy, I will not judge, but if you are not comfortable, do not be coerced into something you do not want to do. At the very least meet first. You would not give some man walking down the street a naked photo of you.

Sally told us she was falling hard for 'Mr Text and Talk' who was much younger. He told her everything she wanted to hear. His messages were captivating and soon she was sending him photos, innocent photos to begin with, she then sent more revealing ones and before she knew it, she was sending explicit videos. All this and she had never met him, 'the love of her life'.

The question has to be asked: can you ever really know someone inside and out without meeting up in person? There are some people who even believe you can fall in love with someone you have never met. I, on the other hand believe, it is difficult to know someone you meet in person, but it is even more difficult to know someone you meet virtually.

They can be anyone they please to be. There can be a connection, even an intense connection as they invade every fibre of your being. Without being able to spend time with someone in person you fall in love with the idea of who they really are. Many invest themselves emotionally in relationships before knowing who they are investing in. Like Sally.

So many have the desire to be loved and can be guilty of making attachments to others despite never meeting them. It is very easy for people to present an idealised version of themselves on dating sites and apps.

You cannot know if you have a true connection with someone until you meet them. I learned early on to meet as soon as possible because the longer you wait, the more likely you are to create a flawless impression of this person in your mind. It was not entirely 'Mr Talk and Text' fault, Sally idealised him in her head.

Sally fell big time. Texting and talking on the phone very often feels more intimate than chatting online. Communicating solely through our phones creates a false sense of closeness and intimacy that may lead to oversharing. She over-shared with photos. Because Sally was not face to face, it was easy to share things that she normally would not early in a relationship.

Sally felt an emotional intensity with 'Mr Text and Talk' so much so, she felt she was falling in love with him. Subconsciously she was compensating for not meeting him in person. Sally was longing to touch and see and feel the sense of this man, but he was not as anxious as her. She was loving what he said, how he said it, and the attention he paid her.

She felt they were forging a real connection but when it came down to meeting, he wanted to continue texting and talking.

Sally eventually got in touch with reality and realised the limitations this kind of relationship had, and she wanted more. It was heartbreaking for her. She begged him to meet her at first, but he said he was working back-to-back right now, but he hoped to be able to meet soon.

We need to remember that dating actually involves in-person contact. Sally's 'Mr Talk and Text' was more into the role-play of being in a relationship. She finally asked herself the question, why he was choosing to role-play at being in a relationship, instead of actually being in a real-life one with her. Moreover, she asked herself the question why she was willing to settle for this. She enjoyed the fantasy for a while but now she was fed up pretending, but the cycle was difficult to break. Her family were putting her under pressure to meet her new man, so Sally was putting pressure on him. He promised to meet her three times, but each time cancelled at the last minute.

It took some time, but she eventually found out he was married. He never intended meeting her, he just wanted to enjoy the attention of a woman who had put him on a pedestal. It took a long time and a lot of heart ache for Sally to understand she was settling for less than what she really wanted and deserved. It is understandable that she gave up internet dating. I hope she will be brave enough to try it again, because although there are challenges with it, there is also the potential of finding love.

Mark aka 'Mr. Right Now'

My 'Mr Right Now' was Mark. I met him on my second encounter with online dating. Dating apps, and websites, come in all different types, but they all offer the same glittering hope. The hope of love at first swipe.

I was thrilled by all the opportunities at my fingertips but I was very nervous I would do something wrong or pick the wrong guy. I was very wary of strangers online. I did not want anyone to know I was online because of my job at the time, so I was worried of being recognised. My first entry into online dating was daunting and I didn't have great experiences, so I was trying again but I was still wary. Putting myself out there was scary. I knew I had to put in the work. When I logged on, I was fishing within minutes. However, I was not having quality experiences. I was not entirely sure what I was doing.

One evening after a day out shopping, I logged on to find a message from Mark. He looked nice, tanned, younger but not too young and a nice t-shirt. We chatted over and back and he told me he would be in my area in a week, so we planned a meet up. I sent him my number to call first to test his personality. Mark rang me a week later by surprise. I was more surprised to hear his accent; not German this time but Dutch. I blatantly said 'you are not Irish' he said, no, is that a problem?

To which I answered, 'of course not'. He was Dutch, living in Ireland. He was in my town and asked to meet up. I thought why not.

I was Pointe Vecchio bound once more. As I sat there awaiting my Dutch man, I wondered what was ahead. It turned out he was very nice with an eccentric character. Our time together flew, and we planned another date.

Mark fit perfectly into my life right then, I never thought of a future with him. The future was up in the air as far as I was concerned. Mark was a great steady weekend date, he never asked too much of me and was always there for me and I for him. I did not think too far into the future. It was all about surviving from day to day at that point. The fact that Mark was an unusual character added to my fun with him.

He was a great distraction because I never knew what he would do next. My family were unsure what to make of him, but they accepted him because he seemed to make me happy. I needed happiness and someone to make me smile after all the stress I endured the previous years.

I was enjoying his company, but I could not shake the feeling that there was somebody else out there more suited to me. Mark did not make my heart race. He did not excite me as a partner. He did not fill me with enthusiasm, but he was good to me, he made me laugh and I enjoyed his quirks. He helped me fill my empty time, and I genuinely cared for him. There was some excitement with him as we travelled a lot. He worked away sometimes, and I went to visit him.

Some of the places he expected me to stay were suspect, however, and I began to see his frugal side. I didn't need him to spend money on me but staying in decent places would be good.

Mark was a good friend and we had fun, but he was travelling more and more, and I was being treated to dates less and less. He was beginning to see a future for us, but I knew although I cared for him, I could not spend the rest of my life with him. He was nice, peculiar sometimes, but nice.

I was in a situation-ship with Mark for too long, and it was not fair on him. While I knew I should end things because I did not feel anything romantic for him, I felt I was keeping him around because it was better than being on my own, maybe he was doing the same.

I would miss the easy friendship, the comfort of having someone there. I would miss him, and although I did not see him in my future life romantically, ending things with him would leave an empty void. Even though I was not interested in Mark long term, I did a lot for him. I dedicated time and effort into maintaining our friendship. I think I felt if we started out as friends, the friendship would transform into romance.

I knew now I needed more, and I needed to tell Mark. The idea of starting this dating lark all over again filled me with dread. It was easier to cling on to Mark at least we were friends. However, I looked forward more and more to him going away on his work trips. That way we could message and keep each other company but I could avoid the romance and the physical side of the relationship. I am not proud of it.

I knew Mark did not feature in my future, but I was just going with the flow. I was not able to tackle the difficult conversation. I was in danger of letting this relationship go on too long.

I asked myself if it was possible for 'Mr. Right Now' to morph into 'Mr. Right'. Most people would say yes but you need to want it to happen. I was sure I did not want it to happen.

His quirkiness, and eccentricities were cute, and fun to begin with, but they were beginning to irritate me now. I began wondering about the other men I was missing out on by being with him. I tried picturing Mark as my Mr Right and I tried to see him in other ways, but he was not the most exciting man I ever met, he was not even close.

I have to admit it was nice to be with someone, I was not totally invested in. It was non-committal and there was less of a chance of getting hurt. Mark is an important part of my life, just not romantically. I value him as a person, even if I do not see him as a potential Mr Right. I had to face the fact that I was keeping him on the hook, in the way I had been kept on the hook before.

Nonetheless, I am not interested in a relationship that is simply a friendship. I think I wanted to hold on to Mark because he gave me options. It was easy to be with someone who provided a safety net. Plotting my way around the dating world was so much riskier. I like that Mark was always waiting in the wings.

Mark had been away for a month and was due back I knew I had to tell him. In truth, I was not looking forward to him returning. When we met up, he hugged me, and I could not reciprocate, he stood back and looked at me. He knew there was something wrong. He said he guessed for some time, I was not that into him.

He said he felt the distance between us. I had not realised my texts had lessened, he felt I was no longer flirting with him. I felt bad but at least it was out. I told Mark I liked him as a friend, but I do not feel chemistry anymore.

I told him I did not want to hurt his feelings. I wished him well and hoped we could still be friends. The beautiful thing about 'Mr. Right Now' is you do not have dreams of a future with him, so it is easier to walk away. It is easier to put the pieces back together. This was unusual for me as I am the one who invests in the relationship too quickly but for some reason it was not me on this occasion. Again, Mark seemed perfect on paper, he did not float my boat. He was a good friend, but he just fizzled out in my mind. I knew he was not 'Mr Right for me'.

He may have been intelligent, well educated, nice, but there was no attraction for me. I had to let him go. It pained me to throw him back into the ocean but there was no chemistry. I tried to force love, but it was not to be. I threw myself back in the ocean and to the plenty of fish out there, because I wanted more than anything to find my goldfish. There is nothing wrong with living for the moment.

There is also nothing wrong with sharing your time with a man who fits your circumstance for the moment. It is important, however, to be realistic. Know how to differentiate between a man who is right for you right now, and a man who is right for you for the rest of your life.

How to spot a 'Mr. Right Now' and not your Mr. Right

- You both use vague terms to describe your relationship.
- You beat around the bush when the relationship topic is in question.
- You don't know what to call each other.
- You do not discuss becoming exclusive.
- He does not make you forget your ex.
- Most women meet Mr. Right Now, after a long-term relationship ends.
- You just want to be with someone because you are part of a couple.
- You want someone to keep you company.
- You might have a great time with him but deep down, your heart is not in it.
- He is better than a jerk who might hurt you.
- You are not a part of each other's lives.
- You don't know this man's friends.
- You don't know how he spends his days.
- You are not involved in his interests.
- You do not introduce him to your family.
- You subconsciously know he is not here to stay.
- You never make long-term plans together.
- Your intimacy is only sexual.
- There is no bond outside of the bedroom.
- There is no real emotional connection.
- You do not feel the need to spend hours next to him.
- You do not need to look deeply in his eyes.
- You hide your imperfections from him.
- You are not comfortable enough to be your true self in front of him.
- You would not fight for the relationship.

- You are aware that you would not stick together through thick and thin.
- You are not invested in him.
- You could walk away tomorrow.

All the above described my time with Mark.

Michael aka 'Mr. Project'

We all think we can fix and mould the man we are with. Take it from me, we cannot. Most of us have dated the man who we feel is not great, but he has potential. We continue because we think we can shape and model our ideal partner. Dating him feels like a project. I sometimes feel it is my mission in life, to fix every man I meet. I was inclined to walk into most relationships with great patience and a toolkit, ready to fix everything. If he had potential, I was going to give him a chance.

One of my dates, Michael, was very nice. His picture was pleasant, his profile was well put together, we had a lot in common, and for me he was age appropriate. Being age appropriate is important to me. Previously, I met the younger man, and I met the older man, neither was a suitable fit. I hoped to meet someone within three years of my own age. I messaged him and he sent me a polite message back. We got chatting and I broke my own rule of three days messaging then swapping numbers for a conversation. I offered him my number, but he did not seem to notice. He was very good at messaging and very intelligent, so I did not push for a conversation. He was reeling me in. Although there was a delay sometimes in getting back to me, I thought this would be fine when we met.

I am big into communication. I can never understand why someone is too busy to take thirty seconds to reply to a text, even an emoji.

As time went on it became obvious, he was not great on the communication front as he was not consistent with his messages. He had the habit of being in contact a lot for a few days, and then a week could go by before he responded again. I would just decide to forget about him when he would message again, and because I was intrigued, I allowed things to go back to square one. He was ambiguous and noncommittal, but I could fix this when we met.

Michael was good; I will give him that. We had excellent deep messaging, which left me feeling confident we would meet. When we did, I knew we would have so much to talk about. I could imagine staring into his eyes across a table while we discussed the meaning of life. He still did not make any genuine effort to meet. I messaged and said I was more interested in meeting someone not a pen-pal, so I regretfully would have to move on, and find someone on my wavelength.

It was after this message he suggested meeting. At this point I was suspicious whether or not he would turn up. Eventually, we met, and we had a wonderful evening, just as I knew we would. I was feeling optimistic this time. Table L-2 in Pointe Vecchio was bringing me luck. As he approached me, I was relieved he looked just like his picture, and he was nicely dressed. We spent the evening chatting, we were connecting, the eye contact was electric. We both left smiling, if a little shy. I liked that.

Later that night I texted him, about a song I heard on the radio, followed by an inquiry about his plans for the weekend. 'It would be nice to meet again' I said. When I heard back from him, it was twenty-four hours later, he ignored the part about the song, and gave me a short reply about how he was tired.

I mentioned something about the upcoming weekend, which he shot down, by saying he is not really into making plans. He is more the spontaneous type. Fine, I thought, be spontaneous. I was ticked off. I did not bother to contact him the next day, and he did not bother to contact me. But then, I remembered how nice our evening was, so I caved the next day and wished him a good day. His response? 'Thanks, you too.' My heart sank once again. Michael was running hot and cold.

Days went by and I heard nothing. This left me feeling cold and unwanted. I called him out on his behaviour. He said, 'I can't understand why you are in such a state?' To which I told him to stop insulting us both. His texts turned monosyllabic. He said he was busy but could meet me again in a week. I could not believe I was accepting this behaviour but meeting him again would give me the opportunity to determine if I could change his way of communicating.

Another week passed before I forced myself to look in the mirror and admit what I did not want to admit. He was stringing me along. He was breadcrumbing me. This man was only interested in keeping me on the back burner. He made me feel good while we messaged, but this changed to worry when I did not hear from him.

This is not what I was looking for, and I knew deep down Michael was a project too far. I was sad to let it go but I had to. I needed to be true to myself. I needed to follow the advice I would give my friends.

Michael was giving me just enough attention to keep my hope of a meeting alive. He would leave flirty little comments, but never really make a move. He never took the initiative. Part of being me is reading into things. I like to analyse, scrutinise and break down every bit of communication with my love interest, dissect every like, and flirtatious emoji. This can be a curse, but it can also save me heartache if I pay attention. I knew Michael was keeping me interested until someone better came along. Maybe it was karma.

Michael was sending little breadcrumbs of messages. I did not know this was a thing but I soon found out. I had not heard of breadcrumbing unless it was on a chicken Kiev before. Now I was experiencing it. Understanding what breadcrumbing means, makes it much easier to see what is really going on, or in actual fact, what is not going on.

Breadcrumbing is the new 'stringing along'. They are stringing you along and you do not even know, you don't even realise that it's happening. In my experience, men do this to boost their ego. They want to know you are still in the background. I believe they are looking for someone better to come along, and they are keeping you on the long finger. This kind of man will always be looking for someone better, even if they commit to meeting you. Even if they enter a relationship with you, they will keep looking around.

This is not about you. It is simply a fact they will never find someone good enough for their fabulous selves. It is a real case of the grass is greener elsewhere. Take it from me nothing will ever be good enough for someone like this. I had enough of this in my past life. I now wanted to meet a man who knew I was the best person for them.

It is a possibility that some men are shy and are too afraid to meet you. They will keep messaging you, but they will most likely cancel any meeting you try to organise. There are many ways of breadcrumbing, the worst is by an ex. He does not intend to get back together with you, but still wants to stay important in your life. Again, this is about him not you. It is about his ego. He still wants you in the background. This ex tries to keep you from moving on, but is happy to move on himself, while stringing you along a little while longer. Why do they have the habit of wanting to stay significant in your life? Maybe, just maybe, they do not know they are doing it.

I have been the sucker on the receiving end of breadcrumbing. Thrilled when I hear from my love interest, with cute messages, I message back immediately, but the excitement wanes rapidly for me, with each lazy reply, or even worse, no reply at all. It is a real roller coaster of emotions. It took me time to realise I was being put on the long finger with Michael. He was an expert and I thought I could fix him. In the future if someone does not respond within a timely fashion, I will make my excuses and leave.

I lose interest now if I feel I am being breadcrumbed. I tend to shut it down as soon as I recognise the symptoms. It only happens if we allow it to happen. So, no more excuses. If I make plans to meet and nothing happens, I call out the behaviour. We are worth much more than this. Get out while you can as breadcrumbing is a project you cannot complete. Rather than wasting your time dreaming of 'what can be' shake off those crumbs. No one is happy with just crumbs.

I feel the urge to fix everything, maybe it is because it makes me feel good. It took me a long time to realise it is not my job to fix my dates. It is not my job to fix breadcrumbing. It is not my job to fix behaviours. Us women have tried to fix problematic partners for centuries. Some who were at best emotionally unavailable, and at worse abusive. This is because the concept is fundamentally a symptom of a patriarchal society. Those of us in our fifties will remember what it was like to live and work in a male dominated society. I feel this has changed somewhat, but not entirely. It is not easy to change the mind-sets of centuries. You can only change your own mind-set.
We need to remember the men we hope to meet now, will also be in their fifties or older, and we can only hope they have evolved with the times.

Michael obviously had his own issues as to why he wanted to keep a woman at bay. He had not evolved. He wants someone who will dance to his tune, and that someone was not going to me. The important thing here is to get yourself away from this behaviour and recognise you have done nothing wrong. You do not need a project, you need a perfect fit for you.

How to spot a 'Project' or a 'Breadcrumber'

A breadcrumber is someone who leads you on by dropping small crumbs of interest, sending occasional messages, and social media interaction. They plan dates but usually cancel at the last minute. They are not worth your time and effort.

- Periodic messages are the first sign of breadcrumbing.
- The messages are ambiguous with blurred plans.
- The messages lack any real interest.
- Texts usually come late at night.
- The messages you get run hot and cold.
- They make you feel like you did something wrong.
- They never ask to see you in person unless they need something.
- They bail on you when you organise a date.
- He gives you just enough time and attention to keep your interest.
- They manipulate you so that you are left wanting more.
- Their actions do not match their words.
- They talk to you but won't set up dates.
- They make spur of the moment plans, usually surrounding sex.
- They rarely share much about their own life.

In my return to dating, I was looking for a serious relationship. I was determined I would get it right this time. Of course, there are never guarantees but with careful consideration on my choices, I had the hope of finding a loving man to share my life.

I wanted someone kind, honest, intelligent, emotionally available, more than anything he had to want to be in my company. We all want someone whose face lights up when they see us. I am no different. I consider myself adept at online dating, especially after I reset the dating-meter. It took me by surprise when I did not recognise, I was being breadcrumbed. When I realised what was happening, I ended it. My only regret is I did not do it earlier.

You might feel totally fine with hooking up casually and you may be ok with sporadic messaging. That is fine, as long as this is what you want. At this point in my life, I do not have time to throw away on time wasters, and inconsiderate jerks.
If like me you want regular communication and an established relationship, make it clear that you are not willing to wait around. Because my breadcrumber, Michael, seemed ideal as a potential partner, I ignored the signs in the beginning. He was unwilling to connect on an emotional level or to spend time with me, even if his conversations were deep. I feel he enjoyed reeling me in and then, like catching a fish, he threw me back. It took me time, but I eventually rejected the crumbs of attention Michael had on offer, so I said goodbye to Mr Breadcrumb.

John aka 'Mr I'

As the age old saying goes, I went back to the drawing board. Scrolling through one evening a new picture popped up as a match. It was John. He looked very nice, well groomed, well dressed, with nice eyes. I looked at his profile, it read very well, if a bit long. I decided to send a message and see if I got a response.

He was very forthcoming about himself and came across as confident and smart. He certainly piqued my interest. He seemed very interested in me. He was very good at messaging and within a week, he asked me on a date. I was delighted, at last, a man who knew what he wanted, he was very into me, and that was so appealing.

On the evening I met John I took extra effort with my preparation and my appearance. I had my hair done. I chose a red dress, red looks good on me, and red is a colour that appeals to men. I was nervous all day; so much so that I left work early to get ready. I liked the sound of John, and I was hopeful for the evening ahead.

Our conversations on the phone were general but he had a lovely sounding voice. I wanted to meet for coffee, but he insisted on dinner, so we compromised on an early evening light bite. Again, I chose Ponte Vecchio. I arrived early and sat at my window seat where I could see him in the distance when he arrived. I chose a nice red wine to settle my nerves.

As I sat nervously looking out the window, I saw John cross the road to meet me. He was dressed very well and looked relaxed. He approached my table and sat down with ease. He chose a non-alcoholic wine, as he was driving, and we shared a cheese board. It was very civilised. I began to relax as John took charge. It was nice to be with someone who knew what they wanted. He was very appealing, and the date moved very fast. He was talkative, it was easy to listen to him and he was very attentive. I am ready for a relationship, and he seemed to want the same thing. Before the date was over, he was asking to meet me again.

I liked this because it did away with 'who will message who first,' and the 'will we ever meet again' question.

Everything moved very fast. By our second date, John was complimenting everything about me. He declared that he thought the two of us were the perfect couple and to my surprise, he was already planning a future with me. I am a cautious person, but he was sweeping me off my feet. It is a bit soon to be planning a future together, but it was a nice change from most of my dates who were commitment-phobes.

I have to admit it was nice, it was really nice to be in the company of someone who really liked me. He was reeling me in with fantastic plans for the future. He was showering me with compliments and gifts. He was all about the wonderful things we were going to do together. He was so enthusiastic and sincere. He was winning me over and we had only known each other for three weeks. It was like dating on speed. I never stopped to think if we were a good match. I felt we had to be, we were on a whirlwind of romance. On the third date, he told me he was falling for me, and I said, 'I think I am falling for you too'. 'It looks like we are a really good match' he said. I went home from this date feeling elated. I heard of other people enjoying whirlwind romances, but it had never happened to me before.

John was everything I ever wanted in a man, why then was my gut not happy. I decided this was a normal feeling as I was not familiar with a man showering me with attention. We agreed that night, we were the perfect match. It was fast, but we both felt it.

John messaged after this date several times a day. He kept me busy responding. There was no problem with communication. I loved the attention, it was hard work but it was worth it. I found the man of my dreams. He described the great times the two of us were going to have. The trips we were going to take. He could not wait for me to meet his family. I invited him to a family wedding in two months' time and he immediately agreed. My friends said he must be serious as he would not agree to go to a family wedding if he was not serious. I was on the road to relationship happiness. It took me a while, but I finally found what I was looking for.

I know you are thinking this is too good to be true and you are right. I did not know then what I know now. I was actually on the road to disappointment. John was future-faking. Another new term to me. None of what he said was likely to happen ever. I am a sensible woman, but I got swept up in the attention. As a woman starved of attention in life, I was happy to grab on to John. He was so genuine. However, once John knew I was into him, everything changed. The chase was over. There was no longer a need to impress me. The good times faded away. Everything that was positive in the relationship became negative. The great communicator became lazy. I changed from the perfect match to the match with shortcomings. Suddenly, my dress was too long or too short.

John's messages became cold and uncaring. He was so convincing, I bought into the vision. This vision was now fading fast.I kept telling myself it was all very fast and maybe if we slowed down it would be better. I still imagine the possibilities.

I let things slide as I thought maybe he is having a bad day. I had to pull myself aside once again. My previous relationships taught me to take a step back. All too often in the past I allowed things to slide, and I went with the flow to see what happened. Disappointment was usually the thing that happened.

I pulled back, but when I did, John got all interested again. He began showering me with attention, apologising for his behaviour. We arranged another date, this time I took off my rose-tinted glasses and kept my eyes and most importantly my ears open. I knew we had jumped in too fast, nonetheless, I still held on to hope.

When we met next time, it was just for drinks. No romantic meal, no romantic gesture, although he did bring flowers. John began talking about the future, this time I was listening with trepidation. I began to hear the frequent use of the word 'I'. Once I started reading between the lines, I could see how self-centred and insincere he really was. Sometimes it takes hurt or disappointment to see things clearly. He had no problem sharing fantasies about our future life together, because he had no problems reneging on everything and anything he promised.

It took me time to work it out. John was a narcissist. I was annoyed with myself because I saw all the signs before. I have to hand it to him, he was an expert. In fact, he was so good, I think he convinced himself he wanted all these things. I was disappointed, I did not find my match on this occasion either.

After John, I took a break from dating. I needed to heal my wounds. It is difficult sharing your heart and your feelings repeatedly. It did not take long before I was glad the intensity was over, but it took some time to find hope again. I missed the attention.

John was a narcissist, I met men like him before, but he was more subtle starting out. When I told him I felt we wanted different things in life, all he said was 'ah well it was fun while it lasted'. He had no empathy. He was not going to miss me. I would miss him or at least I would miss who I thought he was.
I realised he knew from the beginning what he was doing. He knew he was painting a fake picture. He would quickly move on to the next person with his well-developed tactics. He told everyone the same stories.

John enjoyed reeling women in with romance, and when they weakened, he demonstrated his true colours. I am lucky, I have developed inner strength over the years and although I was disappointed and annoyed to be reeled-in by him, I knew I would move on. Some women are very hurt by the Johns of this world. One of my main criteria for meeting a man is exit-ing immediately when they overuse the word 'I'. John was more subtle than that. In retrospect, I could see the signs. I am sharing them with you, so you can make informed decisions for your future.

John had a magnified sense of importance, a need for attention. He had a total lack of empathy. He had no interest in how I felt after he turned cold. He believed he was special, and for a time he drew me into his fantasies.

He was always looking around, saying, how people were so jealous of us, we were so perfect. What he really thought was, he was so perfect. Be careful, when someone tells you they love you, within the first month. It may be true. I believe in love at first sight, but life is not a fairy tale. Real love needs to be nurtured and grown. Follow your gut. I tried to ignore mine. If you think it is too early to fall in love, it probably is.

Narcissists tend to talk a lot about themselves, John did not start like that, but he did think he was better and smarter than everyone else was. He told me about his high-powered job, which I found to be a middle management job, that of course is an achievement, he just made it sound like he was so important he had his finger on the red button.

If like me, you meet someone like John, talk about yourself, see if they ask follow-up questions, and express an interest in you, or do they make it all about themselves. It is said that narcissists use people who are compassionate and empathetic to supply their sense of self-worth. They need other people to make them feel powerful. Their opinion of themselves can be offended very easily, this increases their need for praise. They like to lift themselves up by putting other people down. We all know people like this.

Many narcissists like John, can be romantic, but it is all to their own end. It is to make themselves feel powerful. They make you feel like it is fun teasing you, but it can become mean. I was in a relationship where everything I did from what I wore, to what I ate, and what I watched on TV, was a problem.

He made jokes that I did not find funny, and he tried to lower my self-esteem and succeeded.

John was not like this, otherwise I would have seen the signs earlier. If I stayed with John, I suspect it would not be long before he began blaming me for his failings. I ended whatever this was. It was not easy to end it, but I did not want to fight back. This did not cost John a thought as he was probably already on to his next shiny thing.

Spot a Mr 'I or a Narcissist'

- They have a sense of self-importance.
- They exaggerate their abilities and accomplishments.
- They crave admiration and attention
- They are fixated with beauty, love, power, and success.
- They think they are unique.
- They have no problem exploiting others to get what they want.
- They have no empathy.
- They do not care how you feel it is all about them.
- They feel superior and entitled.
- They do not have boundaries.
- They are always right.
- They have no problem using you for their own benefit.
- You will never be good enough for them.
- They pick on you constantly.
- They never apologise.
- They blame everyone else.
- You feel they don't hear you.
- They cancel important plans.

Some narcissists will treat you like their partner, this way they can enjoy intimate benefits with you, while keeping an eye out for better prospects. They have no problem looking at or flirting with others in front of you. If you raise this with them, they will make it feel like it is your fault, and they will blame you for making a fuss. There is no compromise with a narcissist because they are always right.

Many narcissists find themselves in on-again, off-again relationships, because they always feel there is someone better out there. Their reputation is everything to them so if you end things with them, they are likely to bad mouth you to save face.

Being in a relationship with someone who is always criticising, belittling, and who is never available, is emotionally exhausting. I waited too long in the past so when John revealed his true colours, I needed out of there. I know I deserve better. As much as you want to fix a narcissist, you cannot. You end up trying to change yourself to meet their whims. You will always feel empty in a relationship with someone like this. Nothing will ever be good enough for them. They will never be happy. There is no second chance for a narcissist in my world. I am implementing a zero-tolerance policy towards the 'I' man.

I was sure I would spot a narcissist on the dating scene. I had plenty of examples of them in my past. I was positive about one thing, if I met someone who was all about 'I' and 'me-me-me' I would be out of there so fast, he would wonder if I was ever there in the first place.

John on the other hand was very subtle to begin with. I will admit because he was good looking, I was a little slow on noticing the signs, but they were there.

Liam aka Mr 'Misleading'

Disappointed, but glad I acquired the tools to recognize the signs of control, it was time now to follow my own advice and log back in. Get back on that bike so to speak. I know by far the majority of men are nice men, but the ones I was gravitating towards were not for me. It is easy to lose heart if time after time, you are disappointed, but I wanted to meet someone, so I had to keep trying.

I took my profile out of hiding and thought I would leave it there and wait for a message. That evening I had a message that intrigued me. The profile picture was faded but I could see it was a tall man in a polo shirt and jeans. It was obvious in his first message he had read my profile. He told me I was interesting, and he felt I might have some appealing quirks. He asked me, "if I met a group of your friends on my way to meet you, what would they say about you?" I was drawn in by his approach. It demonstrated intelligence and a way with words.

I messaged Liam back and was delighted with his response. Honestly, I just wanted to stay messaging this man and never meet him because his messages were so good. They were romantic, respectful and it was like being woo-ed in the life of a period drama. He was Darcy to my Elizabeth.

Liam gave me that warm fuzzy feeling inside as I shared his lovely messages with some friends. After a week of messaging, he sent me his number, and asked me to call him any time that suited me. For some reason this time I was slow to call the number because I didn't want the messages to end, I also didn't want to be disappointed again. However, I had my preparation done, I had my guidelines, it was important I followed them.

I arrived home that Wednesday evening from work and read all his messages again. I knew I needed to move this forward sooner rather than later. I sat down with a cup of chamomile tea and sent a 'WhatsApp' message to ask if now was a good time to call. I put my phone down while I waited for his response. I practically hit the ceiling when my phone rang. It was Liam. He was ringing me. I answered with my best husky voice and was totally taken aback when he spoke. His writing suggested a soft spoken, refined man but it was different, it was loud, he was very loud. As we began talking, I relaxed, he was nice, our conversation was fun and interesting.

It was very exciting to be chatting to someone who listened. We chatted for at least a half-hour, and I know we could have stayed chatting, but I think we were both conscious of not overdoing it on our first interaction. He suggested we meet that weekend for dinner. I said I would prefer a coffee for our first meeting. He lived a distance away so I said I would travel halfway to meet him.

I looked forward to meeting Liam more than any other date.

I am sure it is normal to be nervous before a first date, but some degree of nerves might be a good sign. It means this matters to you, and the man you are about to meet might be your potential new love. If you have no nerves at all, it is probably because you are not all that interested. My nerves today however were on overdrive, so I wanted to get to the hotel early, calm myself before our meeting and be date ready.

Because I was meeting Liam outside of my own surroundings, although I knew the hotel, I was not too familiar with its ambiance. I felt being in a hotel would be nice. Getting there early would help me become acclimatised and would be a calming influence on me.

I purposely chose Saturday to meet, so I would not be going from the office to the date venue. I did not want to have my work persona on. I might start interviewing Liam, instead of chatting with him. I kept myself busy that day, as my idle mind tends to go into overdrive. I spent time choosing my outfit and taking time over my hair and make-up. I was putting my best self forward.

As I drove into the hotel car park, I wished I did not have to drive, a glass of wine would have been very nice, but as I have a low alcohol tolerance, I thought I better skip this. I sat in the car for some time listening to music, a bit of 'Queen' was always good for energising me and it would put me in the zone.

I fixed my lippy, pulled the comb through my hair and went into the hotel. As I did, I breathed through my nose and out through my mouth. My anxiety was lapsing. I took myself into the ladies and had a good chat with myself. I got into a positive frame of mind.

Chasing away the self-critical thoughts attempting to creep into the crevices of my mind. Some of the anxiety we feel is self-induced and some is fear of rejection. When we meet our friends, there is none of that. So, look at your date as a friend you haven't met yet and let the fear and anxiety go. A first date is a two-way street, you are both likely to be nervous. The worst-case scenario is you do not need to go out with them again. I hoped I would want to go out with Liam again. I was tired of looking.

It is natural to imagine a future together, but by investing too much before you go on your first date, you will put too much emotional energy into it. Sometimes we worry if the date does not work out, our future will not work out. This is not so, it is one date, it is one evening, you are just meeting this person to see if you are both a good fit. Leave your hopes for the future aside for one hour and live in that present moment. If you are a good fit together, then start looking forward to the next meeting, but hold off on the wedding plans.

I walked into the bar and took a seat in the corner with a good view of the entrance to the inside. A nice waiter took my order for a cappuccino with chocolate sprinklings. As I luxuriated in my first sip a very tall, very well-rounded man approached the bar. He was looking around him as if he was expecting to be meeting someone. He had a shock of wild curly grey hair, and his clothing had never seen an iron. Surely this was not my scribe. No, my messages came from a well-groomed, clean shaven, gentleman with a slightly bohemian look. I looked around the bar again and as I did Mr Hair-shock limped towards me.

No, no, no. It was Liam. He introduced himself and told me I looked exactly like my picture, and I said I would not have recognised you. 'I know' he said, 'I purposefully put up an old picture because I know a current one would not attract attention, but I hoped my personality would win you over'.

What could I say to that, I invited him to sit down, and we began chatting. He asked if I would join him at the bar as he was having hip trouble at the moment and couldn't sit on low chairs. This I did, but I was not happy. I do not like high stools, at five feet two, my legs usually end up swinging. Not a look I was going for.

His personality was great. He was very deep, and I love deep conversation. However, no matter how long we chatted I could not come to terms with his height, his hair, and his lopsided-ness. Plus, I didn't want to spend the rest of my life sitting on a high stool.

I know we live in a world of political correctness, and you may think I am being shallow, I agree love can grow, because it does for me, but I knew sitting there, I would never be able to overcome my first impression. I told him I enjoyed his company, but I did not feel the spark. That is the polite way of saying, I will never find him attractive.

He said maybe we could meet for another coffee, and I said maybe. I really just wanted to get out of there. I hoped he would stay behind but he walked me out. We were like little and large. He wanted me to sit into his jeep for a few minutes to continue our chat, but experience taught me, it was not chat he wanted.

Not happening. I went to my medium sized car where he opened the passenger door and attempted to sit into the front seat. This was a major operation. I thanked him for a nice afternoon, but I really had to go now. He reached over to kiss me but that was not on my mind at all. I sat back and said I must go, and kissing was not on the agenda.

Honestly, it took him ten minutes to extract himself from my car. I did not know whether to laugh or cry. I had so much hope for this date going on his messages. In fact, I had decided before going to meet Liam, I was going to give him every chance, but I did not expect to meet someone who had little or no interest in himself, someone who deceived women because he thought he could talk them around, someone who could barely move.

There may be a woman out there for him, but it was not going to be me. Driving home, I thought he was nice, and his writing was excellent but underneath it all, he deceived me. I should have asked for a more up to date photograph. I should have spoken to him a little bit more and found out his hobbies. I knew he was a farmer, but I imagined him as a gentleman farmer, not one who appears to have given up on his appearance and fitness.

It would be fantastic if everyone used photos that properly represented themselves. Photos that look how they would appear when they meet you. However, this seems like it is too much to ask. Some people try to justify their lack of photos, like Liam, they hope to win people over with their personality.

Deceptive photos are not as bad as fake profiles aimed to swindle, but they are misleading. People see nothing wrong with applying filters while others think it is worth calling out. I feel putting up the best possible version of yourself is essential but not to filter or put up photos that are ten years old. Liam was older and was determined to meet a woman younger than him, so he tried to shave years off his life in his profile, and his photos. There are many men like this.

In Liam's case, I suspect he was well meaning, and he believed that once he met the woman, she would be mesmerised by his personality and the deception would not matter. The age difference would be immaterial. For me it was just not about the age difference, we were very different in many ways. We both enjoyed deep conversation and romantic messages but on meeting him I realised our attitude and outlook on life was very different.

Starting a relationship with a lie, no matter how innocent it may seem, takes away our ability to use our own judgement, to make a decision based on the true facts. This eats away at trust from the very beginning. Age difference is not a problem for me after-all I dated a man fifteen years my junior, but I did not deceive him about my age. I now want to be in an age-appropriate relationship. I find lies very unsettling. We all use the odd white lie, but we should try to be more careful. The longer the lie is continued, the worse the discovery is, when it unfolds. Relationships that start with a lie, even a white lie, rarely end well.

How to deal with 'Mr Misleading'

I think it is perfectly okay to ask your date about their photos before you meet. Maybe say something like my photos are recent, how up to date are yours? It is not a problem to ask for a recent photo. You could also look for clues in the photo itself. Check out if there is a timeframe. Was the photo taken at an event? When did this event take place? If it is a scanned photo, it is likely to be an old one. I did not have any problem doing a little research. I always ask for a surname, with some basic details, you can get a little bit of information. Doing a little bit of research ahead of time lessens surprises. After meeting Liam, I always asked for an up-to-date photograph.

Perhaps add your date on Snapchat, some of my friends did this. As snapchat is about real-time, they are unable to hide their true self. After you have been chatting with someone for a few days, ask if they have Snapchat. If they do, you can swap photos.

A deceiving photo may not always be the result of unscrupulous behaviour. They may be just lacking in confidence. I met men without photos because they had a great profile, but it never worked. Liam was proof of this. While we can understand confidence issues, attempts at falsification are less forgivable.

If your prospective date claims, they do not have current photos. There is no excuse not to send a current photo by using a phone. Everyone can take a selfie, if someone cannot be bothered to do as little as that, then they may not be worth meeting or taking up your time.

If you find yourself in the situation like I did with Liam, perhaps ask yourself a few questions. Do I go home? Do we address the noticeable discrepancy? Do you push through the date as I did with Liam? You must decide for yourself but after the Liam incident, I always asked for a more recent photo.

I would even accept a photo a year old, but not one ten years old. I like to be kind to others, but I am not looking to meet someone where I have to spend the rest of my life sitting on a high stool, nor am I looking for someone to take care of. Plus, it would be nice if we go for a drive in my car, he can get in and get out without getting stuck.

If you feel you were misled, you do not have to stick it out. You do not need to spend more than a few minutes with someone who misrepresents himself. Be aware the man you are meeting may just feel awkward and maybe a little shy, so be kind and excuse yourself as politely as possible. Liam was not shy, and the chat was good, but I knew I was not interested as I would never find him attractive. If you decide to stay, and address the obvious difference between their profile photos, and their real-life appearance, go about it in the kindest possible way. Maybe say 'I had trouble recognizing you from your photos', maybe it was the camera angle.

Make sure your own photos are a good representation of who you are. Show yourself in a few different environments. I do not like photos of myself, I believe I look a lot better in person, but at least I look like myself. The bad photo is a common scenario, it is best if you give yourself every opportunity to attract a good fit by sharing who you really are.

Spot when he is lying

- When he stalls before giving you a response.
- When he gives you elusive answers.
- When they reply to you with questions.
- When he goes on the defensive.
- When he takes his time before sending you a response.
- When his text is long and complicated.
- When he offers extra information even though you didn't ask for it.
- When he gives you excuses in place of direct answers.
- When he suddenly changes the topic.
- When your instinct tells you he is lying.

Lying may be a long-established coping skill that becomes part of a dysfunctional pattern in people's lives. It is very misleading to others and can be very upsetting in a relationship. I know I will be staying away from Mr Misleading from now on.

Colm a.k.a. 'Mr Love-bomb' a.k.a. 'Mr Chicken fillet'

We have all heard the expression 'I am a gluten for punishment' well I am beginning to believe it is true about me, as once more I upload my dating profile, ready to try yet again, to meet my match. I found him online soon after logging on. My friends were excited about this man too. By all accounts, he was a great person for me to date. He was smart, cute, and had a good job. He was easy to track on social media and had a lot of friends who vouched for him online. He sounded perfect to me.

This time I asked for recent photos and was keen to find out that he was flexible enough to walk on the beach or sit into a car.

Colm seemed like a catch, so when he suggested a coffee that afternoon, meeting in the area where I worked, without thinking I said yes. At least this way, I would not have time to over think and become nervous. I left work for an hour and walked ten minutes to the café. I was nervous but I did not have time to dwell on it. As I opened the door of the cafe, I saw him sitting in the corner opposite, he waved and I walked straight over relieved to see he was as he portrayed in his picture, apart from the glasses he was wearing.

He stood up in his shorts and t-shirt, he had been out for a jog in my area. So, he is flexible I thought.
I explained I did not have long, as I had to get back to work, he was in sales he said, so could devise his own timetable. Good he had a job, and he would be able to take time off when he was whisking me away for the weekend.

We both ordered coffee, mine a cappuccino, his, an espresso. We started to chat. He was funny and friendly. He made me smile, which is always a good thing. He seemed to be an all-around good man. We chatted away very easily, I did not find him attractive straight off, but this was not a problem, attraction usually grows for me, he was at least standing straight.

Overall, it was a good first meeting. I returned to work smiling, to the delight and amusement of my colleagues. He messaged me later, saying he was delighted to meet me, and would love to meet again.

I did not expect that two days later he would message and tell me he was in the area again would I join him for lunch. I thought this was a little fast to meet again but I found myself saying 'yes why not'. We met for lunch, and it was fun. He told me he was very successful in his job, he loved keeping fit and although he enjoyed cooking, he enjoyed dining out also. I enjoyed his company, but I still did not feel an emotional connection. Somewhere deep inside I was not melting. I thanked him for the lunch invitation while we both paid our own bill. I like to pay my own way, but I also like when the man offers. He did not even debate the fact with me, we were going Dutch.

As I walked back to work, I felt that was nice, but I did not have the feels. I was surprised when the next day he suggested dinner at the weekend. I told him I had a course on Saturday and would find it difficult to meet afterwards. He insisted he would collect me, take me to dinner and have me home early to rest. It was nice to be fussed over, and it was nice to have someone insisting on dinner. Without too much thought, I agreed to dinner. In the two days that followed, I persuaded myself to go to dinner but if I still did not feel anything, I would tell him. But who knew, maybe a romantic dinner was what I needed. Maybe I did not feel 'the feels' because the last two times I met him were coffee dates.

On the Saturday evening, I arrived home from my course with an hour to spare before dinner. I had given him my address as he insisted on collecting me, I was ok with that as it was the third meeting.

In addition, I knew the company he worked for, as well as the area he lived in. I did not feel the emotional connection, but I trusted him.

I jumped in the shower and made a real effort as the last two times I met him, I was in my work clothes. Both times I met him he was coming from the gym and in his shorts so I felt as we both dressed up for dinner it would be a nice change. I was just applying my second layer of lipstick when my doorbell rang.

I could see what I thought was a white van through the glass in my door. When I opened the door, Colm stood there in the same shorts and t-shirt he had on during the week. He held two bags in his hands and passed me out asking 'so where is the cooker' I stood there in a spin, what was happening? I finally managed to say, 'I thought we were going out to dinner'. He said, 'I thought it would be nice to treat you after a busy day.' This had merit but was not what I was expecting.

He moved around my kitchen like he lived there, I was very confused and uneasy. He took four bottles of wine out of one of the bags, a bit much I thought, as if he read my mind he said, 'he didn't know what I drank'. I said 'red' to which he asked for a glass and poured me a large glass. At this point, I thought I will just drink my wine and try to relax. I did not feel rail-road-ed, but this is exactly what happened. Some of you might say 'what is your problem? it is great to have someone cook for you!' More of you might say 'what are you thinking? get him out of your house!' Both sides of my brain were saying the same things. I felt numb. I did not know what to do. I took the wine and forgot to sip, I gulped it down and tried to figure out what to do next.

My head was in a spin, he popped something in the oven, and I gathered my thoughts. I decided to have the wine, eat the food, and say good night.

I sat on the couch and put on the tv. I could not focus. I was too busy thinking why had he turned up in a van? Why was he wearing the same clothes? Why was he cooking dinner? Why had he not noticed I was dressed up and ready to go out? Why did I let him in?

I took deep breaths and gave him the benefit of the doubt in that he thought he would do a nice thing. I continued to gulp the red wine and noticed he was having a glass of white while cooking. I sat in my living room with the tv, and thought I would distract myself, after all, murderers do not usually cook dinner first. He walked in when he heard the tv and picked up the remote and changed the channel there was a soccer match on. Silly me, why did I not know that? This evening was turning into the 'why' evening. It was then I noticed he had replenished his wine glass, it dawned on me he was drinking, how was he going to get home? Maybe he had a mattress in the back of the van. Dinner was ready, there was chicken and salmon, I told him, I do not eat salmon, so I had a fillet of chicken, and I mean 'a fillet of chicken.' There was nothing else, a fillet of chicken on the plate, all by itself.

My nerves were gone, and my patience was fast disappearing. I got a little salad out of my fridge and told him to eat up, and leave as it was obvious to me, we were not suited. I had allowed this controlling behaviour to go on too long. To say he was shocked was an understatement. His whole face and stature changed. It was obvious he had an angle.

The shortest answer probably was he wanted to use me. Could it be for money, sex, a bed for the night, a bed for a month, a bed forever. Moving fast is the classic move of a narcissist. I had known narcissists before. They have to move fast, hook you in, tie you down, and maintain control, no one was getting control in my house, least of all someone on a third date that was supposed to be taking me to dinner. He was trying to suck me in by what he thought was dazzling me. Whatever the reason, there is absolutely no reason to move this quickly. Most people can act balanced and honourable for short periods of time.

Colm was showing his character very quickly. He looked at me and said, 'I've been drinking, I cannot drive now'. I guessed that was coming so I asked, 'how had you planned on getting home?' he said, 'I thought I could sleep on the couch,' he thought he could sleep in my bed more like. I felt deeply uncomfortable, and asked him to leave, he said 'but I just cooked you dinner' I said 'you cooked me a fillet of chicken that does not constitute dinner.'

I then went on to spell out when he asks a girl to dinner and she gets dressed up, it would have been nice to go out to dinner. I now understood the two rushed coffee dates, because this became a third date and to most these spells more. He was not getting the message, he leaned in to kiss me, and I jumped backwards, I asked him to go for a walk and sober up. He just kept talking, he was doing his best to sway me. He mistook me for someone who cared.

Colm was a self-absorbed idiot. It was a warning sign that he had controlling issues.

He was certainly testing my boundaries as he was doing his best to talk me around but he was being ultra-rude. He was his best self on the coffee dates, trying to make a good impression, now he was going overboard trying to shower me with a fillet of chicken. I do not know what worked for him in the past, but it was not going to work now. I was confused to begin with, but I was fully aware of what was happening now. I was not going to fall into a false sense of security, allowing him to start taking advantage of my good nature.

The chicken fillet was full of empty promises, because this controlling man was trying to put on an act. It is my belief that this psychological abuse worked in the past. Colm was moving too fast, and I was allowing him to do so. I can only think it was because I was taken by surprise. It usually takes some time for love bombing to become noticeable but really manipulative people may try and overwhelm you right away, Colm tried this but instead of overwhelming me, he sent me running. He was making himself at home in my house before we knew each other at all.

Colm may have appeared perfect on paper, but now he was making me feel increasingly uncomfortable. Unbelievably he leaned in to kiss me again, this time putting his finger to my mouth. I was completely flummoxed, instinct led me to bite his finger which brought him to his senses. He reminded me of how kind he was, bringing me wine, cooking me dinner. It was my fault I had nothing in the fridge, to cook with the chicken. He actually believed what he was saying. I reminded him I was expecting to go out to dinner, I trusted him with my address.

I overlooked that he was still wearing the same shorts and t-shirt he wore on our coffee dates. I ignored his obvious dis-respect for me, as he at no point considered what I wanted while he pushed by me to my cooker.

I wanted this man out of my house, but I could not let him drive. I relented and let him sleep in his van in my driveway. He said 'surely you will not throw me out before the rugby' he knew then he had pushed the final button, my face changed colour, my voice took on a high octave, and steam came out my ears.

You can see looking back, I can take humour from the situation, but at the time I was not laughing. I know you will be shocked I let him stay in my driveway, but I did not feel at risk. He was delusional, notional, bizarre and although he wanted to threaten my thought process, he did not endanger my body. I locked my bedroom door and did not sleep very well. I heard him go at some hour of the night, but I no longer cared, it was good riddance. I was another date down and this one was a shocker.

I was shocked at myself more than anything. I could not believe I allowed myself to be pressurised in this way. It would seem Colm wanted me to be into him for his own benefit. I never found out what he hoped to achieve. There are a number of ways someone can make you fall in love with them.

Colm was trying to pretend he was the perfect partner, he just did not know he was so bad at it. He tried one of the worst ways to lure me in. He tried a manipulative tactic known as love bombing.

This dating manoeuvre is extremely hard to detect when it's being unleashed on you. Love bombing is typified by disproportionate attention and affection. The goal is to make you feel needy, and reliant on them. It is a tactic often used by narcissists, abusers, and con artists. It feels really good at first, as you are made to feel special and loved.

You receive all the love and attention you ever wanted. You are lulled into a false feeling of trust. This is when the manipulation begins. They stop treating you like a queen and start to belittle and devalue you. This is not to say that everyone who shows you attention is love bombing you, but it is good to be aware that this trait exists.

The different stages of 'love bombing'

- Love bombers sweep you off your feet and it feels great.
- The love bomber puts you on a pedestal. This seems flattering, but it is all too fast.
- They idealise you.
- The second stage is the devaluation stage.
- The love bomber alternates between being kind one minute and cruel the next.
- They're savvy enough to be loving in public so others think they're great. But they turn abusive in private.
- Love bombers are adept at finding those who are vulnerable.
- They prey on those who just got divorced or recently broke up.

The signs of being 'love bombed'

- The person takes an extreme interest in your family, career, and hobbies?
- They compliment you, then criticise you in the same breath.
- They are constantly asking you where you are.
- They are angry if you don't answer them fast enough.
- They make you feel nervous, and it all feels like too much.
- They lack compassion for you.
- They exhibit boasting behaviour.
- They ignore your time and schedule.
- They are focused on their own needs.
- They give over-the-top compliments.
- They always seem to know what you want to hear.
- They like big displays of affection.
- They like to manipulate the look of a perfect couple.
- They will remind you of how much they have done for you.
- If you don't answer a text, they will be annoyed.
- You start to fear being punished by them.
- You become uneasy in their company.
- They make issues seem like your fault.
- You second-guess yourself.

Love bombing is a form of emotional abuse. It has everything to do with trade-offs. It certainly was for Colm, he thought if he gave me something I would feel obligated to give something in return. It is not your job to change a love bomber's behaviour.

The best course of action is simple, end things and get the support you need for yourself.

Colm, Mr Chicken Fillet, seemed perfect on paper. He even managed a good first impression but beware of 'too fast-too soon' and be prepared that even if he seems Mr perfect on Paper, he may not be Mr Perfect for you.

Chapter VII
'My Friends Dating Stories'

David 'Mr 'Text – Message' aka 'Sext-message'

As I was online dating, so were some of my friends. We were all having varying experiences. We all also had varying methods of choosing. We met occasionally to discuss tactics and usually ended up drinking wine, swapping stories, and learning very little. On our last meeting, Caren relayed the story of her latest meeting. She told us how she reached out to a man who had a very distinguished photo. 'He looked so debonair' she said, 'a total gentleman.'

Caren messaged with this man for over a month and she became invested in him. They planned to meet but he kept putting it off. He always had an excuse and Caren felt they were legitimate reasons. She had been texting and emailing him for six months. He made it very clear that he found her very attractive. He sent her a naked photo of himself, this gave the rest of us a fit of the giggles, as well as fear for our friend, because this was not dating at a certain age etiquette. But each to their own I guess, as long as no-one was getting hurt.

Caren said she had not been involved with many men and she thought this is what you do now, so she reciprocated and sent a photo back.
She thought this was a lead up to them being together properly. However, six months on they still had not met up. She felt they had a very strong connection. Caren decided to tell this man, David, how she felt. David quickly told her that he did not feel the same way. He thought it was clear that they were both having fun. She also found out he had a partner.

Caren was very cross with herself, she wanted us to help her see where she went wrong and how she would choose better next time.

Deep down Caren had to realise she did not know David. She only knew a made-up persona. She mistook a picture of his manhood to be a declaration of how much attraction he felt for her. She played along with the sexy messages because she thought that this is what dating is like these days. She thought they were making a connection. She knew this situation was not ideal, but it was keeping her occupied in the evenings and it made her feel needed.

If Caren were honest with herself, she would have admitted she was struggling with loneliness. This pretend relationship kept her from looking for a real relationship. In this instance, David reaped the benefits of Caren's naivety.

Why do people think it is ok to send intimate photos? Some even admit to sending intimate videos and once out there, these photos and videos are out there forever. If you met a man tomorrow, in a bar and had a conversation with him, would you feel it was ok if they showed their manhood? Indeed, you would not. You would call the police and have them arrested. Why then do some people think it is ok to receive very intimate photos online?

Think about it, if the expectation is to exchange sexy photos early on in the chat, what do you think would be expected after a month.

Exchanging sexy photos is not a forerunner to a real relationship. Not wanting to do this, does not make you narrow-minded or prissy. Only you know what is right for you. Just because somebody sends you a nude photo does not mean you are obliged to send the same. Someone who is genuinely interested in you will not dodge meeting you on an ongoing basis.

When someone is interested in you, they will make good on their intentions instead of leaving you in a confused state where they put in any real effort. Hard as it may be to admit, you know deep down when someone is not that into you. You will also feel if they are playing with you. This is why I feel you should meet up as soon as possible because no one really knows who is behind the keyboard. If your gut tells you, something is wrong it probably is.

No one wants to be the sidekick, the other woman or the provider of titillation. You may feel you are not worthy of anything more, but you are. Learn to ask questions and tell him to take a run and a jump. Sexting someone before you meet them is unhealthy. It is clear what he wants. Know you are being used and move on. There is a reason if someone does not meet you for six months.

In fact, I think there is a reason if they do not meet you in six weeks. This is a fantasy involvement. If you fall into this trap, use the experience as a wakeup call and be more cautious in your next encounter. Know your worth and cut the idiots off fast. You are nobody's plaything unless you choose to be. It has been shown that married men get their kicks by being keyboard seducers, so it is up to us to be more vigilant.

I advised Caren to run like hell. I knew another woman caught in a similar situation, but she allowed it to continue for years before she realised he was playing her along. In this instance, he lived a plane ride away. She flew to see him when he came up with an excuse not to see her. On other occasions, he would show up late at night, sleep with her, then he would leave first thing in the morning. He messaged for years but never called and never took a call.

This woman sent some sexy photos to keep him interested. It was sometime before she realised he was never going to commit to her. He was married. She found this betrayal worse than her own marriage breakdown as she poured so many feelings into it. She thought this was her forever relationship. If you have any misgivings, or gut feelings, trust your instincts, value yourself, and if something feels off, then it probably is.

Know your own boundaries of what feels safe and fun. Keep the focus on yourself and determine what virtues you want in a partner. Do not settle. You want something more concrete than him texting every day or spending the night once a week. Do not settle for less than what you want. It is good to remember we are the ones who teach people how to treat us. It took me a long time to acknowledge dating to be a sorting procedure. It is also a learning process.
Why not learn from my experience and help yourself to categorise what you are looking for in a partner.

There will always be people who look for attention, who want a distraction from their life, who just want sex, or who want to use you.

Sexting has become very popular. It means sending messages, or photos, or videos of a sexual nature. For some people, sending sexts can be a way to feel intimate. You may feel that it will make someone like you more. It can be fun in a relationship but more and more it is between strangers. If someone is worth your while, they will like you whether you sext them, or not. People may feel pressure to participate in it, but you must remember you do not have to do it unless you want to.

I am not in favour of sexting with a stranger. I feel it needs mutual respect. If the other person does not understand why you do not want to sext they are not worth the effort. You should never feel pressured into anything in a relationship. No matter how much you like the other person or how much pressure they put on you. If they respect you, they will completely understand, and if they do not understand, it is even more reason not to communicate with them further.

If it makes you feel uncomfortable and the other person puts you under pressure, block them. Caren felt uncomfortable but she did it as it made her feel connected. Ask yourself if you feel confident and secure in sexting. How would you feel if your images appeared on social media? How much do you trust the person you are sexting? Even if you trust them now, could you trust them if you broke up?

If you decide sexting is for you, protect yourself. Only share with someone you trust. Avoid showing your face. Perhaps agree on some ground rules beforehand. Make an agreement that you both delete the images or texts after you have seen them.

Learn from Caren, I know Caren learned her lesson from her Mr Text Message who became Mr Sext Message.

If this sexting is more serious, if an image you shared appears in social media, contact a legal professional to get advice in having it removed. Contact the person who shared it to delete and surrender all copies they possess. You have the legal right to have these images taken off the internet under our data protection laws.

Finding out your new love interest only wants a sextual relationship is very disappointing and upsetting. It is a very stressful time, so it's important you take care of yourself. Do not be too hard on yourself, we all make mistakes. I made more than most, hence why I have so much experience to share with you.

You are not the first person who has been through something like this and believe me you will not be the last. Talk to your friends, girlfriends are the best. If it is really upsetting you, maybe consider seeing a counsellor. It is important to share your feelings with someone, reach out for support. Most importantly do not give up. Take it from me there are genuine nice men out there, it is just about finding the right fit for you, no one wants to stay text-messaging forever.

Remember Caren's story and how she felt so let down when she found out she was being used.
When we met her for our wine night, we joked about it, but we realised it was no laughing matter. Caren had us as a group of friends. Girlfriends are the best. They will tell you when to watch out and they will support you when you need it.

How to avoid the 'sext-er'

You just start talking to someone online, you appreciate each other's sense of humour, you seem to have a lot in common. You think it is time to meet up, when he hits you with the suggestive text ending with a winky face. There is no reason to believe he is a creep. You just think he is entering into that zone. Perhaps you are picking up the sexiness and you are ready to engage in a verbal lover's rendezvous. If that is how you feel, go for it. It is all about what you are comfortable with.

If you are uncomfortable and you feel it is way too soon, there are ways you can overturn the conversation and let him know you are not ready to engage in this conversation just yet. If he is a smart man, he will take the hint, and switch back to your opinions on pineapple on pizza.
Attempt to strike a balance

- If he is getting suggestive tell him he needs to go find something to do, he could watch some Netflix.
- If you do not want to take part in sexy conversations before you meet, do not divulge the colour of your underwear.
- Try to steer the conversation in a less sexy direction.
- Maybe suggest he finds someone to keep him company, like a dog. They are a man's best friend. This should bring you back to real talk.
- Take the conversation where you want to or end it.

- Tell him your mother makes the best cookies. This will kill his ideas of sex and make him think of his own mother.
- Simply tell him you are not getting sexy with him yet, ask him to take the time to learn your eccentricities.
- Chances are if you knock him back, he will be embarrassed he tested those waters prematurely. If he is not and tries to control the conversation. Block him.
- Just be completely honest. Mr Sext is going straight for what he wants. Classy. Say no, if he does not take no for an answer, there are plenty other men who want to share what you want.
- If he sends you an inappropriate photo without warning. Run for the hills. You have better things to do with your time.

When you think about it, he has done the visual equivalent of forcing himself on you. You would not accept this physically so why accept it virtually. Move on, and you will be all the better for it, trust me. Sexting comes to all of us as a disappointment.

He seemed so nice initially, but now he is looking for some naked texting tango. You may like him, and you may already be invested in him, but do not let that side-track you from what you really hope to find. The moment you are not happy move on. This may or may not teach him a lesson.

Charles aka 'Mr Enthralling'

As many of my friends and I dated in the late seventies and early eighties life had brought some of us full circle and we were dating once again. We were now faced with this whole new dating scene. We would learn together. This is an account of Gabby's first entry into the dating scene. She was one of the first of us to take to tinder. We thought she was very brave as we still investigated online sites.

She saw a photo she liked and swiped right. They were a match. Gabby sent a short message asking 'Mr Tinder' to check out her profile and see if he was interested.

Living alone in her fifties, Gabby wanted company. We all knew Gabby had been in an abusive relationship for over twenty years and we wanted to see her with someone nice, so we encouraged her to reach out and find a nice man. She was lonely and freely admitted she wanted a man in her life. She lived in a very nice housing estate but as she looked out the window of an evening, she saw houses with doors closed, and windows warmly lit, with happy family scenes inside. At least this is the impression she had. She felt isolated as many of us do after a separation of a relationship we hoped would last a lifetime.

Gabby did, however, have a good circle of friends. We were her support. We all tiptoed around, the all-too-many dating sites window-shopping. It was like looking at a catalogue of men. The choice was incredible; it was actually overwhelming. Thus far I was the one regaling them with my stories of dating.

Gabby decided to dive into Tinder. Christmas was coming, and she did not want to be alone.
She filled out her profile, presented herself honestly, with her true age, her love of food and her round belly as a result. She even put up a self-sufficient financial status, not something I would recommend. Gabby was seeking a life partner intelligent, well-travelled, funny and she stressed no games. We were all watching on with interest in those first weeks, she was keeping us all in the loop and up to date. Gabby exchanged messages and a few calls with nice men. She even met some for coffee. She did not however click with anyone.

We all know that scenario, either they are not your type, or they may not be exactly who they pretended to be. I remember telling her she should become fussier, maybe just contact men who were closely matched. None of us really understood how 'the whole match procedure' worked.

As a group, my friends were reasonably tech savvy, and we knew our way around our smartphones. One evening while home alone, Gabby was scrolling when she saw the silver haired man with salt-and pepper beard, he was distinguished looking and liked jazz and walking. She took the leap and messaged him.

Days went by before she received an answer. She had actually given up. He said 'hello, thank you so much for your contact' 'I am so sorry for the delay in replying, I don't come on here very often.' He went on to say he really liked her profile and as well as interesting, she looked beautiful. He said he would love to know more about her, but he is not on here too often, however, he would be delighted if she emailed him.

His name was Charles, and he gave her his email address. Gabby did not see anything wrong with this and emailed him. Charles replied almost immediately. It was a long message where he described himself as a 'well-travelled business owner' he was Irish American, brought up in Boston, but travelled to Ireland. He was retired there now, as his grandmother left him a cottage. He told Gabby she sounded like someone he would really like to get to know, he said, if she was a perfume she would be called 'Eau de perfect.' He could not wait to meet her, according to him he was already imagining their first date.

Gabby was charmed. Charles was romantic, he was different, he was not like the men she knew. She said she was full of questions, about him and about online dating in general. "I am new here and it is kind of a strange way to meet people," she wrote, "but it is much warmer than hanging around the produce department in Aldi." She also told him about some of her previous dates and the deception she encountered. "I think it is best to be who we are, do you ?" she said. He agreed wholeheartedly. It is amazing what people say and do, he told her.

Every evening they would exchange emails. Charles suggested they list their hobbies, their favourite foods, their likes and dislikes. He indicated he was financially secure, and he hoped she was too. Gabby told him she was preparing to retire and looked forward to spending time in her home in France. He even sent her a picture of a ring he purchased saying he could not wait to give it to her. He also sent her a link to a song, which he said, 'holds the message of how I feel about you.'

They had spoken on the phone a few times, as he was away on business. They would meet next time he was visiting his cottage in Ireland in just a few weeks.

When Gabby told us of this romance, her face lit up. We all thought he was too good to be true, but she had fallen in love. She mentioned his voice as enthralling, she could not quite figure out his accent, but she felt that was because he travelled a lot.

He dropped 'my dear' into every other sentence and he was very complimentary. They soon began talking every day. His teenage years in Boston and his years travelling explained the accent, but there was another sound in there too, she thought, something she couldn't place, but she would work that out when they met. They spoke about all the things you talk about at the beginning of a relationship, hopes, dreams, plans for the future. She opened up about her marriage, her past relationships, her work, her family, and her conviction that things happened for a reason.

Gabby had never met a man who was so interested in her. She was just as fascinated by Charles or was it, Charlie? In his emails, he seemed to switch from one to the other. She found his LinkedIn profile, it was short, and he had a few connections. Sometimes Gabby felt they were in some kind of time warp as sometimes when he was having breakfast, he talked about going out for his evening walk. She knew he travelled, one evening he told her he was calling from India, he was finishing up a business deal. 'Funny how you sound like you are just next-door Gabby said.

We were out for our usual girly get together and discussing our most recent dalliances on the dating quagmire. Gabby was remaining tight lipped, but we got it out of her. She had fallen for this guy, and his charms. It was lovely to see her happy, but we pointed out some of the red flags we thought we could see. We just wanted her to be careful and not get hurt. We all know Gabby's past.

Looking back, we wished she had listened. Hindsight is a marvellous thing. The old adage, 'if I knew then what I know now' makes a lot of sense. Looking back, Gabby wondered would things have been different if Charles had said he was from Nigeria. She may have been on higher alert. We all knew about the people who posed as Nigerian bankers and duped victims with 'business opportunities' over spam email. But this was different. Gabby loved to travel and knew lots of people from overseas. The fact that Charles was living away and spoke with an exotic accent made him all the more interesting to Gabby.

She had a deep-down gut feeling, but she ignored it. Every time she had questions Charles had the perfect answer. She knew when she met him her gut would settle. She knew one thing for sure: Charles was not a swindler. He cared for her too much. There are many swindlers out there, who concentrate on vulnerable people looking for love but there are very few figures, as many victims do not report the crime. They are so embarrassed, they do not even tell their closest friends and family it happened.

Gabby is a very smart woman, but she did not even want to hear us when we raised some red flags.

She was too invested, and wanted to believe more than anything he was genuine, after all we were not the ones talking to him.

The good romance scammers have the ability to manoeuvre their target into a kind of partnership. They know how to get under the skin of their victims. They are professional at what they do, they gain your trust as they get inside your head. Scammers flood dating sites with fake profiles. They steal profile photos from other dating sites and from social media.
Men generally pose as older men, who are financially secure and profess themselves to be professional.

Women scammers tend to use a photo of an alluring younger woman, it has been written that men are easier to influence. Whether men or women it comes down to loneliness. A lonely person is a vulnerable person. After the scammer recognises a dating site innocent, or a lonely heart they begin grooming. They begin with a campaign of little messages, compliments, and love notes.

Gabby said that seven days after receiving the first message from Charles, they were on the phone daily. They would text first thing in the morning, and last thing at night. She filled her emails with minute details of her life. Charles would tell her he saw her in his dreams, as they looked into each other's eyes. Those words cast a spell, they made Gabby feel so good. She was enthralled. The question we all asked was, how do you fall in love with someone you never met? Gabby had never heard of catfishing, and we as her friends had no idea the practice was so common.

It all comes down to creating an idealised, romanticised, fanciful relationship. There are no face-to-face distractions, and the catfish can control how they present themselves creating more closeness than their true selves would. They put you on a pedestal, write exaggerated messages which if were spoken would disappear, but because they were written you can read them over and over again. This makes the message stronger. They say things like 'are you real? 'or 'you are a beautiful exotic dream' or 'you fill my days with wonder.

Gabby thought Charles was all she ever wanted. Her defences were broken down by the overwhelming amount of attention being showered on her. She was getting anxious to meet him at this stage, he promised he was finishing a business deal and he could not wait to meet her. He told her, her dreams were his dreams, her goals were his goals. He was on his way the following week, and Gabby could not wait because then she could not only prove to us, he existed, but she could prove it to herself.

Two days before he was due to arrive, he told her he was sending some documentation ahead and she would receive an email from customs asking her if she would receive them, there would be a small cost, but he would reimburse her as soon as he arrived. Gabby knew it was a strange request, but it was only forty-five euro, and this was little to pay to get to see him. Then another problem came up, he had to pay his workers. He had been paid significantly for his business project, he even emailed a scanned image of the check, issued by a bank, but he ran into difficulties trying to access it.

He would transfer it to her account, if she would send her details.

Gabby had money, Charles knew it, he also knew she was in love with him. She said she would send him some money to get him out of difficulty as long as he paid her back when he arrived. As time went on another problem arose and Gabby asked Charles 'how do I know you are not a Nigerian scammer?' 'Oh Gabby' he said, 'you know me better than that.'

Every time doubt creeped into Gabby's mind, she would read his messages back. She was looking for reasons he was telling the truth. He was on his way. At last, she was going to make him dinner and she could not wait, all her doubts would be whisked away. He would stay a whole weekend and we would all be able to meet him.

We did not know at this point the extent of the money she had given him or the promises he had made her. The day arrived, he texted from the airport he was on his way. After that Gabby's phone remained silent, despite all her efforts to get in touch. Something must have gone very wrong.
He always texted back, this was the first time since they started chatting he had not replied. She was sick with worry.

She called me and I went to chat with her and brought the wine. We sat and looked at his messages and tried to figure out what was happening. I gently told her of stories I heard about scams on dating sites. But I said it cannot be a scam as you have not sent him any money.

Then she blurted it all out, she sent him money, but he was going to pay it back. I stayed with her that night.

I could not believe how this smart, beautiful woman had parted with her money to someone she had never met. I could tell she was still holding out hope. I promised to come back again that evening after work. She was grieving, and all I could do was be there. I wanted her to contact the police, but she didn't want to.

Charles finally contacted her again two days later. Something about being held up by immigration at the airport and he needed money to bribe the officials. She was beginning to see the truth. I showed her a YouTube video of a woman who had been scammed out of her life savings. Gabby watched in horror. She texted Charlie confronting him, she gave him an ultimatum to come and meet her. The daily calls, emails and texts ended.

Gabby was devastated and alone with her thoughts for the first time in months. She googled romance scams and then she saw tinder swindler, but even then she said she thought Charles had been different. But he was not. She was scammed but she was lucky because she had not given him everything. Not like the women she read about who had given them their life savings. It took Gabby a long time to come to terms with what happened. On our advice she spoke to the police and as she did, she got really embarrassed at how foolish she had been.

She also spoke with a psychologist who told her it was like finding out someone you loved had died, and you'll never see them again.

Gabby blamed herself and we blamed ourselves too, because we wished we had been more protective of her.

It was a long way back for Gabby but in the end, she did go online again, this time vowing to only meet an Irish man. He may not have Charles' accent or his romance, but he would be real. I am delighted to say she met a gentle man. A man who is real and funny and he loves Gabby. He may not have enthralled her, to begin with, but she is enthralled now.

When we are online dating it is sensible to remember technology has streamlined communication and given swindlers powerful new tools of deception. It has also opened up a readymade pool of potential victims. The mainstreaming of online dating is becoming normal, but it blurs the line between 'real' and 'online' relationships. Online dating has powered a hidden epidemic. Romance scams are on the increase.

Signs of a fake online dating profile that could help you identify a scammer

- Their profiles have very few images or images that seem to be model photos.
- They work or live in another country even though you searched your locality.
- Many scammers claim to be in the military in another country.
- They do not link their profile to their Instagram or other accounts.
- You start chatting and they try to take the conversation elsewhere.
- They quickly ask you to move to another form of messaging like email or phone.

- Be wary of anyone you haven't met moving the conversation to another platform.
- They profess love early on.
- Within a short period, they say they feel a very deep connection to you.
- They target people who are vulnerable and isolated.
- They over flatter and are overly devoted early on.
- Moving the relationship very quickly is the red flag of the Tinder Swindler.
- They avoid meetups.
- They say they want to meet you, but then there is always some unexpected issue.
- They try to solicit money from you.
- They claim to need money to travel to meet you.
- They avoid video chat or face timing.
- They try to trick you into sending them money by sending you a package that requires customs fees.
- They request financial help or financial investment related to their fictional business.
- They ask for your help
- They might send you money and ask you to send it to another account for them.
- They sometimes ask you to open a bank account for them.
- They may send you a link to an app, game, service, or website they say they want you to try out.

How to Outmanoeuvre a Romantic Scammer

- Check that the same image isn't appearing across a variety of profiles under different names.
- Tinder offers a background check feature.
- You should keep up-to-date on the different types of dating scams emerging.
- Never reveal too much information about yourself to someone you've never met.
- A catfish will use your financial situation to their advantage.
- Do not match with profiles that seem suspicious.
- Never ever send intimate images of yourself to an online acquaintance.
- Protect yourself as much as possible.
- Protect your privacy, you would not give your financial details to someone you just met.
- Ensure you don't share too much.
- Go with your gut if something feels off

Josh aka 'Mr tutor' aka 'Mr Groomer'

Molly was separated and wanted to rebuild her life. To do this she decided to go back to education and immediately enrolled in her local Further Education and Training centre. Her first day was nerve wrecking as she felt all her fellow students would be much younger and more IT literate than her.

She was happily surprised at the range of ages and people on her course. The first day was intense as she put her brain back in gear, but it was also distracting which she appreciated. One month in and Molly was finally looking forward to her days in education.

The tutor was kind, funny and attentive. Molly found herself talking and laughing a lot with him. She often stayed back after the lesson had ended, to keep talking. They had such deep conversations that Molly felt her point of view was really valued.
She was drawn towards him. He was attentive, thoughtful and seemed interested in her. Molly and Josh became friends.

Molly is not sure when lines became blurred between tutor and friend, but it became very blurred. He was sympathetic asking about her separation, he spoke gently and caringly about her future. He reassured her and told her he would assist her any way he could. How quickly things changed from confiding in Josh after class, to him picking her up to go for a coffee.

Josh felt it was best not to let the other students know they were meeting outside of class. Molly confided in her friend Rosa, who was on the course with her. They even joked in class when Rosa saw Josh and Molly exchange eye contact. Rosa did warn Molly to be careful with her feelings, but it was too late. Molly had fallen for Josh, she was so delighted he was separated too, even though he had two young boys they would be able to work it out.

Months of secrecy followed, as the friendship turned physical, Josh warned Molly to keep their secret he said nobody would understand and if it came out, even though they were both adults, he could lose his job. So, Molly kept it a secret. She spent more time at the education centre and did very well on her course. She distanced herself from her family and found herself lying to her friends.

Josh made himself essential to her life and being with him was all she wanted, he loved that. Molly felt consumed by Josh. He was so into her, it felt liked he loved her completely. They had sex at his house during lunch, they even had sex in his office. It was all so exciting. Molly had never felt such attention. Josh made her feel so special.

It all ended abruptly when his wife found out. Josh was not separated. Molly was shocked, after all, she had spent weekends at his house, yes there were toys lying around, but there was no sign of a wife. It transpired she was working away during the week, which gave Josh time to play away and even play at home. Molly was devastated. Se felt guilty and dirty.

Molly was not one to interfere in other people's relationships. She had given her whole self, mind and body to Josh. He had taken advantage of a vulnerable lady, an adult yes, but she was a vulnerable adult, and Josh had groomed her for his own benefit. He was so adept in his actions, it was most probably not his first time luring a vulnerable woman.

What followed for Molly was a pattern of uncertain behaviour that lasted years. This man had coerced her into doing many things that, she could not believe she did.

Molly's subsequent relationships were usually emotionally bankrupt, as Molly felt she didn't deserve better. It was years later before she realised her life's story was not what she thought it was. A groomer had sexually abused her.

Josh had built up a relationship of trust and emotional connection with her and he manipulated, exploited and abused her.

An intelligent and successful woman in her late forties, Molly never made the connection between what Josh did to her, and what was morally and ethically wrong. It left her wondering how many other women did he do this to. Molly's shame ran deep, it was some time before she confided in her friends. Rosa was not surprised but she was helpless at the time as Molly was an adult. Molly wants me to tell her story because she wants other women to know adults can be groomed too.

Being groomed, was not Molly's fault, Josh had definitely planned things out in a way that made Molly feel, he genuinely cared about her, and she could not have anticipated his true actions.

One of the reasons grooming works is that it takes advantage of vulnerable and sensitive people. People with a tendency to decipher the actions of someone they care about in the best possible light. None of us want to believe that we could be the target of someone with bad intentions. The manipulator, the abuser or the groomer is the only one to blame, however, the victim ends up blaming themselves. Molly certainly did.

What is Grooming?

It is a form of abuse where a person is manipulated into reliance on the groomer, this in turn allows them to be vulnerable to mistreatment. It is not often that we hear grooming discussed when it comes to an adult grooming another adult.

Possible stages of Grooming.

- **They target the Victim.**

Groomers will generally learn about potential victims before they decide they are a target, they will focus on the most vulnerable. They usually target people with family problems, people with low self-esteem or people who have already been through abuse because it may be harder for them to recognize the pattern.

- **They Gain trust.**

Groomers can be hard to notice. They appear to be genuine. They manipulate the victim over time to be dependent on them. Grooming is usually about control. They flatter and share secrets. They make the person feel special. they do favours and gradually begin asking for favours in return.

- **They fill a Need.**

They try to fill a space in a person's life by convincing the victim that they can fill this void. This may be as simple as giving the victim attention. The groomer becomes essential in the life of their victim.

- **They isolate the victim.**

Groomers will likely try to isolate the victim from friends and loved ones.

This may refuse to meet family and loved ones. Or they bad mouth them or when they meet friends and family and try to be as charming as possible so that any concerns the victim may express are set aside.

- **Abuse.**

While subtle to begin with the introduction of physical or sexual abuse. Other forms of abuse include emotional, mental and financial abuse. All types of abuse are valid.

Maintaining the Relationship

Groomers will try to keep their victim dependent on them. They may use guilt or emotional exploitation to make themselves appear innocent. One example is that whenever you are hurt by something they've done, they make you feel bad, and you end up apologising.

Grooming in Adult Relationships.

Groomers often attempt to push things to a high level of closeness very quickly. This can make it harder for a victim to see red flags. They often shower their victims with love. They may treat the victim in a way that they have never been treated before, making them feel special. Before long they take control, and the victim is unaware of what is happening.Molly wants people to know that if you have been groomed, it is not your fault. She finally reached out for help by finding a life coach, with a background in psychotherapy. She was recommended to Molly. She was left with self-doubt and trust issues. It took her some time, but she did trust again and she did date again but now she takes her time getting to know someone.

'My Mr Right'

As you will know from this book, I did my fair share of internet dating. I had every experience going, I met all the 'Mr's', but this led to great understanding and knowledge. Learning from our mistakes is a cliché but a cliché that I can attest to. I certainly learned from my mistakes. I knew what I was looking for and I hoped I would know how to find it. Everyone wants to find that perfect partner, a lifetime partner who will compliment you and share your life. I learned that there is no such thing as a perfect partner, but I believe there is a right partner. I was now looking for a keeper.

I want a 'Mr. Right' for me. I want someone who fills my heart with joy every time we hold hands. I want someone who wants to know how my day went. I want someone who has my best interest at heart and who takes a genuine interest in my life, as I will in his.
I want someone who makes me feel secure, he not only tells me he loves me, but he shows me.

I want someone who cherishes the memories we share together. I want someone who trusts me and who I can trust. I want someone who has the same hopes and dreams and someone who has the same values.
More than anything I want to be with someone who makes me laugh.
Someone who shares inside jokes, random dancing, glasses of wine and making great memories. I know I want a lot, but I am holding out to meet that person.

I met all the someone's, the phoney someone, the flaky someone, the more interested in themselves someone, the players, the insincere, and the pretentious.

It may take many uncomfortable first dates before meeting a normal someone. After a while you begin to think what is a normal person anyway?

We all want a perfect partner but if we are honest, we are not exactly the perfect partner ourselves. It took me some time to open my mind and begin looking at things differently. Sometimes finding someone is filled with unfair expectations. Maybe we should consider our own expectations, start to concentrate on what kind of life we want to live, what kind of partner we want to be, as well as what kind of partner we hope to find.

Hopefully, the fakes, the narcissists, the liars, the swindlers, will dwindle into the background. As soon as we move away from the phoneys, we will begin to start making genuine connections with more suitable people. I know, I most likely fixated too much over finding 'the one,' to begin with. But after staggering from one unsuccessful date to another, I learned a very valuable lesson, the best way to find a genuine and nice person, is to be a genuine and nice person myself.

When it comes to online or app dating, it is good to have an open mind, but most of all you need to be honest with yourself. For instance, if you want to spend your days with someone who sees the best in others, then see the best in others yourself.
More than anything I wanted to find someone who lives every day with joy and purpose. Someone positive about life. Someone who lives their truth, accepts me for who I am, and smiles every time they see me. I live an authentic life, so I wanted to meet an authentic person.

I knew I didn't need anyone to complete me, I am complete all by myself. I wanted someone to share my life, a soul mate would be nice to have, but they are not a must-have. If your wish is to meet someone new, then be open with the people around you. Do not be needy. Neediness is not an attractive feature. Remember when you met someone needy yourself, I am sure they did not fill you with confidence. If we change our behaviour to suit someone else, we tend to lose ourselves and become needy.

We may act cool and say the coolest things but if we are just doing it to please others we are doing it for all the wrong reasons and we may appear desperate or needy. It is best not to try acting a certain way to get someone to like us as we will not be living our own truth and will end up attracting the wrong type of person. There are times in our lives we will be needy and that is human nature. When we are with the right person they will understand and support us.

Finding 'Mr Right' or Mr 'Authentic' is something I really wanted to do. I know we all dream of living happily ever after and falling in love with our very own prince charming, it did not take me long to find out there were very few prince charming's on offer. Embarking on this journey to find my Mr, proved to be a great challenge.

Spending a lifetime with a person needs a lot of thought. Now that I am older, that lifetime may not be as long as others, but I am determined to get it right this time. In matters of the heart, it is difficult to say what is right and what is wrong.

Many of us live our lives not thinking about who we truly are, we get ensnared in the habitual routine of life, losing our own identity in the process. We lose sight of what really matters to us, and what we actually want. Many of us continue on that trajectory for a lifetime. It took me some time, and many awkward moments, before realising that to find the right partner I must first find myself.

We cannot choose Mr Right when we don't even know what makes us happy. It is my strong belief that many of us let cultural and societal guidelines influence what we want. We tend to coast along with society doing what is expected. Dating, getting married, getting the house, the car, the dog, the children, giving in to the norm. We feel pressure to marry just for the sake of not being the odd one out. We married in the eighties because it was the thing to do, all our friends were doing it, we felt we were in love and most likely we were.

However, many couples realise after some time, especially when the children are grown up, they have grown apart. When this happens many stay in an unhappy relationship out of the fear of being alone. Being in this type of relationship is unfair to both of you and may prevent you from the happily ever after you long for and deserve.

Too many pick their partner based on what their parents, family, and friends expect of them. You are your own person, pick your right fit, only you know who is right for you. You don't need me to tell you that choosing well is the mainstay of a good relationship.

I feel communication and respect are the keys to a successful and fruitful partnership. You may have other priorities. You need to be able to talk honestly about anything and everything, and respect one another when you have a different point of view. For me, especially now, a good relationship should have emotional compatibility.

When searching online we need to remember we do not live our lives virtually, or on paper, we live in the real world. We need to meet the person to see how they make us feel. Relationships are all about feeling. I am looking for a partner with common interests. I want to enjoy their company, while having fun doing the things we really love. We do not need to be a carbon copy of each other, but having common ground can make life worthwhile.

They say opposites attract, but I feel if your interests are too different it may lead to one person sacrificing their interest, for the happiness of the other, this in turn may lead to resentment. I know as I am sure you all do, that there is no such a thing as a perfect man or woman, everyone has their own shortcomings. We will need to compromise but my advice is to do it on the trivial things, such as hair colour, height, dress sense, but never on any of the core issues. It is best not to compromise on your values, they make you who you are, and they make your partner who they are.
More than anything I wanted to find someone I could be myself with. I am flexible but not willing to change myself for anyone anymore. I wanted someone who would accept me for me. I too wanted to meet someone, I did not want to change.

Our gut instincts and our intuitions are our best guiding light. I know I have regretted it when I ignored mine. My advice is not to fall for someone when your gut tells you not to. There is so much dating advice out there, but it all comes down to the joy of meeting someone you connect with. I wanted that joy that is why I returned to the drawing board time after time.

Third Time Lucky

On this my third time, I decided to narrow my search and stay local. There was a man with a nice profile who lived just across the river from me, but I had passed him by in the past as he had a moustache. Moustaches are not my thing, but I decided to take my own advice and look past the moustache, we could always negotiate this at a later date all going well.

I messaged him and was delighted to receive a lovely message in return. We bantered back and forth, and he seemed genuine and nice. He felt authentic.

I was still coming to terms with 'the moustache' but I was warming to it. One warm August day I was on my way home from work, sitting in traffic listening to the radio, I had my driver's window open and was taking in all the people in their summer finery.

Stopped strategically outside Goosers restaurant, I looked longingly at those sitting in the sunshine having a cool drink. The owner was standing at the pavement also taking in the sunshine when I heard him say hi Kerry. This spiked my interest as Kerry was the name of the man I was chatting to. There are not many male Kerry's in our area. One look and I saw a nice well-dressed man stopping to chat with the owner.
They were smiling together and as Kerry walked away, I could see his moustache, it was my Kerry.

As the traffic moved forward, I thought he knows the owner of Goosers, he must like to eat out. I like to eat out. He looked very casual but well dressed, there and then I thought he is worth meeting.

On my return home I fired up my laptop and sent a message asking him to meet for coffee. I was rewarded by a smiley face and a 'thought you would never ask' response. We arranged to meet the following Wednesday after work.

Kerry messaged me on Tuesday to say he had booked a table as we would both need to eat, and we should have dinner. I was delighted with this as it took any confusion from the situation, and it was a very gentlemanly thing to do.

I arrived at the restaurant feeling excited but apprehensive. As I approached, I saw him waiting. He smiled when he saw me, that was a good start. We began our evening sitting down to eat in a cosy atmosphere. He took charge of the wine list which became a comedy.

He was impressing me with his knowledge but to each wine he chose the waitress said, 'sorry sir that one is not available,' this happened three times before he said bring any red French wine you have.

It later transpired he was not really trying to impress me but would only drink old world wines as anything from the new world caused him headaches. A good thing to find out on a first date. We ate, we chatted, we laughed, and time flew by. I realised as we hugged goodbye, I had not even noticed his moustache. He invited me to pizza and wine in Pointe Vecchio at the weekend, he knew my favourite spot. Once again we found the time flew. We were obviously engaged in something we enjoyed. I was finding out he was really good company.

Next, he invited me to drive to the coast with him. I had no qualms spending a few hours trapped in a car with him, this to me was a good sign. We had a lovely day, and as he kissed me goodnight, I knew I was lucky to meet him and cursed myself for not meeting him sooner because of his moustache. Something I would not change about him now. I was falling for this lovely gentleman.

When I feel love, it always stops me in my tracks. It makes me feel giddy and soft. I was giddy with Kerry. Falling in love can feel like floating through air on a misty warm day. It opens your mind to trying new things and building new experiences. We feel invincible and have a great view of our lives and ourselves.

My heart softens to the point that I become attuned to my partners every need. This can be a problem.
It has taken me time and self-development to hold back a little until I am sure of my feelings, and most importantly sure of theirs. We also need to ensure we receive what we need and what we give. I felt I was receiving what I needed from Kerry.

I have the tendency to lose my priorities when I fall in love, but this was in the past. I am mindful now of keeping my own space and time. We all know that one friend who disappears the minute they start a new romance. It is natural to want to spend all your time with a new partner, this does not last forever, and it is important to keep some elements of your own life and not enter totally into someone else's. We all know what the honeymoon period feels like where we forsake restraint and throw caution to the wind.

New love has you moving to extremes, I press the accelerator and lean into it, others are fearful of hurt and lean out, taking it slow. In the past I tried to take it slow but it is pointless, because my heart always rules my head, so I just go with it. I blame oxytocin for the spike in attraction.

As well as leaning in emotionally, I lean in physically, there is nothing like a good hug from the person you love. This love hormone keeps us bonded and helps us feel good. I am a very affectionate person and I need affection in return. Kerry is very affectionate.

This love thing sounds wonderful, but it can be normal to feel some worry. We can feel insecure and anxious as we may fret about being rejected or abandoned. This is a real and legitimate fear. Anytime I felt anxious or insecure in a relationship, I saw it as a sign to get out. This is not easy, but you need to be honest about your feelings and know what you want. For me I need security in a relationship so if I did not feel that early on, I did not pursue it.

I want that invincible feeling where I feel I could climb a mountain or jump in a lake, I want to feel unwavering and resistant to stress. I love to smile and when I am in love, and feel love, my smile beams out. Feeling butterflies is nice but I prefer a feeling of security and happiness. The more I smile the happier I feel. All these feelings come with a warning though, as we may confuse how the person makes us feel, rather than who they really are. So, although I move quickly, I try to take the time to know the person I am falling for.

I try not to overlook the qualities I find endearing in that moment, that might be deal breakers in another state of mind.

I always feel a better person when I am in love. I am kind, patient, loving, and generous. Love makes me a better version of myself. I know love is no fairy tale, I found that out the hard way, but when it feels right, it feels like you are in one. You dream of the happy ever after and many people actually find it.

As soon as you can be vulnerable with your new love, then I think it is game over. When we feel an attachment to a partner, our minds and bodies become aware of a sense of security, protection and armour. There is nothing like the feeling of a safe space where you can be yourself without fear of judgement. A space in which you can be vulnerable in sharing your inner self. I now feel that.

Most people, say when you fall in love you just know, it is hard to describe, or something equally as vague, but it is true, it is hard to describe. As there are no hard-and-fast rules for falling in love, there are no specifications or lists, to know if your feelings are the real deal. Some people know after a first meeting, others foster feelings, over months or even years.

Kerry and I have been together for almost three years. We nurtured our feelings over time. We feel so comfortable, relaxed and contented with each other. Kerry may not be perfect, but then again neither am I, but we are perfect together. We are happy. We give each other strength and confidence.

I may not have fallen in love with him the first time I saw him. Feelings work differently for me. I wait for them to grow. I fell in love with the little things about Kerry, before I completely fell in love with him. I fell in love with his eyes. Whenever he smiles or laughs, his eyes beam out. When he cries his eyes fill up. I love that he can show emotion.

I love how witty he is, and I really love his belly laugh. I fell in love with how he says my name. We certainly have a myriad of differences, but we always find ways to compromise. I always hope that we'll keep on discovering new things about each other. Kerry is now a constant part of my life and I love how he makes my small world revolve. Those who know and love us are delighted for us. We might seem like a 'Mills and Boon' romance novel but when something feels right, it most likely is right. My advice always, is to persevere, and be realistic about your expectations. Have hope, as without hope we have nothing.

You may think love feels complex or problematic, and you may be looking for things like physical chemistry, sexual attraction, and shared interests, or you may be looking for that spark, but in my personal experience, I feel the key factor to not only falling in love but to staying in love, is compatibility. Kerry and I are compatible and we want the best for each other. For me love is harmony and I hope you find your harmony whatever that is for you.

I am sure Kerry and I are about to discover that like any good love story, life will have twists and turns, but I am confident our story will end in happy ever after.

About the Author

Marie O'Connell is an Irish author of short stories, press articles and her book 'Community at Heart.' A mother of three young adults, she has had a varied career to date. Having worked as a pastoral worker, a teacher, an administrator and receptionist.
Now working in the University of Limerick she is a voice for women and equality.
Marie does her best writing in cafes, on park benches, on any beach, and at home in her community of Ballina/Killaloe.
Marie loves to act, tell stories as well as write. She loved her time as a mature student where she graduated with a BA, PG dip, MA presently pursuing a PHD.
In this book she brings her readers into her world of online dating. It is a real life rollercoaster with a few giggles thrown in. The real life experiences of online dating, may not be for everyone but it certainly has its interesting moments.
Marie's friends awaited her next date, so they could hear the stories she had to tell, they were the ones who told her she should write a book because no one could make it up. This is that book.

Pointe Vecchio Killaloe Co. Clare.

Milton Keynes UK
Ingram Content Group UK Ltd.
UKHW011933220823
427305UK00002B/4

Printed in Great Britain
by Amazon

About Rebecca Chase

Rebecca Chase is an English rose and a pocket rocket with a taste for drama, romance, spice and love. She adores writing, whether it's a short story with unexpected passion or a novel that takes you through the ups and downs of a blossoming relationship. She's always looking for everyone's next book boyfriend. When it comes to her stories, you can guarantee there will be romance, there will be mind-blowing sex, and, most of all, there will be love that lasts a lifetime. You'll be desperate for more while aching for a happy ever after.

CONNECT WITH REBECCA

Sign up for my newsletter - tinyurl.com/Rebecca-Chase

Website - www.rebeccahchase.com

Tiktok - @rebeccachaseauthor

Facebook - www.facebook.com/RebeccaHChaseAuthor

Instagram and Threads – rebeccahchase

Goodreads - 15019280.Rebecca_Chase

COMING SOON

Fake A Chance On Me: A fake dating sports romance (The Bulls Rugby Series Book 3)
Released: Summer 2025

Closest Protection Series Book 2: Strike's and Millie (Title TBC): A second chance, friends to enemies to lovers bodyguard romance
Released: Early 2026

Coulter Racing Team Series Book 2: Niki and Rosie: A single mum, age gap sports romance
Released: 2026

Cloud Family Series Book 2: Flora and…

Also By Rebecca Chase

Head Over Feels: An enemies to lovers steamy sports romance (The Bulls Rugby Series Book 1)

Stalling in Love: A steamy opposites attract romance (The Bulls Rugby Series Book 2)

Regally Binding: An enemies to lovers bodyguard romance (Closest Protection Series Book 1)

Go Cook Yourself: A grumpy sunshine workplace romance (Cloud Family Series Book 1)

Occupational Hazard: An Anthology of Spicy Workplace Stories

Keep in Touch: A sweet coming-of-age love story

support, messages, posts, and likes give me space and encouragement to share stories and give new characters a voice. I feel so lucky to have chatted with you online and briefly been part of your lives. Thank you for everything.

To seajart, who designed my book cover. I adore your work. How do you make my notes into such spectacular pieces?

To the people at the pub where I write who've given me a safe home to create new worlds. It's no coincidence that my stories often feature pubs or bars and the found family trope.

To the women in racing who inspired me to write this book. I'm in awe of you and others who have trailblazed. You are my heroes.

Finally, a massive thank you to my friends 'in real life' and the ones I've met online. Writing can be a lonely passion, but I never feel alone because I have you with me, sending messages, reminding me to touch grass and making me laugh. Thank you, Asha, Gill, Kaz and Anna.

ACKNOWLEDGEMENTS

I must give the most special mention to my husband. Although I watched Formula One with my mum as a child, Mr Chase made me fall in love with the sport and accompanied me to my first F1 race in Hungary in 2019. He also gave me the experience of staying at the hotel on the edge of the Silverstone Circuit. He has answered numerous questions about racing's technical aspects and brought his knowledge as a race marshal. Thank you, Mr Chase! You're amazing.

My cat, Bandit, is a troublesome boy with one Elvis sideburn. He inspired both cats in Start Your Engines. He made me love cats and enabled me to truly understand how it's possible to love and be loved by animal bad boys.

I was incredibly lucky to have the knowledge and support of JL Peridot, Elizabeth Holland, Kathryn Kincaid, and Sarah Smith. They brought wisdom and guidance when beta reading, which transformed this book, and I can't thank them enough. Their romance books are exceptional, and everyone should read them—a special mention to Kathryn, whose messages about her love of Connor Dane have kept me smiling.

Thank you to Joanne Machin, a lovely human and world-class editor. Her notes are invaluable and have transformed this book from nonsensical to polished.

The biggest thank you is for those who read my books. Whether this is your first Rebecca Chase or your sixth, your

START YOUR ENGINES PLAYLIST

The Man – Taylor Swift

The Chain – Fleetwood Mac

Sexy Boy - Air

Edge of Seventeen – Stevie Nicks

Femininomenon – Chappell Roan

Love Story (Taylor's Version) – Taylor Swift

Someone You Loved – Lewis Capaldi

hate u love u – Olivia O'Brien

Formula 1 Theme – Brian Tyler

Kids – MGMT

High Hopes – Shed Seven

Made to Love You – Dan Owen

Rebellion (Lies) – Arcade Fire

Toothpaste Kisses – The Maccabees

Summer of Love – Shawn Mendes & Tainy

At Last – Beyoncé

Flux – Bloc Party

Linger – Royel Otis

Liss spun and gasped loudly. She was in the presence of King Archibald.

The King opened his arms, and a measured smile covered his face. "Please come in and have coffee with my family, Miss Granger, and I will explain everything. And security, unhand her. Felicity Granger is a princess now."

START YOUR ENGINES

offered her his hand, but she ignored it, instead sticking up her middle finger at him. At his chuckle, she barely resisted the temptation to claw out his eyes.

"The ladies are out of the car. We're coming in now," he said with a quiet grunt.

"Who are you talking to?" she snarled. Bear pointed to his earpiece with a roll of his eyes.

Everyone was rushing around the car, noises coming from all angles. Strangers walked out of what appeared to be an old building into the courtyard before them.

Questions about the past and present flooded her consciousness. Her ears pounded, and she planted her feet firmly on the ground. "I refuse to go anywhere until someone tells me what's happening. I've had enough of being forced here and there. Someone tell me something, or I'm going back to my pub. And you"—Liss jabbed a digit at Bear—"you give me my bloody phone, or I'm coming for it myself."

She reached into his jacket, but he wrapped his hands around her wrists with lightning-quick reflexes and pinned them mid-air. Her legs quaked, and her skin blistered as arousal filled her veins. *Why does that do it for me?*

"I will pick you up if I have to," he grunted. "There's very little stopping me from throwing you over my shoulder and taking you to the—"

"I can't apologise enough," a male voice called out in the classiest accent she'd ever heard. Even that couldn't stop the heat burning between her thighs at the idea of being popped over Bear's shoulder. It was so caveman, and yet fuck, it was hot. None of the preppy guys from her past would have considered it, let alone dared to do it. "The secrecy is all my fault, darling Felicity."

START YOUR ENGINES

Rebecca Chase

Happy reading

Rebecca Chase

Copyright

This ebook is a work of fiction. Names, characters, businesses, places, events and incidents are either the products of the author's imagination or used in a fictitious manner. Any resemblance to actual persons, living or dead, or actual events is purely coincidental.

Copyright 2025 Rebecca Chase

All rights reserved

Published by Rebecca Chase

Cover design © seajart

All rights reserved. No part of this publication may be reproduced, distributed, or transmitted in any form or by any means, including photocopying, recording, or other electronic or mechanical methods, without the prior written permission of the published, except in the case of brief quotations embodied in critical reviews and certain other noncommerical uses permitted by copyright law.

This book is dedicated to those who've had to fight just to be seen as equal. Remember, this is your life. Don't let others tell you how to live it.

Apply for that job, wear those jeans, grab the chances people don't want you to have and give your hips an extra wiggle as you do it.

You're fucking awesome.

CHAPTER ONE – SENNA

"**I** am a strong, confident woman. I am qualified. I am knowledgeable. I am enough," I mouth to the mirror for the umpteenth time.

Under the fluorescent lights in the office toilets, I resemble a panda waking up from a year-long bender. The bags under my brown eyes are no match for the foundation I attempt to reapply with fumbling fingers as my dad's voice plays through my phone's speaker.

"You can do this, Senna. You're not my first choice to run my team," he grits, "but your brother ditched us to find himself."

"Find himself" is said with a bitterness that's an increasingly large part of my dad's personality.

It's not my fault the great Jim Coulter retired from managing the Coulter Racing team. A heart attack brought on by bad choices and overwork was the final straw. I sink my teeth into my tongue. The last time I mumbled the words, he wouldn't speak to me for a day.

Dad barrels on like he's browbeating one of his engineers instead of his only daughter. "You will lead the team acceptably until he returns. Don't forget you were named after Ayrton Senna."

As if I could forget. I tap the tiles, sighing inwardly. "Sorry you didn't get two sons, Dad."

3

"Senna," he cautions.

I swipe mango lip balm over my lips. "Dad, Niki needed to work out who he is and what he wants because of his accident. An accident that nearly killed him, remember?" I reply, managing my tone.

"I am well aware. He was going to send my team into the stratosphere this season."

My heart races faster than a car on soft tyres. We've had this argument several times over the last week. Niki should be standing here, ready to speak to the board and drivers in preparation for the new season. He wouldn't be staring into the bathroom mirror, limbs trembling, while Dad lectures him.

"And before you ask," I add, trying to redirect the conversation, "I don't know where he is. He's not checked in since he told me I'm the new boss of Coulter Racing as he left the country several days ago."

"He knew that crashing is a part of racing. He should've manned up and taken on the team. Now it's up to you," Dad grumbles.

I rub the scar on my hand from when my car slammed into a wall in a British Formula Three race when I was a teenager. The silver thread warns me never to race again, and that if I'm to achieve, I have to do it alone. Trusting the wrong person nearly ended my life that day.

The bathroom entrance bangs open, and my best friend Jackie's, aka Jacs, boots smack against the tiled floor. Her mechanic's uniform hangs open. A glare clouds her freckly face and makes her red eyebrows dive together as if they're squaring up to each other.

"Dad, I've got to go. I'll update you."

"That's right, Jumps. Get in there and ensure we win the Constructor's Championship this year. It's all on *you*."

His finger is probably pointing at the mobile while my mum is telling him to calm down. "It was a travesty when we lost it by one point twenty years ago."

"Bye, Dad." I sigh. It's all I can do to keep from asking him for the umpteenth time not to use the nickname he gave me when I started karting and I'd accidentally jump the lights at the start.

He doesn't need to remind me of the story he's repeated every season since I was five, either. He hangs up as I'm visited by the haunting image of tears rolling down his cheeks as he told me how he'd be the greatest F1 boss one day.

I hold a fist to my lips as Jacs taps her foot against the floor. She strides to me, grips my shoulders, and forces me to confront my face in the mirror. "Who is this?"

I try to shrug her off, but she's got the grip of a racing driver competing for first place. "What do you mean?"

"Who is this?" Her Scottish accent makes her words punchier. Her green eyes pierce mine in the glass.

"A woman who could do with a makeover, especially a new haircut and a change in style, but doesn't have the time because she's too busy failing at everything she does."

My average body with hints of curves gives away my passion for running and secret love of doughnuts. My blond hair falls limply to the middle of my back, and my lips are too thin, although I won't get fillers. With my luck, they'd go wrong, and I'd be called Ducky for the rest of my life instead of Crasher. Another nickname that's more about my failures than my achievements.

"For fuck's sake, Senna." Her grunt echoes off the marble sinks. "This is the new boss of Coulter Racing. This is a woman who—"

One of the administrative assistants from the marketing and communications department bustles into the toilets, causing Jacs to roar. The assistant squeals as she turns and runs back out.

"Jacs, don't shout at my team."

Jacs strides over to the bathroom door and locks it. "She's not your team, because you're not the marketing and communications department director anymore. You're the boss of the entire company." Technically, that makes her still part of my team, but there's no point arguing. There's a reason why Jacs hit the glass ceiling of the mechanics team and kept going. "And why are you in these toilets and not in the ones attached to the big boss's office? You have a private bathroom now."

"But—"

"But nothing," she replies. She walks back to me at the mirror and makes me face it again. Her five-foot height means I tower above her at five six, but her power obliterates mine in that second. This time, she says in a softer voice. "You are Senna Coulter. Who knows more about cars than any other person in this place, aside from me?"

"Me," I mumble.

"Who knows more about this team than anyone in this building?"

"Me," I say a little louder.

"Who worked every hour that existed while all the men waggled their little dicks, pretending they knew what they were doing but never coming close to your skill or achievements?"

"Me." I smile at our reflections.

"And who is a businesswoman, driver, mechanic, and ball buster who can bring greatness to this team? Something her brother recognised years ago yet her dad is too foolish to realise because, like so many men in this place, he's decided women don't compare? Shout it loud!"

"Me!"

"Yes, Coults. Exactly." The nickname those closest to me use gives me an instant lift. "And if not for the stupid racing driver who shall not be named—Connor fucking Dane—you'd be the greatest racing driver this world has ever seen and better than him, too."

Mentioning Connor Dane makes me snarl, which is precisely what she intended.

"It's going to be harder to avoid him now," I say. Connor was the guy who'd caused me to crash into a wall, effectively ending my racing career when I was a teenager. I've done a brilliant job of avoiding my brother's best friend for ten years. "What if I see him on the track? Did you hear the latest? Apparently, he was caught with his last trainer in his boss's car."

She pushes my worry away with a flip of her hand. "You're going to lead a record-breaking team—"

"We're floundering at the bottom," I cut in.

She glares back. "While he'll slum it at Vessa—"

"Who are the best in the championship—"

"I'm trying to big you up!"

"Fine. This is our season because, hopefully," I reply, whispering the last word and earning a glare from Jacs anyway, "our two drivers this season, Antoine and Dax, will change that, although neither care about the team. In some ways, I'm taking on a failure—"

"Senna," she barks.

"But this team means the world to me, so I won't compare our crappy performances to anyone else's for at least ten minutes," I say to her reflection. Her smirk makes me wrinkle my nose in amusement.

I pull back my shoulders, and wrestle my hair into a low bun.

"Take a breath, listen to your empowering song," Jacs says, finding Fleetwood Mac's "The Chain" on my phone. The song has a bridge that every old-school fan of racing loves. "Ignore that your dad is still the owner, and tell your directors and drivers you will rule this team and make it excellent."

I smile at her as the music plays. Adrenaline floods my limbs, and as the bridge hits, I bounce up and down and ready myself for a fight. I am the motherfucking boss now, and the team will listen.

"Thank you," I whisper, pulling her to me.

We step out of the toilets and stride through the corridors. Photos of Formula One racing greats adorn the walls, including Senna, who I'm named after, and Niki Lauda, who my brother is named after. My steps falter slightly as the pressure builds in my chest.

Jacs's scent, a mixture of plum and rose, combines with the stench of oil that often lingers around her overalls. I breathe it in an attempt to centre myself. Trophies, including Niki's from the races he's won, glint in the cabinets outside the boardroom.

I stare at the last Constructor's Championship trophy we won. It's been a decade. I squeeze my eyes and sense the wrinkles sinking into the skin of my forehead.

"We won't get any of those this year," I mumble.

START YOUR ENGINES

"Senna," Jacs says. "Don't forget you have trophies in there, too."

I open my eyes to see the couple of trophies from my years as an F3 driver. "I was good. I could have been the best if not for the accident."

"I didn't mean those trophies." She points to the shiniest award in the cabinet. "I meant the one I sneaked in after your dad retired."

I stare at the Best Communications Sports Team award from last year's British Sports ceremony.

"Your hard work won that, and your determination will make you successful this year. With the guys in there," she says, nodding to the boardroom, "you need to be a bitch boss at all times, or they'll take everything. Don't show anxiety for a second. It's you against them. Now, shoulders back and sass on. You've got an audience."

I turn to find my new assistant, Jimmy, staring at me with raised eyebrows, tablet in hand.

"Morning, Jimmy," I say with a nod, giving Jacs's shoulder a quick squeeze of thanks before heading to the boardroom. "Are my board, Antoine, and Dax ready for me?"

Jimmy holds out a handful of notes, which I pocket.

"Everyone but Dax is there. Your brother left a message letting you know he'd changed something before he left. You have a new driver," he calls out as I walk into the boardroom.

The words register slowly as I scan the pinched-lip faces of the suited men staring back at me, several of whom are struggling to hide their belief that they're more qualified to run the team than me, a twenty-seven-

year-old woman. Maybe some of them are still expecting Niki.

I bite the inside of my mouth as I search for the new driver Jimmy mentioned.

I glance at Antoine, who is frowning at the man to his side. My so-called new driver, the man my brother has replaced Dax with without consulting me, looks up from his phone. Our branded clothing covers his lean body. His black hair, beautiful blue eyes, and full lips will probably give me an ulcer. As his eyes lock on mine, he drops his phone and glares.

Connor fucking Dane despises me.

Suddenly, all my plans go straight to hell.

CHAPTER TWO – CONNOR

Senna Coulter stares at me like I'm a piece of shit on the bottom of her shoe.

With her hands on her hips and the man I thought was Niki's assistant behind her, she looks every inch the big boss.

I cock my head to the side in a show of ambivalence, but my hands itch to call my best friend—former best friend as of this second—to find out what the hell he's done now.

The woman in front of me reminds me of the Senna I knew, the feisty driver who was once one of my closest friends.

The memory of the last thing she said to me weeks after she was released from the hospital slams into me, making my chest vibrate. *I hope one day you know what it's like to have your life ruined like you've ruined mine. I hate your guts. You're dead to me, Connor Dane.*

I can't forget the angry tears in seventeen-year-old Senna's eyes as I desperately tried to explain that the crash wasn't my fault. She has no idea what that crash was truly about, and I'll never reveal the truth.

A sour taste fills my mouth. I expected to bump into her as she is—was—the comms director, but this changes everything.

"Are you fucking telling me you're the boss now, Jumps?" I blurt.

Her eyes twitch. She used to hate the nickname because it highlighted her early failures. I grind my teeth. I've used it since I was eighteen in an attempt to remove my feelings for her and turn her into a faceless enemy.

She rubs the scar from where she smashed her hand because of me. Bile rises from my gut as I stare at the action. I could destroy the lives of everyone I know and still not hate myself as much as I do now.

"Yes. Niki is gone, and I'm in charge of Coulter Racing." She pulls her rosy lips into her mouth. Her perfect cheekbones catch my eye, and her eyes sparkle. She's fucking gorgeous, she always has been, and aside from a wedding I sneaked into last year, this is the closest I've been to her in years. *Get a grip.*

There's a grunt from Antoine. He despises the idea that a woman is his boss. I hate that guy.

The way her eyes pinch reminds me of how she took down the male drivers during our teenage races. There is a quiver in those eyes, though. I know that movement. I saw it when we were younger and she'd tried to act aggressively around the male drivers to prove she was as good as them. She's anxious as hell.

"I'm more than the boss," she says, looking at me and Antoine.

"Yeah?" I ask, standing.

"If you're on my team, I own you for the season."

The room remains silent as eyes dart back and forth between us.

I scowl at her, but she doesn't flinch.

I take a breath. "Hold—"

"Own you," she repeats before silencing my comeback with a hand.

START YOUR ENGINES

She turns to the board members, who stare with their furrowed brows. "Everybody out. I want you back in here for a strategy meeting in thirty minutes." I move slowly to the door, but her eyes flash as she swivels back to me. "Not you. I'm not done with you. Sit."

I fold my arms, staring her down. She rolls her eyes.

As the board departs, I reposition myself nearer the wall. My nostrils flare as I square my shoulders, and I clench my teeth so hard my jaw hurts.

"You're the new driver Niki has saddled me with." Her shoulders are tight, and her left eye twitches.

I hold up my hands. "Saddled? I didn't sign up to be 'owned' by you, but don't forget that I'm one of the best drivers on the circuit." Or I was.

"And one of the biggest liabilities, when you're not seducing everything in sight."

The stench of vomit fills my nostrils, and I tighten my lips. She doesn't know exactly how much of a liability I am or why. Maybe this is a chance to get out of my contract. If I was in a better mental state, I'd consider this is fate telling me to recompense her for what I did to her.

"I'm not what you—"

She holds her hand up again and connects her phone to the conference room screen. I will bust a vein if she keeps doing that. I study her fingers as I count to ten. Several marks suggest she's not sitting in her office like a hands-off boss but continues working on cars. The line of the scar has embedded itself in her skin. I fist my hands. If I could go back...

I shake my head. I can't go back.

Niki's face appears on the screen.

Senna gasps, "Your hair." But it's so quiet that he doesn't hear.

13

His head is completely shaved. The burns, still healing from his accident, make my *hello* freeze in my throat. It took mere seconds for the rescue crew to remove him from the car and extinguish the fire during his last race. I'm under no illusion that the damage could've been more than burns and broken ribs. The videos of him stretchered away haunt my Senna-free nightmares.

I close my eyes. This isn't the first time I've considered walking away from racing like he did. At twenty-eight, I'm not one of the young racers anymore. I could retire. Each time I get into my car, the adrenaline no longer fuels a desire to win. Instead, a desperation to stay alive controls my hands.

"What the hell, Niki?" Senna's grumble forces my eyes open.

I eyeball my best mate as he pops a cap on his head.

"I couldn't have said it better myself," I grunt.

The three of us haven't spoken like this since the day before Senna's accident when Niki was ill with the flu and told us he couldn't race. If he'd been there, Senna would have remained safe. I shake the memory away and sink my teeth into my lip again, desperate for pain.

Niki smiles. "Look at you two getting on. You're already agreeing about things."

I want to drag him through the screen and smack him, even though I love the guy.

"If you were here, I'd punch your beautiful face," Senna replies. She needs to stop speaking my thoughts. "Why is Dane the Dick here, and where's my other driver?"

"No 'how are you, bro'? 'Where are you?' I expected better of you, little sis," Niki says, although his smile falters. A plain white wall is behind him. His turquoise Coulter

Racing team tee gives away nothing about where he is or what he's been doing.

"Niki," I snap. "Get to the point. I came here for you. You begged me to join the team." When I was about to walk away.

Senna glances at me with her big hazel eyes. When we were teenagers, I'd stare at her when she wasn't looking, just to decipher the colours swirling through her eyes. She says they're brown, but I've stared at them long enough to know.

I check myself. This isn't the time to reminisce or open the box of emotions I closed when I saw her last year at the wedding. I meet her stare, and she looks away quickly. The room smells like every boardroom in this building: coffee and diesel with a hint of Old Spice as most of the directors are men over the age of fifty. But there's something else. I breathe in and get hints of orange blossom. I want to get close to her and find out if it's her fragrance.

I slam my palm against the wall.

Niki sighs. "Connor drives for us now. I've signed him for two years. It was the last thing I did before I left."

Senna stamps her foot, and I try not to laugh or focus on how her wide-legged trousers hide the long legs I recall from the split in her dress at the wedding. "But—"

"He can't get a contract anywhere else because he drove like a dickhead last season," Niki adds. "Vessa kicked him out, and no one wants him on their team."

She stares at me and mouths, "Liability."

I wink at her, and she glares back.

"Oi," Niki says, drawing us back to him. "Senna, you know that Connor is a great driver and could be excellent if he stopped being Dane the Dick."

15

"We both know why I'm called that, and it's not because of my driving," I banter, earning me a scowl from Senna. I grin and lift my eyebrows at her, the swirls hitting my belly again. "It's not the insult you want it to be, Senna, and many women will wax lyrical about my—"

"I can't work with this idiot. This playboy. He's going to ruin us," Senna gripes at the screen, although it's me she's sticking her middle finger up at.

"No, he's not. Connor will give us a chance to succeed, and he will be a very good boy, too."

"I'm no one's good boy." My eyes snap back to his and away from his sister, although I want to witness her reaction.

"Senna, please leave the boardroom. I need to talk to Connor alone."

She stamps her foot again, and a smile replaces the glare I've aimed at Niki.

"You can't order me out of my boardroom. I'm the boss now. You were the one who told me that before you left. My team need to see me as the boss if they're going to be on my side."

I want to comfort her. Even as a teenager, Senna fought for every ounce of respect from the team.

But I don't. I can't.

"Just this once. I promise. I need to have this chat, but then the room, Connor, and the whole team are yours. Okay?"

She side-eyes me with a loathing that would make me feel like crap if I wasn't certain she's secretly struggling with anxiety about everything forced upon her.

"Fine. You've got five minutes, and then I'll be back."

"All right, Princess," I tease, but she strides out of the room without a backward glance.

"Love you, Niki," she shouts as the door bangs behind her.

As I watch her go, I remember her destroying me before a race when we were teenagers. I'd commented there'd never be a female Formula One racing driver. She beat me that day and changed my mind, too. Something sparks in my chest that I must ignore.

"What the hell, man?" I grunt at the screen. "We had a deal."

"Open the door a second."

My brow furrows, but I walk to the door and yank it open. Senna falls against my chest. The scent of orange blossom with a hint of mango envelop me. My hands skim her hips before she pushes her arms against my chest, huffs, and retreats in the direction of the bathroom. I lick my lips slowly before remembering I'm meant to be angry with her brother.

I return to the boardroom screen.

"So?" I snap, my hands flexing from our brief touch. Fuck, I shouldn't be attracted to her like this, especially as I chat to her brother. "You told me you were signing me so we could realise our teenage dream and make this team the best in the world."

"Nothing has changed."

"Except we're not doing this together." My voice booms. "And your sister, who hates me, is my boss."

"She hates you because you haven't talked to her since you visited ours after her accident."

"Because she wouldn't talk to me."

"Because you didn't tell her what really happened," he replies softly, pulling the heat from my argument. "She still probably thinks you did it on purpose."

I drop my head and sigh. "This is the first time I've seen her close up in nearly ten years. She never came to award dinners or the other big events for drivers, and if we bumped into each other in the driver's paddock, she'd turn on her foot and walk away from me." I throw my head back and give the ceiling a silent roar. I also saw her at her Uncle Ralf's wedding, but she doesn't know, and I can't share that with Niki.

"Maybe it's time you told her what happened the day she crashed."

Niki's calm makes me slam my fist on the desk. "I'm not getting into this with you." My shoulders tighten. "This better not be your way of making us friends again, because me and your sister will never be friends."

Niki grins, and I nearly yank the screen off the wall. "Connor, please listen. You needed signing because no one else would take you—"

"I walked out of Vessa before they could push me. And I could walk out of this team, too."

"Our contract is watertight. I ensured it."

"My lawyers will review it." My head hurts from furrowing my brow. "How could you do this to me? We're meant to be best friends."

He smiles back at me, his hands open. "Mate, we are. Nothing changes that."

"Apart from you double-crossing me."

Niki sighs. Fresh lines display his weariness. The crash did a number on him. I dial back my anger.

"This team is my family," he says gently. "And you must stay, because it needs you. My dad made some crap decisions before his heart attack, and the team might get bought out. It won't belong to my family anymore, not that Senna knows, and you can't tell her."

START YOUR ENGINES

"But—"

"And as much as she'll disagree, my sister needs you. And I need you to be there for her, as there will be knives in her back. She pretends she can cope, and I saw the way she was acting the big boss just now. But Dad told me she's scared. He's not sure she can do this."

"But she's always been a fighter. Do you remember when we used to have to drag her away from the bullies because they targeted her as the only elite female racing driver? She took it all. She's stronger than you think." I swallow repeatedly. She took it all until the day I took the sport away from her.

"She needs protecting, Connor. Do this for me. You need to stay close to her. Even though she was a fighter, we still had to guard her when she raced because those guys tried to hurt her."

"And look what happened when I shielded her. I can't go there again, and she won't let me anyway. She could've died that day." I pace the room, my head in my hands. "Besides, your sister is big and ugly enough to guard herself." There's nothing ugly about Senna Coulter. I remember those hips, big hazel eyes, and kissable lips. She's so damn beautiful I have to sink my nails into my palms to stop thinking about her like that. "So I can't leave? Fine. I'll get myself fired."

Niki sits back. His eyes pinch like his sister's when she reaches her limit. When she does it, I get a secret thrill. With her brother, guilt spikes my skin. "Don't you dare."

I pout. "I can't return to those days when protecting your sister was my calling in life. She doesn't need me. She's always thought she could do everything on her own."

"Which is why you need to help her, protect her, without her knowing."

"Even if I could, she doesn't want me around. I can't work under her when she blames me for ruining her life."

"Get over yourself, Dane. It's time you thought about someone other than yourself and what you want." My mouth drops. "Besides, it's not just the people out there wanting to hurt her. You need to keep men away from her as well." He folds his arms and eyeballs me through the screen.

I roll my eyes. "She works in Formula One, which is seventy per cent men. How the hell do you envisage me doing that?"

"I don't care. Just do it. Loads of them will try to get with her now that she runs the company. They're either going to try and destroy her or date her. You must protect her for me because I can't do that from here."

I catch the weary look in his eyes and how his fingers tremble as he readjusts his cap. I don't doubt for a second that he'd be here to help Senna if he could be. Niki was the only one there for me when my dad left my family, and he stuck by me even when his dad told him I was worthless after Senna's accident. I owe him and, to some extent, his sister, too.

I slump in a chair. "Fine, whatever."

"One more thing," Niki says, pointing at me through the screen. "Although I trust you to protect her without her knowing, I know your reputation with women, Dane the Dick. The pact we made as teenagers when we fought over Antoine's sister still stands. Even though I had a chance with her, I walked away because of you." That's not what happened. Antoine's sister never wanted Niki, and I was crushing on Senna but couldn't tell him, like I can't say anything now. "We don't go after the same women, and you don't get with my sister, ever."

START YOUR ENGINES

I laugh loudly until Niki's glares force me to stop.

"There's no danger of that. I can't stand her, but we're too old for teenage pacts," I explain.

"Not when it comes to Senna. This is the only way I can make you behave. Promise me on your life. I can't watch my sister get hurt like all your women have in the past. Your reputation is deserved."

I throw my hands in the air and rock back on my chair. "Niki, I've always been clear with women that I'm not the settling-down type."

"I don't care. Give me the promise we made as teenagers. Promise me you'll protect her and that you won't try anything with her."

The door opens, and Senna stares at me, her eyebrow cocked. "I heard Connor laughing. Are you two done? I've got balls to bust, and I'll be starting with yours, Connor fucking Dane."

Why does that sound so appealing?

"Promise me, Connor."

I look between the woman I have messy feelings for and her big brother. Senna hates me, and I can't let my thoughts about her own me again. This will be fine.

"Sure. Whatever," I say with a roll of my eyes. "But I'm not going to make this easy for anyone."

I glance at Senna, who says in a way that has me pressing those nails deeper into my hands as my belly coils, "You want trouble, Dane? Bring it on, because I'm all in."

21

CHAPTER THREE – SENNA

"Come in," I holler as the knock hits my door again.

"Please don't be Dane. Please don't be Dane," I hiss like a mantra.

Anxiety tightens in my chest.

I've avoided Connor for a week, although he's hung around my office, cracking his knuckles and huffing loudly. Ignoring his attempts to intimidate me or piss me off has become my Olympic sport, and the casualties have included my worn socks from my nervous tapping and the work trousers I've put a hole in from my relentless picking.

A grey-haired man with questionable dress sense pokes his head through the door.

"Uncle Ralf." My face breaks into a beaming smile, and I run to my mentor. He embraces me, and for a moment, I still as safety and comfort overwhelm me.

"Little Boss," he replies in his gentle German accent.

"You don't have to call me that," I say, gazing up at him.

"Senna, that's been your nickname since you were four years old and bossing your brother and me around like the independent little thing you were. I will keep calling you that even after you retire."

"Like you?"

"Like me," he says with a grin.

I pull away, and I point at the chair. "Take a seat."

22

START YOUR ENGINES

"Still bossy, then," he teases.

I offer a wry smile to the man my dad employed as a driver in the heyday of the Coulter Racing team. Once I have time to request them, photos of some of his many wins will adorn the walls of my office.

I settle in my seat. "Is this a flying visit, or are you back to advise the team like you used to?"

I lean towards him. Although Ralf has lost his love of racing and, some say, his edge, he is still the best man I know.

"I'm afraid I'll be on a plane to the Caribbean in about four hours with Myles, but I got a feeling you might need me." He relaxes in his chair. His belly, a sign of his happy retirement travelling the world with his husband Myles, tests the buttons of his neon pink and green Hawaiian shirt. While my dad calls daily to discuss progress, Ralf proves there's life after racing.

"Dad phoned you, didn't he?" My stomach drops.

Ralf shakes his head, which makes his bushy eyebrows resemble dancing feather boas. "Niki did."

I pick at the bottom of my team shirt. The top half strains against my chest almost as much as Uncle Ralf's strains against his belly. I wish I could blame happy living, but it's because there are so few females working at Coulters that they don't make a female-cut shirt. I need time to change that, too.

"But this is what I've always wanted," I stutter, readying myself for battle.

"Inheriting a failing team and a car not fit for purpose and doing it all alone?" I bloody love this straight-talking man, even as he confronts me with the truth.

"Dad cut corners and focused on the short-term." I cradle my head as I study my laptop, which shows an image

23

of the car we're unveiling to the press tomorrow at Shakedown—the day we'll run the car around a track for the first time to make sure it stays together. "You know how big a deal tomorrow is. And I'm petrified by how Dad has decimated this team with his management over the last few years."

Out of the corner of my eye, Ralf nods. "This team has been mistreated for years."

"He doesn't believe I can make this team a success."

Ralf nods.

Gloom grips me.

"Little Boss, look at me," he directs.

I lift my head slowly to study those big blue eyes and soft smile. He leans forward, his elbows on the desk. It's one of his signature moves, and as much as I'm struggling to deal with my dad's lack of belief in me, I still nod because Uncle Ralf is here, and he's never doubted me.

"Your dad is an arschgeige." I grin at the playful German term for dickhead. Ralf has said much worse to my dad during their arguments. "It was your dream to run this team. You've spent your life around this place, learning everything about how the cars work and how to get their greatest performance internally and on the track."

"I know, but it's not enough. I also know what it's like to fail."

He cocks an eyebrow and offers me a sour face. "And to come back fighting harder."

"I presumed I'd get advice and not a pep talk. But you're just like Jacs."

He waves my comment away with his hand. "You kick arse while respecting the opinion of others. You know what it is to be a champion. Niki has lost the wide-eyed excitement. That moment came for me when I realised

every drive could be my last. He's not in the right place to be around this team. But you came through that."

I hold my hand up to stop the ego-massaging chat.

"No, Little Boss, you need to hear this. I am here to remind you who and what you are."

"Dad taught me never to show vulnerability in racing. I've tried to be a bitch boss with the team, but it's not me," I reply flatly.

"Exactly!" His voice booms around the office. "You are not your dad, and you can't boss like him. You are a strategist, a car expert, a racing driver, and someone who makes things happen. You won awards for the team's social media and branding. You pulled this team into this century when everyone else decided it was an old boy's network and an extension of your dad's deteriorating strategy. The mechanics respect you. Everyone respects you. So it's time you respected yourself and ran the team like you know how because you are brilliant, and you will rule this team with an iron fist and a listening heart. And you will achieve it on your own because that is what you do."

He shouts the last part with conviction.

Connor passes my doorway.

"Someone doesn't respect me." I nod in the direction of my liability.

I bloody hate him and his heart-fluttering body. That man in my team's hoodie gives me a thrill that makes me clear my throat with all the anger I can muster.

Ralf turns his head. "Dane? He respects you, but he can't show it. In fact, he respects you too much."

I laugh off that suggestion.

"Trust me on that, Little Boss." I open my mouth, but he silences me with more wisdom. "It's your other driver you need to monitor."

"Antoine? He's harmless. He's a punk with an ego bigger than his d…" Ralf cocks his eyebrow. "Not that I've seen it."

"His ego?"

"No, his dick." My face flushes. I've never liked Antoine, even when we raced together as teenagers. He's a petulant child with an eye for danger and an attitude to match, but he's all I've got.

"You need a partner. It will calm you. You need someone to care for you."

I grind my teeth. "Would you say that to Niki if he was leading this team?"

Ralf rolls his eyes with a grin that reminds me of days karting with Niki and my parents. Ralf could outrace all of us, but instead, he'd coast behind Niki and me and note how we could improve to give us pointers later.

"Of course I would, and he'd probably listen. A boss doesn't *need* a partner, but it helps. Your dad had your mum to support him. You have Jacs, but she has her own team to manage. You don't even have Niki at the moment. Who else do you have to support you?"

"I don't have the support you're talking about, and I don't need it."

I'm not getting into this with my dad's best friend. I have a vet in Australia who I see when I'm in town and need a hookup. The last time I saw him was after an argument with my dad. I don't have relationships and never have.

I've only liked one guy enough to want a relationship, and that was a silly crush when I was seventeen.

There's a knock at the door, and Connor walks in without my permission. My blood boils at his audacity, but I can't help staring at his full lips and those damn grey joggers that hang off his hips. My gaze sticks.

No. I fix my jaw and glare.

My silly crush at seventeen ended the day I crashed because he didn't care who he hurt. He was willing to do anything to get signed by a team and move from Formula Three to Formula Two. That's what the other drivers told me when they visited me in the hospital, and he never explained otherwise, only blaming them and not apologising.

That's when Connor went from the object of my affection to the person I hated. He's why I'll never have a relationship and why I'm all in to win the championship single-handedly.

Don't show vulnerability. Don't trust men who can break your heart. And don't fall in love.

Connor Dane ruined my past, but I refuse to let him ruin my future.

CHAPTER FOUR – CONNOR

Senna's avoided me all week, but it's the Shakedown tomorrow, and I need to know if I'll be driving in the new car for its first time on a track. I always drove for that first session when I was with Vessa, but some teams don't let both drivers try the car. And if I'm driving, I must prepare.

I'm terrified of getting in a car with everyone watching and having flashbacks of Niki on that stretcher as I grip the wheel and take on corners—something no one gets to know.

I need to sit in the new car and know it's safe.

I clear my throat and take a breath as Senna stares at me, her eyebrows raised. Her blond hair shines under the lights of her new office. She's so damn beautiful.

That's when I remember my other task. As per Niki's instructions, I need to check if Senna is okay. I've hung outside her office as much as possible, checking who comes in and who leaves. All I've learned is she stays until midnight every night, doesn't eat dinner, and listens loudly to Harry Styles.

Niki owes me.

"What do you want, Dane?" Senna asks. She taps at her desk as if I've already pissed her off.

Before I respond with more than my pinching glare, Ralf jumps up and pats me on the back. He practically wallops

me to the floor. "Connor, how's it going? I hope you're ready to ditch your showboating and risky driving now you're finally with Coulter."

"I can't promise anything." I chuckle as I hug the big man.

"And we wouldn't have you any other way." He laughs. "You'll do great things with the team."

Senna makes a noise that's a cross between a guffaw and choking. I raise my eyebrow at her over Ralf's shoulder, and her face flushes in a way that reminds me of when she was a teenager and Niki and I caught her spray painting "Boys suck" on Niki's go-kart.

"I haven't seen you in ages, including at my wedding last year."

I do everything I can to avoid Senna's stare. I was there but hid in the back. I ran out straight after the ceremony because of a certain blond-haired beauty. I can't think about that now.

"He wasn't there probably because he was too busy seducing his former trainer," she grumbles.

"You heard that rumour, too? I thought you'd be too wise for idle gossip." If only she knew what problems seeing her at that wedding has caused for me.

She flushes again, and I give myself a silent cheer. Score one for me.

She clenches her jaw. "So why are you here?"

"I need to talk, Coulter."

She glowers at me. I can't bring myself to call her boss. She'll love it too much, and I can't have that. It will make the amber in her eyes sparkle and her lips quirk in a way that used to make my heart beat faster. I shake my head and grit my teeth.

A waft of sandalwood chokes me as Antoine strides into

the office. "I must be in the car tomorrow. I'm your shining star and leading driver, and the press want me."

"Hold up, buddy," I reply, squaring up to Antoine.

Ralf returns to his seat by the desk.

"You got this, Little Boss. Do it your way," he whispers to Senna.

Antoine gets in my face. "Hey, pretty boy."

"There's nothing pretty about me, dipshit, and there won't be anything pretty about you once I've finished." Antoine's clipped me several times "accidentally" over the years. I don't know if it's payback because his sister wanted to date me or because I didn't grow up in a rich family like him. "I don't trust you, and I don't like you."

"Number two has a big mouth for someone who'll fail this year. What you going to do, pretty boy?"

I tip my head and raise my eyebrows in a challenge. "That depends. Can you fight like a man when you're not hiding inside a car?"

He pulls back his shoulders and squeezes his hands. I can take this punk, and the desire to grips me when I think about how he's been hanging around Senna and making digs about her to some of the mechanics.

"Oi!" Senna shouts, jumping up and wedging herself between us.

Fuck. Her body is against mine. It's soft in ways it wasn't years ago. Her breasts press into my chest, and my stomach bottoms out. She smells of the fantasies that have continued to plague me for ten years. I jump back like she's made of blistering fire rather than beauty and strength.

"Both of you, sit down while I tell you the ground rules."

My body twitches, and blood rushes down. I grind my teeth. Angry Senna shouldn't pull a reaction from my body. I'm so fucked up. I'm here to protect her, not to enjoy her

30

authority.

"Bonjour, Senna," Antoine starts as I sit.

"Don't 'bonjour, Senna' me, Antoine, and don't walk into my office without waiting to be allowed in. That's for both of you." She scowls at me, and goosebumps rise on my naked arms. I push the sleeves of my hoodie down. She sees the action, and something clouds her face briefly. "You don't fight in my office like a pathetic pair of schoolboys. You don't fight anywhere. You are teammates, and you will behave as such. You support each other off and on the track. And if you can't do that, you avoid each other. Am I clear?"

Her voice reverberates off the walls. I hold back my smile and shift against my grey joggers. She's breathtaking, like the ultimate fighter, but with the beauty of a goddess.

I shake my head. I can't have these thoughts.

"Did you shake your head at me, Dane?" she shouts.

I go to shake my head again but think better of it in case she accuses me of taunting her. "No."

"No what?"

She stands so close that one more step would put her between my legs. I fist my hands and will my body to behave.

"No, boss," I reply between gritted teeth. It sounds so good coming from my mouth. She's hot as the boss, even more than when she told me what to do as a teenager. I'm nearly breathless.

"That's right. I'm your boss, and I decide, Antoine, who does what tomorrow." She's staring at him, and I miss having those eyes on me. "Understood?"

He tips his head and gives a smile that a particular faction on social media calls his "panty-wetting smile." I check Senna, relieved she's glaring rather than fanning herself.

31

"Yes, boss," Antoine says, and it's all I can do not to smack that smirk off his face.

"Good." Her fingers swipe her scar, revealing that, as much as she's trying to be the big boss, she's struggling. I don't move, instead putting all my energy into scowling at Antoine, who licks his lips seductively as he stares at Senna. "Tomorrow, you will both get to drive. We don't know if the car will work; that is the point of Shakedown, after all. Now, get out and wait for my call about who is starting tomorrow and what to say to the press."

I leave with Antoine behind me. He calls over his shoulder, "I look forward to your call," in a voice too gravelly for my liking.

As we leave the office, Ralf says to Senna, "Well done, Little Boss."

In the reflection of her door, I see her wince and drop her head. It reminds me of my mission, and I practically drag Antoine by his designer shirt collar into the empty men's bathroom.

"Hey!" He pushes me away and straightens his clothes. "Dilfano gave this to me personally."

"I presume that's a designer I don't give a shit about," I retort.

"Obviously. You dress like a university student, which is ironic for someone too stupid for—"

"Just stay away from Senna." I stand close enough to flick my fingers against his forehead, although I resist the action.

His smirk makes my stomach roll. "How do you expect me to do that, mon cheri? She's our boss."

I grit my teeth. "You do what you have to workwise, but don't flirt with her or do anything that will make me slam my fists in your face. Okay?"

START YOUR ENGINES

"She wants me, Dane. Trust me on that."

Someone crashes through the bathroom door, which is lucky for Antoine because every neuron in my head demands I sucker-punch the bastard.

"Stay away. Or I'll make sure you won't drive on this or any team again."

He shrugs as I walk out of the bathroom. I want him away from Senna because I'm protecting her. There's no other reason.

CHAPTER FIVE – SENNA

Jacs sidles up to me and whispers, "Take a breath before you hyperventilate."

I glare at her as the press meanders about the garage. Cameras flash as Antoine drives around the track. We're in the last thirty minutes of Shakedown.

"Not wanting to jinx anything, but we might have a chance this season," Jacs says. "The water leak fix is holding."

"The day isn't over yet, and Dane still needs to drive a full lap. That water leak happened when he was halfway through his first lap," I reply as Connor paces the garage. As much as I can't stand him, he needs this opportunity so we can give the team a chance at success. My phone buzzes with a call.

Jacs raises her eyebrows. "Your dad again?"

I nod and pull a hand down my face.

"He isn't going to be a silent owner, then."

Dad's lecture about Shakedown and that I need to rule the team more forcibly when I was trying to sleep last night has left me on edge. My mum banned him from coming today, but that hasn't stopped him from calling every hour for a progress report.

34

"Could you stop pacing, Dane? You're making me nervous," I hiss so the press, who have been watching me for hours, don't hear. I shove my hair into a messy bun and glance at him out of the corner of my eye. "We'll get you back out there in a moment."

He freezes in the middle of the room. His eyes are wild, and he cracks his knuckles. A question about his anxiety teeters on my tongue. I shake my head. He wouldn't tell me the truth anyway.

"Can you come in, Antoine?" I grunt into the radio the track staff and my French driver can hear.

"Ma belle, I'm showing the press what the car can do. All is well."

The people who can hear him chuckle, and I stare each one of them down.

The chuckles transform into coughs and sulking faces. If I need my competitors to see me as a contender, then I need my team to recognise that I'm the boss and can kick their arses. That's what Dad said. "Antoine, Dane needs a couple of laps in the car. It's only a fortnight before testing in Bahrain and then a week until the season starts. He needs this opportunity."

"He'll have that opportunity in Bahrain. I'm doing this for the press, and he can't showcase a car like I can." Antoine's French accent drips through my headphones. I expect most people melt under his charm, but instead, my back freezes under tension. I pull my bottom teeth over my lip, scratching flesh.

"I need to get out there, Senna." Dane's gravelly voice behind me makes me jump. His breath caresses my neck, giving me a pleasant shiver, and I shake my head at my body's betrayal. It's muscle memory from when I crushed on him at seventeen. "I should drive the car."

"I know," I reply without turning. "I'll get you in the car before the end of the session."

"You've let me stand here since the leak, getting more and more anx—annoyed."

I turn and catch him pursing his lips and shaking his head.

"You're anxious?"

He glares at me and steps closer. "Of course not. I'm annoyed because you're wasting my time."

I tilt my head as I take in the sweat beading his brow and how he wrings his hands. I soften my voice. "What is wrong, Dane?"

"I'm standing here while you chat up Antoine and leave me to wait like a fucking idiot." He fixes me with his stare. "What is your problem with me, Senna?"

"Aw, is pretty boy jealous of me driving the car?" Antoine says from the radio. He can hear what's happening from my mouthpiece. The last thing I need is for Antoine picking up on whatever is going on with Connor before I can work it out for myself.

I step away from Dane, but he steps closer. The heat from his body infiltrates my bubble, and I remind myself I can't back down from these moments. I round on him so he has to deal with me getting in his space. But the proximity doesn't deter him. His mouth curls up, although the action is so brief that it's gone before I can comment.

He leans down, and for one ridiculous moment, I imagine his lips brushing mine. *My fucking head.* It must be stress. The last thing I want is a kiss from him, yet I imagine it, licking my lips in expectation.

Dane grabs the mouthpiece of the radio and holds it still. His skin touches my cheek, and I barely hold onto a gasp. "Antoine, I will fuck you up before the start of the

season if you keep pissing me off. I'm a better driver, teammate, and person than you'll ever be. You're the real liability and a selfish bastard, too." His words are aggressive, yet his eyes are gentle as he stares at me.

His eyelashes brush my face, and I hold my breath.

"But are you a better lover? I can handle a woman's curves as well as I can drive. Do one of the many women you seduce sleep with you twice? No. You're a playboy without skills."

Dane's eyes blaze, anger coming off him in waves.

"When you get back here, I'm going to rearrange your face," Dane shouts down the microphone.

I step back at the volume, but his hand sinks into my hip to keep me close. I flinch at his heat. It gives me an unexpected snap in my belly, and he recoils.

"I didn't mean—" he says, his emotions jumping from rage to panic.

"Press," Jacs says as she fakes a cough behind me.

A photographer lifts his camera to get an incriminating shot of Dane and me to accompany whatever they intend to write about the team's mess. If the investors catch me at war with my drivers, it won't matter that the car is doing well after the initial water issue.

"Antoine, we're done. Come back in," I say with faux calm. I nod at our chief race engineer, Macca, who talks Antoine back to the garage.

"After that debacle, you owe me, Dane. You're giving the press five minutes to ask whatever questions they want, or they'll run a story about the team that will ruin us before we start."

"Not before I get in the car."

Connor pierces me with his glare. His lips are too plump for my liking, and just like that, I'm back to imagining us kissing again. I slam my hand down on the nearest desk.

Antoine parks outside the garage. Dane makes a beeline for him, his shoulders tight and hands curled into fists.

I stare at the new comms manager, imploring him for support. The press can't watch these two fight.

"Ladies and gentlemen," my press guy calls, "please follow me. We've laid out a spread of champagne and canapes. We wanted to give you a taste of what will be a winning season for the Coulter Racing team. This won't be the only champagne flowing this year. We've got goodie bags, too."

I let out a puff of air as he leads them from the garage. Dane rounds on a smirking Antoine, who's removing his helmet. Dane's pointy finger presses into Antoine's shoulder.

"Hey!" I holler. Silence descends inside the garage, and every engineer and mechanic stops as I storm over to the men. The only movement is Antoine pushing Dane's finger away with a hand flip.

"Ma bell—" Antoine says with open hands and a lazy smile.

"No 'belle.' No terms of endearment at all. All I want from either of you is 'yes, boss.' If you two carry on like this, I will terminate both of you. I'm not with this team for a season; I'm here for life, so if we have one crap season just so we can ditch two of the most petulant, childish, and arrogant drivers I've ever met, then so be it. There's drivers who'd jump into your suits before you'd finished removing them. Neither of you are irreplaceable."

START YOUR ENGINES

"You wouldn't." It's the first time Antoine hasn't been smug.

Dane's reaction is something else. His lip cocks to the side again, and he gazes at me with a look that, on anyone else, I'd call admiration.

My dad's words about how I should rule the team bite at me. These two wouldn't treat him like this.

"I would terminate both of you, Antoine. Ask any of my former comms team what I'm capable of. You're not special or important. I'm your boss and your god. Do you understand?" It's like my dad is speaking. My words are full of confidence, yet inside, I'm cringing. My comms team would tell him we were a family and that I was a boss who was supportive, not cutthroat. This isn't me. This isn't who Ralf told me to be.

Antoine's eyes tighten, and I briefly witness the sly, authentic version of him I've waited for. He returns to relaxed charm. "Yes, boss. The car is a dream. I shall enjoy driving it in a race."

I nod, dismissing him. Dane's cocked head and furrowed brow fascinate me.

Once Antoine leaves, I clear out the rest of the garage. Shakedown is officially over, and we've run out of time for Connor to drive because of the men's fighting.

I busy myself, stifling a yawn.

"And, Dane," I say, keeping my distance from Connor for fear of how my body will react. "Next time I tell you to speak to the press, please don't question me or argue. Just do it. You need to get used to the fact that I am your boss. Not my brother. Not my dad. Me. Just show me some respect. I will tell you when you drive. I will tell you when you speak to the press. Fuck, if I tell you to wear a chicken costume and dance like a cat on speed, then—"

39

"Then I do it. Although I'd be wondering why I'm dressed like a chicken if I'm dancing like a cat," he says in a gravelly drawl that has me tapping my heel against the concrete. "But I'll do it because you're my god, boss."

"Just go, Dane." I point to the exit. "I don't want to see you until Bahrain for pre-season practice."

I turn and busy myself tidying my headphones at the desk.

"I hope I get to drive the car then," he says.

I close my eyes and wait a minute.

"Has he gone, Jacs?"

"Yes, Sen."

I slump to the floor, leaning against my chair.

"Connor Dane is why I gave up my childhood dream of being a driver. If the last week is anything to go by, he'll be why I give up my dream of being a racing team boss, too. I'm not sure how long I can keep fighting with him." I pull my knees against my chest.

I don't voice my thoughts about his anxiety or how edgy he seemed about driving.

"It will get better. It has to," she says. "I've got to go and deal with the car. But are you okay?"

I nod as my phone buzzes with a call. I don't need to check it to know it's my dad. After today, it's probably just a matter of time before he finds a way to get rid of me.

Maybe I won't even make it to the start of the season.

Chapter Six – Connor

I stretch out on my hotel bed in another nondescript hotel room in another city before climbing out.

The sheets may be luxurious and the hotel beautiful, but I've tossed and turned for hours. Pink flowers bloom from the vase in the corner. My lack of sleep and inability to control my thoughts, especially when combined with those flowers, trigger a flashback: watching Ralf marry Myles in Bali last summer. They stared at each other, tears rolling down their smiling cheeks as they declared their eternal adoration to one another. Everything in my body screamed that I wanted that—a love that changes everything.

Senna stood in the front row, hiccupping with sobs. All the love I'd once had, albeit the love of an eighteen-year-old lad with no understanding of the world, crashed over me.

Sitting in the back row at the small ceremony, I was enraptured by the woman I would never have. And I couldn't speak to anyone about it, especially not to my best friend. A pink flower was tucked behind her ear. It matched her dress, which skimmed the floor, revealing she was barefoot when she moved. It framed her curves and reminded me how much had changed since we were close. I wanted to dab her tears. Unbeknownst to Senna, her presence chased me away that day when I only wanted to ask her to dance and

find out how she was.

Even though Niki's crash solidified my realisation that my feelings for Senna weren't going away, I could push them far down—at least until the last fortnight.

I remember Niki's shaved head. My head drops, and anxiety itches my throat. Niki's crash also made me fear driving.

My phone tells me it's three a.m. The morning of qualifying. The glamour in my life pales when loneliness sits so heavily on my chest. I used to have Niki when I needed company. My mum will be working at the hospital, but one other person will take my call back home at eleven on a Friday night.

"Hey, Layla," I say to the yawn on the other end of my phone. "What you doing?"

"Studying," my baby sister replies, with a grogginess that was cute fifteen years ago when she slept in my arms as an angelic-faced five-year-old. "I've reached the top five per cent in my year."

"You're amazing. I knew you were smashing it, but that's incredible." She's messaged me photos of her grades every week. I throw on my gym clothes. There's no way I'm sleeping tonight. Insomnia wins again. "But are you having fun? It doesn't always have to be about studying. I could set you up on a date, although no one is good enough for you."

Her chuckle warms me.

"Con, don't be trying to set me up because you can't date the woman you want. How is your boss, the beautiful and too good for you Senna Coulter?"

"If I hadn't seen you after Ralf's wedding, you wouldn't suspect anything." That day, I realised all my years of trying to hate Senna were pointless. My heart had kept a secret place for her during the years we weren't speaking.

START YOUR ENGINES

"I'd have worked it out eventually."

I grunt my response.

"Please tell me you're not just grunting at *her*?"

"You know I could stop paying your tuition at any point, right?"

"What did you tell Dad that time?"

I remain silent, hoping she won't repeat my conversation with Dad when I was signed to the Lapoire Team at eighteen.

"You know, when you told him he could spend more time with the family because you didn't need him to be your coach anymore?"

"We don't need to go over that again." I thought joining Formula Two and giving my dad the freedom to be with the family would be perfect—until he left us for the mother of another driver.

Layla performs an impression of me but adds an extra huff because she loves making me out as the grumpy one. ""Fine, Dad, we don't need you. Even if I had pittance, I'd do everything I could to help my family, including paying for Layla to train in whatever career she wants." I was only ten years old!"

"Whatever." I roll my eyes. My mum can't afford the exorbitant costs of her study. She's the best cheerleader from a distance, but Layla's media degree and my racing career are far removed from Mum's happy life working in a remote Scottish hospital, where she disappeared with Layla after my dad left. "Fine. I'm honoured I'm part of your life and enjoy helping you reach your dreams. Now get lost."

Her laughter makes me grumble louder, especially when she adds, "Back to Senna."

"I'm avoiding her. Technically, I've dodged or been pleasant to her before extracting myself from every Senna-

43

related situation as quickly as possible." I don't add that it's because when I'm with her, I want to press all her buttons, and when I'm not, I feel guilty for not protecting her. "I'm pretty sure, based on Shakedown a couple of weeks ago, that she's on Antoine's side. So, whatever, I don't care."

I fold my arms and glare at my lying face in the gilt-edged hotel mirror.

"Are you going to leave like you said you wanted to do at the start of the season? Because I need you to keep her sweet."

"I can't leave. I promised Niki I'd stay and protect her. I just wish I could get more sleep."

I shield my sister from the worst of it. She's been through enough with our dad and should be enjoying university life. I can't tell her that I'm getting three hours of sleep a night and struggling to eat. Last night, I walked the streets, just like the night before Shakedown. I've sent countless unanswered messages to Niki.

"Con, you need to tell Senna what driving does to you and how you've barely driven since Niki's accident. She'll understand more than most bosses."

"Because she was in a crash that I caused?" I shiver against a cold sweat.

"Yeah, and because it was her brother who was seconds away from…you know."

Images of Niki's car, flames rising from the engine, sucker-punch me. I clear my throat, but no amount of swallowing clears the dryness.

"Connor, I love you, but you're torturing yourself. You promised Niki you'd protect her, but your mind is a mess. You can't keep hiding your feelings about driving or your guilt from what happened when you were teenagers. Sooner or later, she'll find out that you still want—"

START YOUR ENGINES

"Don't say it," I cut in. "If no one says it, then we can pretend it's untrue. And if it's not true, I can protect her like I promised." I squeeze my eyes closed. "I owe Niki. But I owe Senna more, because our crash ended her career. And her dad is thinking of selling the team, so the best way I can help her is by staying out of her way and succeeding. Qualifying is later today. I need to drive my best and get high on the grid to stand a chance of doing well in the race on Sunday."

Layla's voice softens. "I understand that you care about her, but you need to see a professional and deal with this. You've got too much in your head. It's no wonder you're not sleeping."

"Or I could keep going and hope everything will be okay. I managed to get through practice in the car." I know my decision-making is irrational, but that's all I've got.

It's her turn to grumble.

"Anyway, you said I needed to keep Senna sweet. What are you planning?" I ask as I walk to the hotel gym to lift weights and ease my panicky energy.

"I'd benefit from a chat about my future. Senna was the director of marketing, and she won awards. I'd love to speak to her about my next steps."

"Maybe she could get you an internship or even a job."

"I'm no nepo baby."

I chuckle. My sister listened to me moan about the sons of drivers who got everything, whereas I had to struggle for sponsorship and funding. If not for Niki and Senna imploring their dad to finance me, I wouldn't have raced at all—another reason why I owe the Coulter family.

"Okay, I'll speak to her. I'll be in touch, Layla. Thank you for the chat."

"And remember what I said. Get help. Love you."

"Love you too. Try to have some fun at university."

45

I need to smack a punching bag until sleep comes. As I weave through the basement corridors of the hotel, I consider finding Antoine and hitting him instead.

Pressure rushes my ears. If only Niki knew why I am the worst person to defend his sister. I miss my best friend so much. This time last year, my only worries were deciding which woman to bed and how Niki and I could avoid the paparazzi while tearing up a new city. My rep was well deserved, and I revelled in it. I saw Senna at races, but she was always at such a distance that I didn't have to deal with my buried feelings for her.

Maybe I should see a specialist, but Senna might find out and stop me from driving. I need to keep her safe while not letting myself care too much about her.

But I remember how she licked her lips when I spoke on her radio last week. I made her livid, and yet I swear, in that moment, she wanted me. I've replayed that moment all week, except instead of speaking on her radio, I pin her to the wall and kiss her like I always wanted to.

"Hey, bro." Senna's voice carries down the corridor from the gym. Why is Niki answering her calls but avoiding me?

Her soft sobs catch my attention. I peek through the gap in the door. Tears slide down her cheeks. She pushes them out of the way with the sleeves of her Coulter team hoodie. I need to protect her and take all her tears away, but I'm frozen in my spot.

"I don't know what to do. I can get Antoine to toe the line, but what about Connor?" She hasn't said my first name without an expletive in years. It grips my heart like it did the night before she crashed and I watched her sleep. "He acts like I'm nothing. He won't let me tell him what to do, so I lose it with him and try to be aggressive, but he smirks in my

face. It's humiliating and gives the people in the garage another reason to laugh behind my back and disrespect me. I know what they're saying."

She's crying because of me?

My head drops as shame prickles my skin. The fear of racing has got to me, but it's also my reaction to her that I've been countering with my dickhead behaviour. I vowed once to protect her at all costs, and although it ruined everything and hurt her beyond reason, there's still a part of that Senna who needs people on her side.

Hatred fills me as her sobs continue and she tells Niki more of my behaviour. From her perspective, I sound even worse. If I were him, I'd want to protect her against this prick.

But I'm the prick.

My vow didn't work when I was younger, and I was more stupid than I am now. But as I return to my room, I make a new vow. I'll do everything possible to make this a successful year for Senna. I never want her to cry again, especially not because of me. This will be Senna and Team Coulter's best year, and then I will move on because driving isn't for me anymore.

This isn't my future, but it can be hers.

But how do I deal with my fear of driving?

CHAPTER SEVEN – SENNA

A sound in the corridor brings my tears to an end. Fuck. It's bad enough no one respects me, but if they find me crying to my big brother because I can't manage my team, I'm screwed.

"I'll talk to him, sis. He'll behave better once we chat. I will make him listen," Niki says.

"No, I need to fight my own battles. I'll sort it. Don't worry about me. I needed to get everything out." And I had no one else to talk to.

I walk to the door of the gym and peek through the opening. No one is there, although there's a faint smell of wood and lavender. I know who smells of that, but if Connor had heard me cry, he'd have made a point of showing me he'd heard.

I rub my thumb over my scar as anxiety grips my throat. Not that anxiety is ever far from me these days, but this is another wave for me to drown under.

"Senna—"

"No, Niki. I don't need you to protect me or do the big brother thing. I need you to listen."

He grumbles down the receiver. I shouldn't have spoken to him, but he'd called me amidst a bout of insomnia, and I let everything out.

"Anyway, I wanted to tell you about the car," I say. "Dad

cut costs. We got through pre-season and practice okay, but qualifying is today, and we won't have enough spare parts if something happens. We need investors."

"You need to talk to Dad."

"And let him see he was right and that I'm not good enough to run this team?" I flip my trainers off and start pacing the gym. "He wanted you to lead Coulter Racing."

I should ask him how he's doing, but Niki's avoided that question since he walked away from everything he'd worked for and disappeared after signing Connor. I study my scar. After my accident, I walked away, too. Although at first I was devastated, over time I realised that my accident allowed me to consider other options for my future. I miss racing, but I'm lucky that I had other skills. I thought I'd find other ways to make my dad proud.

"Dad picked me because sometimes he's a misogynistic arse," Niki adds, dragging me back to the conversation. "You're good enough, and most people at Coulter know it. And eventually, Dad will, too. But for now, you continue with the team. Once we win races, investors will flood in."

"That's easy then." My chuckle is hollow.

"You got it in the bag."

This time, I do laugh genuinely, although my heart aches. I miss my brother so much.

"So how are you? How are your scars?" I mean the emotional one as much as the physical ones.

There's a noise in the background of the call, and I tip my head. "That's the door. I'd best go," he replies.

He'll tell me when he wants me to know. As much as he's the best older brother, he's also independent and obstinate, like me.

"Please stay safe, okay?"

"Yes, sis. You too. Good luck with qualifying later and

the race tomorrow. And try to get some sleep, even a couple of hours."

We say goodbye as I hang up.

I need to get to the track and check everything for qualifying. This means putting my power suit on and listening to the songs that get me ready to face the shit that's going to be flung my way, including whatever Connor has prepared for me today.

I slip my earbuds in, pop "The Man" by Taylor Swift on, and head back to the room. My gaze swings left and right as I hunt for my earlier eavesdropper, but there's no sign of them. As I step into the lift, I catch the reflection of my red-rimmed eyes and pinched features. I flip the volume and let Taylor obliterate the exhaustion of the last week.

I rub my scar, remembering what my dad said after Connor had made me crash at seventeen. *You were never going to be in Formula One, sweetheart. Everyone knows girls don't do that. Maybe it's time to find out what you're good at.*

Those words have acted as my personal motivation and boss origin story for the last ten years.

It's time to kick ass and show the fans, my dad, and all the teenage drivers who used to bully me precisely what I'm capable of.

CHAPTER EIGHT – SENNA

He's doing it. He's actually doing it.

I swallow the lump in my throat.

Connor is speeding around the track.

My first race as team boss and the first race since Niki crashed.

Memories of the flames burning my brother's car as he was dragged to safety replay in my head. I thumb my scar and count to ten slowly.

Connor's car wobbles on the corner, and he moves close to the barrier at high speed before wrestling the car back.

"Fucking oversteered. He needs to get the car under his control," I mumble as I get a flashback of the moment Niki oversteered and ended up flying towards the barrier. I don't know if I can do this.

Jacs watches the screen with me. "It's going well. He's doing fine. It's just first-race nerves."

I nod but don't look away from the images of cars zooming around the track. Connor seems to slow and back away from other cars. He's not fighting, and he's still making mistakes.

I drag water from my bottle.

"Would it help if I distracted you?"

I side-eye Jacs. "And how are you going to do that?"

51

"That mechanic that used to work at Vessa, the one that brought us together, asked me for a job."

I choke on my water, and Jacs taps me on the back.

"I know, right?"

"Maybe we should offer him one. If not for him, then we wouldn't be best friends," I say as I recall the night I met Jacs at an end-of-season dinner. A jumped-up engineer from Vessa explained how she'd never amount to anything because there wasn't space for women like her in Formula One.

She tips her head and glares at me. "Don't even think about it."

"You need to get control of the car. Watch the track limits," Macca, Connor's race engineer, says over the radio, referring to Connor driving slightly over the edges of the track, which will incur penalties.

Cars bunch around the track in different spots, but Connor has a straight track without many cars around him. His driving should be as smooth as Antoine's.

"I'm trying, Macca," Connor replies, his voice wavering. "Some of these corners are really testing the car. That's why I oversteered."

He's not the driver he was.

"You're doing really well," I say into my microphone.

Jacs waves at me and heads back to her team.

"Hey, boss." Connor's shaky voice is lighter.

"Hey, Dane," I reply. "You're doing well on the tyres. Are you happy with the strategy?"

It isn't my place to talk on the radio. It should be between Connor and Macca, and I wouldn't do the same with Antoine. But this helped Connor when he was younger. Although I've tried to distance myself from him, I've listened to his after-race interviews, and he's commented that

START YOUR ENGINES

chatter can help.

"Yes, Coults." He drops in my nickname and introduces a familiarity that I've tried to avoid. "Is there anything I can do to improve?"

"Let's not share too much with everyone," Macca says, reminding us the radio is open and anyone can listen.

"Dane, do you remember the race where you were first called Dane the Pain and why?"

"Yeah." He chuckles, and I hide my mouth with my hand so no one sees my smile.

I watch the screen as his car speeds up, as if he's chasing another driver.

"You and Niki teased me mercilessly before that race. You showed me a photo of Layla wearing a T-shirt you'd designed and sent her," he says.

My giggle slips out at the way he grumbles. It said on the front, *Senna is the best driver ever*, and on the back, *Connor Dane sucks.*

"Well, if you don't bring Dane the Pain to this race, I'm getting T-shirts made for the whole team and insisting they wear them around head office and the factory for the next week. The back will say, 'Connor Dane sucks.' I won't tell you what the front will say. I need to work out how many N's are in Antoine, though."

His growl fills my ears, and my belly flutters.

"You're not ready for the adrenaline I'll be bringing back into the garage with me."

"I look forward to it," I reply. "Macca, he's all yours."

Jacs stares at me from across the garage with an eyebrow raised. Shit, I'm smirking. I force my face into a blank look as Connor overtakes a driver from Force Brazil. He doesn't do it as smoothly as he would have in the past, but there's hints of Dane the Pain.

53

I lean back in my chair. I want to support and celebrate him, but the knowledge that he made me crash still sits deep in my stomach. My head and heart battle. When I avoided him, I could pretend he risked everything to be the best, including forcing me off the track so I never raced again. But I haven't thought about the race a year earlier, when he got the nickname Dane the Pain, for years.

After that race, he checked in with me to ensure I was okay. Although he drove like a demon, he wanted to be certain that our friendship was safe and explain I wasn't in danger at any point.

I sink my teeth into my lower lip as Connor nears another driver at a corner. My emotions spiral as I remember the moment he hit me, and I have to look away.

I pull my headphones off and toss them onto the desk beside the screen, sighing with relief. A couple of race engineers pat me on the back, and Jacs pumps her fist in my eyeline.

We did it.

The first race under my charge is over. We weren't podium-worthy but came in eighth and tenth, which is impressive for our first race. I'm proud of my team.

My cuticles bleed from me gnawing on them. My hair hangs limply around my face, and my poor-fitting polyester trousers have probably left red marks all over my legs from where they scratched me up.

One of the models—I expect a guest of one of my drivers—sashays past, drawing stares from some of my garage team.

I blanch. I should be celebrating. I need to up my outfit game, not to get that reaction from the drivers, but so I don't focus on my lacklustre appearance. I consider the other team bosses, all men. Some of them are dishevelled messes. Some insist on wearing racing suits, though they spend the whole race staring at screens, but others dress impeccably. The boss of Vessa is the pinnacle of style. He never sweats, and in recent years, as team boss, he's never had a hair out of place. His clothes don't crease because he doesn't allow it. I need to be taken more seriously, which means dressing like a winner and not a teenage intern.

The model walks to the cars. *Please don't be here for Connor. Please be here for Antoine.* I cross my arms and purse my lips as I track her. She steps between the cars. Connor gets out first, high-fiving his trainer, Silas.

I hold my breath.

But Connor barely notices the beauty with full lips, legs that go on for miles, perfect features, and wavy blond hair spun from gold. Instead, he catches my eye. His brow furrows as he sees my eyes flicker in her direction.

My jealousy must be like a banner across my face. Antoine gets out of his car, pulls off his helmet, and swaggers to the model, who jumps and squeals. He tips his head, and she wraps her arms around his neck. Antoine winks at me over her shoulder.

Connor sees that wink and me blinking before looking away as if caught out.

Shit. I'm not staring or even happy because Antoine winks at me. I'm dealing with my secret, shameful relief that she wasn't here for Connor.

"Leave her the fuck alone," Connor grunts. "She's too good for you. Stop playing games with her."

Antoine laughs. So Connor *does* want the model. My

emotions somersault so fast I don't understand how everything goes from celebration to chaos in seconds. I shouldn't care if Connor desires the model.

"If you want Claudia here, you can have her. She likes drivers, don't you, baby?" Antoine teases. The blond buries her face in his shoulder before whispering something in his ear and walking to where her designer handbag sits.

"I don't mean her," Connor snaps as he rounds on Antoine. "You know who I mean."

Antoine winks at me again.

My mouth dries up, and my palms sweat. A crumb of hope stabs my heart, but I dismiss it quickly. Connor can't be jealous because of me.

I hold my breath. I wouldn't want that anyway.

I see the flush of adrenaline on Connor's cheeks. He's amped up because of the race. He steps closer to Antoine, and I hold my breath. He always looked sexy when he came off the track, but now he's a man. My gaze slides down at how his racing suit grips him. His biceps flex as he stands toe-to-toe with Antoine.

I shake my head, but my attraction lingers even as the men eyeball each other.

Antoine whispers something that only Connor hears. With wide eyes, Connor grabs the collar of Antoine's driving suit, but Antoine tips his head and smiles.

My dad's voice tells me that having them fight might make them better drivers. But this isn't the kind of team I want. I rub my scar as I debate between my management style and my dad's.

"Come on, pretty boy. You know how she feels, how she's always felt. She loved racing against me."

"That's enough," I bellow before clearing the garage of everyone but Connor and Antoine.

START YOUR ENGINES

The last days have shown they can behave and stay out of each other's way, but as soon as they're together, they are a pa r of fireworks I have to throw water on.

"Dane, just fucking stop," I shout.

Connor's head whips around, and he stares at me. "Did you hear him? I didn't—"

I hold my hand up, and his eyes widen. My lips quirk briefly. I shouldn't enjoy getting a reaction out of him this much. I should be calming him down.

"Antoine, I don't want you winking at me, attempting your charm on me, rewriting history, or generally willy wanging around this place. You don't own this team. I own you. Get that?"

He cocks his head, and his eyebrows furrow. "What is this willy wanging?"

It's typical that all he hears is the phrase involving a man's appendage. "It's…" I throw my hands in the air. "It means walking around this place like you have an eight-inch dick."

"But I do have an eight-inch dick, ma belle." He winks at me. " can prove—"

Connor grabs him by the collar of his racing suit and picks him off the floor.

"Dane, stop!" I shout. "Antoine, get out and go to press."

Connor drops Antoine, and Antoine walks out. I stare at the biceps rippling beneath Connor's driving suit rather than the alleged big dick in the Frenchman's pants.

"You need to stop fighting, Dane. I can't have this garage erupting because you two have too much testosterone, or you're fighting over some model, or because you're in some competition on who has got the biggest dick."

He raises his eyebrow at me. His lips are tight.

I need to calm his after-race adrenaline because it's doing neither of us a favour. In every interaction between us since he returned into my life, my anger has slid right off him. Maybe I can make him laugh like I did in the race.

"We can establish Antoine has a huge dick," I say.

"Hold off on that opinion until you see mine," he snaps. Okay, I guess it's not the time for jokes. His eyes narrow. "And stop having a go at me when it's his behaviour that's out of line. The guy is a problem, and he treats you like you're here to service him. You're his boss."

My skin flushes with anger. "I'm well aware of what he's like, but I'm handling it."

Dane walks closer to me, and I swallow. He pushes a hand through his soft black hair. My hands tremble, and I sweep my tongue over my lower lip. My stomach flutters, and a silent thrill crackles around my body. I can't work out what's a remnant of my past crush and what's my current anger.

"I'm protecting you, Senna," he says between gritted teeth.

I step back, and my voice pitches. "Protecting me? Are you for real?"

"Stop rubbing your scar," he growls, his stare on my thumb rubbing the line from the operation on my hand.

His words slap me like the wind when I'm racing down the motorway with my windows open. I didn't know I was doing it.

"You can't pretend you're my knight in shining armour now when you're the one who did this just so you could win."

He closes on me. "You don't know the truth," he snarls. "Others are to blame. I tried to protect you that day."

"What, by hitting me so I'd crash? I know the truth about that day because others told me while I was lying in the hospital. The people who cared about me, people like Antoine, came to see me as soon as they could. They said you'd try to blame others."

He steps back, colliding with my desk.

Memories of him storming out of my bedroom weeks after I'd been brought home, when he wouldn't say sorry but was adamant I had to listen to him about the race, are like boots on my chest. He steps close enough for me to smell the mixture of his sweat and woody lavender scent. I smelt that in the corridor after my call with Niki. He must be acting like this because he heard me crying.

Great. Another man in my life who's decided I'm incapable and must protect me rather than support me. I squeeze my eyes to stop the tears threatening to burst free. I will not cry in front of him again.

"If you really want to protect me, then leave me alone and stop fighting with Antoine. Drive the way you're capable of, and then maybe, you can stop being the man I can't bear to be around because he ruined my life. Can you do that?"

Instead of answering, he walks away, and I swear I hear the word "crasher." It's the nickname other drivers have called me—a name to humiliate me.

My whole body is on fire. I stalk towards him and grab him by the shoulder, yanking him around to face me. He stares at me with a mixture of hatred and something else that makes my skin prickle, even as my whole body flames in anger.

"Don't ever call me Crasher again," I reply shakily.

"I would never call you that. I would rather die than hurt you. I hate what I did to you that day. I meant to protect you and keep you safe."

His eyes pinch, and his lips are tight. My chest heaves as I stare at him. Adrenaline sparks through my body, making my limbs burn. He holds my stare as my fingers press into his racing suit. Anger bubbles between us. He licks his bottom lip slowly. I suck in a breath, and he parts his lips as he stares at me. I lean in, and his chest brushes against my breasts. Heat bursts between my thighs, and the fire of his touch threatens to consume me. He lifts his hand to my face, and my lips tremble. All the tension in his shoulders disappears. His eyes soften, and the earlier lines disappear. The contrast is so overwhelming that my pulse rises, and turmoil flips around my body.

I won't let this happen. I can't.

"Can you just keep driving like you're capable of?" I whisper, repeating one of my requests.

I hold my breath in anticipation.

"Yes, I can do that, Miss Coulter. Boss." His last word is like a punch. He pulls back so quickly I nearly fall, his suit ripped from my hand.

It's what I needed to hear. I am his boss. Nothing more.

He walks away. I'm left standing alone in the garage. Goosebumps cover my skin, and I can't forget what he said. What does he mean by saying he meant to protect me that day?

Chapter Nine – Senna

"He said what?" Jacs asks as I stare at the pink sparkling varnish on my toenails.

"He said he'd rather die than hurt me."

"Bloody hell," she says, puffing out her cheeks with one long breath. "And what did you reply?"

"I didn't," I stutter.

Jacs shakes her head as she tops up my second glass during one of our after-race prosecco and pedicure evenings. Two and a half is my limit, or I start making mistakes, and after today and with no sleep, it would end in a fuck or a fight.

"So what now?"

I stare at Jacs with her bobbed red hair and freckles highlighting her nose and cheeks. I thought I'd discovered a real-life unicorn when I found her. The number of women in racing is increasing, but there's still not enough.

"Now, I avoid him and get a makeover."

I sense her stare and grimace.

"Because you fancy him?" Jacs waggles her toenails, painted in our team colours, but with the addition of silver stars. "You'd change your look for him?"

I jump off the bed and study myself in the mirror. "Of course not. The avoiding is because of him—"

"Because you're attracted to him. It's hard not to be. I bet those lips could do amazing things all over a woman's body, and maybe his dick really is as big as Antoine's." I catch her dancing eyebrows in the reflection in the mirror and giggle.

"Hey, those are your thoughts, not mine. I don't think of him that way."

I drag my teeth over my lower lip. Connor's lips are kissable. They always have been. When he was eighteen, I spent too much time staring at them and imagining pressing mine against his. But that was a teenage crush. The things I've imagined lately are R rated.

"Of course you don't. And you didn't just have the filthiest idea. Your eyes give away everything."

I stick my tongue out at her and choke on the scent of nail varnish.

She adds with a cackle, "I bet he can do the sexiest things with his tongue, too."

I smirk and roll my eyes. I need to keep any attraction to Connor locked firmly away. He's not mine to pursue. The guy has more changing moods than I do. And more importantly, I can't let anything get in the way of this job. The race went better than I hoped, but it was *one* race.

"The less we talk about him, the better. There's another twenty-two races to go, and with Antoine peacocking and Connor wanting to smack him, not to mention the lack of money to improve the cars or replace parts after crashes, we don't stand much of a chance of regularly doing better." I breathe slowly, closing my eyes and tucking my lower lip into my mouth.

"Fair. I bet you count your lucky stars that I'm your lead mechanic," she says with a fake chuckle.

I pin her with my stare. "I count them every day. You

START YOUR ENGINES

are one of the best racing mechanics in the world, and I'll never be able to tell you enough how lucky we are that you chose our team."

"You chose me, too." A glow trips across my skin as we match each other's smiles. I wish I had the money to spend on the cars rather than make her team bust themselves for mediocrity. "So if the makeover isn't about him, then what?"

I study the furnishings to avoid her penetrating stare.

"Senna," she pushes.

I wrinkle my nose, walking around the room before staring at her. "I need to upscale my look. Firstly, I must match Filip, Vessa's team boss extraordinaire." I stand in front of the mirror and study my tired eyes and limp hair. "He's stylish perfection. We're not in the same league when it comes to preening, let alone power dressing. And…"

I don't want to say the other thing. Jacs stands behind me, eyeing me and sensing my reluctance. "You can tell me anything," she says, imploring me with her stare, a strand of red hair catching in her long eyelashes. "What is the issue?"

"I'm fed up with everyone trying to protect me. My dad's decided I'm incapable. Niki tried to orchestrate some protection intervention, and Connor said what he said because he heard me crying. To the men, I'm a pathetic teenage girl, and that might partly be because I haven't changed my look since I was seventeen, but my body has changed a lot."

My eyes drop to my chest and my slight curves.

"I've spent years hiding who I am in order to fit in, whether that was a hairstyle I could easily fit under a helmet when I raced as a teenager, or wearing polo shirts and plain trousers as Comms Director so I'd be known for my abilities and getting the job done."

63

"And there's nothing wrong with that if that's who you want to be."

I close my eyes and sigh. "I don't think that's who I want to be anymore. I want to command attention when I walk through the garage. I know I do that with my voice, and I'm starting to have an impact on some of the team." I hold out my hands. "I need to show it's me against the world and be that bitch boss, or at least a woman who came to do business, not a teenager planning her university choices. I want to show I'm here to kick ass and look good while doing it, and if I stop hiding my body, then even better."

Jacs claps her hands. "Does this mean you'll finally show off your perfect legs?"

I smile at her reflection. "I have good legs?"

"Are you for real? I have a footballer's calves and a rugby player's thighs. That isn't the best combination. On the upside, I have an arse that features in the dreams of every man and woman that's spent time with me." I giggle as she spanks her butt. "But you have the legs of a ballet dancer. You run miles every week, so show off."

My face heats with a blush. I wouldn't change my family for the world, but growing up with men and a mum who didn't bother with clothes or make-up meant I didn't think about my body. My favourite clothes are Coulter Racing hoodies and shorts. "But how do I sort out this makeover? I don't want to end up overdoing it and resembling the time Niki turned my Barbie doll into a troll. He was awful to that poor doll, shoving her down the toilet and tying her to his kart."

"I bet he regretted making you angry. You gave up your toys, took up karting, and beat him," Jacs says. I was a typical little sister, equal parts adoration and competition for my big brother.

"I really miss him."

"I know you do. I wish I could bring him home. I can help you with the makeover, though."

"Yeah?"

"My ex, Aida, from when I studied in Australia, is a personal stylist."

Jacs swallows, and I'm reminded of her drought when it comes to relationships and sex, mainly due to work and our sector's lack of eligible options. Neither of us would date someone from the team because it would get around and we'd lose all the respect we've painstakingly built as independent women.

"I'll get Aida to help you before qualifying. Then you can walk in like a bitch boss and shut all those overprotective arseholes up. Aida and I stay in touch, and when we race out there, I pop by for some stress relief"—she winks—"like you do with your vet."

"He's not *my* vet."

"He's a sexy man, awesome in bed—your words—and he loves animals," she replies as I drain my glass. "Isn't that what you want in a man?"

I shrug.

"Don't give me that. The photo he sent you with his top off, muscles everywhere, holding a puppy nearly destroyed me. You'd have it as your screensaver if every nosey bastard didn't ask questions. Is there no chance with you two?"

"He's a hookup. Yes, he's hot and caring and good with animals. And the night we first slept together after a shitty day on the track is firmly in my 'self-care' bank, but even if he lived down the street from me, I wouldn't want long-term with him. It's nearly impossible to have a relationship in this job when you're working every hour that exists and in a different country nearly every week."

"You'd make it work if you liked him," she argues while pointing at me with the nail varnish brush.

"True, but I need someone who challenges me and excites me and who I can chat to for hours and someone who at least understands this industry and—"

"Who has a nine-inch dick and is called Connor Dane?"

I throw my pillow at her. "He's the last person I want to date. Ever! And I don't want to date someone who lies about the size of their penis."

She cocks an eyebrow. "But what if he's not lying?"

I lick my lips at the idea of Connor Dane undressing in front of me. Suddenly, a chocolate bar smacks me in the head.

"Down, girl. Save those saucy faces for when you're alone," Jacs shouts.

Chapter Ten – Senna

"Just don't tell anyone, okay?" Connor says to Silas as I walk into the gym.

"Tell anyone what?" I ask before I see him for the first time since the race in Bahrain days earlier.

Connor pounds the treadmill. His baggy shorts ripple, and sweat drips down his bare chest. Drops slide across tattoos that I've never seen in the flesh. My tongue swells as I take in the whole delicious look complete with a backwards cap. I focus on his eyes for fear that my face will reveal the fantasies that are desperately clawing through my consciousness. I shouldn't have come down here.

Connor winks at me, and I glare before forcing myself to focus on Silas, who is making notes on a tablet.

"Tell anyone what?" I repeat. My voice rasps this time.

"I didn't want Silas to tell anyone that I got a request from my agent. He asked if I would do a naked photo shoot," he pants as he runs, but his stare never leaves mine. A drop of sweat rests in the bow of his full lips. Fuck. I want to lick it. "They asked for the driver with the biggest dick."

Silas chokes.

"You're such a liar. I'll find out what you're hiding," I reply.

"I'll show it to you anytime you want, but only if you

ask, because consent is important to me."

I close my eyes and count to five. Consent is nearly as sexy as the image of a nearly naked, sweating Connor Dane in a backwards cap, bracketing me with his arms as he asks me how much I want to see what is hidden underneath his boxers. I shake my head.

"Are you blushing, boss?"

"No, I'm just pissed off, as my day is going to fuck, which brings me to you." I force a smile. "Firstly, we need to talk about your race at the weekend. How are you doing?"

His eye twitches, and he looks down and focuses on the treadmill. "I'm grand."

I debate my options. I need his truth, but we're not at a stage where he can trust me. "Okay, maybe it's not the time for a review." He continues to avoid eye contact. "I do need a favour, though."

He stares at me with a furrowed brow, and for some hellish reason, it makes my heart beat faster than when he smirks and winks.

I clear my throat. "I need you to do a meet-and-greet for a competition winner. Antoine was booked to do it, but he's disappeared and isn't answering calls. The guests are arriving in fifteen minutes."

"You're done," Silas comments.

Connor jumps off the treadmill and wipes his body with a towel. "What's in it for me?" he asks before slowly licking the bead of sweat on his cupid's bow.

My breath hitches.

"What do you want?"

He lifts his eyebrows twice quickly, and I ready myself to knock him out. "I'm your boss, Dane, not one of your grid honeys."

He squeezes his lips like he's trying not to laugh. "Grid

honeys. That's a new one." He wipes down his chest. I want to study the tattoos. Fuck, if I'm being honest, I want to trace them with my tongue. "Boss, could you call my sister?"

"Layla?"

"Yeah, she's at university studying for a career in comms, maybe social media. It would make a huge difference for her to speak to an expert and trailblazer like you."

My mouth drops. Maybe he's only saying it to get me to do him a favour, but that's one of the biggest compliments I've had from anyone, and it came from Connor fucking Dane.

"Okay," I reply, my throat drier than a Finnish sauna.

"Nice. She should be free now. I'll message you her number before I shower."

I nod my thanks and start towards the exit. That's an image I don't need, but my mind still fills with Connor leaning against a shower wall, his hand sliding down to his—

"And Senna," he says. I turn back. "I would have done it for you anyway. I hate Antoine, and if I can make him look even more like the shit he is, the better."

I take a breath, but of course, he's not finished.

"And I love it when you tell me what to do. I'm here for all your requests."

He winks, and the image changes to me directing him to stroke himself in the shower.

My mobile rings. It's my dad. I cancel it as I walk out.

"A million thank yous, Miss Coulter. It's been so helpful to chat with you," Layla replies from my laptop screen. She's

got the same dark hair and full lips as her brother, and although they have blue eyes, Layla's are brighter and hidden by glasses. She has two cute dimples when she smiles. The Dane family are too beautiful for words.

"You don't need to call me Miss Coulter, Layla. I remember chasing you with Connor around the house when you were in a nappy and you'd stolen his favourite cap. Senna is fine."

Layla laughs. "Okay. Thank you, Senna. You always were lovely to have around, and you made Connor a much nicer older brother."

"For real?" I ask as I note things I've promised to send her.

"Nah, he's always been the best, but you helped him through those tricky teenage years. At least, that's what Mum said."

"I'm sorry I didn't stay in touch after the accident. I should have, but..."

She shrugs. "It's okay. It was a difficult time for all of us. We had a lot going on, with Dad leaving and then Mum and me moving to the middle of nowhere in Scotland."

"What? That happened around the same time?"

Layla nods. "A lot happened, while you were recovering, but Connor looked after Mum and me, ensuring we were comfortable and had money to relocate. There were desperate moments when he lost his funding from your dad, but then Lapoire recruited him into Formula Two."

My blood runs cold. I didn't know my dad cut Connor's funding or about his dad. I knew Connor had signed to Lapoire and moved to Formula Two. It makes sense. My dad could be a petty bastard.

"He must have been delighted when he was recruited." I force a smile.

START YOUR ENGINES

"Yes and no. That's when Connor told Dad he could focus on being with our family rather than spending all his weekends and evenings coaching Connor. Dad announced he was only staying with Mum because of Connor's career and went off with one of the women he was secretly sleeping with." Layla lifts her glasses and rubs her eyes. "Dad nearly destroyed us, and Connor felt guilty for starting that snowball that turned into an avalanche. But we're better off for it. Don't tell Connor I told you all this. I know he's private about things, but this is stuff he should have told you at the time. If not for Niki, I'm not sure if he would've gotten through it."

I'd never thought about what Connor was doing while I was in the hospital. I was selfish, convinced by other drivers that he'd done it on purpose, especially after he was accepted into Formula Two.

I fist my cuffs out of shot. "I'm sorry I wasn't there for him."

"Things happen. A lot was going on, and you were traumatised because of the crash. I only know some of this because of conversations I've overheard and what Mum said. I just wanted you to know that Connor isn't your enemy. He acts up and is a dickhead sometimes, but he's a good guy. Just give him a chance, yeah?"

I nod. In the little image of me at the bottom of the screen, my forehead is lined, and my face is pale. I need to see Connor, even though there's much to process.

"Send me the stuff for when you write your dissertation, and I'll give you some thoughts. And if you ever want a job, we'd love to have you here."

"I want to earn that job. I know that's what you did at Coulter. Connor told me you've had to fight for respect and your roles. You're an incredible woman, Senna. Connor

71

speaks highly of you...most of the time. But please don't talk to him about anything I said."

I grip my desk, debating my options, but Layla's wincing face makes me agree. "Okay, I promise."

"Thank you. Bye, Senna."

"Bye, Layla." I smile as I hang up.

I don't know how to work through everything Layla shared.

"Jimmy, could you find out where the meet-and-greet with the competition winner is right now?" I shout to my assistant as I grab my phone.

As I leave my office, Jimmy pulls up the itinerary. "They should be in the showroom. By the way, your dad called again. He wants to speak to you about Connor's 'shitty driving' during the race."

"If he calls again, tell him I'm in meetings all day," I reply and head to the lift.

I can't speak to Connor about Layla's revelations, but I need to be close to him.

CHAPTER ELEVEN – CONNOR

Margot, the ten-year-old I'm showing around Coulter offices and the factory, stares at the Lego car in our display area.

I smile as she investigates it from every angle, but I'm distracted by my recent chats with Senna. I shouldn't tease her to avoid serious conversations, but I can't talk to her about the race.

I want to be the racing driver I used to be, but there's no chance. At least I survived my first race.

I glance at one of Niki's old helmets sitting on a display stand. If he'd been me in the last race I'd probably tell him he needed sleep and to focus on how to stop being scared about getting in the car. I tried some tactics, like blinking several times before the race. They seemed to release enough tension so I could get in the car.

I look at the helmet again. Niki would probably tell me to suck it up and drive.

I'm training all I can, and Silas is impressed with my progress. Then there's Senna. I'm lucky our radio conversation got me through the race, but I can't rely on her to speak to me every time. Senna is more than a coping mechanism. Did I really declare to her that I'd rather die than hurt her? Fucking adrenaline. I've replayed her big

73

hazel-eyed stare and gasp too many times in the last few days.

And I can't stop myself from cheeking her even when I should be an example to others and show her respect. At least I haven't made her cry again.

I crack my knuckles, drawing a stare from Margot. I smile, and she returns to the car.

I wouldn't know if I made Senna cry again. She hides everything and thinks she has to do it all alone. I want to support her, not hinder or protect her. Instead, I end up flirting with her.

I hold my hand to my face.

Margot squeals. The car Niki drove two years ago in the British GP draws her like a magnet.

"You could drive something like this in ten years," I say, walking to the turquoise and black racing car.

Margot stares at me. She's taken everything in on the tour, asking questions about my career, skills, and training. She reminds me of Senna when we raced each other.

"Your mum says you're winning against kids older than you at karting," I say, looking at her mum, who nods enthusiastically. "You could be just like me one day."

"But women can't be racing drivers," she whispers.

"Of course they can," I reply.

She trails her finger in the air as if she's too scared to touch Niki's car.

"There are no female F1 drivers, and Tawny Mackay is the only woman in F2."

"True." I nod.

She stares at me. "And one of the boys I race against told me there'll never be a woman in Formula One because they're not good enough. And he even said women shouldn't be in racing."

START YOUR ENGINES

I take a deep breath and stare at Margot. "He's wrong."

She furrows her brow as I continue. "I knew a female racing driver who was better than every male. She won races all the time. The boys bullied her and told her she wasn't good enough, and they tried to stop her, but do you know what she did?"

Margot shakes her head. Her eyes are wide, and I struggle not to smile.

"She beat them on the track. She also told them what she thought about them, and although that made them mad, they couldn't say anything back to her because she was the best. I raced against her, and she beat me all the time. She was incredible, the best racing driver."

Margot stares at me. "What happened to her? She's not racing now."

"She stopped, but what she's doing now is better. She's always been a pioneer for women in racing."

"What is she doing?" Margot asks tentatively.

"She runs Coulter Racing," I say. I sense someone other than Margot and her mum watching me. I look to the doorway of the display room, and my eyes lock on Senna's beautiful hazel-eyed stare. How long has she been listening? Her soft gaze makes me want to tuck the wave of hair falling out of her ponytail behind her ear. She's stunning. The corners of her mouth curve into a smile.

"She was the communications director but now manages the entire team. She makes the success of the entire team possible. She knows about cars, people, tracks, racing, and everything else! All the things that happen during a race and in the background during the week wouldn't be possible without her." I stare at Senna as I add, "She may not be racing as a driver, but she is a racing leader. She's all-powerful, and I'm lucky I call her boss."

75

REBECCA CHASE

Senna's throat bobs as she swallows.

"She sounds amazing!"

"She is. And if you're really lucky, she might say hello to us today."

That gets me a full smile, and Senna walks up to us, tapping Margot on the shoulder as I introduce her. "Meet my boss, Senna Coulter."

Margot gasps and beams as she stumbles over her hello.

"Hey, Margot. So you love racing? What's your favourite track?"

Margot's hands dance as she talks animatedly about the tracks she's visited and the ones she wants to go to. Soon, they're talking about races, and Senna is giving her tips on improving her corners and the tactics she used to overtake.

"Thank you," I mouth over Margot's shoulder.

She winks back at me, and my stomach does a weird bubbling thing.

"How would you feel if I watched one of your races sometime? Maybe I could chat with those boys and tell them about women in racing. I'll bring my lead mechanic, Jackie Mackay, and one of my old helmets for you to keep when you're big enough for it," Senna says.

"Can she, Mum? Can she?" Margot screams.

Her mum nods, but her face drops. Senna picks up on it, too, and as I lead Margot towards another part of our display area, Senna remains with Margot's mum.

"Miss Coulter also wrote 'Boys suck' on her brother, Niki's, racing car. She doesn't care what boys think of her and will fight them."

Margot giggles. Senna's laugh hits me hard in the chest. Her eyes twinkle as she shakes her head at me. "You'll get

76

START YOUR ENGINES

me in trouble, Dane."

I beam back at her before pointing out another car to Margot.

Senna and Margot's mum are chatting. I miss most of it, but when Margot is distracted by one of Ralf's old racing suits, I watch Senna pull out a business card and write something that could be a phone number on the back. A tear runs down Margot's mum's cheek.

"Thank you, Miss Coulter. My girl loves racing, but I didn't think we'd have the funds to do it much longer." She hugs Senna, and the bubbles in my belly turn into butterflies.

Shit.

CHAPTER TWELVE – CONNOR

I stretch out on the weight bench in the basement of my Australian hotel and let out a puff of air. It's been a month since Senna heard me talking about her to Margot, and I've tried avoiding her ever since.

I know she wants to talk to me about racing and the past based on something Layla said about their call. Every time she sees me, I've got Silas by my side, so she only manages a nod or a few words about training or a race. But when she pauses, I sense she wants to say more.

We're in a better place, and I can't ruin that, although the masochist in me misses fighting with her. She hasn't shouted at me or chucked me out of a room in ages, but I haven't made her cry, either.

When I came fifth in the Saudi race, she congratulated me with a nod. Thankfully, Antoine didn't get much more for coming eighth, but I wanted more.

I grunt loud enough to draw the attention of the woman staffing the hotel gym. Her tongue tips to the side of her mouth. She has the strong body of a surfer, which isn't unusual here.

My phone rings as expected. I put it to my ear as I answer, "Morning, Ralf."

"Morning. How do you feel about qualifying later? How many hours of sleep did you get?" Ralf says, checking in like

he does every morning before a practice session or race.

"Enough. I'm doing okay."

"No, you're not." I love this straight-talking bastard who calls me out on my shit. "Anxious?"

"Yeah. I had a dream like Niki's crash, but it was me in the car and I was burning."

"Were you watching the videos of the crash again?"

"Yes."

"Nein," he shouts so loudly I catch the surfer woman's eyes as I pull the phone from my ear. "Stop with those damn videos. Racing is terrifying once you realise how vulnerable you are, but if you want to continue driving, you must push it from your head."

My breathing accelerates. "I know. I didn't want to see them, but I caught one of the engineers watching them like it was entertainment."

My pulse rises as I remember the flames licking the car in my dream. I woke before I was rescued, but even when I was awake, the terror stayed with me. I won't get any more sleep now, and probably won't tonight, even though the race is tomorrow.

I catch the eye of the surfer again, and she smiles and gives me a wink. I look away. There's only been one woman in my fantasies in the last months, and although I'm not going there, I can't imagine being satisfied with anyone else. I haven't been able to imagine anyone else, let alone sleep with someone else, since Ralf's wedding.

"I'll speak to Senna," Ralf says as if reading my thoughts. Before I blurt anything out, I realise he means about the engineers. "She will terminate the engineer."

"No, Ralf. She can't know you're coaching me." Ralf's pep talks and calls, albeit with his need to fix rather than listen, are my only help. "If she learns about my fears and

my insomnia, she'll pull me from the team. She needs me if she's going to make Coulter Racing a success."

"But at what cost to you, Dane? You need help and time away."

"And I'll find it. But for now, I keep going."

This is the point we always come to. Ralf knows what many team bosses fail to understand. Lots of drivers struggle with their mental health, but instead of working on it, they push and push until they get out if they're lucky or break if they're not. Our sustenance is the adrenaline from knowing you could break records or die trying. But what happens when what feeds you slowly destroys you?

"Fine. If you continue to be like this, settle in, because it's time for your regular pep talk." He adds a chuckle to remind me his wit is uniquely his.

With Ralf's motivational speech hanging off my shoulders like a protection blanket, I survive qualifying.

Maybe I can get through tomorrow's Australian Grand Prix without fucking up. Wearing my lucky boxers and my routine of stepping into the car from the left side after blinking five times seems to have helped, too. The relief these little actions brings gives me the comfort I need to get in the car. If I keep doing them, there will be no accidents, and everyone will stay safe. Silas is the only one who knows, and although he thinks I need help, he's agreed not to tell anyone.

After qualifying and press interviews, I head back to the garage, ready for my congratulations for coming P3. Starting third on the grid has been my best position in a year. I grit

START YOUR ENGINES

my teeth, hopeful for more than a nod from Senna. I'll be okay if Antoine, who didn't qualify as high as me, gets nothing special from her. She's got to give me at least a handshake for that.

I step through the garage to smiles from my engineers. A buzz of excitement and chatter surrounds me, but there's an edge to it, too. A few engineers look at me like they're trying to communicate something.

As I'm about to question one of the guys, I see her. My mouth dries. Senna sits in front of me, but it's not the Senna I know. Her hair has been cut into a long bob with waves like blond ribbons. She wears her usual team shirt, but there's something different about it, like she's popped an extra button or got it to fit her properly. The people around her, including bloody Antoine, make it hard to know what else she's wearing.

My inner voice screams to run, but I step closer even as sweat rolls down my neck. I know she's a no-go for me, but I must see her up close. I lick my lips before pressing them hard together. My nostrils flare, and my pulse spikes. I will my body to calm. It doesn't matter that she's changed her hair and clothes. She's still my boss and not my friend. I shake my messy head and turn to go.

"Dane, you did it! P3," she shouts. "Where did that performance come from?"

That feels like a dig. I turn around. She's walking to me. *Fuck.* Her legs! I run my palm down my face as I imagine what it would be like to kneel between her long, toned legs. I swallow, and my body pulsates as she closes in on me.

"Dane, you okay?" Her mouth twitches as if she knows the effect she's having on me.

I grit my teeth. This isn't about me. Nothing Senna does is about me.

I focus on her face to avoid staring at her body, but that's a bigger mistake. Her hazel eyes swirl with amber and emerald, and they're bigger than ever. It must be her make-up. I want to make her pupils dilate as I drag my fingers across the bare skin of her inner thighs. I want her to lose it.

Suddenly, she's less than a metre away from me, wobbling slightly in her heels. She slams her hand against the wall to steady herself. Her heels bring her closer to my height. I could easily kiss her from this position. My eyes dip to her lips, and her tongue peeks out as if she has the same thought.

"I'm fine," I say so gruffly she takes a deep breath. Her tongue peeks out again, this time sweeping across her lips.

I busy myself undoing my racing suit. If I don't, she'll know precisely what I'm thinking as my blood rushes downwards.

I catch movement behind her. Antoine. I stare daggers at him as he checks out Senna's arse. I bet it looks incredible in her pencil skirt, but that's irrelevant. She's our boss and deserves our respect. Yet my face burns as my cock twitches in appreciation of her body. I'm a shitbag.

Antoine gives me a wink, and I fist my hands, desperate to knock him out.

Senna presses her lips together. She's oblivious to the increased tension around her. "Do you need to chat about anything or go over qualifying? I'm here for you."

Antoine raises his eyebrows.

"I said I'm fine," I growl between gritted teeth.

Antoine grins.

I need a cold shower, a good meal, and a night of sleep. I don't need to be fantasising about knocking out Antoine before pressing Senna against a wall while respectfully calling her boss and kissing those lips that now shine from

START YOUR ENGINES

where she licked them.

"I need to get back to the hotel. See you tomorrow," I say. I slap the wall as I turn on my heel.

I leave the garage, growling expletives. I'm confident I'll spend tonight wandering the streets of Melbourne in the early hours, anxious about the race and my bloody feelings for my boss.

Chapter Thirteen – Senna

Our race at the Australian Grand Prix is fucked.

I watch repeats of steam pouring out of Connor's car, which hit the barrier after clipping Antoine and spinning off the track. Once I knew he was okay, I shouted swear words and stormed around the garage in trainers because I couldn't handle my heels. Maybe I should be relieved Connor is safe and didn't take out Antoine, although I'm unsure if that was his intention.

The one positive is the car isn't completely ruined, although the repair cost is the last thing we need.

"What was he thinking?" I mutter for the umpteenth time, easing my headphones off my ears.

The race restarted at lap thirty-one of fifty-eight. His car is in the garage, and Jacs is examining it with her team. I can't bear to look at it. Another driver has been in a minor accident since, so the race is still going, but all the cars are on a yellow flag and driving a little slower, unable to overtake until they're given the green flag.

I grip my desk when meowing halts my anger.

My head spins as I look for the source of the sound. No pets are allowed on-site. I check under my desk before taking a breath. I must be losing it.

The meowing sounds again as Connor walks into the garage, seizing my focus. He's taken his bloody time. It

wouldn't surprise me if he was waiting for a bigger calamity so I'd forget.

He throws his helmet down. I open my mouth, but I catch Antoine singing in French from where my headphones hang around my neck.

"That isn't for public radio," his race engineer warns. Whatever Antoine is singing can be heard by the other teams.

I press the earphones to my ear. French isn't my first language, but I recognise the swear words Antoine sings. I hear Connor's driving nicknames, too.

"If you don't have anything racing-related to say, shut up, Antoine," I seethe.

"He clipped me," Antoine snaps. This isn't the time to rehash what happened. We discussed it briefly on the radio while they cleaned up the track of minimal debris. Thankfully, Connor's car was easy to remove from a side area.

"Stop stewing on it and focus on racing. We'll deal with it this week. Are we clear, Antoine?"

There's movement around me. The pit crew sit to the side of the garage. They focus on the big screen while waiting for Antoine to pit for a tyre change. The half of the garage I'm pacing is empty. I should capitalise on the privacy and speak to Connor.

I hold my hand to my mouth as I debate confronting him. I need to talk it out and get his side of the story before he has to do press interviews and before Antoine gets involved. It will get out of hand if I don't resolve what happened now.

I count to five. I can do this. I am the boss, and I need him to see me like one if I'm going to get the best out of him this season.

REBECCA CHASE

"Dane, come here," I command. He smirks at me. "And don't fuck with me."

He swaggers towards where I sit. I yank my headphones off.

"Yes, boss. Have you got helpful pointers for my driving, or will you accept I did nothing wrong?" His voice may be all attitude, but there's a sheen of sweat on his pale face, and his eyes are redder than mine.

"How much sleep did you get last night?"

He shrugs. His hair is messy from where he's run his hands through it. I'm hit by memories of social media comments written by fangirls discussing if his hair is as soft as it looks. I shake them off.

"Dane, are you sleeping?" I try to say gently, but I'm hyped.

He had problems with insomnia as a teenager, but I read in an interview he'd dealt with it.

"I'm fine," he grunts but avoids eye contact. His hands cup his chest at a weird angle.

"Are you hurt?" My stomach churns. "I need to get you seen by a medic."

"I don't need to be seen by anyone. I should get out of here."

I throw my hands in the air. "That's not possible. You can't leave—" The mewing is closer now. It distracts me from the argument. "Did you hear that?"

"I can't hear anything," he replies flatly.

There's movement where his hands hold his chest and more mewing.

"Dane," I warn. "What is in your racing suit?"

His mouth quirks. "Nine inches of—"

"I'm not talking about that." I point at his chest. "What is wriggling and mewing against you?"

86

START YOUR ENGINES

He lowers his hands slightly, and the furry face of a tiny kitten peeks out from above the zip of his slightly open suit.

"What the fuck? How did you get that on-site? Where did you find it?"

He gives a slow huff that fills the air between us. "She's a she."

He takes the kitten out and holds it against his chest. His hands appear bigger as he embraces the tiny creature. I curse the longing and needy thoughts threatening to brim to the surface as the tabby patterned kitten licks his fingers.

"Good girl," he huskily tells the kitten.

I scrunch my toes and run my tongue along the top of my mouth to distract from the pulsing between my legs that's appeared from hearing him say those words. "Dane, explain now."

"Stop being so argumentative," he says softly. It's like he's sharing a secret, and my body trembles lightly. "You don't want to scare her."

"Come here." I tip my head to the corner of the garage, away from the rest of the crew, and he follows me behind a makeshift wall. No one overhears our chatter above the race cars out on the track. I should focus on the race, but how Connor cares for this kitten makes sweat drip down my back. I want to fan myself as he coos to the adorable ball of fluff. I talk as softly as he does. "Please explain to me what's going on."

"I found her in the middle of the night while walking around the city." I want to ask why he was walking around, but he might tell me he was returning from a hookup. "She's a stray. When I found her, she was hungry, shivering, and alone. She's a baby and needs caring for, but I don't know the city or what to do. I didn't want her to die."

"How did you get her on site? If she'd gotten out, she

87

could have caused a crash."

"I hid her. I put her in a secure box in the back of the garage, and Silas cared for her. There was never a chance she'd get out. She was a very good girl." I stare at him as he says those words again. My thighs quiver. "But I just got her out because I needed her after that crash."

"Are we going to talk about your crash?" And why he needed to hold a kitten after it?

"Later," he says as the cat mews louder. Everyone remains focused on their earlier jobs. "What do I do with her? I can't take her home, but I don't know anyone in this city."

I'll leave the crash issue for now, but we'll revisit it. I'm buoyed by the fact he doesn't know anyone in the city. Maybe he wasn't coming back from a hookup. But if his insomnia has returned, I need to learn why. I purse my lips. As I stare at how he rubs the kitten's chin, she lifts her head and closes her eyes, relishing the touch. The gentle way he brushes her fur with his finger makes my heart flutter.

I stretch my hand and stroke her head. Connor's full-lipped smile drains all my adrenaline from me, and I take a slow breath.

"I know someone in the city. I have a friend." I nearly choke on the word friend. "I have a vet buddy who can help."

Connor's shoulders relax as he continues to coo over the kitten and stroke her head. "It's alright, baby. We'll have you safe soon."

My belly flips. I need to return to work but want to stay here. "Keep her hidden and safe, okay?"

I head back to my screen, blinking repeatedly to forget the images of Connor's delicate fingers and soft coos.

Chapter Fourteen – Connor

Senna leads me into an empty waiting room with paintings and photos spread across a wall. A snarling bulldog labelled, "Mabel, our cutest girl" is next to one of a python with the name Edna emblazoned across it. I shudder.

My kitten sleeps soundly in a pink and white fleece blanket against my chest. My heart beats in rhythm with her little breaths, and I struggle not to test that she's okay. As we travelled in a car Senna borrowed, my hands brushed the kitten's ribs. This poor girl would have died if I hadn't struggled to sleep and walked the city.

It's the one positive from the last twenty-four hours.

It's always been difficult to sleep the night before a race, especially so recently since I haven't settled in any kind of rhythm due to the time difference and it only being several races into the season. But that image of Senna as a sexy boss, with her usual sass and attitude, did a number on me. Every time I closed my eyes, I recalled her team shirt straining against her chest and those long legs I want wrapped around my head. Inevitably, Antoine and his winks got into my thoughts, too.

Senna hasn't asked any more about my insomnia, but she will. My thoughts are cut short by a male voice. "Senna, you're looking as gorgeous as ever."

My shoulders tighten, which causes the kitten to wake up and chirp angrily at me.

"Sorry, little one," I whisper before turning to a man with more muscles than a powerlifter addicted to protein shakes laughing with my Senna. No, my boss, Senna. She's not mine in any other way.

I grit my teeth and offer the stranger a sour glare, but he only has eyes for her.

"Do you want to come through with the kitten?" He beams at Senna, but then he sees me, and his mouth turns down at the corners. He replaces it with a fake smile, which I mirror. "And your...friend."

When she doesn't correct him with the words subordinate, driver, or nemesis, a genuine smile replaces my faux one. It's a win I'll hold as close to my heart as this kitten.

"Connor Dane," I say, introducing myself, but he's walking towards the back, forgetting me.

I walk behind Senna and the vet as their arms brush against each other's. Technically, his flexing muscles brush against her arms. I bet I could take him in a fight, though. I might not have his bulk, but I'm a scrappy bastard when I fight for something that matters.

Senna laughs at something he says. I turn my cap around so it faces backwards when I witness him touch the small of her back to lead her into the treatment room. I used to make her laugh like that. My heart aches at the realisation I'm more likely to make her cry than laugh these days.

As we crowd into a small sterile treatment room, I clutch the kitten and ease her onto the metal table. She wakes slowly, blinking her big eyes. All the stress of the last twenty-four hours slips away as the fluffy ball of cuteness stares at me like I'm her hero.

START YOUR ENGINES

"Hello," the bodybuilding vet says to my kitten. "You can call me Brad."

Of course he's called Brad. I roll my eyes until I catch Senna staring at me. I blink several times and mumble, "Must have cat hair in them."

She stares into my eyes, searching for the hair. A hint of amber gives her eyes a glow that reminds me of autumns kicking leaves and laughing. I can't look away. She reaches for my face, and I hold my breath, desperate for her touch, yet I still attempt to hide yearning from owning every part of my face. Her thumb brushes my cheek, and my skin tingles.

I whisper, "I think it's still there," when she starts to pull away.

My entire being craves her touch.

I breathe in her orange blossom scent as she hesitates, her hand in the air. My eyes drop to her mouth as she wets her lower lip. I can't breathe as she touches me again, her thumb brushing my cheek. The softness of her touch makes me shiver.

"You know, stray kittens commonly have fleas. You should probably flea bomb or wash everything this one has touched," Brad says, side-eying us. I've never wanted to punch someone more.

Senna yanks back her hand and turns away from me as Brad checks the kitten over, examining her ears and lifting her lips to investigate her teeth while asking Senna how she's been. "I expected a call when I saw it was a race weekend here, but I didn't expect to be enjoying a different kind of tiger."

I choke on my saliva.

Senna's eyes widen as she says to me, "It's a joke. He calls me tiger in jest."

I glare at Brad, who scowls back. "Sure," I grunt and then mumble, although, surely, in this airless examination room, it will be heard, "He's a fucking hoot."

My kitten does the cutest yawn. As she opens her mouth, she reveals all her tiny teeth and a little tongue.

"So how do you two know each other, Brad?" I draw out his name sardonically. I'm secretly hoping to get a glare from Senna, but she's staring Brad down.

He chuckles, and I fist my hands. "Well, Clive—"

"It's Connor," I snap.

"Sure, whatever. Let's say I'm the one Senna comes to when she's in Melbourne and she needs to work out some stress."

"Brad," Senna warns.

Brad holds up his hands, and even they have muscles. I want to believe it's from crying and wanking over Senna, who can't possibly like him. What is there to like?

"We're friends—good friends who like to spend nights together a couple of times a year," Brad adds.

I grind my teeth to stop myself from asking more questions. I don't want to hear about her friend with benefits. I stroke the top of my kitten's head and scratch behind her ear with one finger, which makes her press her head against my hand. Senna does her other ear, and we smile briefly at each other. I won't read too much into the way her eyes soften as she looks between me and my furry baby or how she clucks at the kitten like this is a real fucking moment between us.

"Anyway," Brad says, cutting my happiness short, "we're going to have to give her—"

"She has a name," I add, although I've not named her yet.

START YOUR ENGINES

Brad glares, but it's Senna's stare that seeps beneath my skin. She tucks some hair behind her ear as she strokes the kitten. "Which is?"

"Coults," I say, as if I haven't that second decided to name her with one of Senna's good nicknames.

Brad huffs as Coults, the big-eyed kitten, gazes at me, her eyes fluttering with tiredness.

"I like it," Senna states, stroking one of Coults's big kitten ears. "Hello, baby. You've got quite a name. If anyone is going to kick ass and make the others behave, it's you."

Brad shrinks a little, and my heart does a wild dance in my chest. I cover my smug grin with my hand, but it still peeks out because it's so fucking massive.

The rest of the inspection continues like this. Senna adores the kitten and acts sweeter with me than she has in years, and Brad softens a little and stops flexing the biceps no one's paying attention to.

Before long, Senna gets in the car as I say goodbye to Coults. I can't have a cat due to my job, but that doesn't stop my nose from itching with oncoming sobs. Tears collect in my eyelashes as I whisper goodbye. I kiss her head briefly, and she coos and gives me one last big-eyed stare. If a kitten doesn't think I'm all bad, maybe there's hope. A tear slips down my cheek, and I turn my cap back around, keeping the brim low as I mumble, "You're safe now, Coults."

Brad takes my number so his assistant can update me on her progress.

He checks to make sure Senna can't hear us, and then squares his shoulders at me. "You should know that when it comes to Senna, she needs someone to protect her, and I've been trying to be that guy for her for a while. I'm her future, so leave her alone."

93

"Whatever. We're just friends," I reply gruffly. "And I don't get why everyone thinks she needs protecting. She's a fucking force."

"You don't understand her at all."

I shrug my shoulders at him and blow a kiss to Coults, who falls asleep as he pops her into a carrier.

"Don't forget to flea bomb everything you own," he adds.

As I get in the car, I struggle to relax my furrowed brows. Should I tell Senna what Brad said, but in a chatty, cheery way that doesn't reveal my feelings? I turn to the window. I don't want to hear her laughter when she hears that Brad thought there was something between us.

I yawn wide. It's been a long fucking day. In the last thirty hours, I've rescued and said goodbye to the best kitten in the world, crashed, and met Mr. The Only Pussy He Knows How to Satisfy Eats Cat Food Vet, all on no sleep.

As I nod off, Senna's voice filters through my exhaustion. "I've only seen Brad twice in the last year. I had business in the city in January, which was the last time. I wouldn't have contacted him, but it was after Niki's accident and Dad's heart attack. As I landed, I learned Dad was stepping down from the team and didn't want me in charge. I needed someone. Not that I need to explain myself to you."

"I'd rather you didn't," I reply, although the reasons she's giving to justify herself make me realise she's got a lot going on, and all of us were too selfish to consider how she was coping.

My stomach burns with the renewed sense that I must be here for her, not protect her like Niki's instructions. I want to hold her as she deals with shit, not take it away from her. I want to be the person she comes to when bad things happen and for her to know I'm a call away. She should know

94

that if she'd turned up at mine when she got news about her dad, I'd have done everything to give her a safe space while she processed it and sat with her as she ran through ideas to change the situation. I shake away the images of our relationship playing out differently than it has. She doesn't want me.

"I don't need to know about your conquests," I mumble.

Lights flash across her face as she drives us to the hotel. "Oh, come on, Dane, you're the biggest player in this car."

"And yet, out of the two of us, you've had sex more recently. Not that I'm judging."

"You haven't had sex in nearly six months? For me, that's normal, but for you, that's..."

As she fumbles for a word, I remain silent. She wouldn't believe my reasons, especially as they're related to seeing her at Ralf's wedding.

As a teenager, she did what no other woman has: challenged me, made me smile, and cared for me. However, she's off-limits for many reasons, including the same one that kept her off-limits when I first fell in love with her: she's still my best friend's sister.

I reply between gritted teeth, "You could do much worse than Mr. Bodybuilder."

She grunts but doesn't push a conversation. I breathe in her orange blossom perfume. It's become an entirely new scent on her due to the smell of oil and rubber tyres from the garage that's probably in her hair. As she stops at traffic lights, she swipes a dash of lip balm, and its mango aroma surrounds us. I count to ten as I fight the temptation to taste the mango for myself and show her that Mr. Bodybuilder has nothing on me when it comes to kissing the feistiest, sexiest woman I've known.

REBECCA CHASE

I rest my head on the chair and pretend to sleep so she doesn't ask questions I can't answer.

CHAPTER FIFTEEN – SENNA

I flip my shoes off and press my feet into the office carpet. It's nearly ten in the evening, and I can't keep staring at spreadsheets. I've deep-dived into our finances for hours, and every new file I open makes me want to bash my head against the desk.

My phone rings, and I stifle a yawn as I answer.

"Senna, why did Adam tell me on the golf course today that you're having issues with finances?" my dad asks without a greeting.

"Because my board member was trying to put you off your stroke?"

"Senna," he warns.

I bite my tongue and rub my scar. "Adam has no business gossiping about the company. He's on the board and should be working to fix problems rather than bad-mouthing me. He should speak directly to me if he has a problem with me."

"He said you've been distracted since Australia."

I squeeze the stress ball shaped like a cat that I found on my desk the other week, staring at the way its belly pops when I do.

"Australia was a month ago. He could have come to the office if he wanted to talk to me. I'm here twelve hours a day." It's usually fourteen, but I don't need everyone to

know that, or I'll never have quiet hours to finish things. "And as I have the time to speak to you four times a week, I'm sure I have the time to speak to him, seeing as he works for me."

"You're telling me that I'm calling too much. Coulter Racing was my baby, and I'm still the owner."

I drop my head to my desk as my dad continues his lecture about how he successfully ran the company for years and was a leader in Formula One as if I didn't know. What he fails to address, and I don't confront him with, is that in recent years, his short-term planning has damaged the company. Whenever I think I've seen the worst of it, I pull a thread and end up with a hundred unravelled balls of wool overflowing from my hands.

I stare at the photo I keep on my desk of my smiling parents. Dad has Niki in his arms. Niki and I are both clutching trophies.

"At the end of the day," I jump in, using one of his overused phrases, "Adam shouldn't be talking about me. I've got a board meeting tomorrow, so I will deal with this then. In the meantime, you must leave me alone to run this company."

He grumbles.

"Have you heard from Niki?" I ask, rolling the toy around in my hand.

"Not recently. Have you?"

"Not for weeks."

"It's a shame he never took over team leadership."

I suck in deep breaths, but all I taste is stale air. I've never felt more alone. Ralf sends me the odd message, but that's it. I can't tell Jacs what's happening because she's stressed enough with her team and struggling with the cars on a shoestring budget. I need to fix everything in this place.

START YOUR ENGINES

When I was comms director, my team had my back. They'd fight some of my decisions because they wanted the best, but we were a team, and their loyalty was unquestionable. The board barely talk to me, and now I know why.

Sensing my lack of response, my dad changes the subject. "How are your drivers? I hope you're keeping Antoine sweet."

"Why?"

"No reason. Is Connor staying out of trouble?"

"They both are," I reply. "They've been in the top fifteen in most races, and Connor always leads Antoine. Antoine is not the best driver we have."

"He would be if I was in charge. I should come to the meeting tomorrow. I can show you how I manage the board so you can learn from my example. They always listened to me."

I throw the stress toy across the room. It bounces off the floor-to-ceiling windows that look out on the car park. Even though it's the beginning of June, darkness covers the space.

"I'm fine. I run the team okay. The next time one of the board tells you things, please tell them to speak directly to me." I'm struggling to keep the begging out of my voice.

"If you're sure."

"Certain. Goodbye, Dad," I say.

"I'll call after the board meeting to see how it went."

I hang up to stop myself from saying more. I've never been able to stand up to him. I look again at the photo on my desk. I've spent a lifetime trying to make him proud, and look where it's gotten me. I had a failed driving career, and now I'm a failing team boss.

99

I retrieve my stress toy, but gripping it and squashing it in my hand won't shake the loneliness that fills my soul.

I peek out my door, and as I expect, I'm alone. I replace my designer shift dress with my team running shorts and hoodie.

My stomach rumbles, reminding me I forgot dinner. We're a few days away from travelling to Spain for the next race. I stare at the ceiling as I try to recall when I last ate a hot meal. If not for Jimmy, I wouldn't have breakfast or lunch.

I rummage through my drawers but am out of emergency chocolate bars. Half a breakfast bar with little dots of green and furry edges sits at the back. I gag as I drop it into the bin.

It joins half-chewed pen lids, a bloody staple I removed from a member of the accounting team who accidentally stapled himself when he found another file of bad news my dad hid, and an empty box of chocolates from Jacs because I haven't had time to hang out with her.

I'm losing everything I've wanted and worked for.

At least we're doing well in races. Connor beating Antoine regularly has created tension, but instead of it boiling over, it's simmering. As Dad used to say when Niki beat me on the track, competition is healthy. It was different when I won against him, though. And when Connor beat both of us, we got a lecture.

Connor Dane.

Since Australia, our interactions have improved. He's cordial and sometimes pleasant. We're not besties and never will be, but I can cope.

I prop my feet on the desk and flip on Taylor Swift. With my eyes closed, I imagine falling asleep and getting the rest I crave, but I haven't got time for that tonight. It will be

another one a.m. drive home before returning at six thirty. With my new bitch boss style persona, I'll have to be up at five thirty because doing hair and make-up takes a fucking age.

"Anti-Hero" reaches its crescendo, and I whistle along. When I was younger, I sat on my bed, listened to "Love Story," and imagined it was about me and Connor. But Connor and I weren't star-crossed lovers. I was an annoying tag-along.

"Still sound like a strangled ferret when you whistle, then, Coults." At Connor's lazy drawl, my eyes pop open, and I grip my chair's arms so I don't fall.

"How long were you standing there?" I reply, my face warming with embarrassment.

"Long enough to realise you're still a Swiftie. You used to listen to 'Love Story' on repeat."

He remembers *that*? He winks, sending my face from warm to hot. He's got his team cap on backwards, which reminds me of the cheeky, adorable Connor from the old days.

I raise an eyebrow in his direction as I rest against the back of my chair. "Well, some of us weren't pretending to like Drake while secretly dancing to Katy Perry."

Connor's grin escalates the heat in my cheeks until my face burns. It's the grin I remember from our teenage years when we teased, competed, and spent all our time together. I switch Taylor Swift off and attempt to erase the past.

My gaze flicks back to him, and my stomach churns. "What are you doing here anyway? Haven't you got a woman to seduce? They'll think you're playing hard to get if you keep letting them down."

His face drops. "I told you in Australia I haven't had sex in a long time. I'm not seducing anyone. And no, I don't want

to talk about it." His gaze runs the length of my legs, still propped on my desk. What is his problem with my legs? I've caught him glaring at them a couple of times. I drop my feet to the floor. "I'm here because, as I was leaving, I saw your car in the car park. I presumed you hadn't eaten, so I got dinner for us."

"Us?" That's when the smell of pizza hits me hard— melted cheese, tomato sauce, and pepperoni. I hide my mouth with my hand as drool collects in the corners of my lips. We used to eat this together as teenagers in our down seasons. "Don't you avoid food like this during race season because you need to fit into your car?"

"Are you asking as my boss or my...friend?" He stutters the last word, and I raise an eyebrow. "Are we friends?"

I shrug. "Depends how much of that pizza you're sharing with me."

He steps closer, looming above me. He's wearing the same hoodie as me, although he's combined it with jeans. He's dressed like he was when we were teenagers, and my heart tightens. Goosebumps cover my legs at his proximity. "I'd give you all of it if you'd let me."

He clears a space on my desk while resting the box on his hip to prove his point. When I quirk an eyebrow, he glares at me. "To avoid getting grease on your important papers."

Then, he puts down a paper towel before resting the pizza box on it. I jump up to help, but before I can speak, he side-eyes me and says, "Stop trying to manage everything. Let me do this one thing for you." He slaps my hands away before flipping the lid and taking out a piece.

I swallow excess saliva as the scent of fresh pizza dough fills my nostrils. He offers a slice to me, and as I move to take

it, he whips it away and takes a bite from it. He laughs as he chews.

"I stand by my opinion that boys suck. I hope you choke on it," I reply, jumping up, ripping the piece out of his hand, and shoving what's left in my mouth. I beam proudly, and he laughs.

"The edge of that was in my mouth. It's like we kissed."

I freeze. That was what I used to say to Niki when one of his fangirls ate half a cookie and offered him the rest. Sitting with Connor in the quiet office brings back too many memories, and every time it does, I'm reminded how my pulse rose at his proximity and how I'd steal his hoodies to smell him close.

I shove him away, and he winks, readjusting his cap. It does nothing to stop how my tongue tickles my lips at the idea of kissing him. I huff loudly. "Sit, Dane, before I kick you out of my office."

He sits on the other side of my desk.

"So tell me, are you still listening to 'Love Story' on repeat like you did when you cooked me pancakes when I came over before karting?"

"I don't know what you mean." I press my lips together to avoid smiling at the memory.

"That would be more believable if your lips weren't doing that dancing thing." He stares at my lips, and his chuckle dies.

"You okay? I expected a funny comeback."

He chucks a serviette at me. "You've got a bit of sauce." His hands are in fists as he directs me.

"You're so fucking weird, Dane."

"I learned from the best, Coults." His wink nearly floors me. He's all grown up but no less sexy than he was as an eighteen-year-old.

103

"Whatever." I shrug to hide the tingles in my belly. "So if you're not listening to Katy Perry, who are you listening to these days?"

"Various. I heard this one song you'd like. It has your big boss energy. Have you heard 'Femininomenon'?"

I shake my head. He eats in that laddish way that's always fascinated me. It's like a race to the finish, even when he's the only one eating. Everything is a competition to him.

"You should. I'll send you a link. You'd love it," he says, chatting like we're two people who haven't defined who they are to each other. "What is the worst thing you've had on a pizza, like ever?"

He stares at me as I sit back in my chair, folding my legs under me. "I went out with Jacs once, and they put lobster on a pizza."

He leans forward. "You know that's not weird, right?"

I wiggle my nose. "It is when they make you choose this big-eyed beautiful animal and then kill it in front of you. Never again."

He winces. "I would die."

"You're so fucking dramatic."

I throw my stress toy at him, but he catches it easily with one of his giant hands. He stares at it and gives it a couple of squeezes before chucking it back.

"Nice toy. Is it helping the stress?"

It's warm from his touch, and I tuck it into my hoodie pocket as if Connor's warmth could fill my belly.

I shrug. Is this the time to broach topics that have plagued me since I spoke to Layla?

"When are you going to ask about my pizza toppings?" he asks. "You know I'm my favourite topic of conversation."

"Fine. What's the weirdest pizza topping you've ever had?"

START YOUR ENGINES

He's already on his last piece, and I'm only starting on my third.

"Caramelised banana and peaches. It was a dare. You're right to make that face. Fruit doesn't belong on pizza."

"Not even pineapple?"

"Especially not pineapple. Don't tell me you've become someone who ruins pizza. I can't bear it, Coults, I really can't. You must be evil."

I smirk at him. "I'm the worst. You don't know the half of it."

His grin as I wink back has me smiling. With a sassy wiggle of my shoulders, I lick the tomato sauce off my fingers. His smile falters, and his eyes darken. My eyebrows dart together as he stares at my lips and fingers and his thumb strokes down his swallowing throat. He looks at me like I'm a pudding he needs to gorge on. A flush fills my belly, and I grip my stress ball, fumbling it.

Quickly, he clears his throat and points at the photo of my family on my desk as he wipes his full lips with the back of his hand. "Have you heard from him recently?"

"Niki?" I shake my head.

"Me neither. Ralf had a message from him a few weeks ago, but Niki won't say where he is."

"You've heard from Ralf?"

Although Ralf supported Niki and Connor when we were younger, he mentored me. If Ralf remains in touch with him, why hasn't he called me? Maybe they think I'm doing a lousy job. Imposter syndrome sneaks up on me often, and as much as I try to fight it, it doesn't help that I haven't got someone cheerleading or supporting me.

"Just for a racing chat," he says, shrugging off the subject. "Do you hear from your dad much?"

105

"He calls me most days, checking on me. He's decided I'm failing the company. I'll never be Niki, the person he wanted at the helm."

Connor rolls his eyes. "Your dad is a fool. He should believe in you and be grateful. He ran this place into the ground and then foisted it onto Niki, who doesn't have a business head. This place would have folded by now if he was in charge. You're doing incredible things, and your family are lucky to have you."

My mouth is dry, and I push my hand through my short waves. I never thought anyone would say that to me, least of all Connor. I stare at him, and he pins me with his gaze as if to prove he meant every word. I pull up my legs and shift around until I can cross them in my office chair. His eyes dip as I clamber into the chair to get the perfect position. He doesn't glare at them this time, instead licking his lips. "You're not in your fancy outfit tonight?"

Is he wondering if I'm this odd and so at ease around everyone? I'm not, but once upon a time, Connor was one of my closest friends.

"I always prefer to be in a hoodie and shorts. You know me." I bite my tongue. I didn't mean to say that. Of course he doesn't know me anymore.

But he nods. "Yes, I do, Coults. I know you."

The spark in his eyes as he gazes at me makes goose pimples rise on my legs. I suck my lips into my mouth, and he watches the movement. He licks his lips slowly, and I remember all those times I wanted to kiss him. I shouldn't be attracted to him now.

"How is Layla?" I ask. If I keep talking, I can avoid the Connor-shaped temptation.

"She's doing well. I'm hoping to see her at some point, but she's preparing to travel for a couple of months in her

summer break from university," Connor says. He looks down and then back at me. "I heard from my dad."

I hold my breath.

"What is he doing now?"

"Still screwing his way around the world with the money I send him each month."

My brow must furrow, because he qualifies his comment. "It's our deal. If I send him money, he stays away from us. He can do who and what he wants, but none of my family has to hear from him. Don't tell Layla that part, because she doesn't need to know. Dad doesn't get to betray any of us again."

"I'm sorry." He shrugs, but I implore him. I don't know his excuse for the crash, and maybe I never will, but he was my friend once. "Layla told me your dad left after you were promoted to F2, so your mum took her to Scotland. I'm sorry I wasn't there for any of you. You must have been lonely."

He shrugs again, and I want to shake him.

"Niki was around. He's not good with emotions, but he tried. Besides, it's not like I need anyone." He closes his eyes, and when he opens them, he smiles like he's reset himself. "Did you like the pizza?"

I worry my lip. I could press him to share more, but we're not there yet. We're only just friends again. Trust takes time, and I'm not sure we'll ever have enough.

"Yeah, it was the best thing I've had in ages. How did you know I hadn't eaten dinner?" I say, blustering through the words.

"Your secretary told Jacs you work late every night and that he considered leaving dinner for you, but you don't ask, and he didn't want to assume. And before you get weird about people talking about you, he was worried about you. No one else heard. I happened to be in the garage."

I open and close my mouth, grinding my teeth. I hate that people talk about me.

"Why were you in the garage?" I reply.

"I wanted to help improve the car," he explains with his hands out. "I'm not an engineer, but I want my vehicle to be the best it can be."

"You always were competitive." I tip my head.

"Coming from you. Miss Karting Champion and Junior Racing Champion."

"Until I wasn't."

His smile drops, and I kick myself for bringing it up. It will always be an unspoken issue between us and why we can't be close.

"That wasn't what you think. It wasn't my fault. You wouldn't believe me if I told you what happened like you didn't believe me when I saw you."

I shrug. "It doesn't change anything, Dane. Nothing you say could make what happened that day okay. You never even said sorry."

He jumps up and begins pacing the room. "I tried, but you wouldn't listen. I *tried*." His voice strains as he stares at the carpet.

I hold my hands up. Instead of sparks of joy, my stomach burns like I've eaten ten burritos and downed five pints of beer. I press my fist to my mouth. "Fine. Let's agree not to talk about it, okay? Thank you for coming by, and I'll see you in Spain."

"You're kicking me out of your office?"

"I'm not kicking you out. I have work to do so that I can go home."

He cocks his eyebrow and folds his arms. "Okay. Please eat the last piece and ensure you go home soon, or you won't be safe to drive." He squeezes his eyes closed and

shakes his head. "I didn't mean anything by that. I wasn't referencing the crash, I—"

"It's okay. Go home, and thank you for dinner. I appreciate it."

"Are we okay?" The sadness in his eyes makes me want him close. I don't want to hurt him.

I nod. "We're okay. You're driving well, and I'm lucky to have you on my staff."

"Staff," he repeats, slowly nodding his head.

What does he want from me? Sleepovers and braiding each other's hair?

I bite the inside of my mouth and walk over to him. I hold out my hand. "Truce."

"That's not how we did it."

"I'm not the person I once was." I sigh. "This is how we're doing it now."

"I've not changed." He squeezes his fists as he stares at my hand. It's not the secret hug-handshake Connor, Niki, and I did when we were younger, a way to be friends off the track so we could leave the race competitiveness and arguments behind.

My fingers tremble, and he lifts his head to look at me.

"Please," I beg, unable to meet his gaze.

He takes my hand. His coarse, hot skin against mine makes my belly roll. I guess I'm still some of the person I was, too. I press my lips together as his thumb briefly strokes the top of my hand. Tingles dance up my arms. My pulse quickens, and I pray that he doesn't stroke the inside of my wrist and find out what his brief touch does to me.

"Truce." His voice is too deep for my liking.

I swallow loudly.

Don't let go. Hold my hand because you want this closeness as much as I do.

But he lets go and sidles to the door. I fake a yawn to hide my sadness, although it quickly turns genuine. I'm so fucking tired, although this brief moment with Connor was like a stay of execution from my future.

"Make sure you go home soon. Catch you in Spain, boss," he says, lingering in my doorway, his arms bracketing it.

"See you then," I reply, pulling the stress toy out of my pocket.

He nods and walks away.

"I'm glad you liked the stress toy," he calls from the corridor.

My mouth goes dry. The toy was from him.

Once I'm sure he's gone, I press my face against the glass of my window and close my eyes. It's like ice on my burning cheeks. It's a shame it can't calm the fluttering in my belly.

Chapter Sixteen – Connor

Sunshine streams through my hotel window, highlighting the dust particles in the air. I strain my eyes and rub my forehead as I grab my phone off the bedside table.

Five hours? I slept five hours the night before a race! That hasn't happened since Niki's crash. I stretch out and yawn loudly. It's not nearly enough, but it's still a miracle. Ralf's chats must be working. I recheck my phone. He'll be calling in an hour.

I reach for the soft toy kitten that was waiting for me at the hotel when I arrived. There was no note. It resembles Coults. I breathe in its orange blossom and mango scent while trying not to hope Senna left it for me. That she thinks about me. I kept it in my bed as I slept. I sniff it before striding to the window to gaze at the city square.

I'm in the plushest hotel in Barcelona. Most of the people rushing between buildings will never stay somewhere like this or be offered the comforts I'm given. I pinch myself like I did the day I first signed with a racing team. Unlike Niki and nearly all the other drivers I race against, I didn't grow up with money. My racing career is a mixture of skill and a lot of luck. If Niki and Senna's dad hadn't spotted me karting, I'd probably be like the other people I went to school with, struggling between earning an

honest living and trying to stay out of jail.

I sigh as I step into the bathroom. This room has everything, including an ornate bathtub I'll use later when I'm sore and tired, as my end-of-race day routine. My old routine was drinking with Niki, maybe finding a hookup, and rushing for the plane home or wherever the team said we were travelling.

But I'm not that guy anymore.

I think back to Ralf's wedding and Senna capturing my heart. I was Dane the Dick, the guy with a deserved bad rep and a love for sex and fast cars, but seeing Senna that day made me realise she was the one.

And as soon as I got home, I remembered why she'd never be mine.

If not for that wedding and Niki's accident I'd probably be at Vessa, driving like a beast and chatting with every woman who smiled at me.

I slump against my door. What would have happened if Senna had been there for me after my dad left? I learnt the hard way that I didn't have anyone to look after me. Not that I need anyone. It's my job to protect others, not the other way around.

My phone rings, distracting me from my internal ramblings. I check my screen as I take a breath.

"Niki," I say, putting the phone on speaker as I prepare for race day. "You've not contacted anyone in weeks."

"I was busy." I wait for more explanation of what he was doing.

"Are you still there?"

"Sorry, yeah. You're doing well this season, Con."

"Have you spoken to Senna?" I ask, biting the inside of my mouth. I can't reveal my mess of emotions to her brother. The image of her sitting at her desk from earlier this

week, with her long sexy legs and my pizza in her mouth, sneaks up on me. I pace the room, counting to ten, as my stomach flips and drops. "Or have you spoken to someone else from the team?"

"I just got off the phone with her. She's stressed, man, and I'm worried about her."

Shit. Did I do something wrong? She's been pleasant to me since the truce. I thought we'd had a breakthrough. I fumble through excuses I can give him, but he cuts off my thoughts.

"Antoine is fucking with her head. I spoke to my old engineer, Macca, who is also impressed by you, and he says Antoine bad-mouthed her in the garage and said he's going to get with her."

"That bastard," I seethe. "I thought I'd got through to him, but Senna has kept us apart since we crashed in Australia. What do you want me to do?"

"Keep protecting her. And it might help if you spoke to Antoine again, nothing threatening, because you know that Dad loves him more than you." Niki clears his throat. "But so he's aware we know he's saying things behind her back."

I place the soft Coults toy in my bag, struggling not to sniff it or linger on what a gift potentially from Senna means. "Why does your dad love him more than me? He's a jerk, and as much as all of us drivers are arrogant bastards, there's a line. And I'm outperforming him every week."

"You're also the guy who put Senna in the hospital and destroyed her racing career."

"It was a career he never believed in anyway," I snap. "And you know what happened that day."

"Hey, I'm not blaming you. You protected her and saved her from what those lads had planned. You did everything you could, like we did every race. If I'd not been

ill, it wouldn't have happened. I blame myself more than you. And you know I tried to speak to her after it happened, but she wouldn't even let me say your name in front of her."

There's a knock at the door. I wrap a towel around my waist and answer it as he rambles. I tip the porter and flick through the paper as I close the door.

"You took care of her. She was like a little sister to you, too."

I glimpse a photo of Senna under racing news. She's wearing one of those pencil skirts and heels outfits that make my skin prickle with heat.

I grind my teeth. Senna was never like a little sister to me. She was a best friend who became the person I loved in my own way. And now, she's the woman I fantasise and fall asleep thinking about. My dreams are filled with running shorts and legs that go on for miles. I want those legs on either side of my face.

Niki's still speaking, and I try to erase the image of Senna's hands on my headboard as she rides my mouth. Not the time. Never the time.

"As things seem to be better between you—"

"Is that what she said?" I ask before holding my head in my hands. Fuck. Talk about eager.

"Kind of. She said she hates you less. That's a win, right?"

I smile because I can imagine her saying it as her eyebrows waggle and her mouth tips up to the side. I want to kiss the attitude out of her.

"At least I know you won't break the pact," he adds.

I drop the paper on my bed. "I wouldn't dare."

"It's time you told her what really happened that day. Maybe she'll finally listen."

I busy myself organising my bag again, laying out the

START YOUR ENGINES

lucky boxers I wear for every race. It's one part of my pre-race ritual, though they're more like obsessions. Since Niki's crash, and then mine in Australia, things have escalated. I can't stop them. I must keep doing them, or something terrible will happen.

"What difference will it make now after all these years? And if she does listen, who's to say it won't make her detest me more? I can't make things worse now that she 'hates me less.' It's one of those secrets we die with."

I don't want to lose my and Senna's hard-fought truce.

Niki huffs. "I hate that Antoine was one of the racers we dealt with in those days. He bullied her, not that she knew, because we shielded her, and he's doing it now but in a different way. Please protect her, okay?"

"Sure, I'll watch over her."

"Like the old days," he states, and I can't repeat it like he wants me to, because in the old days, I was secretly in love with her.

Waves sound in the background of the call. "Where are you, Niki?"

"Nowhere important."

"Are you coming home soon?"

"I will when I'm ready." Whatever that means. "It's the crash and what happened, okay? I can't be around people. Anyway, I've got to go, but I'll call again soon. By the way, Dad is coming to the race today. I told Senna, although he didn't want me to. Keep Antoine away from her."

"Sure, mate. Take care, yeah?"

"You too, Con. Laters." He's my one friend, and I can't tell him I'm too scared to drive, that I fantasise about his sister, or that I'm messier than a British stag party on a night out in Amsterdam.

115

CHAPTER SEVENTEEN – SENNA

"**A**nd I said to her, 'You want to be a racing driver?,' and we all laughed, but she was a good driver until the accident," my dad says to his guests.

He's brought four men to the Spanish Grand Prix and hasn't explained who they are. If they're investors, he should introduce me so I can tell them about our team.

It doesn't matter how many times I tell him I'm the boss; he won't step away from the company. I need to get better at confronting him, but things like this remind me of the times he wouldn't listen when I told him about the drivers who were bullying me.

He's sat here for the entire race, sharing stories of his greatest moments as the team boss, lauding how excellent Niki was and adding me as a footnote. "And she became a great communications director."

The men nod. The race has finished, and we're waiting for Antoine and Connor to return to the garage as everyone packs up.

"And now I'm the boss," I add, although the men aren't listening.

"An incredible one," Jacs says, but they're not listening to her either.

I shrug as I watch videos from the day. Anything to not

116

START YOUR ENGINES

engage with my dad when he's willy wanging. I shouldn't let his adoration of Niki's career and ambivalence towards mine affect me. At least he said I was a great comms director, though he didn't want me to do that, either. I worked my way up from intern during my university years and then, over time, convinced the board I should have the job.

I rub my scar. It shouldn't matter what he thinks. I know what I've achieved.

"Boss, can I show you something?" Jacs says. "One of the pit crew pointed it out to me earlier, and you should see it."

Something to distract me from Dad's booming voice. He moves to the edge of the garage, still sharing stories of the team's wins. Obviously, he doesn't mention all the damage he's done to the company.

Jacs runs through the footage. It's a hot day in Barcelona, and I fist my hair into a tiny ponytail and push my sleeves up. It looks a lot sexier when Connor pushes his sleeves up, and not just because he has tattoos relating to everything from his wins to his childhood on his body. My favourite is the map of the Silverstone racetrack on his bicep. It was the first race he won in Formula One. Since our truce, I've googled him a couple of times, and I may have languished over a semi-nude shoot.

"You okay, Sen? You're red," Jacs says.

I choke on my breath before stuttering, "It's June, and we're in Spain at a racetrack, and I'm dressed for business."

"Someone, get this woman a handheld fan, please," Jacs shouts across the garage.

My assistant, Jimmy, appears with three fans. He's feeling guilty because I told him not to gossip with anyone about me. He's apologised every day since. I explained there was a positive, as it helped bring a truce between me and

117

Connor. He's still been attentive as hell, though. He doesn't usually join me at races, but his development is important.

"Thank you, Jimmy," I reply. He nods sheepishly and walks away.

I turn one of the battery-operated fans on, catching a glimpse of my scar. It's still something I hate and am ashamed of. I could have been an F1 driver and made my dad proud. Guilt creeps up on me for making that truce with Connor and enjoying his semi-nude photo shoot. Why hasn't he apologised for the crash? He's always attempted to justify his actions. My head tells me that he ruined my life, but my heart wants to believe that everything he's said is true and that he looks after others no matter the consequences.

When my heart ruled me, I bought a fluffy toy for him that resembled Coults. He's probably ditched it, thinking a fan left it for him. No one needs to know I slept with it a few nights before leaving it anonymously at reception.

"Watch this," Jacs says, nudging me.

On-screen, the team are lined up on the grid before the race. As it's a sweltering day, the drivers are getting into the cars while covered by umbrellas. I catch Antoine talking to another driver. He mouths the word *crasher*. The other driver, Antoine's friend in those days when we raced together, throws his head back and laughs.

"That little shit. What's he saying about me?"

Jac shakes her head. "I wasn't sure whether to tell you that a couple of my team have said they've caught him talking shit about you. He always shuts up when my team walks in."

I rub my scar more roughly now. That punk. He's not my best driver. Although neither has reached the podium, Connor consistently beats him in every race.

"That's not what I wanted to show you, though."

She points at the screen where Connor is about to enter the car. The umbrella partially hides him, but the camera angle shows enough of his face and side. He blinks five times and then starts spinning. I lean into the screen and count the spins. Then, he taps his left hand on his right leg five times. The umbrella hides his movement, but from how his right arm crosses his body, I suspect he's doing the same to his left leg. Then he shakes his head five times and gets in the car.

"What is he doing?"

"I don't know. But he only allows Silas near him before races. Do you want to chat to him?" Jacs points her thumb towards Silas, who looks at anything but us.

I call him over.

"Silas, please explain what's happening here," I ask as I rewind the footage, and we watch it together.

He stares at the screen, unsurprised by what he's seeing, before lifting his head to the garage ceiling. I fix my stare on him, waiting for him to make eye contact, but he doesn't. "It's a normal pre-race tradition," he squeaks.

"Try again, and I want the truth," I continue my stare, challenging him to meet my gaze.

"Antoine, another excellent result," my dad shouts so loudly it filters into the garage. Another situation I need to deal with. "Well done, Dane," he says with much less energy. For fuck's sake. The issues keep coming. Connor is our best driver, even better than Niki, and could help make this team great again. It's time my dad treated him with respect.

Silas's shoulders tighten when Connor enters the garage. He lowers his voice. "He does it before every qualifying race and grand prix race. I don't know why. It

started with the blinking, but since Australia, it's worse. He swore me to secrecy." Silas blusters through his explanation. "You can't tell him I said anything."

I've seen drivers with their rituals before—hell, I had my own—but the number of things he's doing and the escalation have me clicking my teeth.

"I won't. Thank you for telling me," I reply. "You can go."

Connor stares at the three of us, including a jittery Silas. His brows furrow as Silas rushes past him, not stopping to congratulate him on his race.

My dad and all his friends praise Antoine, but he makes a beeline for me. Who do I deal with first? Although both men need speaking to in a private space and probably not today, I sense them watching me.

"Ma belle," Antoine says, and instead of the fake smile I usually respond with, I glare and grind my teeth. "Your dad invited me to dinner with you, him, and his friends to celebrate my driving."

Before I can tell my dad no, Antoine brushes my ponytail, making it swing.

I flinch away from him as Connor barges into the group.

"Leave her alone, Antoine. I've told you not to touch her," he shouts, grabbing his collar.

"Leave him, Dane. You always were a liability," my dad grumbles. Connor tightens his grip on a flustered Antoine. As much as it's nice to see Antoine managed, I can't have a scene in my garage.

"I can handle this," I snap at my dad and Connor. I shake my head, exhausted at men constantly needing to undermine my authority. "Let go of him."

Connor's mouth drops like I've betrayed him as he pulls his hands away. They hang by his sides.

START YOUR ENGINES

"Guys, take a look around the garage. I need to speak to my little girl," my dad says to his visitors. I throw my headphones down as the men walk away. They stare at me over their shoulders and smirk.

"I'm not your little girl. I run this damn team." I fist my hands.

Connor's eye twitches as he stares. Jacs eases back, leaving the situation to me.

"You're still my—"

I turn to Antoine. "I want you in my office on Tuesday at nine am. And if you ever touch me again, you'll be out of this team before you call me or any of the women here belle again." I catch Connor's glance. "I won't be going to dinner with my dad. I have a job to do that doesn't include having dinner with my drivers."

"Unless it's Connor and pizza," Antoine mumbles.

The bullshit I have to deal with. I glare at Connor, who shrugs. I can't trust anyone.

"Get out, Antoine, before I do something we both regret. Tuesday morning in my office." I dismiss him with a wave of my hand.

"Jumps," my dad says, imploring me to change my mind. Antoine smirks before he turns.

"Don't call me that," I snap, turning on my dad.

He holds his hands up in surrender. "But it was funny when you used to jump the lights. Forgive me. After all, you've eaten dinner with Connor, so you've forgiven him."

I turn to Connor. "I can't believe you told Antoine. He's telling everyone."

Connor steps closer. "I didn't—"

"There are too many egos in here. I'm out." I walk across the garage.

"Senna," my dad says. I recognise his tone, but he's not

121

the boss anymore, neither of the team nor me.

"Leave it, Dad. Go for dinner and schmooze your friends. Talk about how brilliant you made this team and not the mistakes you left me to clean up."

His jaw hits the floor, and his ears turn bright red. No one calls my dad out, and I hate that I'm already planning how to smooth things over later with a call and apology.

"And Dane, be in my office on Tuesday at ten," I snap.

CHAPTER EIGHTEEN – CONNOR

I check my watch. It's 9:45. So what if I arrived at the offices a little early in case Senna needed my help with Antoine? Since the Spanish Grand Prix on Sunday, I've replayed the awkwardness with Senna in the garage. There was so much I didn't get to say.

Jimmy tells me Senna is still in a meeting, but where's Antoine's familiar peacocking?

Maybe she has another driver in there, and she's replacing me because I'm too much trouble.

I lean to the side, but my view is restricted.

I fiddle with my phone, pretending to check my socials, but my attention is on Senna's office. My reflection from the glass confronts me: tired eyes, ruffled hair hidden with my cap, and my team hoodie.

My stomach churns, and sweat beads my forehead. Part of me wants to be fired. It means no more driving and dealing with anxiety-induced insomnia. I don't love driving like I used to, and I perform various rituals at every race to prevent accidents. Then, I spend the rest of the race seeing hazards that aren't there. I'm not safe to drive, but no one realises it because I'm performing well.

But then there's the other thing. If she fires me, I won't be able to spend time with her anymore. I want to be more

123

than friends, but that can't happen. I must protect her, though.

"Is Antoine still with her?" I ask Jimmy, whose head remains buried in his computer. "Hey, Jimmy. Is Antoine still with her?" I ask a little louder.

"I'm not talking to you. You got me in trouble when you overheard me discussing her dinner habits." He side-eyes me as I step up to the desk.

"I'm sorry about that. I want to make sure Senna is looked after. I didn't mean to cause problems for you." His mouth drops open as he furrows his brow. "What?"

"You apologised."

I turn my hands up.

"So?"

"You never apologise. Everyone knows that. When you mess up, you shrug and walk away. You never apologise."

"I'm sure that's not tru—"

"Like never ever," Jimmy replies, his voice slightly louder.

I roll my shoulders. Of course I apologise, like that time when Senna got hurt. I run through the things I said to her. When I did it recently, maybe I dived straight into explaining myself...

Shit. I've never apologised.

"I'm apologising now. I'm sorry for getting you in trouble, and I want to say thank you for caring for Senna like you do and making sure she eats breakfast and lunch. Has she been receiving the dinners I've sent to her office in the evenings?"

"Yeah. I've worked late a few nights, and they arrived while I was leaving. She paces when they're due and then beams and eats everything immediately. I've told her it's not me, but she thanked me anyway."

124

The corner of my mouth turns up. "Let's keep it our secret."

Jimmy nods. He cocks his head. "Where's the real Connor Dane, and what did you do with him?"

I twist my mouth to the side. I am different, but I can't tell him why.

"Antoine left after she shouted at him for fifteen minutes. He threw a tantrum and kicked over a potted plant. Senna helped me tidy up."

My chuckle causes a wry smile from Jimmy. "A potted plant? He's so badass."

Jimmy laughs. "It was hilarious. The first time, he missed and nearly fell over. Then he threw his designer jacket across the room—"

Senna opens her door and glares at Jimmy. "Get in here now, Dane. And, Jimmy, what have I told you about discussing my business?"

I hold up my hands in surrender. "Senna, he—"

I stop as soon as I see her outfit. The cream dress is tailored to her curves. The material stretches over her hips. I want to spend time with those curvaceous hips. The dress dips slightly in a V-neck, and there is a belt around her waist that I want to grab and drag her closer to me. Her heels are the turquoise of the team's colours.

I turn back to Jimmy to compose myself and to remind my cock not to get the wrong idea. "Take care, Jimmy." My mouth is so dry it sounds like I've just woken up.

"Hurry up, Dane."

As I stride into her office, my stomach churns again. I take a breath as I face the door. I must remain professional even if I'm torn between bending her over her desk and pushing that dress up or finding Antoine and beating him with a plant pot.

I pull on the back of my neck and flip my cap backwards, remembering I'm here to protect her. Niki would kill me if he knew what I was thinking about her and that damn desk.

"Connor?" Her voice is a little softer.

She used my first name. She hasn't used it like that since I was eighteen.

I sigh and turn, holding my hands up in surrender. "Before you fire me, I want to say—"

"I'm not firing you." Her blank tone and wide eyes confuse me.

"Did you fire Antoine?"

She perches on the edge of her desk. I get a flash of getting on my knees and pushing up the hem of her dress. I should stop sleeping with the soft toy that smells of her. My dreams are like pornos.

"I'm not firing anyone yet, and my conversation with Antoine isn't your concern."

I scratch my chin. Material rustles. My eyes flicker to the corner of the room, where a stranger tracks my movements. I was too distracted to see him before. He better not be who she dressed up for today.

"Who are you?" I say frostily. He doesn't respond, and the churning in my stomach turns so fiery I tighten my stomach muscles. I flip my attention back to Senna. "Who is he, and why is he staring at me like that?"

Please don't say another friend with benefits. I don't want to meet another one.

I peg him as late thirties. He's got a young George Clooney thing going on—all piercing dark eyes, chiselled jaw, and casual stance. The stranger is another guy with noticeable gym-built muscles.

I bristle and then internally shout at myself for bristling.

"He's here to help you."

START YOUR ENGINES

"What?" I push up my sleeves, and Senna tracks the move. I grit my teeth. I'm seeing what I want to see. "What do I need help for? My only problem is my sex drought, and he's not my type."

Senna folds her arms across her chest. All she succeeds in is pushing up her breasts. My nostrils flare. I know exactly how I'd like to work through my sex drought.

"He's a sports psychologist. I've seen your pre-race rituals. They look like obsessions."

"It's under control," I snap, my eyes pinched and mouth tight. My face burns with shame. "I'm not discussing anything with a sports psychologist. Especially not that one." I point my thumb in the direction of the stranger.

"Why not hi—" Senna sighs and shakes her head. "Ric, could you leave Connor and me to talk? I'll call you."

Ric nods. He steps closer to me, and I pull back. "Connor, it's nothing to be ashamed of. You're not the first elite sportsman to perform rituals. But I want the reasons behind them in case they're symptomatic of conditions that affect your performance and safety on the track. I can help you."

I stare Ric down.

"Bye, Senna," Ric says before leaving.

The door clicks closed behind him, and Senna and I are left standing a few metres apart. I keep my eyes focused on hers. I need a distraction from this moment, but I can't let it be her incredible body.

"Is he another one of your 'buddies'?" I regret the words as soon as they're out of my mouth.

She walks behind her desk and sits down in her chair.

My head drops, and I plop into one of her chairs. I should leave before I say anything else stupid, but part of me is desperate to tell her about the rituals and their

127

reasons.

"Why are you still with the team, Dane?"

I hold back my sad sigh. She's stopped calling me Connor.

"You know your brother has me in a water-tight contract."

She presses her fingertips together and creates a bridge with her hands. "I could break that contract and pay you off so you can leave. You'd never have to see me or this team again."

"Is that what you want?"

She rubs her scar, and I want to rip her fingers away from it. It's like a dagger in my throat. Does she understand how deeply it hurts me every time she does that?

"Do you want me out of your life for good?" I growl.

She pushes her fingers through her hair. I want those short blond waves in my hands.

Now she knows my rituals, my thoughts are jumbling. She remains silent.

"Fine, I'll leave because you clearly don't want me here anymore."

I start towards the door. The burning sensation in my chest tells me to go, but Jimmy's words about how I don't apologise have me turning back.

"Ten years ago, when I visited you at home after the crash, I was so adamant that I had to tell you what happened that I didn't say sorry. I've never said sorry." I swallow loudly, waiting for her to tell me to get out, but she looks at me with eyes wide enough for me to drown in. "I never meant to hurt you, Senna, but I did. I destroyed your racing career. You were the best driver, way better than Niki, me, and all those guys who went on to have F1 careers. I ruined that for you, and I am so sorry. I wish I'd told you this before.

START YOUR ENGINES

I'm more sorry about that day and the way I was after than you can ever imagine."

For the first time, I don't attempt to explain what happened or tell her it wasn't my fault.

I stand by the door, my face against the glass, although my words are aimed at her. "I've got some things to do in the garage. I want to speak to Jacs about one of the car's problems. But I'll be gone by the end of the day and you'll never have to see me again. I'm sorry for everything, Senna."

"Connor, wait." She touches my forearm, and her fingers burn my skin. I didn't hear her walk over to me. She's probably not wearing her shoes. It's one of those cute things she does.

I turn, and she's standing so close. The scent of orange blossom fills my lungs. But I can't wait a second longer.

"Goodbye, Coults."

I look at her standing at the edge of her office one last time. I'm sure her stare will haunt me in my dreams.

CHAPTER NINETEEN – SENNA

Connor walked out of my office nine hours ago. I should have asked him to stay.

For the first time, he apologised without justifying what happened or giving excuses. He gave the most honest and raw apology, and I still didn't ask him to stay.

As he sat in my office, dejected and vulnerable, I accepted that my feelings for him when he was younger never disappeared, and in my heart, I forgave him. That's why I wanted him gone: having the man who's remained deep in my heart and featured in virtually every fantasy I've had in the last three months working under me for the rest of the season isn't helpful or wise. I can't control myself around him, and even though I don't know the truth about what happened that day, I've let him in over the last months. My judgement is fucked when he's involved. I've been able to manage my emotions over the years. If I let him back in, I'll be a team boss ruled by others and not in control. I need to be in control like my dad was.

I can't get hurt by him again.

I thumb through the messages Jimmy left on my desk. I ate the dinner delivered early evening, as always, and I changed into my shorts and hoodie like I've done every evening since Connor last visited in the hope he'd gaze at my legs like he did that night he brought me pizza.

He's not coming back. I should search for another driver and sort out his contract, yet I'm sitting here remembering how his forearms felt under my fingers.

I check my phone. My screen shows a voicemail from Ralf. It might distract me.

"Little boss, I'm sorry I couldn't reach you. There's something you should know. I looked into those investors your dad had with him in Spain. There is a rumour that they're potential buyers. I'm so sorry. Leave this with me, and I shall see what I find out."

Betrayal stings my throat. Why does Dad always let me down?

I need to do the only thing that stopped me from overthinking when I had no other options.

I shove on my trainers and head to the garage. I need to get my hands dirty and listen to pop music while I spend a couple of hours deep in the engine of a crappy car I make my team keep.

The lights in the garage are on. I grumble as I walk through the space. It smells of oil and fuel, and I breathe it in: the scent of my teenage years, of laughing with Niki as we tinkered on whatever car we were allowed to play with. I'd hang out with Uncle Ralf as he told me about all the different parts of the engine and how to use that knowledge to maximise performance.

I miss racing sometimes, but I love the backstage stuff, too. I love working with something to make it brilliant. Now, the engine I'm working with is the entire company.

Soon, I won't have anything.

Connor's deep voice rises and drops as he sings to Lewis Capaldi's "Someone You Loved." My heart beats faster. He hasn't left yet.

I listen and immerse myself in the words. His local

accent is gravelly, and he keeps missing the T at the end of words. As his singing fills my body, I hold onto the moment tightly. This is the Connor I remember—the guy who bares his soul when he sings. As the song finishes, I debate whether to disappear without saying hello. He wants to leave the team, and I shouldn't stop him.

"I know you're there, Sen," he says, his face peeking out from behind the raised bonnet of my banger. "Please stay."

Again, that rare vulnerability. When we were younger, he hoped his dad was watching him race before realising he was distracted by a pretty woman, and he'd keep up the banter. But sometimes, when I joined him and Niki karting at night, he'd show crumbs of sadness.

"Okay," I reply, stepping closer.

"I'm having a problem. Please help."

He points at the engine, and we work on it to a playlist of chilled tunes.

As we work, I breathe in his woodsy smell that lingers whenever he leaves my office. I want to smooth the lines on his forehead away. The smudge of oil on his cheek highlights cheekbones I long to touch. When I last spent time with him like this, he was a boy, but now he is all man. Occasionally, our hands touch, or we get in each other's space.

Eventually, when I can't take it anymore, I say, "I'm surprised you're still here."

He shrugs. "I got a bit caught up with this. But don't worry, I'll be out of your way soon."

"Please don't go." I can't look at him as I say it, fearing he'll see emotions that have bubbled to the surface since we ate together. Watching him perform his rituals before the race has only sharpened them. I want to help him, and not just because I'm his boss. "The team needs you." He doesn't respond, and I share my truth. "I need you."

132

START YOUR ENGINES

"Okay. I'll stay." His voice is husky. "For you."

My heart jumps. "Thanks. Although I might not be the boss for much longer."

He continues tinkering, which makes it easier to talk. It's as if avoiding eye contact quiets the tension that usually fills our conversations. "How come? You're doing a brilliant job, considering the egos of your two drivers, especially this one."

I chuckle. "You got that right." I sigh, and the humour drops. "Uncle Ralf left me a message. The men with Dad on Sunday might have been potential buyers. I thought he was finding investors, but I suspect that since I took over the team, he's only searched for buyers."

"Son of a bitch. Sorry." He rushes through his words. "The reason the team is on a shoestring is because of him. You're doing everything possible to make it brilliant, and we're doing well. We're eighth in the Constructor's Championship. That's amazing, especially considering everyone has double the money we do."

Pride fills my chest, and I stand a little taller. It's what I've wanted to believe, but imposter syndrome told me otherwise.

"It's a team effort," I mumble.

Connor puts his hands on my shoulders and turns me to face him. "And it's your team. We wouldn't work anywhere near as well as we do without you. Your dad is lucky to have you. We all are."

I blush and offer him a grateful smile. His eyes implore me to believe him, and I do. For the first time that day, I tell myself I can do this.

"Thank goodness I'm not wearing my cream dress. You'd have covered it in grime." I laugh.

His eyes rake my body from my hoodie down my legs

133

and back up. His stare sets every inch of my body on fire. It will be vibrator o'clock whenever I get home.

"Yeah," he replies with a raspy voice before letting go. "I'd have hated to make you dirty."

A spark of desire pierces my belly. I count slowly to ten before we continue working on the car.

Connor says, "I should get help. You can achieve greatness with this team, and I don't want to be one of the things that stops that."

I hold my tongue.

"This is where you say you'll give me the number of Ric the di—" He's smiling, but I avoid his gaze. He coughs and corrects himself. "I mean Ric, the sports psychologist."

"I'll do that." I take a deep breath, but even with the extra seconds of contemplation, I still say, "And I wouldn't know about his dick. I've never slept with the guy. I chatted with him when I considered returning to racing in my early twenties."

"Cool." Again, I sense he's smiling. "I'll call him, although I'm nervous about sharing my deepest fears with a stranger."

I'm waiting for Connor's catch. When the silence extends longer, I say, "I get that. It took me a long time to deal with my shit. Talking with him helped me understand that my love of racing was partly because I adored being with the two men who meant the world to me and winning."

"Your dad and Niki?" he asks tentatively.

I hip bump him. "*You* and Niki. You two meant the world to me."

"Cool," he says again, sweeping his hand through his fluffy hair. A half smile ghosts his lips, but it disappears as he clears his throat. "I don't love driving like I used to. It was the only thing that brought me energy. Fuck, the highs were

higher than anything I've ever experienced."

"What changed?" I ask casually, although my heart speeds because he's opening up.

"Niki's crash," he replies flatly. "I'm scared I'll have an accident, a nasty one that will break me for good. So I do the rituals. I'm terrified something bad will happen if I stop them."

I'll do everything I can to help him love driving again. But I need to work out how. I can't help with the obsessive-compulsive aspect—that's for Ric to manage—but I can help with the driving. There's a pain in my chest from knowing all he's gone through, and tears brim my eyes. I swipe them away, pretending to wipe sweat from my brow.

"Thank you for telling me about it. It means a lot."

We continue to work in silence, but it doesn't bring me the calm I need. I debate asking him the question that has plagued me for years—the one Niki refuses to answer, that could hurt me beyond reason. My breathing accelerates, and I grip the car against the dizziness.

I can't hold it in anymore, because helping him means spending time with him.

I blurt out, "What happened the day of my crash? What have you tried to tell me? I need to know."

CHAPTER TWENTY – CONNOR

I close my eyes and wince before swallowing the lump that's lodged in my throat. It's like having tonsilitis and eating a chunk of bread. It won't go down, no matter how often I swallow.

But she needs to know. She deserves to know.

"Don't worry. It's okay," Senna says, pulling off her gloves. She walks away, but I'm behind her instantly, yanking off my gloves.

I turn her to face me. I choke at the redness of her eyes. I take her hand and lead her to the edge of the room. I lay down paper to protect our clothes and pull her to the floor to sit propped against a wall. Goosebumps cover my skin from her body against mine, but I don't let go. As we sit side by side, I smooth my thumb over her skin.

I turn the music off, and we sit in silence.

"I will explain." I count to five as I breathe in and to five again as I let it out. "Just give me a second." I continue to smooth her hand with my thumb.

She nudges my knee with hers. "It's going to be okay, Connor."

I furrow my brow. "That day, I didn't mean to hurt you. I was trying to protect you."

"From who?" she whispers, as if an invisible enemy can

136

hear us.

"The other lads."

"Oh."

I look at her beneath my dark eyelashes. Her face stills. I snag air with a deep breath.

"I was trying to stop a particular group of drivers from hurting you. They'd planned to get in front of you and brake, making you total your car and scare you into never driving again."

She trembles, and I don't let go.

"Why?" It's more like a gasp than a word.

"Because no one wants to be beaten by a girl – well, not no one. Me and Niki always grumbled when you won, but it's always better to be beaten by the best, and you were. But those bastards hated you. It sounds ridiculous. Niki and I were the oldest ones racing in that championship. I was looking to move to Formula Two, but secretly didn't want to go because I wanted to protect you."

She turns to face me. Her eyes are wide. I want to cup her cheek and assure her it doesn't matter, but she needs to know.

"The boys in that group talked shit about you. You know how hard it was to be a female racer. You told us about it whenever we talked about our crap days." I give a hollow chuckle at the memory. "But it was worse than you knew."

She gulps air, but I continue. "Every second Niki and I spent with them when you weren't around, they told sexist jokes and made misogynistic comments. They were in a gang, egging each other on to be the worst versions of themselves. We tried talking to officials about it, but they said it was the heat of competition. One guy said, 'All's fair in racing,' but it wasn't. Not for you."

"My dad said the same. It was like a racing mantra. And

it was a different time. There were no women bosses, barely any women racing, and few high up in race control. We still had grid girls."

She's so animated, her shoulders tight, and she gesticulates with her spare hand.

"But that doesn't make it okay." She's fought harder than every racer out there trying to give other women a chance, not that she'll admit that.

"I know. We still don't have a woman driver in Formula One, but I hope to change that one day if I keep my job." She settles back down against the wall. "Why did they hurt me that day?"

I thumb her hand as I talk. "They'd talk about doing it every race, but with Niki and me protecting you, they never got close. A lot of it was talk. Not that it makes it forgivable."

She grunts in agreement.

"But that day, Niki couldn't race because he was ill." The night before, I'd watched her sleep next to me through a movie and wanted to kiss her. I was happy Niki wasn't with us then, but everything would have been different if he'd raced that day. "I overheard them talking about how it was their chance because I couldn't protect you alone, especially as I needed to win that race for my future. Lapoire was scouting me, and I believed that signing with them would help my family. I tried to protect you anyway and keep everyone at bay."

She leans against my shoulder. Her hair brushes my chin. Every word is essential, but I want to stay like this, keeping my secret and stopping her from hearing the truth. I close my eyes and run my finger against the scar. She shivers.

"They said on the twelfth lap, on Gutter Corner, the driver in front of you, Slater, would slow so it held you up

and another one would sneak up the inside, push you wide, and it would slam you into the tyre barrier."

She gasps. "I could have been seriously injured."

"You were, and it was my fault." I drop my head. "Knowing what was happening, I tried to keep you on a tighter line as we came up to the corner so you weren't behind Slater, but instead of saving you, I oversteered and nudged you. You careered into the wall, crashing and smashing your hand. You never raced again. It was all my fault."

Bile rises in my throat as I wait for her to walk away, but instead, she cups my face between her hands, lifting it. I stare into her hazel eyes, expecting to see them tight as colour flares through them, but instead, she blinks softly. They're deep hazel brown.

"You were trying to save me," she says.

"But—"

"No, Connor," she says firmer. "Those bastards could have seriously hurt me, and you tried to save me. It went horribly wrong, but that wasn't your fault. I remember you tried speaking to me before the start of the race, but I was too busy smack-talking. Did you try to tell my dad or an official?"

I close my eyes and nod. "Both."

"Look at me," she demands, and I do. Tears sit in the corner of her eyes. "You did everything possible and then had to get involved yourself. It was the only thing left for you to do, and it backfired. Instead of listening to you, I believed the same lads who'd taunted me. When they said you'd hurt me to win and be signed, and then you were signed, I thought the worst of you. My trauma was no excuse. I knew you. I should have trusted you."

A tear trickles down her cheek.

My face drops at the memory of when I attempted to speak to her at her house. "You thought you'd never race again. You were grieving because everything you'd planned for your life was ripped from you. It's understandable. I should have come to you at the hospital, but I was scared, and your dad told me I wasn't allowed. I only came to the house that time because Niki told me he could sneak me in. I had minutes to explain what happened. I still should have apologised instead of blaming others."

She pulls her hands away from my face and tucks herself into me. Her orange blossom scent teases my nose. "We made mistakes. I hate how I treated you. You were my best friend, my…" I wait for her to continue, but she doesn't. "I should have let you speak. I'm sorry, Connor. I'm so sorry."

I wrap my arm around her and hold her close.

"I'm sorry, too, Coults." Her body is warm against mine. The concrete floor makes my butt sore, but I won't move. "I should have tried again, but your dad told me never to go near you again, and I was scared that he'd find a way to stop Niki from being my friend. Dad left, and I couldn't lose Niki, either."

"Connor, I told you I hated your guts and that you were dead to me."

"I remember." I shake my head. "But it wasn't just that. From then I vowed to be the best so that my dad saw what he'd lost out on. Trying to be back in your world just made me feel so guilty that, in the end, I chose Niki and being a success over you when, instead, I should have apologised and made things right. I owe you, not just for the accident, but for how I've acted since."

"You don't owe me anything. I'm sorry that my dad treated you like that. I had no idea. It was no coincidence that Niki signed you as soon as he wasn't in charge. You

START YOUR ENGINES

were—you are—the best driver, and yet Dad never wanted you on our family team."

"He told me once that I was an exceptional driver, but it wasn't enough. I don't think he liked how a poor kid was so close to his darlings."

She bangs her fist on the floor. "How ironic that the man who tells me to be more professional is ruled by his prejudices."

I drop my head to her shoulder. I want to kiss her forehead and tell her it's all okay, but that won't help. "Your dad stopped funding me after the crash, but thankfully, I was signed to Lapoire. Everything was happening for me, but I lost you."

"You didn't lose me. We just took a timeout," she says with a half-smile.

"So you're not going to fire me again, even after hearing that story?"

She chuckles, and it makes my heart flush. "I wouldn't dare—well, not for that reason. I make no promises for any other reason. So that's everything?"

Everything but that I fell in love with you at eighteen, the driver who planned to knock you off was Antoine, and your brother is desperate for me to protect you.

"Yeah, that's all of it," I reply as she stretches her legs and waggles them.

"Pins and needles," she explains. "I'd best get back. I have a few things to sort out before I go home."

I resist the temptation to hold her close and stop her from ever walking away from me again. "I should probably get home and rest."

"Good plan. Catch you later." She stands and shakes her body out. She stares at me from above, and for a heartbeat, I imagine asking her if I can sit with her while she

141

works or if she wants to get coffee. But I'm not that guy to her and never will be.

"Bye then," I say with false cheer as her long legs carry her away.

CHAPTER TWENTY-ONE – SENNA

Connor didn't do it to hurt me.

I slide my key in the lock of my parent's house. I need to confront my dad even though Ralf said I shouldn't. Or maybe I just don't want to be alone after speaking to Connor.

"Hello," I call out. My voice echoes around me as my feet hit the marble floor. I should have called. I never pop by unannounced.

An aerial photo of Silverstone takes pride of place on the wall. Next to it is a photo from Dad's first team win. It's all smiles and cheering faces, although the darkness under the eyes of my dad and his team reveals the sacrifices to get there.

"Senna? Is that you?" Mum calls, and a warmth fills my heart.

I make my way to the snug beside the kitchen.

"What are you doing here?" she asks as I walk over and kiss her forehead. "Oh, none of that. I want a proper hug."

She grabs me tightly like she senses something isn't right.

Mums always know.

"I wanted to say hello, and I haven't visited recently."

She raises an eyebrow but doesn't say more. "Have you

eaten?"

I dismiss the question with a wave of my hand as I stare at the photos lining the fireplace. One of Niki and Uncle Ralf, laughing, sits beside a selfie from my graduation. Mum is beaming as she holds my hand, and I'm waving my certificate. I love that photo of me and Mum, but it reminds me that Dad didn't attend because he was in Austria watching Niki race.

"Let me get you a tiny bowl of pasta," she replies with a smile. "And before you say no, I've got leftovers because I made enough for two, but I forgot your dad was out tonight. Come with me."

I follow her into the kitchen and perch on one of the bar seats as she prepares me a dish of ravioli, my second dinner and exactly what I need after Connor's revelations.

"It's spinach and feta. I've been trying to reduce his meat intake since the heart attack. No doubt he'll eat steak with Jean tonight, the silly man."

She pops it in front of me, and my mouth waters instantly. "Jean? Antoine's dad?"

"Yes, he's in town. I'm not keen on him, but I can't control who your dad sees. As long as I don't have to see him."

I drop a piece of ravioli into my mouth as she busies herself around the kitchen. The creamy feta bursts on my tongue.

"Why don't you like him?"

"He always liked to get his own way and didn't care who he hurt to do so," she says, making herself a tea. "I remember the dads around the track when you were a teenager. Connor's dad was just as bad, although he tended to spend his time chatting up the mums."

I raise my eyebrows.

START YOUR ENGINES

"Not me. I was always very clear. He didn't care enough for his son, who deserved more. Jean, on the other hand, was an arrogant arse, and Antoine was just as bad."

I sit back in my seat. Mum must have been drinking because her tongue is looser than normal.

I think to what Connor said about the boys bullying me before the accident. Antoine was one of those. "Mum, do you remember my accident?"

She looks up from the kettle. "Every day of my life."

"I heard something about it, and although I believe it, I'm struggling to process it. I've spent my life thinking one thing, but what if I was wrong?" I rub my scar until she clocks the action.

She joins me at the counter, sitting at the table with a sigh. "Do you want to tell me what it is?"

"Do you promise not to get angry or take sides?"

Her crow's feet disappear as her eyes soften. "Senna, the only side I'll ever take is the one involving this family. You are my girl, and your mind is full. You've rubbed your scar too many times since arriving. Tell me what's happening in that head of yours."

My dad taught me to be strong and that relying on others shows weakness. I grip my fork tightly instead of taking her hand.

"Connor told me he tried to look after me because boys were bullying me, but then he accidentally hurt me." I chase the last bit of pasta around my bowl with my fork, but I can't avoid my mum's raised eyebrows as she waits for me to say what I'm struggling with. "I've hated him for years, and I shouldn't have. He was doing something good, and I banished him from my life. I don't know how to be around him or how to apologise for ostracising him from our family."

145

She cups my face. "Sweetheart, that wasn't just you; your dad and I are to blame for that, too. Niki was the only one on his side. Connor was a good kid, albeit headstrong at times, but then you have to be if you want to be a racing winner, especially when you're not brought up in the industry or with money like you and Niki were. Trusting him in both your heart and your head will take time."

I sigh and rest my head in her palm. "I don't know how I do that."

"My girl doesn't know how to let her best friend back into her life?"

I shrug. Maybe I don't know how to do it without falling in love with him again.

"There's more, isn't there?" she asks, blowing on her tea.

"There's lots. But one thing stuck with me as I drove here. What if one of the people Connor was trying to save me from is Antoine? Do you think he would have done that?"

My mum looks to the ceiling. "It's possible. But he won't admit it to you. If he's like his dad, he sees it as a success. I'm sorry I didn't protect you better when you were racing. Your dad told me that you needed to be tough and face battles alone." She locks eyes with me. "I should have stepped in before it was too late."

I rush around the counter and hug her tightly. "It wasn't your fault, or Connor's. Let's not blame the wrong people anymore. I need to work out how to make things better. I love you, Mum."

"I love you too." She hugs me so hard I can't breathe.

"I'm going before Dad comes home. I need to keep processing without his opinion getting in the way." I extract myself from her mama bear grip. "And I've got Silverstone

START YOUR ENGINES

in a couple of weeks and need to make sure we can be contencers at our home Grand Prix."

As I reach the door, she says, "Don't work too hard."

I smile back at her. She knows better than anyone that a team boss will always work too hard.

"And don't keep thinking you're alone in this. Drop by anytime for a chat."

"Okay."

But I won't.

I've listened to too many people over the last years, and maybe if I hadn't been so pig-headed and believed the worst about Connor, I wouldn't have lost his friendship. I need to do this alone. Dad was right about the life of a racing driver facing battles alone. That stretches into the life of a team boss.

No one can bring success to this team but me.

Chapter Twenty-Two – Senna

Connor jumps out of his car and bounces towards the cheering pit crew hanging over the barrier.

"P3!" they shout, and I watch the screen with a beaming smile.

Connor came third in front of a home crowd at Silverstone. It's his first podium with us and the first podium we've had in nearly two years.

Jacs stands by me. On-screen, Connor springs up and down the asphalt.

"He needed this," I say, unable to pull my gaze from his joy radiating off the screen. He earned every lap and pushed the car to do what was once impossible.

"We all needed it," Jacs replies.

I nod. Watching him bounce and beam makes my body flutter like a million butterflies have gotten loose in my chest. I've barely thought of anything else since he admitted what happened when we were young. We've lost years of friendship, but maybe there's a chance for a new friendship.

Antoine limps across the finish line, grumbling on the radio that Connor tapped him and got the podium Antoine deserves. None of us pander to it. Connor raced fairly.

I couldn't grin harder as Connor swaggers to the interviewer.

"We need to go out tonight and celebrate," Jacs adds.

START YOUR ENGINES

Connor beams during his television interview with five-time championship winner Petre Piaf. I used to have the biggest crush on Petre, and yet, as Connor fluffs his hair and his eyes dance, he's all I see. I bite the inside of my mouth as I remember some of the fantasies I've played out in my head this week while trying to sleep. When he puts a cap on backwards, I tap my fingers restlessly against my thighs. I want him, but I can't have him. I'm his boss. The only female team boss. I need to make strides for women, not fall for the bad boy on my team.

I would be a laughing stock, and my dad wouldn't forgive me.

And Niki would freak out.

Connor answers Petre's question about the car. "I want to thank everyone back at the factory for today. It's a team effort. They're doing great things with the car. It's impossible not to do well when you have a car like this."

Jacs giggles. I shake my head and cover my smile with my hand. Did he have to get a dig in about Antoine's performance? That's going to piss him off. But Connor has a point.

"There was unrest in the offices recently. One rumour was that you were fired."

"I'm fully in. Boss Coulter has believed in me since I joined the team, and I wouldn't be on the podium without her. She's the best team boss I've ever had."

My skin flushes at his words and how his big blue eyes stare into the camera as he licks his lips. It doesn't mean anything, and he's an arse, but I still find myself rubbing my fingers together at the memory of holding his face between my hands.

"So what do you say?" Jacs asks.

"Huh?" I turn to her, still side-eyeing the interview. My

149

stomach flips as I stare at Connor's baby blues and smug grin.

"We need to celebrate tonight. We could go to a bar or go dancing. I'll ask my sister. She won the F2 race earlier, and she's always up for a night out. You're coming, right?" I nod absentmindedly as Connor winks at the camera. My neck tingles. "Awesome. I'll let the crew know. Now, let's get to the trophy podium ceremony."

I remind myself not to become mesmerised by Connor's face or the way he'll have champagne poured over him by competitors as I grab my phone. I'll be wholly professional, and there will be no sign of my swirling emotions.

Jacs babbles as she waits for me, "I'll get Jimmy to book us hotel rooms in London where the other teams are staying. I'll let Connor know once he's finished. He'll totally be up for it."

She's right. He'll definitely want to come, and I've already agreed, so I can't get out of it. It's just a work night out. Nothing can happen.

My stomach flips again, and my mouth goes dry as scenarios play on a loop.

I arrive late to the bar.

Since the race, I've endured meetings with Antoine and his dad about putting Antoine first, spending more on his training and not allowing "that boy Connor to disrupt Antoine's career, or else." Threats mean nothing to me, but it left me overthinking how I need to go this alone and remain professional with Connor.

I yank down the hem of the slinky silver dress Jacs left

START YOUR ENGINES

for me in my hotel room while I was working. The dress is bad enough, but she's paired it with black heels that are going to destroy my feet.

The bouncers let me in and point me in the direction of the roped-off VIP area. I'm in no rush to get to the group, although I want to congratulate Connor face-to-face. It will be a friendly "well done."

My skin heats at the prospect of being close to him. I stop at the bar and neck a shot of tequila. My driver nearly threw me out of the car when I couldn't stop tapping my feet against the floor. It's just Connor, for goodness sake.

As I step closer to the VIP area, the alcohol giving me the slightest buzz because I'm a lightweight who hasn't had time to eat, I see him. He's wearing black chinos. His long-sleeved grey top clings to his muscles. It's a simple outfit, especially compared to my dress, but I lick my lips. He's speaking with Jacs's sister, Tawny. Her auburn hair falls in waves across her shoulders, and she tucks it back as she listens intently to whatever Connor is saying. I purse my lips as she throws her head back and laughs. Her lips are so full, whereas mine are thin, and she's slim like I was when I raced.

She's also an incredible person. She's raced in Formula Two for nearly four years, yet no team's given her the opportunity to race for them in Formula One. She does things for charity and she's lovely to everyone.

But I want to grab Connor, pull him away from her, and say he's my friend and not hers. It's like I'm five years old and in the sandbox with my Barbie. I shake my head and turn away. I down another shot and walk towards the door, speed-dialling my driver. I shouldn't have come here tonight. I could be at the hotel in thirty minutes with Netflix and junk food.

151

A warming breath caresses my neck.

"Where do you think you're going? I haven't had my 'well-done' hug yet, Coults." I close my eyes and swallow before turning.

It's just Connor, your driver and brother's best friend.

But when I meet his sparkling blue eyes and admire his upturned lips, I'm sucker-punched.

He holds his hand in the air as if to touch my hair before fisting his hand. His dark spice scent is heady, and I lick my lips. He watches my tongue slide over the red lipstick I added in the car.

"Well done," I say, my voice raspy as he stares at my lips. "You did brilliantly."

I lean closer, and he envelopes me in a hug. His hands warm my back, and his spicy aftershave makes my skin burn with possibility. He whispers, "It was all for you, Coults. Thank you for believing in me."

I press against him. My body tingles. He's all muscle, and I can barely resist clinging to him. I'm pulsing with need as he holds me tight. His scent is like a shot of sensuality, and his hum is so deep my toes curl.

Oh shit.

I have a crush on Connor fucking Dane.

CHAPTER TWENTY-THREE – CONNOR

Senna pulls away, and I miss the contact immediately. For the past hour, I've been sitting here, talking and joking with everyone, but my eyes lingered on the door the entire time.

Her dress sparkles under the bar's spotlights. I want to hold her curves while staring at her and taking in everything she is tonight. She shivers, yet I sweat under my long-sleeved T-shirt.

"Are you cold?"

She shakes her head, and her short waves swish around her face. I can't stop staring at her bright red lips, blond waves, tight dress, and black fuck-me heels. But I also want her thoughts on the race. I must have a praise kink with her because I've never cared what my bosses thought before. I know when I'm good, and I drove excellently today. But I want it from her lips. I want her to say my name like it's the best thing she's wrapped her tongue around.

"Did you like the race?" I say, my pulse thrumming in my throat.

A group of girls rush me, and I lose Senna in the crowd.

I search for her over the heads of the women. My heart beats faster. *Please don't let her leave.* I want to chat with her away from work, dance with her, and pull her body against mine.

By the time I've signed various women's arms and

153

chests, I return to our tables. She's sitting in a corner with Antoine. I scratch my forearms under my top. I can't get to her with the wall on one side and Antoine on the other.

I sit close enough to eavesdrop on their conversation. Drivers from other teams join us, wanting my perspective on the race. They're young and impressionable, acting first and thinking later. The passion and need to be the best burns through their eyes, especially the dark stare of the fluffy-haired Australian Billy Nister, who's gaining a reputation for taking risks that could get him killed. I don't miss being like that. Taking friends out without understanding the consequences leaves you lonely. Luckily, I had Niki to set me right. This guy doesn't have a responsible team boss holding him to account.

"I swore you were going off at one point," Luca, another driver, comments, leaving me space to tell them about the near miss at one of the corners while gesticulating wildly.

My gaze flicks to Senna, trying to read her shiny lips. She's not smiling, but there's no anger, either. She crosses her legs and reveals more of her thighs. My hand twitches. Her skin is creamy white, and her legs are toned from running. She sucks on a straw from her cocktail. The combination of her thigh and mouth gives me fantasies that have me shifting in my seat to hide my reaction.

Jacs and Tawny backchat the drivers at our table. I crack a joke, and Senna meets my stare as she listens to Antoine, who slides closer.

The music throbs through the club. Although my seat is padded and covered with velvet, my skin itches. Women stare at me from different booths, but it's Senna I want to spend time with.

I could ask her to dance.

We used to dance in her kitchen when we were teenagers. She'd always tease me when I was in a lousy mood, usually because of my dad, grab my hand, and make me spin her around the kitchen while I sang. It usually stopped my grunting, except when Niki caught us and laughed. But that didn't matter, because my singing made Senna smile, which was all I wanted.

We'd giggle when we chased a cheeky Layla, too. I want to hear that giggle.

My head is a mess of past and present. Before, I loved her like an eighteen-year-old loves his best friend, who he believes will be in his life forever. But now my feelings are more like a clock with dying batteries, sometimes moving forward and freezing. I want to take her to bed and show her how insignificant her exes are while brushing my lips against hers and making mine red with her lipstick. I want to tell her she can conquer the world and that anyone who underestimates her doesn't deserve a second of her light while also getting on my knees and lifting that dress higher.

"What do you think?" Jacs says, staring at me.

"About?"

"We could tweak that part of the engine. It might help the speed. It's a risk, but Tawny said other teams have tried it."

Tawny explains in more detail, and we debate different options to improve my car's performance. My gaze flicks to Senna, who's now with Jimmy. He says something, and her smile lights her entire face. My chest opens up. I want to kiss that smile. I want to taste the joy on her lips.

She catches me looking and winks. My stomach bottoms out.

"I'l speak to you in a bit," she mouths.

My palms sweat with anticipation. I nod and lift my

glass in a cheer, and she does the same.

My feet are so jittery. I need space.

Lights hit the faces of drivers celebrating the end of another race as I walk past booths. We've got one more race before a desperately needed summer break. I head into the quiet corridor, towards the bathrooms.

"Oi," Antoine shouts from behind me. I instinctively hunch my shoulders. "That podium should have been mine."

"You didn't have the edge today. You started badly and got in my way. You were ahead of me on the grid and messed it up. I didn't do anything to stop you from getting the podium," I say, hands wide.

"I will fuck you up the next time we race." Antoine steps closer, and I'm hit by the alcohol fumes wafting from him. If Senna catches us, this will ruin her night, and she deserves a great night.

I sigh loudly, checking no one is nearby. "Don't be so ridiculous. We're on the same team. We want to make Coulter successful."

"Fuck off. You don't care about the team," he scoffs. I roll my tongue around my mouth. I want nothing more than to smack the sneer off his face, but that won't help. "Apart from a particular boss. You always were protective of her. It didn't pay off that day you smashed her hand, though. Crasher was supposed to have an accident, yet you saved her and stopped her racing. And then we convinced her you did it on purpose." He cackles.

"Why did you do that?"

"Payback for all the times you got in my way in races. And because we could."

My fist itches. I want to shove it in his ugly face.

"Save yourself for the track." I bare my teeth. "She'll fire you if you keep acting like a dick."

START YOUR ENGINES

He laughs, his face creasing like I've told the funniest joke. "She's a puppet, and her dad pulls the strings. He wants people to buy the team, and guess who's looking for a new investment?"

My whole body tenses. I don't like that future. I need to walk away, yet I've had enough of Antoine not taking responsibility for his actions. "You're drunk and rambling. Maybe if you put more effort into racing and less into being a shithead with a complex about having a female boss, you'd get a podium yourself."

"I will be in charge of this team, and I'll make Senna get on her knees and show me exactly what she's willing to do to keep her job."

I grab him by his designer shirt and shove him against the wall. "You don't speak about Senna like that. If you say anything like that to her or about her again, I'll make you pay."

"You've got some issues you need to work out. I know exactly who you should work them out on, but she'd rather have someone with class like me. Someone her daddy respects." He cackles. "Why would she desire a bit of rough with issues like you? She'll never want you, Dane."

I draw back my fist to hit him, but a shout freezes my hand.

"Put him down," Senna bellows. "I thought we'd dealt with this. Antoine, go. I need to speak to Connor."

Antoine walks away, winking at me. I give him a death stare over Senna's shoulder.

"Oi, Dane," Senna says, pushing me against the wall. In her heels, she's nearly the same height as me. Her dress shimmers, and I want to hold her and keep her still, but she shoves me again. "What the fuck was that?"

I shrug and roll my eyes. She grabs my jaw and holds it.

157

There's a fire in her eyes that gives my body all the wrong ideas. Her fingers burn my skin, but she doesn't let go.

"Was he right?"

I don't know how much she heard. I hope that she heard Antoine say he caused her crash, but I can't answer. Is she referring to me wanting her? I'll deny it forever if I have to, because she can't know. I won't have her ignoring me because she thinks I want to fuck her. Her eyes pinch as she attempts to decipher my thoughts, but I remain quiet.

"Do you want to work out your issues with me to prove something?"

I clench my jaw, and she lets go as if I've confirmed her fears.

"So this friendship we're trying to resurface was you were proving you were the big man, and I was what, another silly fangirl who praised you?"

I shake my head. I try to speak, but her body is so close to mine it's like her heat fills my veins while her anger has me on the edge of falling. "It was never about proving something."

"Then what was that hug about? Why have you stared at me all night? I thought..." She shakes her head. "It doesn't matter what I thought."

Goose pimples cover her arms, and she stares at my lips and then licks her own.

"What do you want from me, Senna? Do you want a friend? Because I can be a friend."

She sighs, and her breath whispers against my lips. I should stop this conversation. I should be protecting her, not trying to seduce her. She's my best friend's little sister. Yet I hold my tongue desperate for her answer.

"Were you staring at me because you hate Antoine? Is this about being better than him? Because when I look at

START YOUR ENGINES

him, there's nothing, but when I look at you, I..."

As she swallows, I fixate on her throat. I run her hair between my fingers, and my body comes alive as her pupils dilate, and she lets out a sigh that ghosts my lips.

"What happens when you look at me, Coults?"

She leans into me. I hold her hip, and she stares at me with this need that is like a drug injected straight into my veins.

"When I look at you, I want you."

Fuck it.

My lips crash against hers. I grip her and pull her around a quiet corner where no one will catch us. She whimpers into my mouth. I suck on her lower lip, and she puts her arms around my neck, pulling me close.

She tastes of berries and alcohol. It's like the sweetness and the sin all at once, and I turn her so her back is pressed against the wall. I pull up her leg, and she tucks it against me so I can grind against her. She makes the sexiest gasps as my hand slides up her thigh and under her hem. My dick is so hard against her. Everything is out of control. I need this. It's like the last ten years of wanting her are exploding into this moment.

A ringtone stops me dead. It's "Kids" by MGMT. Niki is calling.

I pull away.

Her face falls.

"It's Niki—"

She steps back and out of my reach. "You'd best get it," she says without bitterness. Her eyes soften. "My brother is important. It's okay. Let's pretend this never happened. It was an alcohol-fuelled mistake, and we're boss and driver. Can you imagine what someone like Antoine would say if he saw us?" She gives a fake laugh that sets my teeth on edge.

159

"But—"

"Leave it, Connor. It's okay. Our lives are stressful enough." She forces a smile, and she strokes her scar. I don't believe she does it to hurt me and remind me of the accident, but every time I witness her fingers against that silver line, it's like someone has wrapped an elastic band around my gut. "Well done for the race. Honestly. You were incredible." She winces and then fakes that smile again. "Catch you at the factory or something. The last race of the season is in a fortnight, and then we have a lovely month with time off. Take care, yeah?"

I swear she takes a slow breath as she turns.

As she walks out of my eyeline, I answer the phone to Niki, who praises my podium place. For Niki, I manage a cheery response even as my hopes die.

Chapter Twenty-Four – Senna

I stretch my neck to one side and down a couple of paracetamol, gulping the water like I've returned from the desert. I don't know if I have a hangover or if kissing Connor last night means my body is punishing me for the years spent not kissing him and having mediocre moments with incomparable men.

Connor fucking Dane can kiss.

I run my thumb across my lower lip.

"Senna?" Ric, the sports psychologist Connor has been speaking to since our chat on the garage floor, says, dragging my focus back. "I must tell you something. As Connor's boss, you need to know."

A timely reminder that Connor is a driver on my team and, therefore, off-limits, even though if last night's kiss is anything to go by, a night with him would be everything I've fantasised.

I shake my head, deleting the things I spent the last night imagining when I returned to my hotel room.

"Before you tell me anything, has Connor consented for you to share this?" I ask.

"Yes, we met at lunchtime, and he said it was helpful for you to know."

I take a deep breath. "Okay, Ric. What is it?"

"Connor doesn't enjoy driving. I know we've only had a few sessions, but even with his third place this weekend, his love for it has gone," Ric explains.

I hold in my gasp. His celebration on the podium and the interviews I've watched while hiding in my office convinced me otherwise.

"Why is he still driving? Because of the contract?"

"He's asked that his reasons remain confidential."

I write reasons to stop overthinking them, but one makes me pause. He said when we chatted in the garage that he wanted me to be a success. Is he still racing because of me?

A shadow passes my office. Nearly all the staff have today off, which suits me fine, as I don't want to see anyone and fake that I'm doing okay.

"What do I do, Ric?"

"You celebrate his wins and help him improve after his losses. He wanted you to know, which is encouraging. He respects you, but ultimately, only Connor can solve this. I'll get him safely to the end of the season, but be prepared to let him out of the contract early for his mental health."

My head drops. I want to hug Connor and make everything okay. "Should I let him out of his contract now?"

"No. It has to be his decision. I know you were close and that he's Niki's friend, but you're still his boss, and the friendship will add to his guilt, which means he'll continue to drive. He has to make the decision, and you have to support it. Try not to let your emotions get in the way."

"Okay," I murmur, but my heart hurts for the future.

"If you want to chat about it at any point, give me a call."

"Yes. Thanks, Ric."

I hang up and hold my thumping head in my hands. I

START YOUR ENGINES

have to be professional with Connor. I have to do it for him. There's also the Antoine problem. I heard what he said to Connor about being the reason I crashed as a teenager. I have an angel and a devil on my team, and I can't see a solution. But I have to sort it out.

I can't protect Connor from Antoine and his dad without remaining professional. If I'm to keep him on the team for as long as he wants to stay, then I need to be seen as a fair and reasonable boss, even if on the inside, I just want him. In the meantime, maybe I can find a way to replace Antoine.

I search the system for the contracts when a knock sounds at my door.

"Come in." *Please don't be Dad.*

Connor, with his bright blue eyes and fucking kissable lips, enters my office.

My heart stops.

"What are you doing here, Connor? You get today off." I stutter, offering a measured smile as I try to remember I'm his boss, but I know it wavers as I struggle to find the sweet spot of a professional friend.

"I thought you might need hangover food," he says, passing me a shopping bag.

I rifle through it and squeal in a way that makes him beam as I place an energy drink, chocolate bars, and crisps on my desk. "You're amazing."

He blushes. "I wasn't sure what you preferred after a hangover. If you need pizza, I can get it. There's paracetamol in there, too."

"This is perfect." I smile at him, and he grins back. It's like butterflies with spikes for wings torture my belly. I can't forget Ric's words. "Thank you. I really appreciate it. I, um, spoke to Ric just now."

163

His lips turn down.

"I want to look after you as a boss. If there is anything I can do to help, will you tell me? That includes if you need to get out of your contract."

"Yes, boss," he says with a nod. "I appreciate it. I'll catch you later, Senna."

I've said the wrong thing while trying to say the right thing. His face is unreadable as he walks out.

"Connor," I shout. I don't want to be alone today, but I can't fully admit it's him I want around. It's enough to want support.

"Yes, Coults?" He grips the doorframe as if he can't face stepping back into the room.

His biceps throb.

I rasp, "Do you want to stay and eat chocolate? Your head must be hurting, too."

His smile makes my heart ache to have him by my side again. And then he shakes his head. "No, because then you'll have more reasons to stay when you should go home and rest. Promise me you won't stay all day."

He locks eyes with me.

"I promise."

"Good g—" He clears his throat as my eyes widen. "That's good boss behaviour."

The ache in my heart has turned into a different ache, and it's between my legs.

"Take care, Connor."

Why does this feel like a goodbye to what we could have had?

"Always. Laters, boss." He gives me a wink, and I fist my skirt under the desk so he can't see my heart breaking as my body breathes for him.

Chapter Twenty-Five – Senna

Jacs paces my office. The team is packing for Hungary for the last race before the summer break.

"Are you sure Antoine confessed to trying to make you crash when you were teenagers?"

I nod.

Connor and I have continued to be professional with each other for the last week. When he sees me, he gives me a head dip or talks with me in a group setting about the car's performance. It's for the best, even though my belly is like a fucking tornado every time he's in my vicinity.

"What are you going to do about Antoine?" Jacs asks before sliding into the seat in front of my desk as I pop an antacid in my mouth.

I lean my chin on my fists. "I don't know. I can't trust him. He's not a team player, and the last months suggest he'll do it again without caring about consequences." I rub my forehead with my finger. "Antoine's dad calls every day asking me when I'll get rid of Connor. Connor isn't the problem."

Well, he's my problem, but Jacs doesn't know about the kiss that will never happen again or that I need to protect him.

At his voice outside my office, I close my eyes and fantasise about him walking into my office and pushing me up against the wall, his body between my thighs as his hands undo the buttons of my blouse. "Senna, what is going on with you? Your face is red, and you keep licking your lips."

I suck in a breath. "I don't—"

She turns to the door, and Connor's eyes catch mine, and for a moment, it's like the kiss is happening all over again. Heat floods my veins as I imagine his hands brushing my skin.

"Something happen between you two? Is that why you've avoided me since our night out?"

"Close the door."

"He's acted weird since he came third at Silverstone. I thought that was just what happens with some drivers after a race. I've never seen him act so professional." She squeals in delight. "What happened between you two?"

Connor drops his stare and then looks back up. I nearly fall off my chair when he sucks his lip into his mouth.

"Close the door, Jacs." My tone has an edge, but her mouth is upturned as she swaggers to the door.

"We'll have words later, big boy," she fake-whispers to Connor.

"Jacs, please."

We're coming up to the big season break, where no one can work on the cars, do any development work, or touch anything. The drivers usually go away and are surrounded by beautiful groupies, returning at the end of August with tans and models on their arms. Maybe that's Connor's plan.

Operational departments like finance continue, so although I've got two weeks booked off, I'm not going anywhere.

START YOUR ENGINES

My phone flashes with a message. It's from the vet, aka my former fuck buddy, reminding me there's somewhere I could go. But I won't. I can't.

"Okay, something is going on with you. You've gone from blushing and grumpy to...well, I've no idea, but your brow is so damn furrowed that you've got a monobrow. What is going on, and who is that message from?"

"Mr. Vet."

"Your Australian fuck buddy with all the muscles?" She throws her hands in the air. "The drama! What does he want?"

"He wants me to stay with him for a week during the summer break." I drop my head, bashing it against the desk. The pain is nothing compared to my distress.

"Are you going? You'd benefit from stress relief. Unless Mr. Vet wants more, because your heart is clearly with a certain bad boy racing driver."

I lift my head to glare at her. "My heart isn't anywhere. I might go for a week. It would only be for a change of scenery. Friends without benefits."

"Do you want to go?"

My breath catches in my throat, and I stare through the glass of my office door to Connor, who is laughing with Jimmy. I drop my head back on my desk.

Jacs starts on at me again. "So Mr. Vet wants you. Connor wants you—"

"Connor and I can't be together. We had a drunk kiss, and then he got a call from Niki. It was what I needed to convince me we shouldn't have kissed. I'm his boss, my dad hates him, and he's my brother's best friend. I need to remain professional." My words are muffled against the desk, but she catches every word.

167

"And yet, minutes ago, he gave you fuck-me eyes through your doorway, and you blushed. And he's arranged for food to be delivered to your office every evening to ensure you eat."

I lift my head, and my eyes pinch as I stare at her. "He did that?"

She nods smugly and puts her hands behind her head. Her chair tips back slightly.

"But—"

Suddenly, my door flies open, and my dad strides in. The season break means everyone panics and must conduct as much business as possible. My phone vibrates again. It's Mr. Vet. I pop it in my drawer.

Dad's ears are the colour of beetroot, and I prepare for a rant about a decision I've made. I still need to confront him.

"Give me a minute, Jacs. And close the door behind you. Not that it makes a difference, because some people are too rude to knock," I add. It's like water on oil with my dad.

Again, I catch Connor's eye as Jacs leaves my office and closes the door. They can't be fuck-me eyes.

"What do you want, Dad?"

"You need to treat Antoine better," Dad huffs.

"Antoine needs to be a better driver," I retort. "I thought we agreed that I was in charge."

My reply is half-hearted because I suspect he's continued to speak to board members behind my back.

"That was when I trusted your decisions." My dad slams his hands on my desk. The temptation to recoil is strong, but I raise my eyebrow instead. "You're favouring Connor because why? He's the reason for your failed driving career and accident."

"Connor is the better driver. That's been clear all season." I don't add that Antoine is the real reason I crashed as a teenager. Dad won't listen, and I suspect there's another reason for his adoration of Antoine.

I bang a fist on my desk to avoid stroking or hiding my scar. It's not something to be ashamed of. "Is Antoine one of the investors you're lining up?" My dad's face doesn't change. And the truth hits me. "What Ralf said was right. You're not looking for investors. You're searching for buyers, and Antoine is one of them. That's why you've been hanging out with Jean. I thought I could trust you. I knew, sure as shit, I shouldn't trust them."

My dad refuses to make eye contact. Instead, he continues to huff as he walks across the office to stare out the window.

"You don't believe in me, do you? Why have you let me run this team if you were going to sell it?"

He turns, and his features soften. "Jumps." I bristle. "Niki was supposed to run this team before he disappeared. Don't get me wrong, you're not doing badly—"

"I'm doing much better than you did when you ran this place into the ground last year."

His shoulders hunch, and his face reddens. Shit, I don't want to give him another heart attack.

"Don't give me attitude, Senna. I'm selling this team at the end of the season because it's the right thing to do. It's right for my health and for this family. Niki disappeared because of his crash. You're working every hour you can and not having a life. You should be having babies."

I grab the arms of my chair to prevent from striding over and smacking him in the face.

"I don't want babies. I want to run this team," I shout. Everyone outside my office will hear what I just said,

169

including Connor. It's true I don't want babies, but that doesn't mean I don't want a relationship, which is entirely possible. All the other team bosses have partners.

But the only man I want is the one I can't date.

My dad collapses in a chair. I can barely keep up with my moods, let alone his. "What is going on, Dad? Where did the baby thing come from?"

He sighs and holds his hands up. "Your mum has told me that I must walk away from the team before it's too late. But I don't want to watch you get hurt again. After your accident, I thought about how to protect you, which included keeping Connor away from you."

My jaw tightens. "Antoine was responsible for the crash. He and some other lads were trying to hurt me, and Connor was saving me from them."

"By crashing into you? Don't be ridiculous. What they were doing was tactical, a bit of roughhousing to make you drive better. Connor hurt you. If not for him, I'm not sure where you'd be, but it wouldn't be here. I know racing was important to you, but it was a bit of fun for you, not a career, unlike Niki."

I throw my head back and grunt.

"Don't be so dramatic, Senna. You're a team boss now."

"Exactly. And I have another half of the season to prove to you and every other fucker out there—"

"Language."

I fist my hands as my rage threatens to overwhelm me.

"I can swear in my office. You always did." I quickly continue before he says something about girlie tantrums or petulant children. "Give me until the end of the season. Niki trusted me with this team, so you should, too. Have you spoken to Mum about it?"

START YOUR ENGINES

"Your mum sings your praises. She doesn't know I'm considering selling it. I'll tell her when I'm ready. We don't need any more theatrics."

I shouldn't have to beg my dad to believe in me, but I have my entire life. Begging him to let me drive, race, and join the company as a marketing intern. Why can't I say this to him?

"Please let me show you what I can do, and if we're in the top six in the Constructor's Championship, don't sell it, okay?"

His shoulders slump. "Fine. You win. For now."

I've promised something I'm not sure I can deliver.

"And about Antoine," I add. My dad's shoulders tighten again, and I ready myself for another fight. "I don't like the guy. He takes things too far, shows me no respect, and is a misogynistic bastard. I'm used to some of that in this industry, but it's a risk to the team, and I don't care what you say about the crash; he caused it." And lied to me about Connor.

My dad leans forward, pinning me with his stare. "Where is this going?"

"I reserve the right to make any decisions about him I need to make as the boss. I don't care if you're keeping him and his dad sweet so you can sell to him. I need to know you've got my back if I have to make a difficult decision." My nerves have jangled about Antoine for most of the season, but they continue to escalate. "Have you got my back, Dad?"

A knock sounds at my door.

"It's your mum," Dad grumbles.

I shout to her to enter, and she rushes in, kissing me on my forehead. "Hello, darling. I'd stay and chat, but your dad has a hospital appointment."

171

REBECCA CHASE

"Just a check-up," my dad snaps before I can ask if I should be worried.

"I saw Connor outside answering your assistant's phone. Your team really do support you. Millionaire drivers acting as secretaries—whatever next?" she says, sensing tension and smashing it out of the room, like she's always done. She doesn't get enough credit for the successful parts of Dad's career. "It would be lovely to see you when you get a break. There's always a pasta dish ready for you." She scans the papers littering my desk as my mobile buzzes from my drawer.

I hug her tightly. "Yes, Mum. I'll visit when I can."

As Dad approaches the door, he turns. "Any news from Niki?"

I shake my head. "He's not called me recently."

"Okay. Hopefully, he'll come back to us. I miss him."

"Me too," I reply. "And Dad, about Antoine—have you got my back?"

"Just don't do anything rash, and don't let Connor get in the way of this team's future."

My mum waves as she pushes Dad out the door.

Before I can contemplate anything else, Jimmy rushes into the room. "A couple of things." He reels off messages, but one catches my attention. "And your vet friend called because he wasn't sure you were getting his texts."

Jimmy tips his head as he tries to read the note. "Sorry, I can't read Connor's writing."

"Connor took the message?"

"Yeah. I was in the bathroom. It says, 'Please tell her I'm looking forward to seeing Tiger in August,' and there's a number and a drawing of a bat or something."

Shit. Connor thinks I'm staying with Mr. Vet in the break. I examine the piece of paper. It's not a bat but a badly

172

drawn cock and balls. Childish Connor used to scrawl those on Niki's notebooks when they were in a mood with each other and he wanted to call him a dick but couldn't because they were giving each other the silent treatment. My head drops on my desk for the umpteenth time that day.

"Is that all?" I mumble.

"Yes." He walks out, pausing at the door. I can sense it even with my head on my desk.

"What now, Jimmy?" I sigh.

"As you're away with your 'Mr. Biceps Bigger Than His Head Vet'—Connor's words"—I bite the inside of my mouth so hard that I taste blood—"I've asked Connor to catsit while I'm on holiday. He's staying in his beach house for the summer break."

Jimmy walks out.

My phone vibrates loudly from my drawer. As if life weren't complicated enough with the Antoine issue, having to be in the top six by the end of the season, and dealing with the memory of Connor's kiss.

With all my thoughts snapping at once, one seed of hope remains. Connor isn't going on holiday to surround himself with models during the break.

I can't be with him, though, especially after Dad's parting words.

CHAPTER TWENTY-SIX – CONNOR

The last race before the summer break in one of my favourite cities.

Although I don't love driving like I used to, I adore returning here. I had my first win at the Hungarian Grand Prix, and even though many of the stands are filled with fans of Vessa's number-one driver, blue and red British flags wave for me. Ralf is here, too. We chatted on the phone this morning. Between him and calls with the sports psychologist, I've reduced some of the things I do before I race. I want to do them, and intrusive thoughts tell me I'll crash if I don't, but I'm practising mindfulness.

I breathe in and centre myself as I prepare to get in the car. The other drivers wear headphones, playing pre-race songs to get themselves fired up. I've not got one. I've spent hours searching for one, but nothing hits me right. Too many songs remind me of Niki, and then I remember his crash, and I'm back to square one.

I close my eyes and attempt calm, but I get flashes of Senna. I can't forget that kiss. I've tried. I ensure she gets her dinners, and hang out with Jimmy in case she leaves her office. I can't get enough of her laugh. I smile at her and stare at her eyes and lips and...

Fuck. I need to focus. This race counts.

I lick my lips and remember the taste of her cranberry

cocktail. She jump-started my senses that night in the bar—her scent, her taste, and the softness of her thigh... I shake my head. That kiss was better than anything I'd ever imagined, and I've had a lot of kisses. I've enjoyed a lot of women and had them screaming my name. But that kiss was the one that deleted all the others from my memories.

"T me to get going," Silas says, and I climb into the car. I'm not as focused as I need to be.

Macca says, "This is your race, Connor, but watch out for Valetini on the first corner. He's gunning for you. And ignore Antoine."

But I can't ignore him. I'm starting ahead of him, and he hates it. Since we nearly came to blows, he's threatened me multiple times. I don't care what he says to me, but his promises of hurting Senna are the other reason I've hung outside her office.

I want to get on the podium again as a fuck you to him. And I want Senna's praise before she heads off to Australia to be with that bloody vet for the summer break.

I struggle to concentrate as I drive my formation lap, warming my tyres and preparing to race.

"Focus," Macca says through my radio.

I can't, though. I squint and clench my teeth. I don't want to drive anymore, but I need to for Senna. I need to protect her and—

The lights turn green, and I go. All my thoughts fall away, and as much as I hate driving, it's like I'm in the right space to do something great.

"**W**atch yourself, Connor," Macca snaps through the radio.

I raise my voice. "He's getting too close." Antoine has been behind me for a lap. He can't get around me, not that he's trying. He slides behind me as if nudging me. "He's trying to make me crash."

There's no code word for this. Other teams can hear us. They're probably laughing at Senna's mismanagement of her drivers, which makes me want to bare my teeth and scream. Antoine is risking so much for a vendetta.

"His race engineer and Senna are talking to him," Macca comments. But it doesn't matter. He's been enabled by his dad and Senna's dad for too long.

We're entering a DRS, Drag Reduction System, zone on a straight, which means he could attempt to overtake. I want to fight Antoine and stop him, but letting him overtake is the safest option. He'll probably crash as soon as he passes me, anyway.

"I'm going to let him pass. It's best for the team," I say. If I'm protecting the team, then I'm protecting Senna. I need to do that for her.

"No." Senna's voice fills my ears. "You can't let him believe this is acceptable. He'll do it again."

I want to tell her not to go to Australia. With everything going on, that shouldn't be my thought.

I grit my teeth. We're two laps from the end of the race. "Okay. I'll hold him off."

"Good." The tension in her one word has me gripping the steering wheel tighter.

My stomach lurches as I take the next corner. I'm flying at speeds across this track. Everything I hate about racing is shoved in my face. If I could, I'd leave it today. I used to love the adrenaline and the pressure to be the best, but I'm only racing for her now. I want this team to succeed for her.

I need to be around Senna every second. It's not to

START YOUR ENGINES

protect her; it's because I still love her. It's a different love than before. It's the love of an adult. I've fallen hard, but I can't do anything about it. I'd be complicating her life and her future.

I remember Ralf's wedding. I should be focusing, but all I can see is Senna in a beautiful floor-length pink dress, her blond hair in some intricate do, with the pink flower tucked behind her ear. Her softness and tears as Ralf married the man he loved. I only wanted her, and nothing else made sense, including racing and screwing around.

We're on the last lap now, but Antoine continues pressuring me, getting so close I pull to the side.

This is it for him now. It must be as clear to him as it is to me. He was already on his last warning; Jimmy heard her tell him after Silverstone. But this will mean he's out of the team. I need to survive for the rest of this lap, and then he'll be gone. I don't doubt for a second that Senna will fire him. She makes the decisions her dad was always too scared of.

I turn into the second-to-last corner that loops behind the garage, and suddenly, he's beside me. He's too close. I'm running out of space. I'm driving too fast to do anything. I hope I can squeeze through. Macca shouts, but it's nothing compared to the rush of panic flooding my ears.

His car is so close. At this speed, a crash is inevitable. The guy might kill me. There's a wall to my side and him on the other. I jerk the wheel away, but he still hits me. Suddenly, it's like I'm in slow motion, and my car is in the air. I'm flying closer to a wall and death. I close my eyes and wait for the inevitable. As I pray for a swift death, my last thought is Senna and never telling her how I felt.

CHAPTER TWENTY-SEVEN – SENNA

The camera focuses on Connor's car, which has smashed into the wall.

There's no movement.

"Please be okay," I whisper to the screen, but still, there's nothing.

The crowd is silent. The pit crew is frozen. Wetness covers my cheeks. I didn't know I was crying.

"Please, Connor," I whisper. And suddenly, I'm throwing my headphones down, jumping off my chair and running.

Where he crashed means he'll be on the other side of the garage. Because of safety measures, I won't get to him, but maybe I'll get closer. It won't help—nothing can—but I need to do something.

What if Connor needs rehabilitation or someone there for him? Connor has others, but he needs me.

I push past engineers and crew as I near the back of the garage. Steam rises from his car, and suddenly, there's another threat. His car might spark! He could burn in there.

Tears continue to stream down my face; I might lose my best friend again. We'd just reconnected. I fired Antoine as soon as he started driving dangerously. Maybe I should have waited until the end of the race, because that must have spurred on his vendetta. He was possessed.

START YOUR ENGINES

I reach the fence and relentlessly rub my scar as I hunt for movement.

Please, God, let him be okay.

My body is ice, and I'm sure my heart stops. My eyes are swollen from crying. The steam isn't helping, either. I rush back and forth against the fence to get a better view.

And then I see him.

Connor slowly climbs out of the car. His body shakes violently. My fist is against my mouth. I'll scream if I don't keep my lips pressed tightly together.

He shakes his limbs. He needs to escape the car, but he's frozen. Of course he is. He's in shock.

"Connor," I shout, although it's more of a cross between a gasp and a shriek. He can't hear me with his helmet on, but I won't stop shrieking his name even as my throat is hoarse from steam and screaming.

Suddenly, he looks up and starts walking to the fence. There will be a gap—there's always a gap. I search for it, but the steam hides everything.

As I investigate each part of the fence, a marshal points to an opening, and Connor slides through.

He pulls off his helmet. His face is the palest I've ever seen, and I reach for him. His skin is freezing.

As he opens his mouth, his lips tremble. He whispers something.

I lean in and catch his words. "Please don't go to Australia."

And then he falls to the ground.

CHAPTER TWENTY-EIGHT – CONNOR

"Thank you," I say to the nurse who accompanied me on the plane back to England.

"Thank you for the signed photo. My niece is obsessed with you. She'll love it."

He disappears back into the airport to return to Hungary, and I'm faced with a sobbing Jimmy.

"I'm so glad you're okay. I would have come to the plane and helped you out, but I've got Fluffers in the car, and I couldn't leave him and—"

"Come here, Jimmy, it's okay," I say, enveloping him in a hug. He cries against my chest. "Let's get to your car. This is the longest I've stood for the last two days. That's when the accident was, right? I'm still a fuzzy with the hospital and travel."

"Yes. Two days. Oh no, I'm so sorry. I shouldn't be crying on you."

I hold him at arm's length to look into his eyes. "Mate, it's fine. Going down to my house on the coast and looking after your fluffball is the perfect recuperation. I'm grateful you're giving me a lift because I'm not sure I can drive right now." Will I ever drive again? I've been on the cusp of resigning since I woke. But then I wouldn't be near Senna.

Jimmy eases me into the car like I'm a baby deer.

"Nice car. Where did you get it?"

START YOUR ENGINES

Jimmy shrugs as his cat shouts at us from his carrier in the footwell.

"You be quiet, Fluffers. This is Connor, and he's going to take care of you," Jimmy replies before running around and jumping into the driver's seat.

A black and white grumpy cat with one Elvis Presley sideburn sits in the carrier. His glare reminds me of Senna when she first saw me in her boardroom.

"How is everyone?" I ask casually, although I'm only thinking of her.

I don't remember much after I crashed into the wall. My memories of getting out of the car and seeing Senna are fuzzy, as is the hospital trip where I saw her face, but that could have been a dream, too. If she was there, that was the last time we were together.

I pull down the visor to check the mirror. The scratches on my hands and the black eye that's like a child's painting where they've run amok with purple and black paint are the only physical hints that I've been in a crash. The true damage is psychological.

"I've got so many messages from people who didn't want to bother you with calls while you were in the hospital. Silas says he'll have you in training before you know it. Macca is proud of how you handled the car and knows you'll smash it as soon as you're back on the track. I told him those words weren't appropriate, but he insisted I pass it on," Jimmy grumbles as he drives us out of the airport and towards the motorway. "Engineer humour."

"Anyone else?"

"Did your mum and brother speak to you? They called Silas initially, but he said it was okay for them to call you."

"Yeah, I had brief video calls with both of them. Layla was still travelling during her university break, so I told her

not to come home. She deserves freedom after her hard work. I was insistent with Mum, as she wanted to fly to Hungary and wrap me in a blanket, but her job is critical. Other people need her more than me." And I refuse to be a burden.

"Ralf and Ric said they'll be in touch when you're in your holiday home. Jacs made you a secret care package. I sneaked a look at it, and it's energy drinks and a candy penis. I don't understand that woman," he says, shaking his head.

I smile. "Me neither."

"Everyone else is on holiday or finishing work before the summer break. I'm grateful that you're looking after my boy while I'm in America. I haven't seen my family in a year."

"It's my pleasure. You deserve a holiday."

I want to ask if he's avoided mentioning Senna for a reason. Maybe she's travelling to Australia to see Mr. Can't Even Say He Has A Good Personality Because All He Cares About Are His Muscles Vet.

"And you heard about Antoine?"

"No. I'm guessing his dad tried to talk the FIA out of punishing him. How did he spin it this time?"

"Senna fired him. She did it during the race just before he crashed into you."

I fumble for words, but my mouth is so dry that my tongue has stuck to the roof of it. I thought she would. But fuck. That means something else. She doesn't need me to protect her anymore. There will be other issues, but she's starting to handle the board and winning battles.

I can leave.

I scroll through my emails and find the draft of my resignation. My finger hovers over the send button. Fluffers shouts at me. He's eyeballing me with his eyes half closed.

"You're so cheeky, Fluffers," Jimmy says before looking

START YOUR ENGINES

at me. "I've got the stuff you requested from your apartment and extra bits. There's tonnes of food in the car. You're going to have the best time together. Fluffers is so loving."

I'm too scared to look at Fluffers. I swear he's trying to psych me out. I pop my phone into my pocket in case he shouts at me again. "Yeah. And it will be nice to spend time in my house. I bought it five years ago after a recommendation from Filip at Vessa, but I've never spent time there."

"Because you're usually on a tropical island with Niki and lots of...fans?"

"And the rest," I say, giving a fake laugh. Most of my summers were spent getting drunk and doing something dangerous during the day and sleeping around in the evenings. "But it will be good to enjoy the quiet this year."

"I couldn't cope being completely alone. You've got a car for when you're lonely?"

I give a non-committal grunt sound. I've no intention of driving.

"Cool. We'll be there soon."

Fluffers shouts and stares at me again. He's going to kill me in my sleep.

183

Chapter Twenty-Nine – Senna

"**H**ow is he?" I ask, jumping out my door as soon as Jimmy parks outside my apartment.

My cuticles are bitten to hell. I'm glad paparazzi can't get near my place because I'd be plastered over the Internet with my scraggly hair, dirty joggers, and hoody.

Jimmy chucks me my car keys. "He's shaky. He's got a black eye and some cuts. But it's not his body I'm worried about. From what I can gather, he hasn't got a car down there. I suspect he won't be driving for a long time."

I cover my sigh with a nod.

"I'm not surprised." I can't ask him to drive for the team again. He needs looking after, but I'm not the person to do it. I'm why he crashed, and I can't forgive myself for firing Antoine during the race. If I hadn't done that, Connor would be okay. "He didn't need this. He was already struggling with driving. I was so stupid."

Jimmy hugs me, and tears slip down my cheeks. "It's not your fault, Senna. You didn't know Antoine would try and hit him."

"But I should have known. I shouldn't have let it get this far."

"We've all heard how close he is with your dad."

"I'm the boss, the person in charge. I let this happen

when I should have gone with my instincts. I knew what Antoine was capable of. Connor could have died."

"But he didn't. You're doing what you can to help. I think he wants to hear from you."

I step back and shake my head. "He doesn't need me in his life. Look at what I've done to it. I treated him like crap when he tried to protect me as a teenager, and now I'm finding new ways to hurt him." I make a note to ask Ric to call him. He needs the psychologist now more than ever, although not to help him race, but to help him exist. "Did he like the food?"

Jimmy nods as we walk back to my apartment. "Nearly as much as I loved driving your car. I could have driven him in mine."

"It's not my main car. He would have recognised that. Anyway, you needed something with a lot of space so he could stretch out."

"It took me twenty minutes to carry the shopping and house stuff in. You must have been in the supermarket all day."

I shrug. Technically, I was there for two hours in the middle of the night, trudging up and down the aisles. I wanted him to have all his favourite foods. "I need him to be okay. You'll call him while you're away and say it's to check on Fluffers?"

"I mean, I'd call anyway, but yeah. I'll update you. You could call him."

"I can't, unless..." I scrape my lower lip with my teeth. "Did he ask after me?"

I hate that I sound needy. He told me not to go to Australia, so I didn't. But that doesn't mean we have a future.

Jimmy shakes his head, and my shoulders slump. What

did I expect? I've hurt him repeatedly. My chest aches. I wrap my arms around myself to stop the shivers.

"I told him about Antoine."

"Oh," I manage. A driver waves at me from a Bentley. "You'd best get off. You've got a plane to catch, and your car is here."

"I don't want to leave you like this. Will you be okay?"

"I'll be fine. Seclusion is part of being a boss. You deserve a holiday, Jimmy. You're the best assistant ever."

"You take care, yeah?"

He turns and sees the car I'd organised for him. "Bloody hell, Senna. I don't deserve a car like this."

"Yeah, you do. Have a lovely trip. I'll be in touch."

As the Bentley leaves, I grip my phone tightly. I should call Connor. I doubt he remembers me visiting him in the hospital, and it would be nice to hear his voice, even if he's shouting at me about the crash. We can't repeat what we went through as teenagers. I need to learn from that.

I scroll through my phone. I won't beg him to return for the next half of the season. I'll find someone to replace him if I need to.

Before I press call, my phone beeps with an email. It's from Connor and titled "Resignation."

I nearly drop my phone, fumbling to open it. Does he blame me, hate me? I won't beg him to stay. I'll return after the summer break with no drivers, but I don't care. I won't ask Connor to return after everything he's been through.

Dear Miss Coulter,

I am writing to inform you of my decision to resign from Coulter Racing with immediate effect.

Yours,

Connor Dane

START YOUR ENGINES

A sob breaks free from my mouth at the formal tone. This has been his only contact since the crash.

I walk into my apartment to get ready for the office. I need to throw myself into work because that's all I've got left.

CHAPTER THIRTY – CONNOR

"Come here, Fluffers," I call out.

Where is that white fluffball? He's teased me with his refusal to be cuddled unless it's on his terms. He glared at me for the first three days, and then, in the middle of the night, he was there, pawing at me, scratching me until I turned on my side so he could settle in the crook of my arm. He insisted I stroked him and stretched out his paws with menacing claws until I did. And he knocked my cuddly Coults toy out of the bed like a jealous little bastard.

I check my phone for the umpteenth time that week, but Senna hasn't called. It's been several days since Jimmy brought me home and I sent the resignation. The bruise around my eye is fading, and the scratches are nearly gone. Senna's probably in Australia with Mr. Probably Spends All His Time Taking Selfies Vet. It's not like I have anything to offer her. I'm a racing driver who's too scared to drive, hiding away in his beach house, cat-sitting a cat that hates him.

My phone rings, but I ignore it when I see Niki on the screen.

The sand of my private beach fills my view, and a little ways down, the lake laps at the edge. I open the window a crack to immerse myself in the sound of the water. Blue

188

therapy, being near water, can help with mental health, so here I am. It's miles from anywhere and anyone, which is perfect.

Is Senna thinking of me, or am I another stain on her busy life? She'll probably return from summer break with the glow of a woman finally finding the love she's searched for and deserved. It doesn't matter because I won't be seeing her again.

Did she pick up on the word "Yours" in my email?

She must be having sex marathons with Mr. Can't Satisfy You Because He's Busy Finishing His Protein Shake Vet.

The phone rings again—Niki. I can't avoid him forever, and speaking to him is better than seeing anyone in person.

"Finally," Niki says when I answer.

"What do you want?" I'm sullen, and I don't care.

Niki got me into this mess, but his sister didn't get me out of it. Childhood best friends have lost all meaning. They're jerks. And I still love them.

"To check you're okay," he replies.

Hearing his voice softens some of my hardening heart. And remembering Senna's face as I kissed her at the bar makes the other part of my heart soften.

"Me and Fluffers are doing fine, thank you." I crouch down and peek under the generic Swedish catalogue–ready sofa, trying to locate the fluffy bastard. Having never lived here, I've spent no time making it homely.

"Who is Fluffers?" The sound of seagulls rings in my ears.

"Are you at a beach?"

From the intel Ralf shared with me, Niki is renting an AirBnB in a remote area in Europe. For now, we're leaving him to do what he needs to.

"Kinda. Who is Fluffers?" he asks again.

I open the cupboards as I hunt the cat. He's not allowed outside because he's only staying for a few weeks. We don't want him attempting to trek home.

"Jimmy's cat. I said I'd cat-sit because I wouldn't go anywhere during summer break." Or after the break, I add silently.

"Why aren't you going anywhere? Is this about the crash?"

"I'd decided before the crash. Not that it's any of your business. It's not like you're around for me." I sound worse than a grumpy teenager. I could call my mum or Layla, and they'll be here within a day, and so would some of my team, although they'll hate me when they learn I've left. Either way, Senna isn't here for me, and that hurts more than I want to admit to her brother. "It doesn't matter."

"Yes, it does. I'm sorry I'm not around for you. I have things I need to deal with."

"What things?"

"Stuff. You're not the only one lonely this summer."

I'm in the bedroom now, searching under the bed, checking behind my chest of drawers. I catch my dishevelled appearance in the mirror. My hair thrusts out at weird angles, as if I've been hiding under the bed. My joggers and branded T-shirts have seen better days, and I'm starting to grow a beard for the first time in my life.

"Are you lonely, Niki?"

"I meant Senna," Niki murmurs.

My stomach bottoms out at her name. It's the first time someone has said it aloud. The thoughts I've had while attempting to sleep aren't the thoughts you have about your best friend's little sister.

"She won't stop working. She's got to take the next two

weeks off per the summer break rules, and she's not far from where you're staying."

I freeze. She's not in Australia. A zip of joy fills my heart. But she still hasn't contacted me.

Niki's babbling overwhelms my thoughts. "Since Hungary, she's slept at the office every night, and when I called her, she talked non-stop about who will replace Antoine. She blames herself for what he did. She's not sleeping. I doubt she's eating, as Jimmy is away, and if not for the mandatory break, she probably wouldn't be in Dorset. I need you to take care of her."

"I can't. She'd have messaged if she wanted my company. She doesn't need me. She's an independent adult."

I want to explain that if he cared so much, he shouldn't have left her with a mess and should have come home and been with her. But I hold my tongue because Niki's suffered, too.

"Please," Niki begs. My friendship with Niki is breaking. I'm hiding more from him than telling him, yet when he begs, I listen. "Please, if you've ever cared for Senna, reach out to her."

I care about her too much.

"I'll consider it."

Niki's thank you as he hangs up hurts my heart. The guy believes I can help Senna, but I've left the team, which leaves her in the lurch. And all I want is to finish the kiss we started in the bar.

These aren't supportive, caring thoughts.

But she hasn't called me. Maybe she's got nothing left to say to me.

Fluffers mews. He's gotten into the garden. Of course he has, the little bastard.

I storm out, ready to give him hell.

He's playing with a bee!

His little white paws are swiping at it. He opens his mouth but misses. Thank God. I want to run and grab him, but he'll run off. I need to give him space so he'll come to me.

"Fluffers," I call out. But he continues to jab and snap at the bee. The way he dances around it and swipes would be cute if it couldn't seriously harm him. Can a sting kill him? I pull my phone out of my pocket and search for cats and bee stings while monitoring him out of the corner of my eye.

My sweaty fingers slip off the screen several times, but as I get to a page, Fluffers makes a noise that makes my blood go cold.

The bee has gone, but Fluffers's paw presses against the ground.

I creep closer and grab him. Pulling him into my arms, I see what was under his right paw—a dead bee. The cat I'm meant to protect was stung, and I can't get to the vet because I don't have a car.

I can't lose this cat as well as everyone else. I bloody love him.

My heart is frantic as I rock him.

My throat burns, and I will myself to calm as I call the one person I shouldn't.

The words fly out of my mouth as soon as the phone connects. "Senna, I need you."

CHAPTER THIRTY-ONE – SENNA

"Senna, I need you." Connor's line repeats in my head as I race to his holiday home. I take the country roads faster than I should. His voice was ice cold.

I've nearly called him a hundred times since I got his resignation, but he was clear that he was done with the team and so done with me. *Please let him be okay.* I can't have him hurt. Since his crash, I've avoided him for more than guilt. Knowing how I felt about him scared me to my very soul. I can't let him in only to lose him again.

As I do a handbrake turn in his driveway, I see his folded body at the edge as he cradles Fluffers.

I jump from my Porshe and rush to him. Tears stream down his face as he rocks the cat.

"Are you okay?" My voice wavers.

Connor shakes his head, and barbed wire tightens around my heart. I cup his face with my hands and make him focus on me. "Connor, please tell me what's wrong."

"It's Fluffers," he says as a sob wrenches itself from between his lips. He holds Fluffers's swollen paw up. It's like Fluffers is wearing a boxing glove. "He was stung by a bee. He might die."

This little cat, who smirks as he stares at him, has him shaking and choked with anxiety.

I know a bee-stung cat isn't the huge emergency

Connor thinks it is, but I can't bear to see Connor distressed like this. "It's okay. We'll get it sorted, baby." The word slips out, but Connor is so overwhelmed by Fluffers that he doesn't pick up on it.

"And I can't get him to an emergency vet because I don't have a car and—"

I turn Connor around and walk him towards the house, partly so I don't have to look at his devastation because it makes me want to hold him and make all his pain go away. My heart tears because seeing him again lets those feelings I've pushed down out of the box. And I wouldn't put it past this bloody cat to jump out of his arms and chase another bee.

"Let's go inside and call Brad. I've had cats stung by bees before, and it's not as scary as you think."

"Okay," he replies with a gulping sound. He wipes his eyes with his shoulder. His voice changes. It's deeper and carries an edge. "Why aren't you with Mr. Often Forgets Leg Day So His Small Penis Is Thicker Than His Calves Vet?"

I hold a chuckle. Who knew mentioning my old fuck buddy would help stem the tears? Connor is jealous of a man who pales in comparison to him.

Connor scowled the entire time I spoke to Brad. Once Brad established I wasn't calling to change my mind about visiting him, I relayed instructions to Connor on removing the venom and things to be aware of.

I kick my shoes off as I hang up.

"What do we do now?" Connor asks, his shoulders loosening. He stares at Fluffers like he's a baby.

START YOUR ENGINES

He's so precious with this cat and the kitten he found in Australia. I knew he could be sweet; he's been like that with me, but this is an extra level. I want to hold Connor close and protect him so that no one ever comes close to hurting him again. A tickle hits my belly. The box I've tried to shove my feelings in about being his boss and not allowing myself to imagine being with him is opening. I can't lock it shut anymore, and I don't want to. Heat fills my limbs as I stare at him. I need to look after him and be the person he's tried to be for me.

If Connor doesn't have a car with him, that means he's not driving. From the brief messages Jimmy and I shared over the last week, I'm sure Connor hasn't driven since the accident.

"He mentioned antihistamines might help stop the swelling," I say.

Connor has Fluffers's paw temporarily wrapped in a makeshift ice pack, aka a bag of peas. "But I don't have any."

"We'd need a certain type. I'll head out while you sit with Fluffers."

Technically, we don't need them. Fluffers doesn't have a bee allergy, or he would have gone into anaphylactic shock by now. A specific small dose of antihistamines can help, though.

"Okay." Connor nods. His face has regained its tan, and he's wiped his tears away.

My gaze drops down his body. His T-shirt clings to his muscles while showing off the forearm tattoos I've dreamt about tracing with my fingers and tongue. His joggers hang low on his hips, and I glimpse a little hair leading beneath the waistband. With his dark beard, he resembles a mountain hero ready for battle. That he's cooing to a cat makes my hormones spark hotter.

195

I put my plan into action. I make sure Connor is distracted, and then I perform a fake dive dramatic enough to impress a footballer.

I scream in pain as I roll around on the floor, clutching my ankle.

Connor runs over, not letting go of Fluffers, who scrabbles to escape my shrieking. Connor eases him into his carrier before he kneels beside me.

"What happened?" The vein in his neck is out of control as he holds me.

I squeeze my eyes shut, trying to force a tear, but nothing comes. The way his gaze scans me, his hands shaking, which I'm sure is more due to the day's action than anything to do with me, leaves me warm and annoyed. As he tries to touch me, I pull away. He can't learn I'm faking the injury.

"I caught your sofa and went down. I've twisted my ankle." I'm a shit liar, but concern clouds his awareness. I'm a special kind of sick that hasn't got a cure. "Please help me up."

I must move this on before he realises what I'm up to. He helps me sit on the sofa. "Let me check it."

"No," I blurt out, pulling away from him again. "I forgot to shave near my ankles this week. It's embarrassing how hairy they are."

Worst lie ever. And now he thinks I'm a weirdo with hobbit ankles. I clench my jaw. *Get on with it, Senna.* This isn't about turning him on. This is about getting him back in a car.

He glances at my legs. Well, it's more than a glance. He's staring at my thighs like they're made of gold.

"Okay, well, stay here and rest. I'll find you another pack of veggies to put on it, and we'll chill out until it feels

better."

"But what about the antihistamines for Fluffers?" Which he doesn't need because he's okay. He's shouting from the carrier like the house is burning down. He's a demanding little bastard. "I can't drive like this, and Jimmy will be devastated if he knows we could have helped his cat more."

My voice catches in my throat. Doing this to Connor feels cruel, but he needs to get behind the wheel now. It's what I did after my race, and it's what the sports psychologist recommended, not to race, but to drive and be in control again. I'm not doing this because I want Connor back on my team. I'm doing it to help him, but still, I feel like a mega bitch.

Guilt slaps me.

"Actually, don't worry. I can get it for him. I'm sure my ankle is fine." I get up to prove everything is okay, waggling it around near him. I'll never be able to manipulate anyone into anything.

Connor's eyes flit between me and the car keys in my hand. "No. I'll do it. I've always wanted to drive your car, not that you've ever let me. And this is for Fluffers, right?"

I nod weakly. I'm a bitch.

As we carry the cat carrier to the car, because there's no chance Connor is leaving Fluffers alone, he says, "I knew you were faking. Your ankles are hair-free. I noticed your legs when you were on the phone with the Australian dickhead. But if you'd fall like Ronaldo to get me to drive, I guess I can do it."

I go to speak, and he holds his hand up like I did the day I found out he was a driver on my team. My scowl makes him grin.

"For the record, Coults, I don't want to drive, and the

idea makes me want to throw myself and the car keys into the water. But having you by my side as I do it is the best way for me to give this a go. If you drove after your accident, I can, too. It turns out, your presence can get me to face anything, including what I fear most."

Connor fucking Dane strikes again, and my heart pulsates like it's about to explode.

CHAPTER THIRTY-TWO – CONNOR

My hands tremble as I take a corner. Senna sits in the passenger seat, and a mewing Fluffers is safely in his carrier in her footwell. I glance at her legs. Her shorts are denim and teeny, and if I weren't panicked about crashing into a hedge, I'd let my gaze linger. It's been a week, and I've missed her so much that being this close to her and smelling her floral citrus scent clears my head.

"It took me two months before I drove after my crash. I didn't want to. The prospect of getting behind a wheel was like will ngly consuming a pint of sick." I blanch at the picture she creates. "But I did it."

"What made you take the step?"

She gives a mirthless chuckle. "Niki lied and told me you were coming to the house. I needed to get as far away as possible."

"So you're saying that, even then, I helped you face your fears."

Her laugh is genuine. "If that's how you want to see it."

Fluffers has quieted down. My knuckles are getting their colour back, and my pulse is less rapid. It has absolutely nothing to do with Senna's legs, laugh, and general incredibleness—nothing at all.

I clear my throat. "So you didn't want to visit Mr. Thinks He's God And Calls You Tiger Vet, then?"

She wriggles her nose at me. "Look at you coming up with new names for him every time. And people say you have no imagination."

I smile at her and try not to get distracted by her legs. She's also wearing a team T-shirt that clings to her boobs. Fuck. The crash should have been enough to calm my libido a little.

My gaze flicks back to the road. "That doesn't answer my question, Coults. What changed your mind about seeing him?"

"Work," she replies. She stares out the window. I tuck the discussion away for now. "I'm proud of you, Connor, especially as you knew I faked an injury. You didn't have to drive us."

Although I suspect her words are partly to avoid a conversation about the vet, I puff out my chest. "Thank you. I've always wanted to drive this beast. If crashing and nearly dying is what it took, then fair enough."

Her voice quiets. "I was petrified when you crashed. I ran through the garage like a woman possessed. I don't want to lose you again," she stutters.

I briefly squeeze her hand, which she clenches in her lap.

"You won't lose me, Senna. I'm not going anywhere."

"But your resignation—"

"I'm going to try to stay. I don't know if I can, but I'll try." I shouldn't make promises I can't keep. All I've done is drive a car to the village pharmacy. "But I might need your help."

"I'm here for you always."

Even as fears form a lump in my throat and wolves howl in my head, telling me to change my mind, there's something intense growing in my chest. It's hope and

START YOUR ENGINES

something extra I can't label because only platonic thoughts are safe in relation to my boss.

I park, and she climbs out of the car. Her shorts nearly reveal the bottom of her butt.

And there go the platonic feelings.

By the day's end, I'm sitting on the sofa under a blanket with Senna and a movie that lights up her face.

She fell asleep an hour ago. She insisted on staying and ensuring Fluffers was okay. Her mouth parts, and her lips draw me closer. I remember the taste of cranberry that lingered in my dreams after our night at the bar. I added mango lip balm to my shopping request to have her scent when panic overwhelmed me. I'm either a psychopath or lovesick.

Today, we became good friends again, and that's all we can be. We haven't discussed what happened that night in the bar, and as far as I'm concerned, it remains a blip. Like I said to her in the car, I'm not going anywhere even though it'll be torture being around her permanently.

Senna shifts in her sleep, and a waft of orange blossom covers me.

"I want to kiss her forehead and hold her in my arms," I whisper to Fluffers, who stretches in my lap, reminding me he's the only one who can have my attention.

I glance at Senna. That's the final straw for Fluffers. He throws me a death stare, jumps off my lap, and strolls to the bedroom on his healed paw. That's where I should go, but I don't want to wake Senna. If I could watch her sleep for the rest of my life, it would be nearly complete. Just one thing would be missing.

201

She moans in her sleep, and my dick gets harder than a rock. That thing. I want to kiss her, to bring her pleasure she's never known. I want to obliterate Mr. Dickhead Vet and every other guy lucky enough to touch her. None of them deserve her.

And neither do I.

I'm a failing driver who's made promises I don't know how to keep. Doing anything with her would destroy my friendship with Niki forever. And yet, as she snuggles up to me in her sleep, my arm falls around her. Her chest presses against me, and my lips brush her forehead. I thread my fingers through her hair and whisper promises to her. Eventually, my head tips back, and I close my eyes, praying I'll dream of a life where I can be with my Senna.

CHAPTER THIRTY-THREE – SENNA

The battle on screen between Ayrton Senna and Alain Prost continues. Over the last three days, Connor and I have watched countless races featuring greats like Michael Schumacher, Graham Hill, and Lewis Hamilton.

Connor grips my hand. "I used to watch these races with my mum on Sunday afternoons while she rushed in and out preparing dinner."

I want to run my knuckles against his freshly shaved jaw. "And that was where you discovered your love of driving?"

His eyes twinkle as he catches my gaze. "That's where I discovered my love of adrenaline."

My stomach thuds. He has no idea how sexy he is when he says things like this. My stare grazes his forearms, which flex as the rivals force each other to drive increasingly dangerously. I catch the bottom of his Silverstone track tattoo and barely resist tracing it with my fingers. Over the last three days, we've been working on Operation Get Connor Driving. But all it's done is make me want him more.

"I remember when you were thirteen. You were fearless on the track." We're sitting closer on the sofa than we should be if I don't want weird drunk-on-Connor feelings. His thigh is flush against mine. Every movement

203

means his body presses against me. It's doing a number on my nipples, which push against my lace bra. He has no idea what he does to me.

It's been like this for three days, as we barely leave each other's side during the day while playing computer games and entertaining Fluffers.

My legs open wider as if my hormones control my body. "I'm guessing your crashes stopped the adrenaline," I stammer.

"I can find adrenaline in other things." He side-eyes me.

Images of being under Connor as he owns my body flash. If our kiss, which still sneaks into my dreams, is anything to go by, I'm not surprised. My body heats, and I rake my lips with my teeth. Time together has worsened my feelings for him. It's not just the desperation to kiss him again. It's everything. My teenage heart is alive for the first time in years, and she wants to cuddle while listening to Taylor Swift on repeat. Meanwhile, my adult side wants to jump his bones.

He flips his cap so it's facing backwards. His knuckles are tight, and I reprimand myself for being horny when he's suffering.

He clears his throat. "But it's not just that I'm scared of driving. It's that I don't love it anymore."

I gasp and cover my mouth. "You don't love driving? But I've let you drive my car twice."

He laughs and shoves me. His touch makes my skin burn, and I swear he stares at my legs as I tuck them under me. It's nice to be back in my shorts and T-shirts. I glance out of his bay windows. All these touches make me want to dive into the lake and cool myself off.

"And we've played Need for Speed and Mario Kart every day." Nothing stops the internal Connor burn. Gaming

START YOUR ENGINES

against him nearly killed me the other day—all that swearing and banter.

"Gaming doesn't count. And it was fun driving your car even when you screamed as I got close to the hedge to let those tourists pass." He gives me a nudge that has me nearly toppling off the sofa. He wraps his arm around my waist and pulls me back. "It's good to know how you sound when you scream."

I turn to face him. Our lips are so close I could kiss him. Maybe I'm not the only one dealing with forbidden thoughts. Fuck, I'm so confused.

I take a breath. "Anyway, we're meant to work on Operation Get Connor Driving. But we should call it Operation Make Connor Love Driving Again."

He shrugs, but his gaze lingers on my lips. I shove him away. I can't deal with all these emotions. "So you don't like driving because of the crashes and...?"

"And the politics and the enabled shitty behaviour of people like Antoine who can be dangerous twats because they have power and money," he practically snarls.

"I still need to replace him. I'm not allowed to do business right now because of shutdown, but I keep thinking about it." *When I'm not thinking about you.*

"Tawny would be good, and she's got what she needs to move up in terms of license and skill. She has ideas for how to maximise the cars, too."

"Jacs's sister?" I roll my shoulders.

I like her, and she's an exceptional driver who's precisely what the team needs. But she and Connor flirted on our night out, although it was me he kissed. So what if she and Connor flirt if it'd be good for the team?

"She would be brilliant." I'm a prick for being jealous. He's not mine. I retuck my legs as I remember his hand

205

against my thigh under the hem of my dress when we kissed. He smells of beer and spice like he did that night.

"She'd benefit from a female boss who doesn't sideline her success." Guilt bites my ankles. It's hard to be a woman in this business. I could help shield her from the crap. I need to raise women as I've always done, not be jealous of them. "Her boss hasn't given her the respect she deserves, so I reckon she'd move even though she'd go from top dog in F2 to a newbie in F1 in the middle of the season."

"How do you know all of this?" The question is out of my mouth before I stop it. "Do you chat?"

"Are you jealous, Sen?" His lip tilts.

The bastard knows exactly what's going on in my head. It's like cocky eighteen-year-old Connor has entered the room. Only it's not my teenage heart fluttering. It's all adult, and that stare has put the heat right between my legs.

"No chance."

A wave of hair falls out of my ponytail, and he tucks it behind my ear. I make a fist to stop me from grabbing the T-shirt clinging to his chest.

"For the record, Coults." His voice lowers. My belly performs Olympic-level gymnastics with flips and rolls. "She and Jacs called me yesterday. But it's just friendship. She's not my type. I like the bosses, not the drivers."

Fuck.

"Like Graham Hill. He was a boss and a driver," I stutter, pointing at the screen.

I'm too scared to ask what he feels for me.

"Like Graham Hill," he agrees and settles into the sofa with a sigh.

Thoughts itch my brain as we stare at the screen. "So if you no longer love driving, why stay with the team?"

He pulls my legs onto his lap, and I don't resist him. His

heat penetrates my skin.

"Partly for Niki. But mostly for you. I'm not leaving you in the lurch like others have. You need me, don't you?"

As I stare into those big blue eyes, I'm sure he knows all the ways I need him. "Yes. I need you."

"Then, even though I'll run through everything I hate about driving as I wait for races to start, I'll drive and I'll do it for you."

"For me?" It comes out like a squeak rather than a question full of self-assurance.

"For you," he confirms. "It's all for you."

My mouth goes dry. His thumbs tap on my thighs. I can't resist him for much longer, and my reasons for not letting him close are fading into nothing.

CHAPTER THIRTY-FOUR – CONNOR

Her legs are impossibly smooth, like silk. I bite my lip. Does she taste as soft as she looks? Spending these days with her has made me want to shout my feelings from the rooftops. I want to get a reaction and know she wants me as much as I desire her.

She focuses on the cars flying around the track on screen, her hazel eyes swirling with amber and burnt orange.

I need to enjoy the friendship and get over myself, yet I grip her legs again. She must moisturise hourly, or more likely, she's a fucking angel. She's wearing her tiny denim shorts again, but I refuse to look above her knees. I grip her legs tighter to stop my hands from drifting.

"I have a question," she announces. *Please ask me if I love you so I can get on my knees and prove my answer with my tongue.* My cock begins to harden, and I will it to calm.

"Sure." I clear my throat.

"You said that before a race, you'll run through everything you hate about racing."

I shrug. "Yeah."

"You don't wear headphones like the other drivers before a race. Why is that?"

This is an appropriate question from a friend. I can't fuck things up. But I can't stop my eyes from drifting up her

legs and higher. Shit, her nipples are pressing against her T-shirt.

"Connor?"

I move her legs off me and stand, walking a few steps to the kitchen part of the open-plan house. I force distance physically and hopefully in my head, too. "No reason. They all do it because they have music they listen to, but I don't. Do you want a drink?"

"You don't have music, or you don't want to listen to music?" She stands and follows me.

"I don't have music to listen to. Is this important?" I wring my hands together.

"Yes. So you don't have a song you listen to when you get ready to race?"

Her toes touch mine as she lifts her head and pins my gaze. Everything about this woman is unrelenting, and I can't resist it. And I'm trying. I've been trying most of my life.

"I thought that was something only boxers did and people who are crappy townie drivers."

She gives me a playful shove. "No, you didn't."

"I've never found my song, so listening to music before racing distracts me and frustrates me. So what?"

I try to walk away, but she grips my hands.

"But every driver on this circuit has one. I have one for when I go into meetings."

"Fleetwood Mac's 'The Chain,'" I reply with a smile that's erring on cocky.

She shoves me again, although she's blushing and grinning this time. "Yes, and sometimes 'The Man' by Taylor Swift."

I lick my lips. "And do you have a walk when you listen to 'The Man'? Because I'd like to see that. It will help my song research."

"The only thing you'll see is me flicking you the Vs as I walk away."

"I like the idea of watching you walk away," I say with a wink that makes her shake her head as a grin broader than the sky takes over her face.

"Back to the song. I've got a couple, but one jumps out." And then she walks to her bag, her gait slow. I swear she gives her butt an extra wiggle.

A grunt escapes my mouth, and she looks over her shoulder, her brows furrowed. I shrug and lick my lips as I stare at her butt. Senna sticks her middle finger up at me as she grins. I'm a dickhead, but I think she likes that.

She likes me. Fuck. I can't stop messing with her.

She pulls her headphones out of her bag and walks back. As she reaches me, she cups my face. My breath catches. I'm like some giddy teenager desperate for his crush to kiss him rather than a man who's usually in control.

She flips her headphones from the box and slides them into my ears. Her fingers brush my neck, and I hold in a gasp that threatens to reveal I'm not just a cocky guy giving charm to his friend. Her sweet scent of orange blossom lingers on my skin as she grabs her phone from her back pocket. Her eyelashes flutter, and she bites her lip as she scrolls through her music account. I swallow loudly, the sound like a blast of noise with the headphones stuck in my ears. "Here we go."

Her big hazel eyes focus on mine as I listen to the first beats of the song. I can't figure out what she's mouthing, so I try to remove the earbuds, but she holds her hands against mine to keep them in.

"Just listen," she mouths. It's nearly impossible to focus on the music. She hasn't dropped her hands, and her heat penetrates my skin, filling my veins with her. She strokes her thumbs behind my ears.

START YOUR ENGINES

"Close your eyes," she mouths. Half of me wants to keep my eyes open so I can drown in the intensity of her stare, the amber swirling in her eyes, and her tongue edging across her bottom lip. But if I'm going to listen to it, I need to have a view that is much less sensory than her beauty.

I close my eyes as the rhythm builds. There are violins and an Irish melody I don't recognise. The power continues to take hold, and it's frantic and consuming.

It's like a revelation and everything I've needed. Like she's everything I've needed. I can imagine listening to this song before a race. The punch of the rhythm gives me power and presence and makes me want to act, destroy, and control, too.

I wish her hands were against me in the build-up to a race. That would give me power. With her, I'd take on the world, every driver, bastard, and anyone else who gets in my way. I shake my head, and goosebumps smatter across my skin.

The song ebbs and fades, and Senna's hands disappear. I miss her touch instantly. I remove the earbuds.

"Not it? I can try others."

"It was perfect," I say, my voice gruff.

Her smile and puffed-up chest warm my heart. She flips the phone to the speaker and puts it on the counter beside us. The song plays again.

"I knew it. It played in a bar I hung out in years ago, and I immediately thought of you. It has your energy and a melody that refuses to leave the body."

"You thought of me in the past?" We haven't talked about those years where we didn't speak. She wasn't in my life until she worked in the comms department, and then she avoided me. I didn't think I existed to her.

Her eyes widen as if she's revealed more than she

211

intended. "Oh, well, sometimes. Usually, it was thoughts of hate," she says with a stunted laugh.

"Usually? So there were other thoughts, too?"

I'm not letting this conversation go away. I've let too much get away from me. This thing between us is coming to a head.

The song moves through the chorus and is as unrelenting as she is. She's always been this way, pressing and pushing in my heart. The intensity makes me straighten my back, and my shoulders rise.

"Yes." She dips her head, and I tuck my finger under her chin and lift it. Our eyes meet.

"And what were those thoughts, Coults?" The danger of the moment has me fisting my other hand so she's oblivious to my tremble. This feels more significant and adrenaline-filled than any race and podium win.

"I missed you. I missed my friend who made me laugh and filled my days with hope and joy I didn't believe I'd experience again."

She didn't always hate me.

She holds my stare. "Did you ever think of me?"

I take a breath and laugh awkwardly.

"Never mind." She pulls away, but I reach for her hand to draw her back.

I cup her face like she cupped mine. "You wonder if I ever thought of you. Every. Fucking. Day. Some days, you were all I thought about. There was a space in my heart that was all you, and nothing else filled it."

As I talk, new colours join the amber in her hazel eyes. I'm mesmerised by the blue flecks. She's so fucking beautiful.

"There would be days when I got through Senna-free hours, but there were also days when each breath I took was

infused with you. I woke most mornings curious about what you were doing or wishing I could see you and explain. I caught a joke and wanted to tell you it or I'd read something about racing and question if you'd heard the same story. When I visited your brother, I wanted to ask him about you and ensure you were okay, but I didn't cross that line. I kept it inside, although it ate at me. I tried to hate you, but even when I did, I was lying to myself."

She studies my eyes, leaning into my hands as if she can't let herself believe me. "I wanted to ask him about you, too. I should've been able to cut you out of my heart as I cut you out of my life, but you've always been there, filling my dreams and reminding me of the happy times. We were close, weren't we?"

The song nears its crescendo, giving me the energy and presence I need to drive. Only now, it allows me to share my truth.

"The closest. I missed your laughter and your joy. I hoped no other man got to know what it was like to make you smile. I wanted to believe you saved all your smiles for me. I hated that other men got to touch you like I wanted to."

She holds my hand against her cheek and fixes me with a look that makes me shiver. "Like a friend?"

I shake my head. "Like a lover."

Her stare penetrates mine. "I wanted that, too. I imagined it."

I tremble at the admission.

"Some days, I'd punish myself with Google press shots of who you were dating. And then the other days..." She pauses so long that I raise my eyebrows. I grit my teeth to stop myself hurrying her.

For months, I've tried to be the best driver for her, even

while fighting my struggles and the knowledge she can't be mine. But as the song embeds itself in my soul, the music that reminded her of me, I brush her lower lip with my thumb. She runs her tongue across it, as if tasting me.

"Other days," she eventually adds, her voice gravelly and saturated with arousal, "I'd search for your sexier shots and fantasise about kissing you and—"

I press my lips hard against hers, claiming her. She gasps. I need to slow down. If this is my one opportunity, I must remember her. Our moment in the bar was too brief. I want to know her taste so I can revisit it nightly. I want to make her whimper. I need her softness.

My other hand cups her other cheek, and I brush kisses to her lips. "I imagined your kisses," I say between the grazes of my lips. "I longed to be the man in your bed and in your heart." She leans closer. "I wanted to hunt down your dates and tell them they weren't good enough for you. That no one was good enough for you, including me, but you were mine anyway."

I back her up against the counter. She wraps her arms around my neck, and I lift her and ease her onto the countertop. I slide my tongue into her parted mouth, and she moans against me as my hands slide underneath the gap between her shorts and her thighs. We're making out, and although I want to do more, I want to spend time discovering her body slowly, too. She opens her legs enough to let me stand between them. I pull the tie out of her hair and let her short waves cascade down like a drawer of messy ribbons.

She tries to undo my jeans, but I still her hands. "Senna." My gruff voice reveals what this moment does to me. "I want this. I want you writhing beneath me as you say my name and lose everything but your words for me. But for

now, I want to kiss you and enjoy the sexy noises you make and feel your body shake against mine." She trembles. "Do you want that, too, baby?"

"Yes, Connor." I'm not the only one whose voice is saturated with passion. "I want everything. Now fucking kiss me again like I've never been kissed before."

"Yes, boss," I murmur against her lips before giving her everything she wants and more.

CHAPTER THIRTY-FIVE – SENNA

I can feel everything, from the heat of his palms hard against my skin to the softness of his lips as they brush against mine. Our tongues tangle, and I grab at tufts of his hair. He growls into my mouth, and I lose myself in the kiss, in him.

His kisses are quickly becoming my new obsession. My fingertips dance across the back of his neck, and his hands travel up my body until they're sliding beneath my top. And then they stop. I wriggle a little, wanting him to touch my breasts, to thumb my nipples that are straining at my top, but he doesn't. Instead, he grips my waist and controls the moment.

I don't know how long we spend kissing because I'm lost in my pleasure. Occasionally, we break for air, but each time, we return to each other like two lost souls who've finally found their other half.

The ache in my body is more than the need to be touched. It's the ache for him that I've been keeping secret for months, for years.

With my legs wrapped around his waist, I pull him tighter against me. For years my life was empty because he wasn't in it.

He pulls back to stare at me, and I fist his top and bring him straight back against me. He swipes his tongue across

my lips.

"More. I need more," I pant.

His lips brush my jaw and neck, the heat of his touch burning my skin. His teeth scrape at my ear lobe, and I bob against him. His erection presses into me, and I suck in a breath.

He smells of sweat and spice.

"Please, Connor," I beg, and his hands slide to my bum, grabbing it as he lifts me and carries me to the sofa.

He sits and pulls me on top of him, my thighs straddling his lap.

He stares at me like I'm all he needs for his survival. I lick my lips, my brows furrowing as I take in his adoration.

"I've dreamt about kissing these cheeks that flush when you're angry with me," he says, his fingers trailing over my skin. He holds up my hand and kisses my palm. "I've longed to kiss this hand. Every time you held it up to silence me, I'd get so fucking turned on."

"You like it when I tell you what to do?"

"Shush," he replies with a smirk before pressing his lips to my neck. "When I first saw your new hairstyle and boss outfit, I nearly lost it, partly because you looked like the perfect boss to discipline me but also because it meant you were keeping your hair down so I couldn't stare at your neck and fantasise about kissing it and making you moan my name."

He sucks on my neck, and I know he's going to leave a love bite, the mark of his need.

"Please, Connor. I need more."

"When I'm ready," he growls against my skin, making me whimper his name.

"You're fucking gorgeous," he grunts against my collarbone as he pulls away and stares at me.

217

I'm grinding against his erection, practically dry humping him, as his lips press against mine, harder this time. The friction of our clothes against my pussy makes me moan into his mouth. He grips my arse, kneading my cheeks as he pulls me onto him.

I swear he's bigger than he said. His dick is thick and hard, and the thought of it pushing inside me makes me lean back and grind harder. He reclines against the sofa and threads his fingers behind his head. He watches me enjoy his body with a smug smile. It's like I'm performing for him. Everything I'm doing is hitting my clit just right, and I stare at him as I rub myself against him again and again. I'm soaking, but I need his lips on me.

"Kiss me," I beg.

"Yes, baby," he replies, flipping me so I'm underneath him.

I hiss as he stares at me again. Suddenly, he softens the moment, brushing the back of his fingers across my cheekbones and smiling at me. "I've wanted this for so long that I'm scared of fucking it up. It's like all my dreams and fantasies are finally coming true, and I can't stop staring at you."

My heart flutters at the earnest way he looks at me.

I suck in my lower lip and lose myself in his cerulean eyes.

I don't know what this is, and I don't care. I just want him.

His arms bracket my head as he dips his head and presses kisses to my cheek.

"You're fucking perfect, Coults, and I'm..." he whispers in my ear before sucking my lower lip into his mouth. And then he says the one word that ended his resignation letter. "...yours."

His kisses are soft, hard, and everything in between. He strokes my skin, squeezing my breasts and thumbing my nipples, but never ducking his hand beneath my clothes. It's the make-out we never got as teenagers, and for one glorious afternoon, it's ours.

This man can kiss.

But I need more. I want to know what it's like to have Connor fucking Dane inside me.

He starts to slip my top off. My lips are sore, and my body aches from not coming.

Fluffers jumps on the top of the sofa and stares down at us.

His meow is louder than a fire alarm.

"Someone is hungry," he says, and I can't stop my giggle.

Connor's eyebrow quirks as he shakes his head. I cover my face with my hands, but he pulls them away. "Safe to say we're all hungry."

Connor kisses my forehead, eases himself off me, and heads to the open-plan kitchen.

His muscles flex as he opens the tin of cat food. I lick my lips as the muscles in his forearms harden. He catches the action and smirks. That smirk destroys me.

"Do you want your food, Fluffers?" he says softly, bending down to rub Fluffers under the chin. The furry beast makes a figure eight through his legs, his tail swishing like he owns this man, and Connor beams. My heart thunders.

I want to own this man.

I walk over to the two of them as I adjust my clothes. I'm forever drawn to him.

Connor sucks in his lower lip and winks at me. My emotions are in hyperdrive.

Fluffers claws Connor's ankle to hurry him up and

curtail our flirting.

"Oi, you." Connor pops the food down, and Fluffers attacks it with the hunger of a cat who hasn't been fed in weeks rather than a few hours. Connor's forearms flex again, and my body quivers.

"Good girl."

An ache spreads through my body. When I look at him again, his dark and wanting eyes meet mine. "Who are you calling a good girl? Fluffers is a boy." My voice wavers.

He steps closer, and my entire body trembles at his intent. "Maybe I'm calling you good girl. Would you like that, baby?" his lips whisper against my neck.

His kisses trail down my skin. When I think they'll undo me, he gets on his knees and lifts my T-shirt. His lips are hot against my body as my hands fist his hair.

"We need to stop," I say between gasps.

He pulls his head back. "I've gone too far too quick?"

I press my finger to his lips and shake my head.

His sudden vulnerability wraps around my heart, and I kneel to face him. I return his earlier moves and brush kisses against his neck. I lift his shirt. His abs quiver, and the words of his tattoo move like rushing water as I run my fingertips across them.

I push his shirt down quickly and find his brow furrowed. "If I start that, I'll never stop."

"I'm not complaining."

My hand travels lower and catches on his erection. "Your dick is massive!"

"Say it again." His smile is charm and cockiness. "Tell me my dick is huge, baby."

"No." I jump up and stand away. I want to repeat those words and have him drag me to his bed. His eyebrows jump high. "Not no, because I don't want to. I really want to. Fuck

me, your cock is the biggest I've had near my hand, and I've not seen it to know that." He smirks, and I glare. "We need to go out and get dinner—"

"I have everything I want to eat right here."

I choke on my gasp.

"Have you ever straddled a man's face while he worships your—"

"That's it. We're going out."

I want everything he's offering me, but I need time to contemplate the lines I'm crossing, and having my legs wrapped around Connor's devilish face won't help that.

He chuckles as I stand frozen. I'm too saturated with need to move.

"Come on then, beautiful. I'd best drive as you won't be able to concentrate with the thought of my tongue in your pussy. I'd hate for you to scratch your car knowing exactly what I have planned for you when we get back."

I get my bag as he tracks my movements. He's like a hungry panther playing with his food.

"By the way, do you need to make any notes about your plans for the rest of your time off?"

I turn to him, my head hurting from the change of conversation. "Huh?"

"Once I fuck your brains out, baby, you're not going to remember your name, so if there's anything important you want to remember, you'd best make a note."

"You're such an ass." I hold my keys out to him. "I'll let you drive, but promise you'll be careful with my baby."

He grabs my keys and pulls me against him. "Only if you promise to be my good girl when we return and let me do all the things with you I've fantasised about for years."

My mouth dries up, and I nod.

As I follow him out of the house, my eyes firmly fixed

221

on his butt, I can't imagine dinner will last long. I can barely remember my name, let alone how to eat.

CHAPTER THIRTY-SIX – SENNA

"**A**re you enjoying the fondue?" he asks as I pull my fork with bread on the end out of the cheesy mixture. Scents of rosemary and cheeses I can't distinguish mix with Connor's spicy aftershave.

I nod as I blow on the bread that drips over my plate.

"You're beautiful," he adds, his blue eyes twinkling from the glow of the fake candles that light our table and the fairy lights dotted around the coffee shop that transforms into a village bistro at night.

I look around at the other tables. This place seems popular with locals, holidaymakers, and walkers returning to the village after their hikes.

"I'm wearing shorts and a hoodie. I hardly look like a model," I reply with a roll of my eyes.

"You look like everything I've ever wanted and needed."

I rub my furrowed brow. Everything has changed in one day. I can't—

"Tell me something about you I don't know from the last ten years," he cuts into my overthinking.

"I could tell you how I met Jacs." He nods as he fills my water glass. I take a quick sip. "I thought I'd discovered a real-life unicorn when I found her. A female best friend who

is as passionate about racing as me. Best day ever." He raises his eyebrows at me. "Okay, today is pretty close."

He chuckles and winks. I nearly fan myself with my serviette.

"At the end-of-season dinner, I overheard a mechanic from Vessa tell her she'd never amount to anything because there wasn't space for women like her in Formula One."

"Dick."

"Exactly. But then he added that he'd enjoy watching her never climb the ladder over the next few years and walked off. So I "accidentally" pushed my bag out in front of him."

"That's my girl," Connor says and my belly flutters.

I sip my water to stop from squealing.

"His faceplant was perfect. I was apologetic, but I got away with it because of who Dad was. I hate the whole nepo baby thing because I've worked for everything I've had. But when I needed to bring that arsehole down without consequences, it worked in my favour."

"You're no nepo baby. You're the hardest working person in racing." I hum my appreciation. "But then what happened? How did you catch your unicorn?"

"For the rest of that evening, I made my way around the room, learning all I needed about Jacs and by the end of the night, I'd petitioned the head of the mechanic's team to sign her to Coulter Racing, hoping she was as good as her reputation. She was better, and within two years, she was one of the head mechanics, and the dickhead from Vessa now asks her for a job. She refuses."

Connor claps his hands and beams at me. "That's why you're the best."

I scrunch my nose, but he repeats, "You're the best, baby."

START YOUR ENGINES

The wait staff takes our plates, but we only see each other.

"Your turn. I have a specific question for you, but it might be too much," I say as my lips tip down.

"I won't hide anything from you anymore. You can ask me anything whenever you want."

His words calm my pulse. "Your dad. I'm sorry I wasn't there when he left."

"Senna, you've been thinking about this a lot?" I nod. He holds out his hand, and I take it. "Don't ever feel guilty for what happened. My dad is the only person who should feel guilt," he says softly.

"How did you get through it?"

He leans his head back and looks at the ceiling. He lets out a long breath, and I squeeze his hand to remind him that I'm here for him.

"Don't worry, it doesn't matter, Con."

Connor fixes me with his stare. "It matters to you, and so it matters. I want you to know everything about me; this is part of who I am." He drags in a breath and lets it out slowly. "For a while, I didn't get through it. I lost you and your parents and then my dad and mum and Layla in one hit."

Sadness creeps up my body, and I suck my lower lip into my mouth.

"And it wasn't your fault, Sen. It was the best and worst time of my life. Signed to a team but at a cost at the age of eighteen. For the first time in my life, I had money and attention, and I didn't have anyone telling me to behave. I sent money to Dad to keep him from the family and to Mum to start a fund for Layla's future. But there was so much."

"And you had Niki, who was signed and eighteen and trouble."

225

Connor's lips quirk. "We thought we were the shit. We swaggered around nightclubs and said the most stupid things in interviews. Groupies laughed at everything we said and entertained us."

My jaw hardens. The wait staff bring our pasta, and I tuck in like I'm totally fine. Connor never lets go of my hand.

"Senna, I spiralled, baby. I knew I didn't want to be my dad and cheat like he did all the time, so I avoided relationships. I was always upfront about it, but..."

I look at him when he doesn't finish his sentence.

"Does my past freak you out?" he says, winding me.

"I know you have a past, and I have no right to have an issue with it." I run my finger against my gin glass, and condensation wets my skin. "It's not like I don't have one."

"Including with Mr Giant Muscles and Ego Vet," Connor says. "I'm surprised you didn't go to him."

"I wouldn't, I couldn't. I considered visiting him just to get away from work—"

"And me?" he asks with a raised eyebrow.

"Yes, because of the boss thing. But ultimately, I didn't want him, and I didn't want him to think I did. I just wanted you."

He grips my hand and hooks my stare. "Good. Because I've never been so fucking jealous in my entire life." He strokes my skin with his thumb. "And when it comes to those models or exes or anyone else, you have nothing to be jealous of because the day I saw you at Ralf's wedding, every woman that had been in my life faded away like sunshine when a storm comes."

"I'm the storm?"

"You're the fucking cyclone that I can't stop chasing. At Ralf's wedding, your presence dragged me under your spell, and I never wanted to be anywhere else. You were it for me.

I never slept with another woman after that day."

"Oh." Cold air crosses my arms, yet his hand burns my skin.

"You're it for me. You have written over every memory until they've become days when I saw you and days when I didn't. After that wedding, my heart told me I didn't want any more Senna-free days even though my head said that's exactly what I'd be having. Then you walked into the board room and changed everything."

"That day was…memorable." I smile as I look down at the empty table. I've no idea when our plates were taken. I take a breath and utter words that I know will lead to questions, but they slip out of my mouth anyway because I need to let him in. "I wish you'd stayed for the wedding reception."

My heart swirls with emotions I'm scared to share.

"Did something happen?" I look into his blue eyes, which are infused with concern.

I press my fingers against my mouth, and he squeezes my other hand. "Baby, who hurt you?"

"I'd never felt more alone as I did at the wedding. Niki was distracted by women vying for his attention, and Dad tried to set me up with the son of one of his former business partners. I tried to tell Dad I wasn't interested in his traditional dreams for me because I wanted to run the team. That night, I overheard him telling Mum that the team would never be mine but that it would be Niki's one day. I always suspected it, but he talked about me like I was a silly girl."

"Oh, Coults. I'm sorry about your dad. He doesn't deserve to have a daughter like you. I'm proud just to be able to call you a friend. You're incredible."

I smile because I know to him that's true. "I realised something else that day. Stood at the side of the marquee,

looking at all the people, I realised that if I wanted to be a team boss, then it would be the loneliest thing in the world because I would always have to fight Dad. Niki would support me, but he's always been about his dreams with his charmed life." Sadness wells in my heart. "At least he was until the accident."

"It will be interesting to see who he is when he returns."

"If he returns."

"Take my other hand, Sen," Connor says, gripping both tightly. "I know you think you have to do this alone and that you have no one on your side, but you have Jacs, the whole team and you have me. I will always support you. I'm here for you in whatever capacity you want."

"Thank you," I say, and he holds my hands to his mouth and kisses them.

He didn't push me to talk more or agree that I would always come to him when I felt lonely. He's planted a seed in my head so I can think about it and ask questions later. Connor Dane is everything, but I don't know what to say now.

And then he whispers, "And because one of my skills will always be to lighten the mood. I also need you to know that my best friend became my own hands after that wedding."

"So that's why you have such impressive forearms," I reply, leaning back to gaze at them.

"I knew you were staring at them." He flexes them and winks. "I've got the strongest forearms, and it's all because of you."

I throw my head back and laugh.

His face softens. "You're the one woman I desire, and everyone else fades into fiction. You were the first girl I

wanted to kiss and the only one I want to kiss. If nothing else happens between us, at least I have the memory of your lips against mine and the touch of your skin."

He finds it so easy to share what's in his heart, yet every word is a struggle for me. I focus on the dried splash of pasta sauce on the tablecloth, rubbing my scar.

Out of the corner of my eye, I witness his smile drop.

"Sen, I hate seeing you do that. My heart hurts every time because I caused it. I'm so sorry I caused you pain and destroyed your future. You should be the one on the podiums, not Niki or me. I should have given up racing that day."

I shake my head as I rush to his side of the table, nearly knocking our glasses. I hold his head between my hands. His closed eyes and trembles stab my chest. "Never think like that." I sit on his lap. "I wanted to be a driver. I loved it, and although I'll never be that person, I know I can do other things. I partly raced to impress Dad like Niki did. I loved the adrenaline, too, although being the boss gives me plenty of that. But I wanted to win for him. When they said I should rethink racing, I had the opportunity to think differently. I miss it, but I still have a future and can help women, too."

"Like funding Margot, the girl who came for the meet and greet several months ago."

"Yeah, something like that. Although you weren't meant to hear that." I poke him in the belly. Fuck, he's pure muscle.

"And you don't miss being a racing driver?" His face creases as if he's hurting, and my chest tightens.

I brush his lips with mine and run my fingers through his hair. "I love driving like a speed demon where it's safe, and I'll always miss professionally racing on the track, fighting for a win. But I don't miss the lectures from my dad

or the bullying. Racing will always be my life, but I like running a team and helping others reach their potential."

"And you're amazing at that. You've revolutionised the team. I wish your dad could see that." He gifts me forehead kisses. "You're better than he was."

I take a slow breath as Connor hands me my drink, giving me a moment. "I love my dad, but his influence is one of the reasons Niki left the country. If he were still here, he'd be racing even if he wasn't ready for it because Dad would pressure him."

Connor stares at me. "Your dad's opinions are hard to get away from. I overheard him tell you he wanted you to start a family and not be the boss."

"Did you hear my response?" I bite the inside of my mouth.

Connor and I haven't defined us, but I can't lose him again. But if he wants kids, I have to stop this.

"Yes."

"And what does your future look like?"

CHAPTER THIRTY-SEVEN – CONNOR

What a loaded question. I briefly trace the patterns on the blue gingham tablecloth. Until last week, I didn't think I'd drive again—and now, the future.

"Senna." I brush kisses to her scar. "I don't know what the next year or years hold, but since I lost you at eighteen, I've tried everything to move on." I hold her hand against my heart. "This beats because you're in the world. I would rather die alone than have a future without you. At the wedding, it was like I'd found the only person who completed me. The only person who'd ever complete me. It was a journey to get here. But I'm here now. I don't make sense without you, and I never want to let you go. If you said we needed to move to the jungle in Congo and open a soy latte coffee shop, I'd do it. If you told me we would have twenty kids, even though I don't want any, I'd do it. You're it for me. You're everything."

She ducks her head, and my stomach eats itself from inside out.

I've fucked up. I needed to build up to that. And it's like I've forgotten the added complications of her brother and that she's my boss and her relationship with me could mess up her career. And yet, there was no chance I could hold it in.

When she looks back up, she's rolling her lips together. They're wet from where she's swiped them with her tongue.

"Take me home," she demands. "Take me to your home and prove that everything you said isn't just words. Take me to bed, Connor."

I swallow so loudly I swear the waitress furrows her brow. "Yes, boss."

"I'll meet you at the car." Her voice trembles as she hands me her car keys. I love that she's as terrified by this as I am. She knocks back her drink and stands. "I need a second."

I rush to the car, hoping she's not pacing in the bathroom and regretting her decision. Maybe she's calling Jacs to chat through her panic or, worse, getting her brother's consent to fuck his best friend. It's like I'm riding rapids as I consider the options. This could ruin everything, but I don't feel guilty. I'm horny from all the truth bombs and the way she shared her fears.

Suddenly, she's in the headlights of the car. In her tiny shorts and T-shirt, she's all my dreams come true. And then she puts the phone on speaker. I poke my tongue against the inside of my mouth as I lower the windows. I hum to the last bars of "The Man" by Taylor Swift.

My sexy boss and best friend is scared and needs her confidence song. She gives a bum wiggle that has my cock fighting for freedom from my jeans before striding to the passenger window.

"Get in the car, Coults," I growl. "I need to bury my tongue in your pussy."

A blush runs from her face down her body and under her T-shirt as she opens her door and slides in. The leather cracks as she sits beside me. She's barely got her seatbelt on as I pull away from the curb with squealing tyres. She

doesn't tell me to keep the car safe. Instead, she removes her T-shirt, which leaves her in a bralette with her nipples pressing through the lace. Her blush travels all the way down her chest.

The drive is a blur. As we get to the end of the long driveway that leads to my holiday home, there's more tension in the car than before a race. I knew what adrenaline was, but that was before I considered making the woman I adore orgasm. I lean over and unclick her seatbelt. It gives me ideas of tying her to my bed. My head is Senna porn, and she's not even seen me naked.

"Get in the house, beautiful," I growl.

She tips her head as she winks at me. "We're not having sex on the bonnet of my car?"

I fixate on the bonnet and gulp. I can imagine her on her back as I take her roughly.

"Maybe tomorrow," I reply with a throat so dry I'm rivalling the Sahara.

"It's a deal."

I can't check if she's serious because she's out of the car, looking for the key I keep under the plant pot. She runs through the house, kicking off her trainers.

"Don't remove any more clothes," I shout as I storm in. She freezes outside the bedroom. "I'm ripping them off you."

This should be two people finally making love, but my body demands something else. Her eyes bulge from her head as I yank my belt from my waistband. She sucks on her lower lip as I drag my T-shirt up from the back and pull it

over and off. Her eyes pin to my chest. I flex my abs, showing off my muscles and tattoos. Senna is in teeny shorts and a baby-blue bralette. Her tan from hanging at my house makes her skin glow, but the rosy hue of her nipples blooms from beneath the lace.

I cock my finger. "Come here, Coults."

Her hands fist at her hips. "I thought I was the boss."

I flick open the top button of my jeans. "I'm the boss in this house."

She shivers but doesn't move.

"I can stop if you want." But I would die. My thumb rests on the next button. "Or you can come here so I can fuck you—a fuck like you've never had before."

"Those are big words."

"Not for me. Now come closer so I can feel your hand on my cock."

Her stare flicks to my dick, which is still hidden by my jeans.

As she walks towards me, I stride closer, pick her up, and throw her over my shoulder. Her gasp is so satisfying that I judder in my jeans.

Within five short steps, we're in my bedroom. I throw her on my bed and stare down at her. Her gaze tracks from my eyes to the remaining buttons on my jeans and back up again.

"Hurry," she says, undoing the buttons on her shorts. I still her hand with mine.

"There's no rush," I grunt, even though my dick tells me I should listen to her. "We've got until the morning, and I'm built to last all night."

"You're so cocky."

"I'm with the woman I've spent years dreaming about. I'm allowed to be the cockiest guy in the world." I flick the

buttons on her shorts before yanking them down, pulling her knickers with them.

"You're soaking." I run a finger across her pussy and slide it in my mouth. I've never seen her eyes wider as I suck on my digit. "Fuck, I'm going to enjoy you."

"Dane!" She bares her teeth like a wolf, but she can't be hungrier than I am. Teasing her is even more fun than driving her car. I undo the rest of the buttons on my jeans and push them down and off.

"Take your bralette off," I order, and she starts to pull it up. "Slowly. I've fantasised about your tits for years."

Her chest rises and falls quickly with shaky breaths. "But what if you don't like—"

"That's not an option. Your body is all I've ever wanted. From these legs..." I crawl onto the bed, lift one ankle, and brush her calves with my mouth. As much as my language is dominant, I am gentle. I want to build her fire until we're burning this place down. My lips travel higher, kissing her inner thighs, which makes her squirm until I place a palm against her belly to keep her still. "...to these thighs." I cross to her other calf and repeat my moves. I bypass the wet spot between her legs, which causes a grunt of frustration so loud I cock my eyebrow. "Patience, Senna."

My lips brush her belly, and then I reach her breasts. "They're even better than my fantasies, and that is not fucking possible because they were glorious every time I fisted my cock to my filthiest thoughts of you." She lifts her hands in submission as I lick and suck on her nipples. Her occasional hiss causes me to lift my head and wink at her. She glares at me with furrowed brows. "That's right, baby, channel those years of hate."

"I didn't hate you as much as I do right now," she replies, and I laugh against her, my lips vibrating her skin.

"When do I get to feel you inside me?"

"I've got a promise to keep first."

Her brow furrows so damn hard I imagine fucking a migraine out of her head.

I press a kiss to her lips and revel in the way she grinds against my rock-hard dick. "You're huge," she stutters as she opens her thighs wide.

"I'd best get you needier so you're really ready for me."

"I can't get needier."

I flip us around so my head is on the pillow and she's straddling my chest. Her pussy soaks the hair on my stomach. I grip her hands. There's no chance I'd last if she touched me. "You can, baby. Grab the headboard and straddle my face. I promised you a ride, and it's time you collected."

"But—"

"I said grab the headboard." I wrap my hands around her butt and drag her onto my face.

CHAPTER THIRTY-EIGHT – SENNA

"I probably won't be able to come like this, and what if I suffocate you and—"

He silences me as he squeezes my butt, his palms wide as he grips it tightly.

"Good girl," he murmurs before his tongue laps. The arousal flows through my body, but I can't focus. There's too much in my head.

"Are you sure I'm not too—"

He lands a palm on my arse cheek. At this angle, it's not much more than a tap, but it still makes me squeal and grind against his mouth. His chuckles at my reaction bring another wave of pleasure. I've never been bent over and given a good spanking, and I want Connor to do it.

The men I've been with were either too scared because they knew about my family or went too far, dominating me because my power emasculated them—their words, not mine. But Connor isn't. He's literally tongue fucking me and authoritative at the same time.

"Connor, more." He wraps his arms around my thighs, holding me against his tongue as it swirls around my clit. My words turn to moans, and my head lolls back as he pulls me onto him again and again. I have to grip the headboard to stop from falling as his tongue flicks inside me.

I'm sucking in air for fear I might forget to breathe. His

fingers dig into my flesh. My teenage crush owns my body like an expert. I let out a sound like a cry. I've never made that noise during sex before. He pushes me off his mouth. His grin is devilish, and if I weren't already soaking his chin, I would be now. "That's my good girl."

"Fuck."

He yanks me against his mouth. I grind and twist as he takes my arousal higher. My knuckles turn white from gripping the headboard. My thighs shake, and my biceps tense. He kneads my bum with the occasional butt tap that has me writhing against his tongue.

I sneak a look behind me. His cock judders like it's inside me. I need it inside me.

He takes a breath. "I want to drown under your wetness. Now ride me like you mean it. I want your orgasm, baby."

With one hand, I grip his hair, and with the other, I clutch the headboard. He squeezes my thighs, pulling me onto him again and again. My stomach clenches, and my muscles burn as his teeth nip at my clit. I've never felt more used and in control at the same time.

I'm panting, desperate to come. My hand moves to my breast. I twist and pinch my nipple while staring down at his beautiful face. His vast eyes fix on mine, creasing with his happiness. That's what pushes me over the edge: the pleasure, the pain, and his adoration.

My orgasm wrecks me. He eases me off him, rolling me until I'm cradled against his body.

"That was..." But I can't get my words out. My chest heaves as I draw in oxygen.

He's so damn smug that I want to beat him. However, there were no losers in that moment. I'm not sure I'll be able to walk tomorrow, but I want more and to see him come

START YOUR ENGINES

apart.

"Shorts off, Dane."

"You don't get to take control, boss." He kisses me hard. I taste myself on his lips. "You taste like heaven."

"No, I don't," I reply. "You can't think that."

"Your body is perfect. You taste perfect. I will punish you if you disagree." There is an irresistible glint in his eyes.

"How about we say it's okay rather than perfect?" I reply with a smile.

"Get on your knees."

I side-eye him, and he stares at me. His eyebrows are high as he waits.

"I want to see your cock first. I've imagined it for too long."

He licks his lips slowly as if he's still tasting me. "If you insist. But then you're getting on your knees, and I'm going to give you the spanking you need." My body throbs. "Keep watching, baby."

He stands and yanks down his boxers in one move. His dick is huge. I'm imagining him against my tongue, filling my mouth. Would I gag on him instantly or—

"Stop licking those beautiful lips. Assume the position. All fours. Now." He reaches for a condom.

He sheaths himself. I'm lifting my pelvis in anticipation.

He holds out his hands as he kneels on the bed. "You have no idea how sexy you are, do you? Whether you're in your boss dress or your shorts or naked. You are the sexiest woman I've ever seen. Staring at you makes me nearly lose it. I need to sink my cock in you and make you come. It's all I was made for. Now get on all fours so I can fuck you hard. And this time, we're breaking the bed. If it's not in pieces by the time I'm done with you, I've failed."

When I bend over, he groans loudly. I look over my

239

shoulder and catch him holding and squeezing his dick, fisting it slowly in his hand. His stare licks my skin.

"Fuck me, then," I say between gritted teeth.

"When I'm ready." He spanks me, and I tremor at the sting.

"Maybe you're too tired."

He spanks me harder at my sass, and I whimper. "Maybe I'm enjoying the moment."

I bite my lip and stare. "But—"

"The woman I've wanted since I was eighteen, who I didn't think would speak to me ever again, the most beautiful woman in the world, is naked in front of me after a day of laughing with me. You want to help me love driving again. You're everything, and now you're in my bed and demanding I fuck you. You are perfect. And you're all mine."

And with that, he grips my hips and slides his dick inside me. He waits for my body to adjust to him, and then he pulls out and pushes back in. I've never been this full in my life. His bed smells of his citrus woody scent, and I immerse myself in it.

"Good girl. Take me like you've wanted me for months."

"Years," I pant.

"Yes. Squeeze your tits for me. You're my sexy, good girl. No one else's. Ever. That's right, Coults. Pinch your nipples like you want me to. Show me how you like it."

I touch myself while he demands more, and my other hand grip the sheets. I pant and hold on tight.

"Now, your clit. It's all sensitive and swollen, yes?" I reach to rub my clit. It's still wet from his mouth. "That's right, baby."

I cry out as he goes deeper, and his nails dig into my skin. "Rub your clit harder. Own it like it's my fingers on you,

playing with you."

His dick goes deeper and deeper, his heat penetrating me. He slams into me so hard. His body covers me as he presses kisses to the back of my neck. I turn to watch the way he holds my hips as he fucks me. I burn with need for him as he pounds me repeatedly. Sweat drips between my breasts as a whimper bursts from my lips.

"Louder. I want to know how much you want me. Scream my name."

"Connor."

"Louder." He spanks me, and I cry out. "What do you want me to do?"

"Make me come," I shout.

"That's my girl."

My forearm is flat on the bed as I continue to rub my clit. I'm gasping for breath as he pulls back and slams hard into me again. My orgasm smashes through my body, destroying all the barriers I'd built over the years. He penetrates me faster and harder until he bellows with his orgasm. His kisses cover my skin as he finally lets go.

He drops a kiss on my back and then disposes of the condom. We're the kind of mess you only get into after the best sex of your life. He pulls me under his duvet, and his hands reach around me to hold me tight to him. Sex with emotion while sharing what you really want is terrifying, but the payoff is even more incredible than I'd believed.

His lips return to my neck. His fingertips caress my skin, playing with my clit as he holds me. "You're so fucking beautiful. You're my soft, filthy woman. You're all I've ever wanted."

CHAPTER THIRTY-NINE – CONNOR

I open my eyes and reach for Senna. Hazy memories from the middle of the night, spooning as I slowly thrust into her, my fingertips against her clit and nipples, seem more like dreams than reality. Her gasps and requests for more are whispers that refuse to leave me.

She's not beside me. I jump out of bed, nearly face-planting on the floor. Maybe I was too demanding or pushed her too far with the spanking. It was our first time together, and I was possessed. All my fantasies came true in an instant, and I forgot to hold back.

I rush into the open-plan kitchen dining area and freeze. She's winding her hair around her finger in a way she should save for when speaking to me. She sits on a bar stool at the kitchen counter. Her legs hang down beneath my hoodie, which barely covers her thighs. I remember the softness of her legs against my face, how I traced every muscle and made them flex with my facial hair.

She hangs up the phone. Did she do that because she didn't want me to hear?

I turn to go, and she calls out my name. "Connor?" Her voice wavers.

My shoulders hunch. I don't want to apologise for what was the best night of my life and what I hoped was the best night of hers.

START YOUR ENGINES

Her footsteps tap against the floor as she comes closer, but I can't move. I opened my heart last night.

She breathes kisses against my shoulders. I grit my teeth.

"Connor, are you okay? Did I do something wrong?"

I turn. She wears the same fear. Instincts control my moves, and I pull her close and wrap my arms around her.

"I'm sorry, Senna. When I woke and saw you'd gone and then found you on the phone…oh my God, I'm such a twat. I've never been jealous of anyone before, but with you, everything is different. I'm so sorry. You didn't do anything wrong. It's all me."

I rock her, but she pushes me away. I wait for the Senna torrent of abuse I know so well, but instead, she stares at me and says, "I'm the same. When you were with Tawny at the bar, I thought you wanted her. When you asked about her joining the team, I nearly said no because I couldn't cope being around the two of you as you flirted and—"

My lips crash against hers, and she pushes me back. "Connor—wait. Are we in a relationship? How do I know what last night was for you? How do I know it wasn't a blip?"

I press my lips to her scarred hand, brushing against the silver mark. I'm not used to the vulnerability that fills my words. "Because nothing about how I feel for you is a blip. We shouldn't have fucked last night—" Senna steps back, but I grab her, pressing kisses to her wrists where her pulse is out of control. "We shouldn't have fucked without talking. You're my best mate's sister and my boss. I should have checked if you were sure, discussed the consequences, or established if this was a one-off or a long-term thing for you."

"What is it for you?"

I wrap her arms around my neck, and my hands slide

243

under the hoodie to her bum. "I'm all in, Senna. I want to shout how much you're it for me from the rooftops, but I don't want people at work to treat you with less respect, which, in our industry, they will."

"And I don't want my brother to hate you. I know about your pact," she says, referring to the pact Niki and I made as teenagers, which said I couldn't date her.

"The pact is the thing of teenagers, and I don't care about it. How about we don't call it..." I trail off. I want to be with her, but her job is her life.

"A relationship? We don't have to label it, but just date, exclusively and privately. We don't even know if we can do the relationship thing. I've never been in one."

"Me neither." It's for the best, but I wish it weren't.

"And so Niki doesn't have to know until we know what we're doing. He'd kill you if he knew what we did last night."

"And what we're going to do again now. I will have you gripping the headboard like it's the wood stopping Kate Winslet from dying in *Titanic*."

She smirks and my earlier anxiety fades under the glow of her smile. "And when it breaks, knowing you, you'll find a way to wear it like a badge of honour."

"The whole town would know. I'd have to tell them the filthy words you shouted when it cracked." She rolls her eyes, and even that makes me puff out my chest. "Now get in the bedroom, Sen."

"Now? But I'm not sure what decision we came to about us."

I squeeze her butt, and my erection nudges at her knickers. "We decided we need to fuck again and that we're exclusively, secretly dating." Saying that gives me heartburn. I want to tell everyone Senna is my girlfriend and that my heart is only for her, but I can't let her risk everything she's

achieved and her relationship with her family for me. This is the right thing for her. "If that's okay with you?"

I want her to tell me it's not okay and that she's willing to risk everything, although I wouldn't let her. She nods and says, "I hate it, too. When I spoke to Jacs, she knew I was happy about something."

My shoulders ease slightly. She wasn't speaking to another guy.

"She heard your grin down the phone, eh?"

"She asked me who I was fucking and if he had a sibling."

My eyebrows quirk. "And you said?"

"I said I didn't know what she was talking about. I was enjoying the break."

"Did she believe you?"

She avoids eye contact briefly. "Of course she didn't. I spent all night fucking the man of my dreams. I'm not that good a liar."

My stomach thuds. Right now, she's the one significant thing in my life. I could lose everything, yet I want her screaming my name and telling me again I'm the man of her dreams. It's enough for now.

I back her against the wall. She's so willing and needy for me. Her freshly bitten lips cry for me to soothe them. She reaches into the hoodie pocket and pulls out a condom.

I raise my eyebrows, and she smiles shyly. "I was hoping we'd do it here when you got up."

"Then let me make your fantasies real." I lift the hoodie up and off her, and she trembles against me. This is enough for now. "Put the condom on me."

Her eyes are wide as she obeys. She rips open the foil with her teeth and strokes down my length as she slides on the condom. I push her soaking knickers to one side. Damn,

she's ready for me. Her eyes flutter closed as I lift her leg and tuck it against my hip.

"I'm the man of your dreams, eh?" I murmur as I slide my dick inside her. "You're all my dreams and fantasies come true."

I pin her hands her above her head, and her brows furrow. "Please keep your eyes open. I want to see all the colours as you come."

I lace my fingers with hers as I slowly push inside her. Her smile falters as arousal takes over.

"Connor," she moans as I brush kisses to her neck.

"I know, baby," I reply.

"I'm yours. All yours."

"And I'm yours," I reply as my hands travel down her arms until I cup her face. She wraps her legs around me, but not to control the movement. She wants every part of her as close to me as possible. I want it, too.

She makes a cute whimper as I lick the seam of her lips. Our tongues tangle as I continue to press into her, our bodies speeding up as her need overwhelms us. Her arms are still high in surrender.

My lips brush her nipples, and she tightens around my cock.

I could spend my life like this and still want more.

"Yours," she whispers again as she comes.

Somehow, Senna has dragged me out of the house. I'd go wherever she leads, but I'd rather we stayed in my bed as I make her moan or where I can listen to the cute snores she denies she makes.

"Why can't I drive today?" I don't care how petulant I sound.

"You don't enjoy driving," she teases. She's swapped my hoodie for a summer dress. She's bra-free, and as she grips the gear stick and takes the car into fifth gear, I glance at her lap. She promised me sex on the bonnet at some point. Maybe that's what we're doing today.

My dick grows in agreement.

"I enjoy driving your car."

I marvel at her control as she takes the corner at speed. I haven't watched her drive in years, and it's so damn arousing. Her legs are wide, and her hands occasionally rest on the gear stick. It's like she's caressing the head of my cock as she squeezes it absentmindedly before turning the wheel on another corner.

"Although I'm enjoying how you drive it, too," I add, my mouth dry as I watch the leather slide through her hands.

"Down, boy," she sasses. "We're heading to the village."

"For lunch, hopefully. I need sustenance for what I have planned for you."

She giggles. I do want her beneath me again, but I'd also be happy to hold her and talk more about what she did in those years we weren't close. Between snoozes and orgasms, she's shared stories about university and about joining the comms team, but there's so much more I want to hear.

"A late lunch because it's already three in the afternoon. *Someone* wouldn't let us leave the house."

"Damn right. I'm still annoyed you put clothes on, although you look fucking delicious in them. Are you wearing knickers?"

My stare rakes over her body, and her skin flushes pink.

"None of your business. After our ridiculously late lunch, we've got an appointment. The appointment is for me, but I need you and lots of sweets to get through it."

I stare at her as she parks outside a pub.

"What kind of appointment involves sweets?"

Her smirking face tells me she's not sharing her secret. "I also brought cuddly Coults. I found him under your bed. That's no way to respect a toy your boss gives you."

She pulls out the cuddly toy cat that was left for me at the Barcelona hotel, which I've carried everywhere since.

"I hoped he was from you." I grab it off her and smell her orange blossom perfume lingering on his fur. "It's not my fault he was under the bed. Fluffers hates him."

She nods her head. "That I can believe."

As I clutch the toy tighter, I fix her with my stare. "What appointment includes sweets and soft toys?"

She shrugs and gets out of the car, snatching the toy back.

I laugh, but in truth, I would walk through fire with her if she asked.

I'm totally screwed.

CHAPTER FORTY – SENNA

I knock on the door of the small cottage. At the flamingo-shaped doorknocker and bright pink flowers from the rocking basket, Connor eyes me warily.

"You need to tell me what we're doing. Is it a swingers meet-up?"

"No." He's thrown guesses at me over the last couple of hours.

He grumbles. His eyes drift upwards. "You took painkillers at lunch. Is that because of how hard I rocked your world or because of where we are?" I ignore that one, but it doesn't deter him, although his voice drops in panic. "I didn't hurt you, did I? Your arse is so fucking spankable, but if I went too far, you'd tell me, right?"

I brush kisses to his knuckles and drop my voice in case someone comes to the door. "Your spanks nearly made me come, especially when you did it again this morning. You have nothing to apologise for. And I'd tell you if you went too far."

"Good. So where are we?"

The door opens and reveals a woman in a vest and baggy jeans. A paisley square of cotton is rolled up in her hair, and she has a big grin. "Senna, come in. The studio is next door, and I'm finishing an appointment with another client. You're my last one for the day."

"Thank you for fitting me in, Polly."

Connor's brows dance in confusion.

"When my wife told me your reason for coming, I had to fit you in. Take a seat in my sitting room." Polly points to the room at the side. "There's lots for you to look through in there. I'll get you when I'm free. Kel is heading out soon for the evening rush, but she'll get you a drink before she goes."

Kel, the woman who runs the bistro where Connor and I were the night before, bustles in and takes our coffee orders. Connor taps his foot repeatedly as she hands us our drinks and rushes out the door with a wave.

An old indie song plays from a smart speaker. I glance at Connor, who sips his coffee in silence. It must be scalding. I blow on mine. He's glaring at his mug and has a wrinkly forehead. I could put him out of his misery, but instead, I wait for him to burst.

He crosses his arms and glares at me. "I can't take it. Where are we, and what is going on? Why is the woman from the bistro making us coffee in her house, and who is her wife?"

He's like a little boy who's been told he has to believe in Father Christmas if he wants presents. I hide my smirk behind my mug. I love that he brings out this cheeky side of me. Everywhere else, I'm all business, but with him, I get to be free.

"When you were getting the car last night, I asked the lady that runs the bistro if she knew of any tattoo artists, and she told me about her wife Polly."

"You're getting a tattoo? Since when?"

I put our cups down and take his hands between mine. "Last night, you said it hurts you when I rub my scar."

He shakes his head. "Don't listen to me. I'm a selfish dick. It's your scar and my issue."

"I know that." With one hand, I brush his cheekbones with my fingertips. "But what you said made me realise I was ashamed of this mark, this branding. It proved I couldn't race with the men and was a failure."

He gasps. "But you aren't a failure."

I smooth the lines on his forehead away, but he takes my hand and kisses my scar.

"I'm starting to believe that now. But I made this scar a reason to feel humiliated."

"I'm so sorry. To me, you're strong. You fought past the accident and drove again. Even when I told myself I shouldn't care about you, I was in awe of you. People have been scared to drive again, but not you. And some drivers have waxed lyrical about their accidents and never done anything else but moan. But you trained and fought to be a leader in a world that put barriers in your way. You inspire me and many others, including Tawny and everyone growing up who wants to be part of this world professionally. You're incredible."

My cheeks flush, and as much as I'm tempted to rub the scar shyly, I don't. Instead, I press my lips hard against Connor's. His eyelashes tickle my face, and his finger traces a heart around my scar.

"You say the best things," I whisper against his lips.

He shrugs, but his smile is more extensive than his dick, and that's saying something.

"I want to make this scar a feature. I crashed and came back from it. I was a successful racing driver, and I want to celebrate that. And if it makes you hurt less, that's good, too."

I worry my lip as I wait for something, anything.

"Connor?"

"Don't do this for me. I don't deserve it." He stumbles

over the words.

"I'm doing this for both of us. I'm doing this for all those times I failed but didn't give up."

"You're incredible," he repeats as his lips brush my scar. I get a pull in my stomach that reminds me this thing between us could be forever, but we've only just reconnected. I can't risk everything yet. "What tattoo are you getting? What about your old racing car or a map of your favourite track?"

"I'm going to get the time of my fastest lap around Silverstone."

He beams. "From the week after your seventeenth birthday? I love that idea."

I sit back in my chair and stare at him. "You remember that's when I got my fastest lap?"

He drags both of his lips into his mouth. His eyes crease as he winces.

"Connor?"

My pulse rises as he stares at me.

"Promise me you won't laugh," he says.

I squint and twist my mouth. "Why would I laugh?"

"Just promise. Pinky promise?" He holds his little finger out. His teeth scratch his lip.

I hook my little finger in his. "Pinky promise."

With our fingers still joined, he uses his other hand to lift his T-shirt slowly. I hold my breath as he reveals his panty-wetting abs. Tattoos cross his body, but he points to a small one near his armpit. With all our fun, it's one I hadn't noticed.

"It's well hidden, and it's not been in any of your photo shoots. When did you get it?"

"Have you enjoyed my photoshoots? Do you play with yourself when you stare at them?"

"Connor," I warn.

"Yes, baby?" he says in a low voice that makes me quiver.

"Can I touch it?"

"Only if you promise to let me watch while you do."

"I don't mean my pussy."

"Shame. Maybe we'll do that later. Pinky promise?"

I roll my eyes, but I can't stop the smile from turning up my lips.

"When did you get this?" I trace the tattoo with my finger. He gasps and tightens his muscles. They ripple, and it's like they're all demanding my touch.

"I got it when I was eighteen, a couple of weeks before the crash. It was one of my first. I ask them to cover it up when I'm in shoots." His voice is still low, but the tease is gone for now. My fingertip swirls around the numbers of my fastest lap time at Silverstone.

"I can't believe you never showed me." He hisses as I lick the inking. "Why didn't you?"

"I wanted to. It took me too long to build up the courage. But I never had it removed or covered up by another tattoo."

"Why?"

"Because it was always you. From the first time you beat me on the track to the night before your last race when we watched movies together and you fell asleep in my arms. It was always you."

I kiss him with everything I have. My hand fists his T-shirt as he strokes and grips my hair. We're panting and kissing, our tongues entwining as the missing years disappear. I can't get enough of him. I don't want this to be a hidden fling, but there's so much at stake.

Connor hasn't had enough people on his side in his life.

His dad left him, and his family are busy. My brother is the only one who has always been there for him, and he shouldn't lose that. And I don't want my brother to get hurt, either. I don't know what is going on with him or why he's so distant, but until I can work that out and until we understand what Connor and I can be to each other when it's not just us two in a bubble, then we need to hide it.

A cough has us easing apart. Over his shoulder, Polly covers her eyes with her hand. I'm not sure which of us blushes harder at being caught.

"Sorry to disturb you, but I'm ready for you to come through," she says.

Connor grabs the sweets and toy Coults and takes my hand.

It's time to embrace my future and not focus on my past.

Chapter Forty-One – Connor

I can't stop looking at her hand. It's covered by clear wrapping, and beneath is her best lap time like an embossing on her skin. My feet tap as I study it for the umpteenth time.

"Should I drive us home?" I ask, reaching for the keys. "I don't want you to hurt your hand, and it might be sore or—"

Senna raises her eyebrows and holds her keys tight.

"Or you could drive because you're perfectly capable," I stutter.

She shakes her head as she walks to the driver's side, and I slide into the passenger seat. She kisses me on the lips, and I taste the fruity jelly sweeties she's sucked on. "Maybe we should pick up some ingredients so I can cook you dinner?"

She speeds down the road as I click in my seatbelt. She hasn't mentioned the tattoo I got since she kissed me. Maybe she's realising I was a bit obsessed with her. "Or we could eat out. Whatever—"

She trails her fingers up my thigh.

"Or we—"

"Connor," she growls. I wink at her. "You're a right chatterbox this evening."

"You're too quiet, and it's freaking me out." I'm playing it cool as I chuckle, but I lost my calm about an hour earlier.

She grabs the gear stick, and I instantly miss her warmth. I'm whipped, and although I'm terrified, I'm excited, too.

"Your laughter isn't fooling anyone," she says, side-eyeing me as she takes another corner. Her hand lingers on the gear stick.

I've shown enough vulnerability over the last day. I must remember that you don't show all this emotion when it's just dating.

She spies me warily but doesn't say anything more as she drives us through the country roads. I tap my thighs as I glance out the window. "This isn't the way to my house. Have you got another surprise planned?"

"You'll see."

I press my palm to her thigh, sliding it under her dress. She's so sexy when she drives. Being in the car with her helps me to love driving more. I'll remember the sweets on her lips and the caress of her spicy floral perfume.

"Don't move that higher, or I'll crash."

"Totally worth it." She side-eyes me. This time, my smirk reaches my eyes. But the temptation of the surprise stops me from moving higher. Her quads tense as she presses the clutch and pushes the car into fifth gear. "Out of curiosity, are you wearing knickers?"

"You'll find out later...if you win."

"What?"

"Just enjoy the drive."

My little finger catches on the hem of her dress. I pull it slightly, which makes her strap fall. My dick presses against the zipper of my shorts with a desire only she gives me.

"Yes, boss."

START YOUR ENGINES

"Connor, we're here ."

I squint against the bright sunshine. It's nearly seven in the evening. A security guard opens a barrier and waves us through.

"Where are we? Is this… Why?"

"It's part of my mission to get you enjoying driving again."

She parks outside the main building of Dunsfold Aerodrome, the airfield used in the BBC car television show *Top Gear*. I gape at the track with the curves and straights I've only imagined driving on. The grass surrounding the asphalt is mostly green, although the brown biting the edges reminds me of the hot summer I haven't had much chance to enjoy due to racing.

I've conquered tracks worldwide, but I also grew up watching some of my favourite drivers on *Top Gear* take on this track. Childhood Connor bursts from my chest and tells me how this was one of his dreams I'd forgotten about. But the show doesn't film here anymore. Maybe Senna wants me to drive her Porsche here. I love her Porsche, but I'd rather drive a Ferrari around this.

Something shiny and orange catches my eye. I gasp as I stare in awe at the Lamborghini Hypercar I've only seen online. "Only twenty of these were made! Where did you get it?"

I run to it, hold my hand out, but quickly pull it back. "Can I touch it?"

Senna chuckles behind me. "Of course. You can drive it, too. But don't forget the other cars. They're feeling left out."

I'm so blinded by its beauty I hadn't noticed the others.

Next to it is an Aston Martin in gunmetal that makes me drool, and, next to that, a Bugatti in bright blue. It's the colour of cloudless summer days.

I walk around the vehicles, staring in the window like a wide-eyed child outside a candy shop, waiting for it to open after school.

"Get in, then," Senna says.

I whip my head around. "Which one? I've never driven any of these rare cars."

"Whichever one you think you can beat me in."

I jut out my head. "Beat you in?"

She presses her lips to mine, and for a second, I'm distracted by the heat of her body, her candy taste, and her hands under my T-shirt. Her breath tickles my skin when she pulls back and says, "Yes, Dane, beat me in. This is your surprise. When you were younger, you dreamed of driving the best cars. When we were karting as teenagers, your eyes lit up whenever you were allowed near a supercar. I want you to recreate that happiness and buzz you felt then. Try each car out. You've got until the sun goes down, and maybe we can race each other if there's time. The helmets are in the cars."

I grasp her hands tightly and cover her face in kisses. "You did this for me?"

"I called in a couple of favours. Jacs helped me arrange it."

My pulse is out of control. It's because of her, not because I have the opportunity to drive without the pressure of being judged. It's not about winning a trophy to make a business prick somewhere happy. This is all for me, and she did this.

As I climb into the Lambo, I turn to her. "You said if I win, I find out if you're wearing knickers."

START YOUR ENGINES

"He finally remembers," she says with a smile. She folds her arms and licks her lips slowly. "If we have time to compete, then the bet is that if you win, you get to find out what's underneath my dress."

"And if you win?"

"*When* I win, I'll come up with something. Don't you worry, baby."

"I don't doubt that for a second, boss." I give her a quick grin and reach for my helmet. All my dreams are coming true tonight, and it's because of her.

CHAPTER FORTY-TWO – SENNA

Emotions rush me as Connor parks beside me. He's driven around the track for the last ninety minutes. Dusk is coming, and the transporter will collect the cars in about half an hour and return them to their owners.

As I stare at his beaming face and flushed cheeks, my heart threatens to burst from my chest.

"Are you too scared to race me?" Connor asks as he leans his elbow out the window. Damn, those forearms are good. Maybe he'll use them to pin my hands above my head later.

"Sure, I'm shaking in my trainers." I bend over so my ass is in the air as I look in the car, pecking his lips. "Are you sure you want to race, though? You could fit in a couple more laps."

"Coults, I need to know if you're wearing knickers, which anyone behind you would be able to see or not see right now."

I laugh, and he pulls me further into the car with his hand softly on the nape of my neck. He takes the kiss deeper, and I relax into it. I would give anything to battle against him like we used to before it all went wrong.

He eases his hold, and I lean back. "Okay, if you're sure. Are you sticking with this car?"

"The Aston is the best one, so yeah. It decided for me.

START YOUR ENGINES

Which one are you going for? Or will I have to be a gentleman and let you have the Aston?"

"Hell no." I stride to the Lamborghini, adding a wiggle to my bum that makes him groan. "This is the one I'm going to beat you in. Prepare for humiliation. I've missed whooping your sexy butt."

Helmet on, I meet him at the start line.

Our time at the track is private, so with no one to start us, we struggle to communicate when we begin. As I'm about to go, Connor tears off the start line, his tyres squeaking as dust kicks up behind him.

"He's forgotten how good I used to be," I growl as I take off. Within a minute, I'm gaining on him. It's been years since I raced like this. I come to this airfield several times a year alone to work out my frustrations or anxiety, so I know this track better than him. And I've driven this car before, too.

He cranks his engine and speeds up.

I take one of the curves, nearly spinning out. Is he laughing at me or panicking I'll get hurt? I want his competitive spirit, not his protection.

He gets away from me, something he wouldn't do if he were worried. This is the Connor I want, the guy who gives it all. To him, I'm not a pathetic creature who can't race like a speed freak.

I grip the paddles. I'm climbing at over one hundred miles an hour. I lock it in high gear and gain the distance I lost.

We agreed to two laps, and as we pass the start line to

signal we're moving into the second, he's still ahead and not letting me pass. While he's not getting in my way to the point of danger, he's pushing me, and the missile of the car I'm driving wants to burn rubber and destroy him.

Fighting for the win, which will be a win for both of us, is a turn-on I wasn't expecting. When I'm usually here, I'm racing against myself. But competing against him and wanting to obliterate him fills me with the power and aggression that bleeds from my skin. This is like pure arousal mixed with adrenaline and the intensity of the high speeds that nearly killed us both in the past.

I didn't realise how much I missed racing against him. I don't know if I want to beat him or fuck him more, but either way, I'm screaming in delight. It's the last stretch, and I briefly level with him before firing past.

I hope his eyes were wide as I sped past. I was too busy cheering and pumping my fist. I sail over the line and relish the victory and the speed that carries me to the other side of the track. He catches me, and I pull over, yanking my helmet off and ready to wave my victory in his face, but I don't get the chance.

He walks towards me, the same fire in his stare that flamed my body during the win. He closes in on me, and suddenly, the joy of my win transforms into something sensual and power-driven. He lifts me and places me on my bonnet. I lie back as he surveys my long legs.

"Even though you beat me, you're still my prize. Now show me what's under this dress." He pushes my legs apart and shoves the hem of my dress up to my hips. "Hmmm, you sexy brat."

A warm breeze makes my skin chill at the naked wetness between my thighs. "You're so fucking naughty, aren't you, baby?"

START YOUR ENGINES

I drag my lips into my mouth as he grips my thighs, keeping my legs apart. His gaze burns my pussy. I can't get any words out. It's like I'm on show for him as I pull down the straps of my dress to reveal my hard nipples.

"Fuck. I want every part of you." But the sun has set, and it's nearly dark. The car transporter will be here in minutes. "And when I get home, I'll own my little speed queen."

"But what about my prize for winning?"

"You never told me what you got if you won."

"Your cock inside me on the bonnet of the winning car."

"Good girl." He flicks open the buttons of his shorts. He puts a condom on in record time. Then he leans over me, biting my nipple and thrusting a finger inside me.

"We don't have time before the car transporter," I say between gasps.

"I'm making time. If I want to finger fuck you to orgasm, I will."

I cry out as his fingers curl, and he hits my G-spot. He licks and sucks at my nipples. I'm moaning as he pants, and as I'm about to panic that there won't be enough time, he pulls out his fingers, sinks his hands into my hips, and penetrates me with his cock in one swift movement.

"Fucking soaking, baby. Racing does it for you, eh?" His eyebrow cocks. He grits his teeth.

"You do it for me, Connor. Beating you in a car that's going fast enough to pour adrenaline through my limbs does it for me."

He penetrates me repeatedly, sinking his cock into me, dragging me to the edge of the bonnet before pushing his dick so deep that he grips me harder. My breasts are bouncing. My back bangs against the bonnet of a car that costs more than his summer home, and my lips are painfully

sore because I'm biting them, but he doesn't stop.

His stare eats me up. My hair is all over the place from the passion-filled fuck, and then he puts my ankles over his shoulders and goes deeper. I can barely breathe. The noises of our sex are so loud I can't believe the guard on the barrier hasn't heard.

"You're so sexy like this, baby. You're a speed queen, a boss, and all mine. No one else touches you but me. You don't fantasise about anyone but me and my hard cock. Is that right, baby?"

"Yes," I whimper. The scent of burnt rubber is like an aphrodisiac, and I'm on the edge of coming.

"Are you going to let me watch you play with yourself on the way home?" I pant, and my chest heaves. "Senna, are you?"

That growl, the depth of his cock, and the pure need on his face all do it for me, and I scream my climax and agree to everything he wants as I come. With one last push, he climaxes, his rippling forearms holding on tight as my orgasm obliterates me. His kisses cover my neck and between my breasts as my breathing slows. The lights of the car transporter fill the runway as driver guides it through the barrier, thankfully not shining on us.

We jump up and readjust ourselves. I check the bonnet, but the darkness hides any imperfections.

"I hope we haven't damaged it," I say through panting breaths.

"Totally worth it. You were incredible," he whispers in my ear before his lips brush the nape of my neck. "I'm going to remember you like that forever."

CHAPTER FORTY-THREE – CONNOR

Senna lies against my chest, and her orange blossom scent dances in the air between us. Her heart's rhythm has become my rhythm. Her heat warms my soul. I wind sections of her hair around my finger and ghost her forehead with kisses. Fluffers sits beside us on the sofa, too grumpy to sit on her lap, although he's warmed to both of us. We've become an odd family over these last two weeks of summer break.

"This half-season is going to be the best one yet. Tawny can't wait to sign the contracts tomorrow." Jacs's Scottish brogue surrounds the living space. Even though she's not on speakerphone, I hear every word. She's the loudest person I've ever met. She probably has the same ear damage lots of us have from too many years near noisy engines.

"It will be amazing. I wish I'd fired Antoine sooner," Senna replies.

"Me too," I mumble, and she puts her finger on her mouth.

"Who's there with you?" Jacs asks. "Is that Connor?"

Senna huffs as she puts the phone on speaker.

"You all right, Jacs?" I holler.

"Not as okay as you two. Are you hanging out as friends or…" She leaves us to fill in the word, but secret exclusive

dating has rules, including that you don't discuss it. "Okay... Either way, I'm glad Senna finally took time off. You needed it, chick. We were worried about you."

Senna tenses against me. "Is everyone talking about me?"

Oh shit.

This is the last thing she needs to hear. I smooth my fingers down the nape of her neck and swallow the newly formed lump in my throat.

"No, but I was worried you wouldn't take your summer break, and when I saw Ralf in passing, he mentioned Niki called him suggesting someone should look after you and—" Jacs rambles.

"I don't need protection or people to worry about me. I bet my dad didn't have this," Senna replies.

"He should have," I grunt, and she tips her head. "Maybe if he'd had people worrying about him, his health would have been better, and he wouldn't have left the team in a mess for you to deal with."

I've kept quiet about her dad. Senna told me he's considering selling the team unless she gets us to the top six in the Constructor's Championship, something he couldn't do in the last five years.

Her head drops, and she closes her eyes. "I'm not a pathetic woman who can't run things." The phone sits next to her. The call with Jacs is still open.

"Your dad made you jump through hoops. We've spent nearly two weeks together." In absolute bliss. "But before that, you were exhausted, working all the hours and only eating because of the meals I sent to your office."

I want her to understand that she doesn't have to do this alone and that real relationships are possible. I want to care for her.

"Even Niki, who barely calls you, was worried about you," I add.

"How do you know Niki was worried about me?"

I can't tell her he asked me to protect her. She'll rage. And I haven't protected her for weeks unless she's wanted me to. She presses her fists to her forehead.

Jacs jumps in. "Senna, chill. This team matters to all of us. I know it means more to you, but we care about you, okay?"

"Okay," Senna grunts, but it's not.

"I'll bring Tawny to your office tomorrow to sign the contracts, and then we'll get everything ready for the first race in the Netherlands in a couple of weeks."

"Sounds great."

"I'm guessing you don't want me to mention you two to anyone? Not that I would." Jacs's voice quiets as Senna takes her off speakerphone and walks to the bedroom.

Senna looks at me warily as she pauses in the doorway. "We're not a two. We're just friends hanging out and..."

The door closes, and the rest of her sentence remains a mystery, but I can't tell if she's lying to Jacs or if that's how she sees us.

I start cooking dinner, although I'm shuffling around the kitchen like a man carrying fifty-kilogram dumbbells. The heavyweight I'm carrying is embedded in my heart. I want to wake up next to her every morning like I have these past weeks. I need to be the first person she thinks about when she allows herself a break and the reason she leaves work on time.

I could call Layla, but I'm not ready for her opinions, and she's in a significantly different time zone. I owe Ralf a call. He's left several messages because he knows what returning to racing after the crash will mean to me.

"Connor," he booms as I continue to make dinner. It's our special last meal together before we return to our everyday lives. I've got candles, and I made a playlist like I'm a lovesick teenager.

"Hey, Ralf."

"How are you feeling?"

Like my heart is slowly being ripped out, and there's nothing I can do to stop it. "I'm okay."

"Are you sure? Are you worried about the Netherlands?"

"A bit. But over the last ten days, I've spoken to the sports psychologist every day. You'd like him. He's straight to the point and funny with it. We're working on how to prepare before races."

"Are you sleeping?"

I glance to the bedroom, where Jacs's muffled voice tries to seep under the door. "Yeah, really well."

"That's good," Ralf says, filling the silence. "There were times I worried you wouldn't get to this place. It will take focus when you're back, but I have hope for you. Have you got any tactics you can take into the next half of the season with your sleeping?"

"Ric gave me tactics. I've struggled with sleeping for years, but these weeks were different." *Because every day, I get to sleep beside the woman who brings me peace like nothing else does.* "But enough about me. How are you and Myles? Where are you travelling next?"

"Hawaii! I've bought a magnificent new shirt. He hates the swirling green bears on it, but he loves me, and love conquers all." My imaginary dumbbells get heavier. "But I'm not done with my questions. I've got one more, and then I'll talk your ear off about my travels."

"Go for it."

"Have you got back in a car after the crash? Is it why you didn't return my calls?"

He's right, although the other reason is once Senna filled my world, aside from messages to my family, I avoided anyone who'd ruin our bubble.

"I've driven loads. It took a while and a bit of cajoling from a friend, initially." I clear my throat. "But I love driving more than I have in years. I raced for fun last week. There was a blue Bugatti you'd have sold your Hawaiian shirts for."

Ralf chuckles. "Not possible."

"Not even Myles can make you get rid of the neon things." I laugh. "But Ralf, I haven't loved racing or driving for years, and now I can't get enough of it. I want my name to be up there, but more than that, I want to keep driving." I grab the empty pasta packet and slam-dunk it in the bin as I babble. "So much has changed. I'm the happiest I've been in forever."

I freeze and sigh. I was until Jacs's call.

"Now tell me about your travels. What are your plans in Hawaii?"

As he shares his itinerary, Senna wraps her arms around me. I lean my hand back and tuck her close. We stay like that until Ralf and I say goodbye.

"I'm sorry for kicking off earlier. I was scared, and I panicked," she whispers. "I'm scared about the next half of the season and people thinking I'm not good enough. I need you in my life."

My heart is a little lighter, and I take deep breaths. I turn and bring her with me. I stare into her red, glassy eyes full of unshed tears.

"I'm not going anywhere," I whisper back to her. One corner of her lips turns up tentatively. She closes her eyes and sucks in the air. My kisses ghost her eyelashes. A tiny

tang of salt covers my lips. "We'll make it work. We have to."

I rock her in my arms and hum the song she plays me when we clean our teeth together.

I don't want a day without her in it—a day without this.

CHAPTER FORTY-FOUR – CONNOR

My heart lifts as I take the corner. This is what I spent my life working towards. But it's not like it was before. I grip the steering wheel and flip a gearshift paddle as I speed out of it.

"Yes, Connor, you're smashing it," Macca tells me over the radio. "This is the best you've driven in years."

"Thanks, Macca."

He's right.

I no longer think driving is my sole purpose in life. I know what, or rather who, my life is for, but as I speed around the track, adrenaline rushes through my body. There's still the temptation to use some of my obsessive tactics, like tapping my leg or spinning before I get in the car, but Ric has helped me see that those techniques aren't stopping me from crashing.

Luca, from Vessa, is a couple of seconds ahead of me. I need to get closer to pass him, and I will. My car will get me there.

"Keep chasing," Macca says. "You're still eight laps from the end, so if you can get close, I reckon you can pass him on the last couple of laps. There's a chance. Your tyres are fresher than his."

"That's enough for me."

Our car is improving. Senna is managing the money well

271

and has made some changes. Of course she has. She's a freaking business goddess. She's a goddess in every way. I wouldn't love driving if not for her.

She's the reason this is different. She's the reason for my happiness.

In my mirror, I spy my favourite Australian, Billy Nister, speeding up behind me. He's young and makes mistakes, and I know the risk of having him behind me.

"Do you see Nister?" Macca says.

I know his words are more than to make me aware.

When drivers as cocksure and dangerous as Billy approached me in the first half of the season, my anxiety would have shot up. But not anymore. I know the risks, but I can beat them, because when I do, I get to drive, and as a bonus, I make my woman happy.

"Yeah, I got him."

I smile as I block Billy. I can fend him off easily. He's still young and making obvious mistakes. It's Vessa I want to beat.

"How is Tawny doing?" I ask.

"She's four cars behind you. She's doing well for only her third race in Formula One. Her confidence is soaring. Well done for the pep talk you gave her."

"I'm always happy to help the team," I say. "One last thing before I shut off the radio and focus on Luca. Is everyone watching and enjoying the race?"

"Hells, yes, Connor. I have a feeling that even the boss is smiling."

"I heard that," Senna cuts in, and fireworks go off in my belly. Three words, and I'm a power horse whose only goal is to make its boss happy. "And yes, I'm beaming because my drivers are burning up the Italian track. Bring it home, Connor, and get past Vessa, too."

START YOUR ENGINES

"Yes, boss," I say with a smirk. "Radio off unless it's urgent. Catch you later."

My smile carries me around the track until I'm within a second of Luca. As I pass him, I squeeze my hand and pump my fist. That one is for her.

CHAPTER FORTY-FIVE – SENNA

Another podium for Connor and the team. I can't wait until he returns to the garage, but he's got press interviews first.

My phone vibrates with a call. It's my dad. It's always Dad.

"Hi," I say, struggling to keep the tension hunching my shoulders out of my voice.

"Tawny should have done better," he says.

"Hello to you, too."

"Senna, the board are moaning because you brought someone into the team that's never driven in F1," he snaps.

"I'm aware. They told me at the meeting this week, and I told them to get over it, as she is an exceptional driver. Did you see her today? It's only her third race with us, and she came seventh. Antoine barely scraped that in his last races."

"I'm not happy you fired him."

I cover the mouthpiece and scream. Silas, Connor's trainer, looks over at me, and I give him a fake smile. I have to do this alone. My dad doesn't need to be the team's problem.

"And I'm not happy that he nearly killed Connor, who was third again today." And drove like a sexy speed demon. "Don't you think it's time you left me to lead the team rather than get involved in everything?"

START YOUR ENGINES

"I spoke with Antoine and his dad. Antoine wants to meet with you to apologise. He's sorry for what happened," he says, ignoring my request.

I don't believe that for a second, but there's no point explaining this. I knew Antoine wouldn't leave it alone when I fired him.

"He knows where to find me. But I'm not taking him back. I'm building a team, not managing an arrogant prick," I snap.

I spy Macca staring at his phone with a frown. He's always the first to celebrate the team.

Dad continues, "Another thing—"

"No, I've got to go. Tell me another time. Love you."

But he hangs up without hearing my last words.

Silas comes over. "Are you okay, boss? Is there anything I can do?"

I shake my head. "No, but thank you." It's my job to act as a buffer between the board and my team. "Is something wrong with Macca? He seems down."

"It's to do with his kid's birthday. But you didn't hear that from me."

"Thanks, Silas." I raise my voice as Silas walks to Tawny's trainer. "Macca, can I have a word?"

Macca quickly tucks his phone in his pocket as if he's been caught doing something he shouldn't. No doubt a legacy of my dad's management. Rule with fear, not with support. That's not my way.

His brow furrows as he joins me. "Did I do something wrong? Connor had a good race. I was only joking on the radio."

"Macca, you were incredible today. We're lucky to have you as our chief race engineer. Connor knows he's got the best." A hint of a smile plays on his lips.

"Oh, well. You know, I'm all right."

"You're the best, Macca. I want to hear you say it."

He presses his lips together, but his smile appears anyway. "I'm the best, boss."

"Damn right," I say. "But if something is up, you'd tell me."

He shrugs. "It's just family stuff."

"Family is what enables us to do this and do it well. What's on your mind?"

He avoids eye contact and wrings his hands.

"Macca," I press.

"When we're in Austin in a couple of weeks, it's my kid's birthday after."

"Monday after the Sunday race. She'll be three years old." I don't know the birthdays and ages of all my team, but some stick with me.

He grins. "Yeah. I know it isn't a milestone, but I've never missed her birthday. Half the day will be gone when I get home from the race. I wanted to be there when she woke and opened her presents." He shrugs again. "But it's nothing. There will be other birthdays."

My dad never raced home for my birthdays, and while I understand why, more than ever now I'm the boss, it's not the life I want for my team. "Your girl matters. We'll get you home for it. I can't have you miss the race—"

"I wouldn't want to. My wife and I knew this life when I joined. She makes my dreams possible."

Like my mum did. Always behind the scenes.

"I'm glad you've got her. But I have a private jet, Macca. As soon as the race ends, we'll get you a helicopter to the airport and you'll be home to wake up with your girl or we can bring your wife and daughter here and book a suite in my name."

Macca embraces me with tears in his eyes. "Thank you, boss. I just...thank you. You've made this team a place I want to be. You're the best."

I hug him hard. "It's the least I can do."

"There's no other bosses like you, and we've never had anything like your support. And thank you for what you've done for Connor and Tawny. You've made this a team to be proud of."

"Ma belle," Antoine calls out, and my head throbs.

I wipe a hand down my face as he walks over.

"Do you need me to get him kicked out?" Macca asks, and I nearly hug him again.

I shake my head. "I've got this, but thank you."

He nods and steps away, shooing a couple of other staff so no one can overhear my conversation.

Antoine attempts to kiss my cheeks, but I step back, folding my arms. "No, Antoine. I don't want your greetings or whatever bullshit you have up your sleeve. What are you doing here?"

"I've come to apologise." His smile is as fake as his words. His eyebrows waggle. "I promise not to willy wang."

I set my jaw and give him the sourest look in my arsenal, but it goes unnoticed. "Apologise, then."

"You are cross with me. How can I make it up to you?"

"You can apologise and then leave. You'll never return to this team, and I'll never trust you again." A dark look crosses his face, but I need to say this, or his family will keep pushing me through my dad. "I don't care what deal you think you have with my dad. I run this team, and as long as I do, you'll not be welcome back into my offices, garage, or anywhere else related to Coulter Racing. You're dangerous and always have been." I drop my voice. "I know you're the real reason my racing career ended. You're an arrogant prick

who thinks he's better than everyone else. Get out of my garage before I kick you out."

Antoine grabs my shoulder hard enough to bruise it. "Senna, you'd best be careful who you're speaking to. You might not be boss forever."

"Get your fucking hands off her!" Connor strides over. His face burns red.

Over Antoine's shoulder, I see every member of the garage stare at Connor and then me and Antoine.

"I can handle this, Connor," I reply, but he's already grabbing Antoine's designer cashmere sweater.

"Get your hands off me, pretty boy," Antoine replies, pulling himself out of Connor's grasp before brushing himself down.

"Go now, or I'll pick you up and throw you out myself," Connor snaps.

"Connor, I've got this. I can do it by myself."

"But you don't have to," Connor replies, and I stare at him. "You have a team that will fight for you."

He points at the whole garage, who look at the ceiling or floor before picking up tools or their phones to appear like they're not watching.

"Antoine, come with me," I say. Antoine doesn't move. Instead, he eyeballs Connor. "Now, unless you want Connor to make good on his word and have the world's press watch you on your arse."

Antoine follows me through the garage. Connor watches us go with pinched eyes and a sneer that I know I'll have to sort out.

"I meant what I said. You're not welcome here, and you'll never drive for me again. If you push me, I'll ruin your name. I'm sure it wouldn't take long to dig up dirt on you."

Antoine smirks. "Things will change by the end of the

season. Tell your dad I said hello. Actually, I'll tell him when my dad and I meet him for dinner."

He walks away, and I return to the garage to find Connor pacing. I want to grab his hands, hold him still, and tell him it will be okay, but I can't in front of my team. Instead, I trace my tattoo in front of him. He looks down at it and back into my eyes.

I take a deep breath. "Connor, I'm grateful you were there for me, but you don't need to protect me. I can do it alone and need to be seen to."

He drops his head and says between gritted teeth, "You also need to know that I'm here for you and that you're mine."

I check behind me, but if anyone heard the last part, there's no sign.

"If something goes wrong, then it's on my head. I can't lose the respect I've worked hard to earn." I don't add that if something goes wrong between us, I won't have anyone.

He nods. "I know."

"Thank you."

I place my hand on the desk beside his, and his little finger brushes mine. A warmth spreads through my chest, and he stares at me like I'm all he needs.

CHAPTER FORTY-SIX – SENNA

Two podiums from four races. We're a month into the second half of the season, and I beam with the rest of the crew as Connor shakes his champagne and covers the two drivers from Vessa.

"He's doing well," Jacs says in my ear as I laugh.

"He is. And so is Tawny." The first female driver in Formula One for years is consistently top eight in every race. "It's a matter of time before she's up there."

"I hope she'll be less of a tosser when she is, but it's unlikely."

We laugh as Connor chases Luca, threatening to make him drink from his shoe. No one's done that since Daniel Ricciardo was on the podium, but Connor's so damn giddy, and it's infectious.

"He's happy." We both know she's not talking about racing.

Connor catches my eye and winks. My belly flutters.

"He is." The engineers and pit crew are oblivious. We're getting away with our secret, spending every evening together this past month except when we're travelling. "We both are. Thank you for giving me a talking-to before we returned from summer break."

I needed her phone call on the last day.

START YOUR ENGINES

"I told you what you already knew. It doesn't have to be everyone's business. You want to be with him even if you're just calling it dating. Denying that would have made you both miserable, and we had enough of that at the start of the year."

I elbow her. "You're very wise."

"I know," Jacs replies while pretending to blow on her nails. "Are you keeping the 'no hotel beds sharing' policy when you're away with the team to stop you getting caught?"

"Yeah, but it's annoying as hell. We both sleep much better together. Although we take it in turns to have cuddly Coults."

Jacs makes a gagging noise. I raise my eyebrows at her.

"Poor Senna and her bad boy with the giant dick."

"Oi, you. You'll be happy to know that tomorrow we're meeting back at his summer house by the lake for a few days. For rest and—"

"Noisy fucking," Jacs says, and I shrug, although I'm smirking so hard. "Have you specified if you're more than dating yet?"

"No. I'm in the most complicated relationship possible that isn't technically a proper relationship, and I've never been happier. Although," I stutter, "Niki called the other week."

"Your brother who'd end Connor in a heartbeat if he knew what you two were doing? And?"

I drop my head. "He still won't say when he's coming home or where he is. I don't understand what he's doing. Why can't he talk to his best friend or me? We've always been there for him. We know what racing is like better than anyone and what help is available."

"Maybe he doesn't want help."

281

I wring my hands while studying the tattoo celebrating my racing career. A cheer from the crowd makes me look up. Connor stares at me, his brow furrowed, as he catches signs of my stress. He's holding his shoe in the air and waits for my full attention before pouring champagne into it. When I nod, he drinks it all, his stare never leaving my face.

He's such a massive dickhead. A giggle rises in my throat. Everyone in the crowd screams his name. They love him nearly as much as I do.

"You're smashing it this season, and I don't just mean Connor's junk," Jacs teases, and I roll my eyes. "We're climbing the table, and you're showing your dad he can't sell the team. We're top seven, Senna. Top fucking seven!"

I pull my shoulders back. "We need to get top three in several more races to reach number six, but for the first time, it's possible."

"And your dad is proud?"

"Of course he isn't. But he's stopped speaking to me about Antoine or telling me about the board. I rarely answer his calls."

"Any more problems with Antoine? I can't believe I missed the drama in the garage a couple of weeks ago. Bloody Tawny dragging me to all her interviews."

"She's proud of her big sister, the mechanic."

Jacs shrugs.

"I haven't heard again from Antoine. I don't think he's completely out of the picture, but he believes I'll make good on my threat. It wouldn't surprise me if he has a lot of dodgy business dealings. I have to keep him away from this team, and the only way I can do it is by making this team a success."

"And you're doing it."

Pressure builds in my chest. But what if it isn't enough?

START YOUR ENGINES

"Anyway, enough about me. Have you got anything going on that I can make fake vomiting sounds about?" I ask, nudging Jacs.

Jacs laughs loudly. "I have plenty of hookups, but I'm bored. And who am I going to date? I'm not going near any men or women in racing. They'd break my heart or try to be the most dominant person to prove something, especially the guys."

"There was a reason I never dated in the industry until now."

Connor licks his lips, and the heat between my thighs grows. I know what I'll be getting tomorrow. I spend a lot of our time together with his face between my legs. He's like an oral god, and I never get tired of his hands holding me against his face as I scream my orgasm. That's the other reason we can't share a hotel room. Everyone would learn within seconds that the best racer in the team was fucking the boss, especially with his dirty talk.

"As there's no one in the industry I'd date, I'm left with someone I'll only see a few times a year because of our impossible schedule. Please don't tell me you're going to be one of those friends who so desperately wants me to be as happy as her—yuck—that you start setting me up with people? Because I don't want you to."

Jacs elbows me, and I wrap my arms around her.

Connor swaggers around the podium. Everyone else is ready to pack up, but he's doing it for me. He catches my eye to make sure I'm watching. I shake my head at him, which makes him grin wider. He's a bellend. Yet my stomach does somersaults. Twenty-four hours until I'm back in his arms.

"God no," I reply to Jacs before whispering, "If everyone has what I have, I don't get to be smug. And I love being smug around you."

283

"Oi," Jacs says but wraps her arms around me. "I'm happy for you and your self-satisfied ass. I really am. But can you get your man to stop being such a wanker? He's drinking out of his shoe again."

"I have no control over him." I laugh.

But as I shake my head and raise my eyebrows, he puts his shoe down. Maybe I have a little influence over him.

Jacs whispers, "He'd go to the end of the earth just to see your smile."

She's repeating what I told her Connor said in my office last week. I nearly fucked him on my desk when he dropped that comment into our conversation. Fuck knows how we'll be able to get to the end of the season without getting caught.

But we must.

Chapter Forty-Seven – Senna

I cross the threshold of the summer home and drop my bags. Beyonce's "At Last" plays from a speaker. I kick my trainers off, narrowly missing the candles littering the space.

"Connor?" I sneak around the one-floor house in the teeny shorts he loves. Thank goodness for the ongoing high temperatures. "I was pissed off that the situation at the factory made me later than planned, but I nearly broke the speed limits coming down."

I humph at the lack of response. "Where are you, Connor? I can't fuck you if I can't find you."

The scent of baked bread and cheese draws me to where the back door is open a crack.

I sneak through to the decking, and my breath hitches.

Connor stands on the deck in front of the lake. His eyes sparkle in the moonlight as he fixes me with his stare. Candles line the decking, giving him an ethereal glow. His eyes travel down my body, pausing at my legs long enough for him to lick his lips before lifting back to my eyes.

His stare reflects my smile, and he presses his hand to his heart as he greets me.

"Welcome home, baby," he says breathlessly

I'm running, my bare feet slapping against the wooden slats. He opens his arms, and I jump into them. He spins me

as he buries his face in my hair.

"It's been too long, Coults."

"We were on the plane together," I say, although my voice catches. He smells of fresh showers, of oak and cherries.

"And I couldn't touch you then. I couldn't get close enough to feel your skin against mine. You laughed with Jacs and chatted to the team, and the whole time, I wanted you laughing at my jokes or revealing the smile you reserve only for me." I stare into his eyes as he kisses my palm. "Like all my real smiles are only for you."

I bite my lips, and his gaze drops to them.

"Your fucking lips get me every time. There was a moment on the plane when I stood behind you. I was so close to leaning in and licking your skin." He licks my neck, making me moan. "I was desperate to make your pulse rise against my mouth."

I swallow loudly. "I felt you behind me."

"I know you did, baby. You blushed, and I was a heartbeat away from turning you around to kiss you and slide my hands into your blouse and thumb your nipples."

He lifts my T-shirt and rubs his thumbs across my nipples through the lace of my bra. I gasp.

"That's right, baby. Did you miss me, too?"

There's a trace of vulnerability in his voice. I pause. My fingers are jittery.

"Cat got your tongue, or are you teasing me?" He kisses my neck again, and I shiver. "You're scared of this. Why? I've got you. If we were drowning in the deepest part of that lake, my one thought would be to save you. Tell me you know this."

"I do," I whisper.

"Then talk to me."

START YOUR ENGINES

I clench my belly as he unsnaps my shorts and slides the zipper down. His hand eases into my knickers, but then he stops. I press my pussy against his hand.

He chuckles. "Hungry for me. I'm not doing anything until you tell me what's scaring you."

I lift my face to meet his gaze. His jaw is tight, and his eyes are dark as he stares into my soul. "I spent all my adult years hiding how I felt about you, including to myself. I'm scared.."

"Of?"

"Falling. Of telling you exactly how I feel about you and getting hurt."

"Senna, I wasted so much of my life not accepting my feelings, and even when I did, I couldn't act on them and chose to distance myself from you. I'm terrified that one day you'll wake and realise I'm too much of a dickhead for someone as incredible as you." I push him away, but he holds me tighter. "But I'm all in, baby. I'm not going to hurt you. I'm going to worship you."

My breath catches from the adoration saturating his voice until it rasps my name. "Senna, tell me you missed me."

"I missed you, Dane," I grunt. It's as if saying his surname removes me from possible heartbreak.

"Say my name. Say Connor. Did you miss me? Did you wish you could touch me and kiss me? Did you imagine coming as you rode my face? Did you struggle to focus because you wanted to play racing games, or be held by me? Because that's all I thought about."

I nod as I grip the waistband of his shorts.

"Then say it."

"I missed you, Connor. When you were behind me, I wanted you to whisper my name like only you can. I wanted

to curl up next to you on the plane and get the best sleep, because I only get it with you. I wanted you."

"That's my girl. My best friend. My everything." He licks his fingers and slides them into my knickers.

I moan as he teases me. "I wanted to wrap my legs around your head—"

"Your legs are one of the seven wonders of the modern world." He calls them that often.

His fingertips brush my clit, and I press my pussy into his touch. As I talk, he slides his fingers inside me gently, and it's like I'm finally in the place I should have been for weeks. He rubs my clit with his thumb as he continues to press his fingers inside me.

I stammer as he continues to own my pleasure, "And I wanted to be like this. In your arms forever. I missed you, Connor. I always miss you." I barely finish the sentence before his fingers thrust faster.

"I always miss you, too, baby."

He dips his head and bites my nipple through my bra. I'm writhing against his hand as his thumb endures against my clit, and he finger fucks me in the candlelight on his decking.

"I'll never wake up and think you're too much of a dickhead. I like that you're a dickhead." Stars are starting to spin as he finger fucks me harder. "I hope I'll always be enough for you."

"You can't be anything but enough for me. You're it. You're the sun and the moon. There's no part of my day that I'm not thinking of you, and if you'll give me all your trust, I'll show you." His voice is deep and rough. "Give it to me, Sen."

I hold my breath as if I can keep my control a little longer.

"Give me everything you have, because nothing would stop how I feel about you. *Nothing*. You are enough. You're more than enough. You're mine."

My orgasm explodes, and soon, I'm shaking against his hand.

I sink my teeth into his shoulder as emotions overwhelm me. It's like my brain is filled with fire, sun, and diesel, all combusting at once, yet peace overwhelms me, too, making me throw my head back and stare at the star-filled sky in awe. My body sags, but he holds me up and covers me with kisses.

"Hungry, weren't you, baby?"

"Hungry for you," I gasp. "I'm all yours. Only yours."

He hums against my neck as he flutters kisses to my skin. My body is still electric, and I want more. I gasp for breath, but it doesn't dilute my need for him. Nothing can.

I reach for his shorts. "Now it's your turn."

He pulls his T-shirt from the back, dragging it over his head. The move is so sexy that I pause. His biceps flex. His tattoos call to me, and I trace them with my fingers as I run my tongue across my upper lip. He pulls my hands to his mouth and kisses my knuckles before pressing his lips to my palm. In a dreamlike state, we undress between kisses and loving touches.

"Have you ever had sex in this lake?" I stutter.

He quirks his brow and twists his mouth as he stares at the dark water. "Not yet. It makes me nervous. I rarely go in."

"But you said if I were drowning in the deepest part of it, your only thought would be to save me."

He tips his head as I stroke his cock. Thank God we've chatted about contraception and when we were last tested. Water and condoms would be way too complicated right

now.

"I'd follow you to the ends of the earth and beyond." His admission carries on the wind, creating an aura of protection around us. "Even though this lake at night scares me."

I swallow repeatedly. I love every version of Connor, but my love for him terrifies me too much to tell him. Sometimes, he lets me be the boss away from the office, and he's not too proud to admit he gets anxious.

"Then know I've got you, Connor. I would dive down and give you the kiss of life while people dragged me away. You're it for me, and I will always be here for you."

"Always is a big word," he replies.

I wrap my arms around him and press my lips to his. His heartbeat thuds against my chest. "Always."

He grabs my hand as we run down the deck and dive into the water.

The lake is freezing, but this is our last chance to enjoy it before the summer ends.

I shiver in the shallowest part of the lake as I wrap my legs around him. His erection presses at my belly. His body is like a wall of heat, and as water drips down his shoulders, I burn.

"Are you ready, baby?" he asks.

I wrap my arms around his neck tightly. His gaze drops to my chest rising above the ripples of water. His pupils are stormy, and his grip on my breast is possessive.

"I'm always ready for you. Fuck me, Connor."

With that, he slides inside me as he whispers, "Always," again and again.

He moves gently, easing out before pushing back inside me. He sucks and licks at my neck while rocking me against him. One hand rests on the back of my neck, holding me

tightly as I use my thighs to move with him, lifting and dropping. It's more like lovemaking when he skims his fingers across my cheek and tells me I'm the most beautiful sight he's ever seen.

"Connor," I moan.

"You feel so good around my dick, baby," he says, his voice deep enough to reach every part of my aching body. I press him tighter against me with my feet, joining our bodies as I slide up and down against him. "I want to make love to you. It's all I think about. And once I've made you come hard on my dick, I'm going to take you inside and worship you. Do you want that, Coults?"

My yes is more like a cry of desperation.

He bites my ear lobe. "I never stop thinking about having you. I'm always imagining new ways to make you moan and gasp. When you're in meetings telling us what to do, I fantasise about bending you over the conference table and sliding right in."

My orgasm already builds again. I grip him harder and whimper in his ear, "More."

"I want to fuck you in your office, your hands on the glass as you lose yourself. I sit opposite you, desperate to pull up that sexy boss dress and thrust inside you."

I mumble my agreement. It would be risky, yet I want it. The danger works because of the safety between us.

"Do you imagine me on my knees under your desk, licking you to climax before I make you stand and fuck you from behind?"

My moans are as messy as my control as I immerse myself in the thickness of his dick that continues to push inside me. His muscles ripple against me. My thighs burn from keeping the rhythm, but I don't stop. I need him inside me. I take a deep breath, overwhelmed by his desperation

for me. The scent of the salty lake and the beer he must have drunk before I arrived mingle on my tongue.

His jaw clenches as he presses his lips to mine. His tongue is in my mouth. He presses his palm to the back of my neck, controlling the kiss. Although he has the power to drag an orgasm from my depths, he's not ready. He pulls his lips away and licks at my neck.

I whimper and moan as his dick fills me.

"I know, baby. It feels so good."

And that's when something switches. He fucks me with abandon, thrusting in and out as I squeeze my thighs and take him as deep as I can. The mixture of pleasure and pain sends me soaring.

"Come," he grunts. "I need to watch you come."

I go over the edge. My body shakes as I respond to his demand. My nails dig into his skin as I grip him. My climax overwhelms him, and he fills me with his orgasm as he groans his praises.

"That's my girl," he says repeatedly as I shiver and tremble. I hold on tight as he kisses me again. His mouth covers mine. His kisses are never-ending. "Mine."

Love for him bursts through my chest.

This is it. This is everything I've ever wanted. The intensity of the last half hour flows away on the quiet waves of the lake.

CHAPTER FORTY-EIGHT – SENNA

We have a few hours before I head back to the office.

Connor cooks us breakfast. The scent of bacon and pancakes drifts through to the bedroom. I stretch out on the bed like a cat that's finally found a beam of sunshine. Meetings and decisions have made my shoulders sore and my legs tight, but here, with him, peace descends, and endorphins tickle my belly. We haven't talked about the sentiments we expressed while having sex last night, but weirdly, I don't need to. Connor's actions and words have shown me what this is. I sigh happily.

My phone rings. I glance over, expecting one of the team.

It's Niki.

I look through the doorway at Connor, who stirs something while flipping a pancake. Calls from Niki are rare. Maybe he's coming home. Excitement and dread mingle as I snap up the phone and answer, holding it to my ear.

"Hey, big bro." I squeak the words.

"Hey, you. How are things? You smashed the last race."

"Thanks." My throat tightens, so I grab the glass beside me and gulp water.

Music plays in the background. "Bringing Tawny to the team was a genius move."

I can't tell him I came up with the idea with Connor.

293

"She's doing brilliantly. It was the move she deserved, but she needed someone to take a chance on her."

"And you were that person. You're doing well, and I'm so proud of you."

My stomach lurches as Connor appears with the kale smoothie he's prepared for me. He's always taking care of me. I hold a finger to my lips, and his brows knot.

I mouth, "It's Niki," and the furrow turns to wide-eyed panic. As he backs out of the room, he crashes into a chest of drawers. A photo of Connor and me crashes to the floor.

"What was that?"

"Nothing," I bleat. "I knocked a glass on the floor."

He chuckles. "You're at home, then?"

"Yes." It sounds more like a question than a statement. I'm already lying to my brother. "Are you nearby?"

I hold my chest as I wait for his answer.

"No, not yet." I let out my breath as quietly as possible. My hands are clammy, and I grip the phone tighter. "But I called to tell you I'll be back at the end of November, a couple of weeks after the end of the season."

I blink rapidly as I push a hand through my hair, still knotted from the lake. I don't know whether to be delighted or gutted. After six more weeks of Connor-filled bliss, everything could come crashing down. But I get my brother back.

"I can't wait to see you," I admit.

I catch Connor's eye. My sexy tattooed man worries his lips, nearly missing the plate as he attempts to drop a pancake on it.

"I've missed you, little sis."

I take a sip of water.

Maybe I could share something about Connor so he knows we spend lots of time together. It might help in the

START YOUR ENGINES

future. "I've missed you, too. And—"

"I'm also calling about something else. Dad wants to have dinner with you."

My lips curl, and I put my glass down before I drop it. "Then why hasn't he called me himself? Oh yeah, because I'm avoiding his calls."

There's silence at the other end, and I pace the room.

"I don't want to meet with Dad. What's the point? So he can tell me he doesn't believe in me and I should hurry up and have babies?" I snap. I kick a shoe and hurt my toe, my face creasing.

Connor walks tentatively closer, but I hold him back with my hand. I don't need him to protect me from my shitty family.

"I didn't know Dad said that. He wants to make amends. He hoped you, Connor and Tawny would meet him when you returned after the Mexico Grand Prix. He's been a dick to Connor since the crash—"

"The crash that wasn't his fault."

"Yes," he concedes. "And he wouldn't have allowed Tawny to join the team halfway through the season. He doesn't deserve your time, but this is big for him, Senna. Give him a chance, okay?"

"I'll consider it."

Maybe if Dad and Connor get on without him knowing about us, it will be easier to tell Niki about Connor. I can't have their relationship break because of me. I don't want to have to strategise my own life and a company my dad doesn't believe I can manage.

I catch Connor's eye again. He's pointing at the food. "I'd best go, as I need to eat something. But don't do Dad's dirty work for him next time."

"I won't." I start walking to Connor as Niki adds, "By the

295

way, do you speak to Connor much outside of telling him how to race?"

"Oh, you know. A little. The usual amount," I stutter.

Connor holds his hands up with a silent question.

"And he's looking after you, right?"

"Looking after me? I guess…"

"Good."

I huff. "But I don't need anyone to—"

"Got to go." He hangs up.

Even while travelling, he's still trying to be my controlling big brother. I slam my phone down next to Connor's. Connor wraps his arms around me and brushes my hair with his lips.

"Everything okay?" he asks as he drizzles the perfect amount of syrup onto my pancake from behind. I wrestle with the temptation to push him off. Why does one call with my brother set me on edge?

Maybe he senses it, because he steps away. His phone vibrates with a call. I spot that Niki is calling him. He flinches but doesn't answer it.

"You can answer it. It's okay," I say, watching as his jaw hardens.

"I'll speak to him later."

Something is off, but I can't figure out what.

"Niki's coming back," I blurt.

"When?" His eyes are massive, and he flips his cap backwards.

"A couple of weeks after the end of the season." Connor stares at me as I slice the pancake with rough cuts. "And Dad wants to meet with me, you, and Tawny for dinner in about a month when we return from Mexico. Fuck knows why he wants to wait until then. There's three races left after that."

I shove a lump of pancake into my mouth, glaring at Connor and daring him to attempt to improve the situation or protect me as he did with Antoine.

"Okay. I'm eager for both of those things already," Connor says before going to wash the dishes.

I stare at his back. "Why?" Shame creeps up on me as he turns. I should be easy-going like he is, but I'm still stung by Niki being on my dad's side. And why is Connor the person Niki calls as soon as he's spoken to me?

Connor turns and rubs his hands on the tea towel. I refuse to be distracted by his muscular forearms.

"You have every right to be angry at your family, but—"

"But?" I fix my jaw.

"But you don't get to take it out on me," he says, dropping the tea towel on the counter and walking closer. "I'm not happy with how they try to protect you when you're excelling at things they can't do in a mediocre fashion. But I'm not here for you to be annoyed at."

My arms hang limply by my sides, and my voice cracks. "I'm sorry. I hate how they make me feel. And when I saw Niki calling you, I got it in my head that he didn't trust me and needed feedback about me."

"It's okay." He reaches me and cups my face. "But I'm not your protector. You don't need one. I'm attempting to be your equal. I want to speak to your brother about us."

Panic flutters in my chest. "Not yet. I'm not ready yet."

"I thought you'd say that, so I didn't answer his call. It's getting hard to hide how I feel about you. I don't need his consent, but I want to tell him. If he's coming back, then maybe he's okay, and so it will be the right time to talk to him about us."

"Okay," I reply. The need to control the situation itches

at my skin. But he's got this, and he's got me. "My brother doesn't deserve a friend-to-friend chat with you about us. But I get it. And if you're willing to meet with Dad, then we will. I'm sorry for being a brat."

"You've said sorry already. It's okay. You've always had to fight in your family, but you don't need to do that with me. We've got each other's backs. Always." His words are saturated with confidence, but his hands are clammy, and his jaw clenches. "I want to be your boyfriend."

I do a double-take. It's like all the air is dragged from my lungs.

"I planned to say all of this on the deck last night, but you were so fucking sexy, and I went all caveman." His face flushes, and he takes a deep breath.

His smile is broader than his tattooed chest as I lead him into the bedroom.

"I need you close," I murmur. "I'm not used to these feelings or letting someone in like this."

We sit on the bed together. I pull off his cap, and he lowers his head and rests it on my belly. I run my hands through his hair as his fingers trip up and down my legs. He draws a heart shape on my thigh.

"We've got each other. With the end of the season coming, your dad acting weirdly, and Niki coming back, it's all about to kick off, but I'm not going anywhere." I slide down the bed and hold Connor between my arms. He meets my stare. His eyes are soft and his smile gentle. "So will you be my girlfriend?"

My fingers are jittery, but I'm beaming. "Yes. It's just between us for now, but I want to be your girlfriend more than I want to win the championship."

"Fucking yes," he says with a cheer and a fist pump before dropping kisses to my forehead. "You're mine. All

mine."

He kisses me on the lips and sighs. I sink into his chest as he strokes my skin. I scratch his scalp lightly with my nails.

"As your boyfriend and, therefore, someone who is allowed to care about you." He clears his throat, and I pause, my hands on his back. "I was wondering, are you nervous about the rest of the season?"

"I'm anxious when I'm not here," I admit. "I'm terrified that I won't be in the top six."

"We're getting there. You're a success, Senna."

What makes my nose itch with potential tears isn't his words that I'm certain he means but that he cares. He's listening and respecting me, not because he has to, but because he wants to. He wants me. I still, and he holds me against his bare chest. He smells of pancakes and his natural musk, and I barely resist pressing my lips to his skin.

"I want success for the entire team. I want to do well, for all the staff. Everyone's worked so hard, and we deserve to do well. You deserve to do well."

He hums in agreement. "What can I do to help make that happen, then?"

"Keep doing what you're doing. Your driving is incredible. You were seconds off first this weekend."

"I was fucking awesome."

I giggle. "Yes, you were. And driving doesn't scare you anymore?"

He holds me tighter, his hands stroking up and down my back under my T-shirt. "I love it. I've got another meeting with Ric later, but he can see how much I adore it. When I was racing last weekend, I felt so alive, and not just because I knew you were watching."

"It's hard to look away. You have such power, control, and energy when you drive now."

"Because I know the risks, and I'm not scared of them. I couldn't give up driving now. You made me love it with my pre-race song and sports psychologist mindset. And, anytime I get nervous, I remember how much fun it was to race you at the aerodrome and how sexy you looked on the bonnet of that Hypercar."

His fingers curl around my back. His chest warms my cheek.

"That was pretty memorable."

"Pretty memorable?" He tickles me, and I shake and scream, pulling away from him. He pins me under him as I drag air into my lungs. I'm gasping for breath as he stares at me. "That night was the best night of my life. Every night, every second with you is the best of my life."

"Don't let Layla hear you say that, or she'll think all those times you sneaked her into theme parks without your mum knowing weren't special. You made her love adrenaline too much. I spoke to her again the other day, and she said she's considering getting a motorbike."

"The fuck she is. They're too dangerous. I told her I won't fund it."

"Oops," I say.

Connor cocks his eyebrow. "Senna, what did you do?"

"I said if she was willing to intern with us one day, I'll buy her a motorbike."

Connor turns me so I'm underneath him.

"And you can't get annoyed because you drive F1 cars, and they're dangerous."

"But you love how dangerous I am. You always have."

I shrug as he stares at me. "Whatever. I was always better at driving than you."

He wrinkles his nose. "Maybe."

I pull my lips into my teeth, although I feel I'm glowing

under his inspection.

"I love staring into your beautiful hazel eyes. They have all these colours."

"They're brown," I correct him.

He caresses my cheek with the back of his fingers. "I've stared into them since I was a boy. They're hazel."

I suck in a breath and close my eyes as he presses kisses to my eyelids. "We've got an hour before I have to go," I whisper.

"We'd best make it count, then," he says, pushing my T-shirt up and brushing my skin with his lips.

And then he makes love to me. There's no other name for it. It's more than sex or fucking. It's the two of us connecting on a level we haven't until now, and it's all I've ever wanted.

CHAPTER FORTY-NINE – CONNOR

"I pushed that car as much as I could," Tawny says with her arms folded. Her auburn hair falls across her shoulders, but she reminds me more of a grumpy kid with a sour pout than a Formula One driver.

I nod from the front passenger seat of Senna's car. "So did I. What happened in Mexico is down to the car."

Senna pays us no attention. Her stare fixes on the road as she drives us closer to the meal with her dad. Her skin still carries some of the tan from the race in Mexico. I look away from her, although my gaze is drawn back as if she wears a string from her heart to mine.

Jacs taps my chair, and I rub my brow. "I know what you're going to say," I grumble. "You've said it every time we've talked about the car's performance over the last month."

She lets out a loud puff of air. "But—"

"No buts, Jacs." I turn in the passenger seat to stare at the sisters leaning forward from their back seats. Jacs strains against her seatbelt as Tawny glowers at her with her arms still folded. "For the last two races, since the team upgraded the car, it's slower. Tawny and I haven't done anything different. If it were just one of us, that would be on the driver, but neither of us has been top five. We're scraping

302

START YOUR ENGINES

into the top ten each race, and the upgrades are the key difference."

Tawny throws her hands in the air. "Exactly this. I've tried to tell you, but you wouldn't listen to me. Maybe you'll listen to Connor."

Jacs scowls at her sister. "The ultimate decision lies with Senna. We know why we did the upgrades. We needed to be a podium contender and get top three after the tricky first half of the season, but it doesn't seem to have worked."

"Doesn't seem?" I raise my voice. "We're telling you it hasn't worked. Get used to this bullshit in F1, Tawny. No one listens to the drivers. We're just the ones in the car trying to win races."

Jacs grumbles, and she and Tawny argue from the back seat. Senna is silent. Her hands grip the steering wheel as she drives us to an exclusive hotel on the outskirts of London. Her knuckles are white, and her jaw tightens. Her tattoo shines bright as we stop at traffic lights.

"Senna?" I'm a shitty boyfriend. She's been panicking about this meal since Niki called her weeks ago, yet I've been arguing with Jacs like we're children. I rest my hand on her thigh. I know I shouldn't where Tawny might see, but I need to comfort her. The hem of her woolly dress warms my palm. "I'm sorry. How are you feeling?"

She worries her lips, which are a pretty shade of pink. I draw a heart on her leg with my finger, and she takes a slow breath.

"They're dating?" Tawny whispers loudly. As I turn in my seat again, Jacs shoots her a look.

"As far as you're concerned, they're boss and driver and nothing more," Jacs replies. "And I'm here tonight for solidarity and not because I'm the only one who knows about these two and can distract any questions that get too

303

personal."

Tawny holds her hands up in surrender. "Noted. I don't know anything."

I squeeze Senna's knee.

I'm trying to be supportive, but I'm going to a dinner with Senna's parents, and although they can't learn I'm her boyfriend, I know I am. I've never been to a dinner with a partner's parents before. I should be as nervous as the trembling woman beside me, but I'm jittery with excitement about making a good impression.

"Work is the most important thing to Senna, so we've tried to keep everything separate and secret."

Senna links her fingers through mine on her knee. "Not the most important thing. Not anymore."

I stare back at her, but she's focused on the road.

"Wow! This is an F1 romance," Tawny whispers to Jacs.

"Doesn't it make you want to vomit and hug them all at once?"

I drop my head in my hands and laugh.

We turn into the hotel's car park, and Senna drives past the entrance.

Tawny leans forward. "Aren't you going to get them to park your—"

I laugh. "Senna never lets anyone park or drive her car."

"No one but Connor," she says, her beautiful lips shining.

I pull on the back of my neck. "Yeah. No one but me. Senna is headstrong, which is why we love her."

She parks the car, and as we climb out, she gathers us in a group. "Tonight is about getting through. My dad can be an arsehole, but he's passionate and still owns the team. Here are the rules—"

Jacs rolls her eyes, and Senna points at her. "Rule one:

less attitude from you," she says with a wink. "Rule two: enjoy yourself. The food and wine are good here, but don't enjoy yourself too much, because secrets will come out. Rule three: if it gets too heated, ask my mum about gardening, dogs, or her favourite city to visit. She loves to share but doesn't always get a word in. Rule four: don't mention me and Connor. My dad still hates Connor, so let's not worsen that situation."

"A though tonight, I'll do my best to make Senna's parents like me so they realise I'm the best person for their daughter. That way, when Niki returns, and we announce it, they'll already be on my side."

Senna squeezes my hand tightly, and my pulse performs a jig. Her eyes twinkle under the security lights in the car park, and it takes everything I have not to gather her in my arms and kiss her.

She turns back to the group "Rule five—"

"I'm getting cold." Jacs shivers in her green tailored jumpsuit.

Watching Senna be the demanding boss makes me impossibly more in love with her. And unfortunately, blood rushes to my dick, too. I shouldn't meet the parents with a massive hard-on.

"Rule five: no lip from any of you, and don't commit to anything my dad suggests."

"Rule six: Connor needs to think about less sexy things because his erection is obvious from here. Could you have worn tighter trousers?" Jacs asks.

Tawny stares at the sky to avoid the sight of my manhood straining at my zipper. She's giggling loudly, and Jacs joins in.

"It's not my fault. Senna is mouth-watering in those high heels and her smart sweater dress. And then she got all

boss-like and—"

Now they're all chuckling at me. Senna bends over, shaking with laughter.

"That's not helping," I shout, turning their laughter into belly wobbles.

A grumble from across the car park stops us. "When you've finished, some of us are hungry."

"Sorry, Dad," Senna shouts back. Fuck. My whole body tightens, and I hug myself. "We'll meet you inside. I've got one more bit of business."

"That was your dad? Do you think he heard what we were laughing about?" Tawny asks, yanking at the sleeves of her jacket like she's been told off at school for wearing the wrong blazer.

"Nah, but get behind me, Connor, until your cock goes down," Senna says, which sets Jacs off again. "And you made a good point about the upgrades. I've examined the timings and how it's changed performance, and you're right. It didn't work. We'll change the cars back in time for the next race. Thank you for being patient about our experiment."

Jacs and Tawny walk ahead as I tightly hold Senna's hands in mine.

"You let us work our rants out and then cut through the bullshit and made the decision. You're amazing. It's one of the many reasons I love you," I whisper as we walk towards the hotel. She freezes. "I mean..."

"You love me?" Her voice drops and is filled with a wonder that makes me want to kick myself for saying it right now.

Her hazel eyes dance with gold and blue, and her smile grows, creating little lines near her eyes.

I gulp loudly. "Coults, I love you. I love you more than I believed possible, and I really would go to the end of the

START YOUR ENGINES

universe just to see you smile."

I get an elbow in my back as someone jostles us.

"Oi," I grumble, turning on my heel to face Ralf.

"Good for you, Connor. But I'm hungry," he replies.

He moves me to the side and tucks Senna's arm in his. "Your dad invited me to dinner."

They walk into the restaurant. Senna gazes back at me, standing like a dickhead in the car park, but I quickly catch up.

As we're led to the private dining area, her mum rushes to hug her as everyone seats themselves. Her dad stares at her and doesn't even say hello to me.

As I sit, I can't stop myself from looking at her. Her shoulders are hunched so high that I want to kiss a line down her back to ease her before she gets a headache, but I can't here.

I brush her little finger under the table, and she hooks hers with mine. I will look after her as best I can, and maybe later, I'll learn if she loves me.

Ralf clears his throat and stares at me. Fuck. That he knows about us makes the fact that we're about to have dinner with her dad, who already hates me and wants to sell the team, more awkward.

Here goes nothing.

CHAPTER FIFTY – SENNA

He told me he loved me, but I didn't get to say the same. Hearing those words as I was about to enter the restaurant was like putting on the armour I needed.

We get through most of the dinner in the private room unscathed. Dad is his version of politeness, which means he doesn't start fights, but the knowledge that I need to confront him means I've been picking at my food. Tawny and my mum have found a shared love of cute dog videos. When Ralf isn't talking to Dad about what former drivers are up to, he and Jacs are covering the greatest hits of races they've both loved, sharing secrets about the engineering of those cars.

I look between my dad and Connor.

"You look well, Senna," Mum says softly, studying my face. I smile at her. "I was worried when you became team boss because I know what it can do to people." She observes my dad, but he's speaking to Ralf about the "good ol' days" of track girls and cocky drivers. I glance at Connor, who winks at me. Okay, cocky drivers still exist, and the sport is better for it.

"Thank you, Mum. Jimmy and Connor ensure I eat every meal and take breaks, too."

Jimmy deals with lunch. Connor makes breakfast,

organises dinner and texts me to ensure I walk around the building and go for a run. At night, depending on when I make it home, he runs me a bath, and we watch movies or have the kind of sex that makes me forget all my worries.

"Then I'll thank Jimmy another time. And thank you, Connor, for being a good influence on my girl. You cared about her when she was a teenager, too." There's a twinkle in Mum's eye as she eats the last spoonful of her tiramisu. The more I speak to Mum and Dad since he retired, the more I realise he'd be nothing without her. I hope he realises that, too. "I remember how you two danced in the kitchen when you thought you were alone, and you sang, too, Connor. You had a lovely voice."

"Thank you." Connor coughs and blushes. "And you don't need to thank me. Senna is a good influence on me. I'm a lucky man...I mean, friend...friend man." He stares at the table as Mum grins. "I'm a lucky friend who is a man."

Talk about revealing everything. But I don't care. He loves me. Connor fucking Dane loves me, and I love him, too. I can't wait for this meal to be over so I can tell him.

"Anyway," he continues, "Senna is a considerate but ball-busting boss. She cares about the entire team. She knows everyone by name. She asked one of the interns what they wanted for their future and put things in place to make it happen. She asks about the pit crew's kids and makes sure that, where possible, they can be home for birthdays. She's put the family back into Coulter without losing an inch of professionalism and performance. There's not a word for how incredible she is."

My legs tremble. "You saw that?" I whisper quietly enough for him to hear. "I didn't think anyone knew the things I did."

"She's astounding," my mum says. Her smile as her

eyes flit between me and Connor makes me lift my chest. "No matter what she's done, she's always pushed and tried to be the best without forgetting the people around her. She was the same as a driver, always ensuring you and Niki ate the right things before races and had your equipment together."

"It's a shame not everyone realises how amazing she is," Connor says, glancing at my dad, who stops speaking and stares back. I squeeze Connor's thigh. This isn't the time for a fight.

"They know." My mum sighs. "But they don't always understand."

Silence descends. Then the waiter brings port to the table. I glance at Ralf, who gives me a nod. It's like the nod of comrades going into battle. The port course is when Dad does business. He'll wait for an entire meal, giving polite conversation, but when the port comes out, he goes for the gullet.

I lean back in my chair. He fixes me with his stare.

"Why are your drivers doing so badly at the moment?"

Connor tenses beside me, and I squeeze his thigh under the table. This is my fight. I nod to Jacs, who says something to Tawny about the toilet. I don't want her here for this. I'd already warned her this might happen.

"We tried an upgrade. It didn't work," I reply flatly. I turn to Ralf to engineer another conversation.

"Well done for trying it," Ralf says under his breath before adding louder, "Hawaii was lovely."

"Are you sure it's not because you fired Antoine and made Connor the lead driver?" Dad glares at Connor, who eyeballs him.

Jacs scowls at my dad from the doorway of our private dining room before jostling Tawny out. Ralf laughs to ease

the situation, and Mum grumbles at Dad about ruining dinner. Connor grips my hand under the table. I offer him a brief smile as a thank you. He knows this is my fight, but I don't doubt he has my back.

"I thought you wanted to meet me to apologise for your behaviour this year. I wouldn't have come here if Niki hadn't told me to," I seethe.

Dad leans back in his chair, his arms wide with his trademark power stance, but I'm not backing down.

"Come on. This is a business chat." I lift my chin high and curl my lips. "I'm not sure leading a team is for you. You were fantastic at marketing, but leading a team isn't a job. It's a calling."

I grip the table. "I can't believe you."

"What? You should be used to boardroom chat."

I grind my teeth. "We're not in a boardroom. We're at a family meal. A family you've hurt with your demands. Your son pushed himself to crash and then left the country to get away from you."

"Niki left for other reasons."

I'm relieved Ralf, Mum, and Connor are quiet as we battle.

I pin my dad with my stare. My skin itches at the fight. In a boardroom, I'd have research to hand, and my heart wouldn't be invested or on the precipice of hurt with history thrown at me. But it's different with Dad, and it always was.

"He left because you created expectations he couldn't meet, that no one can meet, not even you. And you've tried to do the same with me. When was the last time Coulter Racing, under your helm, reached the top six in the Constructor's Championship?"

"Hold on—"

"Five years ago," I snarl. "And you still told me you'd

sell the team if I didn't get it to the top six."

"You didn't," my mum says, frowning at Dad.

"It was her idea," Dad replies, thumbing in my direction.

"You pushed me there."

But he's talking to my mum now. "I want Senna to settle down. I want grandkids and not to have my life dictated by a racing calendar anymore. I want to have a proper family."

My mum throws down her serviette. A server backs out of the room. "Then you shouldn't have made our lives about racing. I love everything about Formula One, but you pushed the kids to do it when they were younger, and now you want them out because you're done? That's not how it works."

"But she could have a happy life."

My mum twists to stare at me. "Senna, do you want to continue as team boss?"

"Yes."

She pokes my dad in the chest. "Then problem solved. Stop controlling the lives of everyone around you. And stop trying to protect Senna when you should have protected Niki. You're the reason I nearly lost my son last year, and instead of him coming to us to recover, you made him team boss. He escaped the country to get away from you." She jabs him harder on the word *you*. "Senna is running the team amazingly, and she's happy. Look at her. She is happy."

Even with her anger at my dad, she smiles at me.

Dad bristles. He'll reflect later, but when confronted, he always doubles down. He gulps his port, wiping any remaining drops from his mouth with his serviette, and replies, "It doesn't matter. I've got a buyer for the team."

My mouth drops. Uncle Ralf is staring at my dad, his eyes wide.

312

START YOUR ENGINES

"You didn't believe in her," Connor states. "You told her what she needed to do to keep the team, and you looked for a buyer anyway."

Dad eyeballs Connor. "Hold on, Dane—"

"No, you hold on." Connor leans into the table, his voice low. "Senna brought the team back from the brink. She dealt with Antoine, the same guy you lauded, who is one of the little shits Niki and I tried to protect her from when we were teenagers. Antoine treated her like she was nothing, and you enabled that. You ruined the team with your lack of research and development, hence the recent performance issue. You decimated the finances, all things she's improved because she has the intelligence to do it and the respect of others to ask for their help. She transformed the team."

My dad stands, and so does Connor. He fists his hands, and I moisten my lips, watching in awe and admiration. That's my man.

"You have the fucking audacity to go back on your promises when she's done more for this team than you've done in decades. How dare you not believe in your daughter when you've seen how incredible she is."

No one has defended me to my dad like this. Niki let him railroad me and then did things behind the scenes. But Connor is risking everything to confront my dad with the impact of his behaviour.

I love him.

I stand, throwing my serviette onto the table like my mum did. I grab Connor's hand and squeeze it. "Connor, let's go. Uncle Ralf, will you run Tawny and Jacs home?"

"Of course," Ralf replies with a nod.

"Thank you, Mum. You're the best," I say, kissing her. "I'm sorry."

"You have nothing to be sorry for, my beautiful, strong

313

girl," she replies, hugging me tight.

Hand-in-hand with Connor, I step away from the table.

"I'm not done with you, Senna, and I'm certainly not done with Connor," Dad grunts as we stand.

"Yes, you are," I reply, turning on my heel. "Connor was loyal even when he was terrified to drive. Still, you don't see the light he's been for our entire family. I love this man and have for years."

"And I love her. She's my world." Connor's eyes shine, and I'm engulfed in his adoration. "Let's go, baby."

"Does your brother know?" my dad says, his teeth gnashing. "Niki will return to your betrayal. Don't you remember the rows I had with him after the crash about keeping his friendship with this player?"

I stride back to the table. "Connor is the most amazing man. He's honest and patient and cares about me. I worry about Niki as much as you do. But we haven't told him. Don't you dare tell him in your brusque way. We'll tell him at the end of the season. Now, I'm taking my boyfriend home, and then I'll get my team in the top six because I keep my promises."

I catch up with Jacs and Tawny near the toilets and inform them that Ralf will drive them home. I also give them the highlights of our family argument. It's not even our biggest.

Tears brim my eyes as we return to the car.

"Drive us to the offices," Connor grunts, gripping me tight, his thumb stroking my tattoo.

"But there won't be anyone there," I stutter, my hands trembling.

His warmth resets me.

"That's the point. Tonight can't be about your dad's shitty behaviour. You are a powerful, strong, and fucking

amazing woman and in control of so much. I will do whatever I can to remind you of that. I owe my boss office sex, and that's exactly what you're getting. This night is going to end in an epic orgasm, and it's got your name all over it."

CHAPTER FIFTY-ONE – CONNOR

My back aches from the tension of the Coulter family argument. I rub Senna's shoulders and arms from behind as we stand in the lift in the Coulter office building, although it's more to comfort me than her. Her reflection in the lift mirror offers me a half smile, which makes my stomach jittery.

We could've returned home, where I would've fed her spoonfuls of ice cream or held her close. I'm sure she needs to be in control of something, and while I can't book a secret race track with Hypercars at a minute's notice, I can do this.

We slip into her office. I wasn't lying about wanting to go down on her beneath her desk. I've had a ridiculous number of fantasies about her and this desk, but this is about what she wants and helping her recognise her power.

"Connor, did you mean what you said about me earlier?" she says timidly.

She stands awkwardly near the door. I read her wrong. She didn't need to be the boss. She needs to be cherished and adored.

I gather her in my arms, basking in her orange blossom scent and the softness of her blond waves. "Which bit, Coults?"

"All of it?"

I brush kisses to her forehead. "Yes, baby. I meant every word. You're incredible. And I count my blessings every day that you chose me. You love me. I've waited every day since the summer for you to come to your senses and realise I'm nowhere near good enough for you."

Her lips whisper against my skin, "Never. I adore you. I loved you when we were younger. But this is different. It's like I might die if I don't see your face or hear from you. I never want to be with anyone else. When you race, I'm terrified something will happen to you because my life would be over if it did. But I don't want to stop you being you."

I lift her and carry her to her desk, propping her on the edge. "I don't want to stop you from being you, either."

Her smile breaks my heart into a million pieces and then sews them together again. Now, it's made for her.

"Have you been in love before?" she asks, running her fingers through my hair. I close my eyes and let her grazing touches soothe me.

"I'm surprised you don't know. But maybe there were times when, during the years we weren't speaking, you didn't follow my life because it hurt too much. That's how it was for me."

She hums in agreement. All those years, we were emotionally holding hands through our conflict.

"I've been in love three times." She gasps. I stand between her thighs and pin them with my hands so she can't go anywhere. Moonlight streams through the window. Her curvy earrings spin, and the light cascades off them. "And all three times were with you."

I smooth the lines of her forehead before dropping a kiss against her lips.

"The first time I knew I loved you was the night before

317

your last race. I sat beside you on the sofa. You slept against me, making the same cute snores you do now."

"I don't snore." She gives me a playful shove, but I take her hand and brush my lips against her wrist.

"Yes, you do, baby, and I fucking love those sounds." She twists her mouth into the cutest smile. "That night, as you slept beside me, I knew what I felt for you wasn't a teenage crush. I loved you as much as an eighteen-year-old lad with no sense can. But I couldn't tell you. I was scared your brother would kill me because of that fucking pact or you'd laugh at me. There was stuff going on with my dad, too, but I still had this need to ask you out. And then I hit you, and you crashed and—"

"And I refused to speak to you ever again." She holds my face between her hands.

Tears collect in her eyelashes, and my vision blurs from the painful memories.

"And part of me thought I'd never recover. All I wanted to do was hold you and promise to be better, but you didn't want anything to do with me. Over time, I pushed the feelings down, but really, I still loved you. You were always here." I press her palm against my heart. "And then I went to Ralf and Myles's wedding last summer."

"I didn't see you there. I searched," she admits with a flush to her cheeks. I kiss the little dots of red.

My smile is sudden and unwavering. "Because you hated me and wanted to beat me to death with your bridesmaid bouquet?"

She chuckles.

I curl a wave of her hair around my fingers. Her tears haven't fallen but still make flecks of gold shine from her hazel eyes. "I hid in the back because, as much as I was invited, I also knew it might cause unwanted attention."

"Because you're such a big star?" she teases.

I wrap her arms around my neck. "No, because Myles's daughter had a massive crush on me. Before I slipped out, she chased after me. I explained I was in love with someone else and always had been and that although they didn't love me, there would never be anyone else for me. She wasn't happy, but she respected my issues with unrequited love, and then she went straight on Tinder."

"And I was the person you loved?" Her voice is so light. I want to make love to her and hear her sing my name from her beautiful lips, but I'm not done yet.

"Yes. The moment you stood at the front of the ceremony with your hair in that delicate style, my heart stopped. I wanted to play with that pink flower behind your ears and carry the shoes you would've ditched somewhere so you could be barefoot. You were beautiful."

She shrugs. "I was all right."

"You were a vision. Before I left, you told the best man he couldn't tell a cruel joke in his speech. You were around a corner from me. I couldn't see you, but I heard you. Ralf's brother was such a big bruiser of a man, yet there you were, standing up to him and ensuring the speech must be words of love. That was the second time I fell in love with you."

Her laughter makes me want to close my eyes and immerse myself in it forever. "Because I told off a grumpy bastard?"

"Because I was reminded of the Senna who cares about her people and wants everyone to be happy. I wanted to be one of your people and feel that care. It also helped that in the ceremony, the slit in your dress opened, and I caught a glimpse of your phenomenal legs."

She smiles, and my heart stops again. "I insisted the hair and make-up team make me stunning because Ralf told

me he'd invited you."

I gulp loudly. "You wanted to look your best for me?"

"Yes. Even though I hated you. They said they'd never worked with such a bossy bridesmaid before."

"That's my girl." I kiss her smiling lips hard. "I left the wedding after you berated Ralf's brother and I realised that my love for you hadn't gone away after all those years. I knew you hated me, so I'd never be truly happy. Nothing in my life would be enough because I'd never have you."

"Oh." She fists my shirt, unable to meet my gaze.

"I was a mess. I didn't want to be with any other woman after that. I struggled with driving because it didn't give me the joy I craved. It got worse after Niki's crash. When I started working for you, I hated it because, deep down, I still loved you. But I was reminded how much you detested me. I couldn't have you, so I didn't want to be around you."

Tears slip down my cheeks, and Senna cradles me.

"It's okay. We have each other now. Nothing will change that," she whispers, kissing away my tears.

"Hopefully your brother won't kill me." I'm shaking at the words that were on my tongue the entire drive to her office. "I'd sacrifice everything for you. I'll go up against him and do anything to keep your heart."

"I won't let him hurt you. We'll convince him that we should be together. You're not a fuckboy. You're the most loving man I've ever met. I only want you forever."

"Forever sounds perfect."

I tangle my fingers in her hair, and she pulls my shirt out of my trousers and unbuttons it. I've never allowed myself to be this vulnerable with anyone, but she won't hurt me.

She blesses my skin with kisses. I unsnap my trousers. Her fingers stroke the tattoo of her best lap time under my arm. She can't resist touching it when we're alone together.

START YOUR ENGINES

My nerves spark like lightning as she appraises me.

"You're so beautiful. I could stare at you for hours." Slowly, she pushes down my underwear, and I kick off my shoes and rid myself of my trousers and boxers. She wraps her hand around my dick, and my head falls back. "This is what I want."

"That's my girl," I hiss as she fists my cock.

She strokes me up and down, and my legs shake. Little hairs rise all over my skin, and I moan in desperation for her.

She moistens her lips in a way that is so fucking tempting. "Connor, you've given me more than I hoped. You believe in me in a way no one else does. You challenge me and listen to me. You trust me and give me the safety to be me."

"Yes, baby," I growl. I struggle to focus on her words even though I understand their importance.

My body demands I stay with her hand wrapped around me, yet somehow, I step back. I lift her dress up and off until she's seated in her purple underwear on the edge of her desk. My mouth goes dry as I take my time to stare. She reaches for my cock again, but with an arched eyebrow, I pin her wrists with my hand.

"Not yet, beautiful. I want to remember the moment I finally see my sexy boss in her underwear sitting on her desk for eternity."

Her smile is coy, and my heart flutters. I clear my throat. I pull her into my arms and lift her. She wraps her legs around me, grinding on my erection as I carry her over to her new cream-fabric sofa and lay her on it.

I settle between her thighs. I tuck my fingers under her bra straps and drag them down.

I ghost kisses to her shoulders as she huffs. My lips follow the curve of her bra. I'm hard for her, but this isn't

the quick fuck I initially fantasised when I imagined our time in her office.

"You're so sexy, baby. You're this badass boss woman, and yet you chose me." I pull down one cup and run my tongue around her nipple. She pushes her pelvis up to me, demanding more.

"You chose me first," she says between gasps. "And now you're mine forever."

Her hazel eyes swirl with colour.

She whimpers and moans as I duck down, lathering and biting one nipple while pulling down the other cup and trailing my fingers across the other nipple.

My mouth hovers over her breast as I blow across it. She shivers. My fingers slide down her belly and into her knickers. She's so wet for me. I tease her clit, never pressing hard enough but not pulling away.

"Yours," I reply, pressing my fingers inside her as my thumb rubs her clit. She grinds against the palm of my hand, and I push against her.

My cock presses against her, and I slide down her knickers.

"I love you, Coults."

I ease my cock inside her and wait. She moves and writhes, desperate for me to fuck her, but this is the moment I've waited for. Nothing compares to being inside the woman I love in the sanctuary of her office. We'll remember this moment when I return for a meeting, especially if she's reprimanding me. My cock stretches her. Her legs and arms are around me as I feather kisses across her body.

"I love you, too, Connor," she whispers as I pull back and press deeper.

I lose track of time as we cuddle, kiss, and revel in our

intimacy. The world could burn around us, and I'd still be here with the woman I love, keeping us safe.

CHAPTER FIFTY-TWO – SENNA

I stretch in my bed.

"Good morning, baby," Connor says over the video call we've had all night.

"Good morning, beautiful. Did you sleep okay?" We declared our love for each other two weeks ago, and it's been bliss ever since.

"Like a cat cuddled up to his favourite owner," he says with a wink. He's only on the floor below me, but we must keep my staff unaware of our relationship. "I'm going to head to the gym and call Layla while I'm there. Do you want to join me and say hello to your future intern?"

I chuckle. "She might change her mind. She's still got to finish university."

"She won't change her mind. She thinks you're incredible, as I do, although she admires your business mind and social media skills, whereas I admire that and everything else."

I cuddle into my blanket as I stare at Connor, who beams at me through the screen. "I love you, Connor fucking Dane."

"And I love you, too, Coults. And you're ready for our date tonight after the race?"

"Yes."

START YOUR ENGINES

"And you promise to turn your phone off so you can relax. You need to relax."

"Yes, Con." I roll my eyes. I need to let others look after me sometimes, especially him, even though I worry about the team and how they'll cope without me. "But this isn't about you protecting me, is it?"

"I wouldn't dare."

My phone rings.

"Who's that?"

"It's Dad," I say with a shrug. "I haven't spoken to him since that meal."

It goes to voicemail and then rings again. This time, it's my mum.

"Connor, I'd best get that. You have fun at the gym, and don't get distracted by the slot machines."

Connor jumps up, and I see the famous Dane dick. I can't believe this sexy and kind man is mine.

"Do you think they have them in the gym, too?"

I chuckle. "It is Vegas. I'll message you when I've finished talking with my parents."

"Love you, and good luck. You know where I am if you need backup." He moves into a boxing stance that does nothing to hide his penis.

I roll my eyes as I say, "Love you," and hang up the call on my laptop while answering my phone.

"Mum, what's up?"

"It's me," Dad replies.

My finger hovers over the red end call symbol.

"Before you hang up, I need to talk to you. I had another health scare this morning."

"Are you okay?" I stutter.

"I am," his voice wavers. "But I thought that was it for me. I've tried calling your brother, but I can't reach him. It's

time we found out where he is."

"If you're sure. I haven't heard from him for a few weeks."

"Me neither," he replies.

"Are you all right now? Should I come home?"

"Of course not. You've got the race today. Nothing is more important than that."

"Sorry, yes." I don't know why I'm apologising for caring about my dad, especially based on how he's treated me. I check my watch. I've got a couple of hours before I need to leave. "Dad?"

He clears his throat. "I called to apologise for the meal. I regret how I treated you and for ruining a perfectly good dinner. It's just... I worry about you," he says gruffly.

"Oh, right. That wasn't a good evening, was it?" My words are stilted. I'm not used to my dad apologising for things or sharing anything related to feelings.

"No, and I'm partly to blame." Partly?

"Right. Well, you don't need to worry about me. I was fine."

"That's not what I mean. I worry about you all the time. I worry about you leading the team when you should live differently. That's why I wanted Niki as the team boss. This isn't your life."

As apologies go, this is shit, but I don't want to argue and give him another heart attack. "I love everything about racing."

"Do you? I still feel sick when I remember your crash. That day Connor slammed you into a wall, your mum and I panicked that something more serious had happened. I'll never forget that moment."

"Connor didn't do it—"

"I remember the terror as we waited to see if you were

safe. My plans for your future flashed in front of my eyes. Not the life you'd had but the one you should have. I thought about how I'd never get to walk you down the aisle, hold a grandchild, or have Christmas celebrations with a big family. I didn't think about how you'd never race again, although I know it was important to you."

He never asked what was important to me. Even now, he's telling me what my future should have been.

"When you recovered, which was the best day, and got a university place, I felt you'd be safe from racing and have a future away from this business. Yet you're working every hour of the day and taking on the stress that gave me a heart attack. I want more for you, Senna."

I rub my forehead with my fingers. "But what about the things I want?"

He makes a humph sound. "This business ruins lives, and I'd hate my daughter to have her life ruined."

"Dad," I say gently, "I love this life. Yes, it's hard, and the strain sometimes gets to me. But I have Connor now. I have what I want." My dad, the guy who used to hold me on his shoulders as I waved my trophies in the air, the man I worshipped and wanted to achieve for seems less powerful—I don't need his pride anymore. I need his acceptance.

"But you should have more. You should know that I'm still talking to that buyer. If you can't walk away, I must make you."

"You promised me that if we came sixth, you wouldn't."

"It's in your best interests."

Tears collect in my eyes, but I refuse to back down. "We're still going to be sixth, and we'll do it as a team because we can. And I will continue to work in racing because I can."

"Senna, I love you."

"I love you, too. But right now, I'm not sure if I like you. Goodbye, Dad. Look after yourself."

"**V**egas, baby!" Connor shouts as he swaggers around the garage.

I watch the screens with Jacs and Macca, although my attention occasionally drifts to Connor making finger guns at the team. In one day, he's obliterated all the anxiety left over from my conversation with my dad. I will find a way to change Dad's mind. I must. "Stop putting us off. We're determining if we're changing pit strategy for the race."

"Who cares? It's Vegas, baby."

He dances across the garage, persuading the crew to join him. I shake my head and squeeze my lips tight to hide my grin.

"I know. You've shouted that for the last four days we've been here." And I loved it every time except when he shouted it in my ear while I attempted to sleep on the plane.

He wears his racing suit on his bottom half with the top half hanging down. He's delectable in his white long-sleeved T-shirt under the suit. I want to run over and kiss him, but we're attempting professionalism when we're at work, except the two times we've had sex in my office and the other time in the garage. But aside from that, complete professionalism.

He winks at me as if he knows what I'm thinking as he spins. Tawny runs to his side and performs some kind of body popping. He high-fives her as if they're wrestling teammates, and he's tapping her in. He strides to me. My

toes curl and my stomach flops.

I couldn't want him more.

So far, it's not damaged my ability to run the team. We removed the upgrades for the last race, and it paid off, because Connor and Tawny were P4 and P5. We're on the cusp of sixth in the championship, but it would take another podium and a win.

"Dane, I need to ask you about positions." His eyebrows jump, and I turn away and cover my mouth to keep the laughter at bay. "Positions for the race," I add gruffly.

My whole body will explode at his proximity if I look at him.

"Yes, boss," he says. I'd place bets he's wearing the smuggest smile. "What have I got to do to get us top six by the end of the season? With this race and the last one in Abu Dhabi next week, we can do it."

He's repeating what I said in bed the other morning before we left for the States. He's such a cocky bellend.

"My thoughts exactly," I say with a side-eye. His grin is disarming. "But it will take another two podiums. As much as I believe in you, we can't do it."

"There's no 'I' in can't."

Jacs giggles as Connor showboats. This is the Connor of years earlier, who didn't get scared about driving and slept before races. I know he sleeps now because of our overnight video calls. We take it in turn to have cuddly toy Coults, too, so it always smells of both of us.

"Connor with sleep is terrifying. I preferred you when you were an insomniac," Macca jokes.

"Me too," Jacs replies. "Although I reckon Connor with sleep can get on the podium."

"At least one of you believes in me," Connor adds.

I swivel in my chair and stare at him. He raises an

REBECCA CHASE

eyebrow as I prepare my contrition. My fingers tap my best lap time tattoo. "Ignore me. I'm being negative. You can do this, and you've got the team's full support behind you."

"Do you believe in me, boss?"

A smile tickles my lips, but I remain stoic. "Yes, Dane. You can do it."

He tips his shoulders and rejoins the dancing. Tawny executes a perfect worm move on the dirty garage floor.

"That's all I needed to hear. On it, boss." His wink isn't subtle, but I'm the only one looking into his eyes due to the unexpected Irish dancing and kicking up of his legs he's performing.

"Can I join them?" Macca asks.

I roll my eyes, although that tickling smile is a full beam now. "Have at it, mate."

My nose itches, and a lump forms in my throat. I've helped develop a team that manages their pre-race anxiety by having fun and not by fighting and shouting. Based on the stares from pit crews peeking through our open garage doors, it's unusual, but it works.

"Are you okay?" Jacs asks. Tawny giggles as she high-fives the pit crew.

"I don't want to lose this because my dad wouldn't believe in me. In just over a week, this crew could be broken up with Tawny kicked out because Antoine and his dad or some other piece of shit buys the team. And Connor loves racing now and wants to make this team great. I want this to be the future for all of us," I say as Connor jumps on someone's back. "Oi," I shout, pointing at him to get back on the ground.

"Sorry, boss," he shouts and obeys, but his smile remains.

"Sen, being in the top six doesn't mean anything to your

330

dad, because he's already made his decision, but it means something to your family, your team. We are doing it for each other, but more importantly, we're doing it for you because you're the best boss we've ever had. No matter what happens next, you made something amazing, okay?"

That's when the tears fall. I've never been happier because, win or lose, I've found a family who truly believes in me, and there's nothing more I want.

"Connor told me he's taking you out tonight," she says, handing me a tissue.

"He wants me to turn my phone off. He says I need to relax more than ever, especially after hearing about my dad and his scare. He doesn't want that to happen to me."

"He's got a point, and we can manage without you. If there's an emergency, I'll call Connor. Okay?"

I grip her hand tightly. "Okay. Love you, Jacs."

"Love you, too, Sen."

I check my watch and raise my voice above the music. "Right, enough of this shit. We've got a podium to get. It's tradition time."

Our new ritual replaced Connor's compulsive preparations before he got in the car, but it was also to celebrate what we have and not be another team ruled by fear.

"Everyone, a cheer for Tawny." The crew cheers. "A cheer for Connor." The crew cheers. "And a cheer for all of you. Because we're all brilliant."

"She forgot someone," one of the crew shouts. She's new and the quietest one, but she can holler. "A cheer for the best boss."

The garage goes wild, cheering like they're at a concert. I shake my head before I throw it back and laugh. "You're a bunch of dicks. Now let's do this."

Jacs has a quick word with Tawny as I give Connor his earbuds.

"You can do this. I believe in you more than anyone and anything," I say to him. I want to kiss him, but I can't here. "Now get ready, and don't forget to listen to your song."

"Yes, baby," he whispers. I shiver from head to toe. "I'd never forget the song the most beautiful woman in the world found for me because she always thought about me like I thought about her."

It's not a kiss to my lips but one to my heart. He walks backwards, his stare never leaving mine, and I press the heel of my palm to my chest.

As we reach my corridor after the awesome date Connor arranged, I lean up and ghost Connor's lips with mine. His hands wrap around me, and I whisper against his mouth, "I'm so proud of you today. Your driving was intense, and your support and the discussions with Tawny are helping her, too."

"It's all for you and the team, baby. And well done for relaxing tonight. I'm glad you let me look after you. I've had no calls. The team functioned fine without you."

I wrap my arms around his neck and deepen the kiss. His murmur is filled with words of adoration. I might be about to lose my team, but I will return from that, especially with Connor by my side.

A clearing throat makes us turn to the door of my suite. Niki sits on the floor, his eyes pinched and his mouth tight.

"What the fuck?" Niki snaps.

CHAPTER FIFTY-THREE – SENNA

"**G**et your fucking hands off my sister." Niki jumps up and rushes Connor, but I stand in front of him.

A curl of Niki's dirty blond hair falls on his forehead from beneath his backwards cap. His stare burns a hole in my heart.

"Niki, leave it," I say, lifting my jaw.

Connor tries to get out from behind me. The fool. I can protect him. "It's not—"

"Don't you dare say it's not what I think." Spittle flies from Niki's mouth, landing in the air because I'm forcing distance between him and us. His tan highlights his cheekbones, as do the red angry spots on his cheeks. "You're fucking my sister, right?"

"Yes, but it's not just—"

"Shut the hell up. We had a deal, and clearly, you haven't stuck to it," Niki rages. "I know what you're like, remember? You're a player."

"I'm not like that."

"You had a personality transplant?"

I turn so I'm still facing Niki in case he does anything stupid, but so I can speak quietly to Connor. "Connor, please let me handle this."

Although Niki's lost the lean body of a racing driver and

bulked out a little, I'm confident Connor could take him, but knowing my man and how guilty he's felt over the last months, he'd probably let Niki beat him to a pulp.

"So you need my baby sister to fight your battles, do you? You were supposed to be my best friend." His face is bright red, and he's fisting his hands.

"I am your best friend."

"You're dead to me," he replies, his jaw tight.

There's a ding at the lift. We don't need anyone else to get involved in this. "Connor, you go. I'll talk to Niki and call you, okay?"

He slides his hand into mine. Niki growls in response. "I'm here for you. We can do this together."

I shake my head. "He'll be more reasonable if it's just me."

"I'm right here. I can hear everything," Niki says between gritted teeth. He squeezes his fists again. Where has my sweet brother gone?

"Trust me," I murmur to Connor, whose face drops as he nods.

He glances at Niki and winces, yet still kisses my cheek. "I love you," he whispers, but in the quiet of the corridor, I'm certain Niki hears.

As he steps away and walks to the lift, his eyes wide with worry, Niki aims one last jibe at him. "All this time, you were finding a way to get with her. You promised me, promised you would take care of her. I asked you to protect her this season, and you did this."

Connor looks away from me, but the truth is evident in his pinched eyes. My mouth drops.

"What is he saying, Connor?"

"It's not like it sounds—"

I round on Connor. "You've been talking about me

334

START YOUR ENGINES

behind my back?"

"Yes," Niki replies smugly. "I knew how hard this year would be for you and—"

"Stop, Niki. I'm talking to my boyfriend."

Connor squeezes his lips together as he stares at me. His forehead is squished, but I resist the pull to smooth the lines. "At first, it was about protecting you, but within a short time, I knew you didn't need that. You just needed someone on your side. Out of the two of us, I'm the one who needs protecting. I'm a liability, remember?"

He gives me a soft smile.

"I love you," he says, imploring me.

Niki guffaws. "The player is in love? Sure. Jog on, Dane."

Connor's face drops, and my heart breaks.

"Connor, I love you, too. But I need to talk to my brother. Could you leave us alone?"

He lifts his eyebrows as if waiting for me to change my mind. I kiss his cheek and hold his hand to my heart. "Please?"

"Are you two fucking kidding me with this? Get lost, Connor," my brother shouts.

Connor hesitates, but my pinched stare has him walking to the lift.

"Get in my suite now, Niki," I hiss as I open my room and storm into it.

Niki slams the door as he joins me. "He's not the right man for you, sis. He's a player. He treats women badly—"

I round on him. "This isn't about him, although I'd defend that incredible man until I had no breath left in me. This is about us. You've lied to me repeatedly. Did you know Dad was selling the team no matter what I did?"

Niki holds his hands up.

"You shit," I snarl.

"Sen, I was trying to protect you. I thought if I came home and took over, then we could run it together. I'd be in charge, and I could protect you. With me leading things, I'd convince Dad not to sell."

I square up to him. "Are you kidding me? I don't need you. You should have believed in me. You should have been proud of me like I've always been proud of you. I've made this team a success."

"A success at what cost? Your health? You're not being rational. Look at who you're dating. You can't be thinking straight. I love the guy, but he's not boyfriend material, and he's your driver! You've always said it's hard to be a woman in this industry, but look at who you're secretly dating. What will people say because I know you haven't told your team?"

"What do you mean?"

"I went to the garage to find you, but no one knew where you were. Macca needed you, but you were off with Connor. Connor is distracting you. I told him to protect you this season, and he didn't, and now you're losing the team. All those people depend on you."

"And I'm doing everything I can to ensure we have a future." My shoulders hunch as I pace. I check my phone. Ten missed calls from Macca.

"By getting distracted and going off with Connor the week before your last race?"

It's like he's repeating all my fears. My inferiority complex rears its head, and I don't know what to believe. "I'm an effective boss. We've done well this season. We nearly made the top six. Why can't you believe in me?"

He walks towards me, and I step back. "Because I don't recognise you anymore. Do you remember saying how difficult it was for you to make strides for women? You've struggled your entire career. Don't let it all go for him."

"I'm not." I drag in a breath. "I'm stronger with him and with the whole team on my side."

"If he's really as great as you say he is, and if you love him as much as you say you do, then why didn't you tell me? I heard it from Dad. He called me as I got to the hotel. I didn't believe him because the idea you'd date your former enemy, a player, was ridiculous."

I freeze, staring at Niki.

"We wanted to tell you face-to-face," I stutter. I rub my scar as I fumble with my words.

"Are you ashamed of him, Senna?"

"No!"

"But you know people will think less of you. You'll lose all the respect you've earned like you lost Dad's and mine."

I choke. This isn't my sweet older brother.

"And you've put the company at risk by dating him. How can you make reasonable decisions when you're secretly dating one of the team? You can't. I want you to be happy and have a good life, but you can't do that with Connor. You need protecting, and he isn't the guy to do it."

"You're saying these things because you're hurting."

"Or maybe I'm saying them because no one else can because they don't know."

My hands shake. His words sting. I always said I needed to do this alone. What if letting Connor in has cost my future and that of my whole team?

Niki's brow furrows. "Senna, I'm here for you. I want you to be happy, but—"

I point to the open door. "Just go." His jaw drops. "I love you. I've always been proud of you and put you first, even though you haven't done the same for me. I watched Dad go to your race in Austria and miss my graduation and didn't say a thing. You're my big brother who I would do anything

for, but right now, I need to be alone."

He ambles out the door. He turns as if he has more to say and is rewarded with the door shutting in his face.

I slide to the floor and drop my face to my hands.

My phone buzzes. It's Connor. But I can't bring myself to answer. I love him, but I'm the boss and I must protect him and the team.

With one race to go and my career in the balance, I'm not sure I can.

CHAPTER FIFTY-FOUR – CONNOR

Senna wasn't at the hotel reception when we checked out, although she sent me a message earlier in the morning.

> Senna: I'll meet you in Abu Dhabi. I love you, but I need time to work through everyth ng xx

I've been a zombie throughout the days of travel and preparation for the final race of the season.

Every morning, she sends a message saying good morning, and she video calls me every evening. She doesn't say much but leaves the call open as I try to sleep, but I don't. I watch her sleep and hope everything will be okay at the end of the season. But how can it be?

I've tried to talk to her several times, but she doesn't want the team to know about us, so I've only spoken about the race preparation. She's about to lose her team and everything that matters to her. I can't push her and demand that she decide our future now. I love her too much to put that pressure on her.

"Are you okay, Con?" Silas asks as I get out of the car. He hands me a cap.

I look at Senna, and for a second, we make eye contact. Her eyes are as red-rimmed as I suspect mine are, although at least her make-up attempts to cover it. Everything inside me feels like it's breaking. I want to hold her and tell her we can do it together, but she won't let me help her. I'm nothing without her strength and love.

I put my cap on backwards and give her a half smile. Her shoulders lift in a sigh, and she squeezes her lips in a smile she doesn't have the energy for. It takes everything I have not to rush over and take her in my arms.

Silas elbows me. "Connor?"

"Yeah, sorry. I'm a bit off with the end of the season."

"Same. These could be our last days together if rumours are to be believed about our future bosses."

My heart smacks against my chest at a million miles per hour. "What do you know?"

"Connor," Ralf shouts as he walks into the garage entrance in a Hawaiian shirt covered in neon cats. I'm shocked his husband let him out of the house with this one. He yanks me into a hug so tight that when he lets go, I nearly fall over my stumbling feet.

"It's nice to see you," I stutter.

"You're a crap liar. Come with me. We need a chat."

He slams a hand against my back and practically catapults me out of the garage.

"Do you like my shirt? I got it at the airport. I've decided to stop travelling for a while. I'm going to be a cat daddy."

"It's lovely. Myles will hate it."

"I know," he replies with a massive grin.

"What are you doing here?"

"I'm worried about you," Ralf says as I pace the tarmac. "That was your last practice season before qualifying tomorrow. You were going through the motions, waiting for

it to end. You've lost your spark again."

My eyes hurt from lack of sleep and the tears no one sees me shed.

I shrug.

Ralf shakes his head. "No, Dane. We don't shrug our answers." I love his brusqueness. "She asked me to chat to you."

"There's no point asking who 'she' is, is there?" I rub my forehead, refusing to give in to the temptation to check the garage and catch her eye again.

Ralf's deep laugh makes me smile despite the sadness that's ravaged me since Monday.

"I know she's keeping me at arm's length because she has so much going on in her head with the end of season and Niki returning, but I want to support her and tell the world I adore her while also making sure she doesn't lose an ounce of credibility."

My chest collapses, and I fold in on myself. I can't voice my other worry, but it's sat inside me since she told me to go so she could talk to Niki. What if she doesn't return to me at the end of the season? What if one week without me convinces her I wasn't good enough for her?

"All is not lost, Connor."

"I miss her. I can help her, but her family have got to her. She's not been the same boss this week."

"All will be okay in the end. Deep down, she's still the same person who revolutionised this team. I've seen the garage. You're a family now."

I grit my teeth. "But true families help each other. She thinks she has to do it alone. I need to show her that she can be the best with me and the whole team on her side. She doesn't need to be the person her family want her to be."

"She's scared of so much, including letting everyone

down." Ralf shakes his head and folds his arms. "I don't think she'll admit it, but she's spent all these years fighting alone that she's terrified of trusting others and being public with someone. Her dad's judgement is hard enough, but now she has Niki's, too. They've made her question everything."

I sigh so hard that I'm surprised I have breath left.

"You still have a race to win to get top six in the Constructor's Championship."

I slam my helmet down. "What's the point?" Except I know the point. My life and everything in it has always been for and about her. "I can't win the race. I haven't won a race in over two years. Why would things change now?"

Ralf grabs my shoulders, and his eyes burn with torment. "Where did the self-belief go? You've returned from the brink when you didn't believe you'd race again. You've dealt with Antoine and crashes and crippling anxiety. Where is the fire?"

I drop my head. "It left with Senna. I didn't do it alone. She was beside me every step of the way. Nothing makes sense anymore."

Ever since the summer, my days have been filled with her love and laughter. I don't know where I'd be if not for our nighttime video calls and the gifts she leaves me at the hotel. I reach for the paper tucked inside my racing suit she left for me this morning and scan it, although I know it by heart.

You're the best man I've ever met. You've been the light in my day and the comfort in my weary heart. Thank you for giving me time.

"Connor," Ralf says as I tuck the paper back inside my suit. "She believes in you. She cares about you more than

anything. She sent me to be by your side because she can't be. She's overwhelmed by everything, and her brother and father won't listen to her anymore because they're so damn pig-headed. Show her that you can help and that she doesn't need to do it alone."

I kick the ground. "How?"

Ralf shrugs and grins. "How would I know?"

I chuckle. "So I'm not allowed to shrug, but you can? You're a bastard."

He chuckles. "I know. But I have a plan."

"Seriously?"

"She might still lose the team, but it's worth a try." He offers me a devilish smirk. "Are you in?"

I wince. "Will it fix anything?"

"Probably not, but at least it will stop you being grumpy. You'll have to talk to Niki. Senna isn't talking to him, but he's in Abu Dhabi for the race."

"So I could lose my life after her brother beats the shit out of me, and she could be angry with me for meddling?" I glare at him, although I hold out my hand to shake his. "Fine. I'm in. It doesn't involve any crashes, does it?"

"I can't be held responsible for your awful driving, Dane."

I punch him on the arm as he laughs loudly.

It's worth trying something because, in less than three days, the woman I love will lose everything she's worked for, and I'm terrified of what that will do to her.

"**Y**ou?" Niki snaps as he opens the door to his hotel room. "I don't want you here. I don't want to see you again." He

tries to slam it, but I shove my foot in the way to stop him. "Move your foot, Dane. The only reason I'm not breaking it is because you need to race in two days."

I stare him down. "Let me in. This is for Senna."

He opens his mouth to start on me again, but I beat him to it, raising my voice. "I hate you, man. But I love you, too. If any part of you genuinely cares about your sister like I do, you'll let me in."

"I hate you and love you, too," he mumbles as he opens the door. I don't know if he wanted me to hear him. "Get on with it."

I stride into his room, which is all soft furnishings and muted colours, but it's impossible to tell how long Niki has been here. He hasn't unpacked his bag, and it reeks of disinfectant. I turn on him. "I want to kick your arse like I did when we were younger—"

He scowls at me. "When I let you because you were a weak little bastard."

"In those days, I beat you for fun. If I did it now, I'm pretty sure one of us would damage the other one, so don't be a dick, Niki. I should have told Senna about your request to protect her early into what we had, but you need to know I love her. I've loved her since I was seventeen, and I was too scared to tell her then because she was too good for me."

He grunts in agreement.

I shove my fisted hands in my pockets. I grit my teeth and lock my eyes with him. "And because I was scared it would ruin our friendship."

He rolls his eyes.

I squeeze my hands tighter. His square jaw is perfectly punchable. "But you and I haven't had a friendship in some time. You didn't come to me after you crashed except to sign a contract that trapped me. You left and only called when

START YOUR ENGINES

you wanted something. I was ready to be there for you, but you didn't want that."

He folds his arms like when he was a punk-ass teenager who'd lost a race. "Don't tell me what I wanted—"

I pin him with my stare. "Am I wrong?"

Niki raises his eyebrows. I prepare for a smackdown.

I shift to get a solid stance as I reply, "Hit me if you have to, but be prepared for me to hit you back, because I've got to do something with all this emotion I can't deal with."

He shakes his head. "I'm not going to hit you, although I should. We had a pact."

"Fuck off with the pact. I only made it to shut you up. I'm not a player anymore, and we're not teenagers. I love her more than anything." His eyebrows knot together, and his lips tighten. "What was going on with you? Where have you been?"

He huffs. "It's no one's business—"

I turn away. "This is a waste of time. Ralf was wrong. We don't have a friendship anymore."

"Wait," Niki calls.

I turn.

His hand hangs in the space between us. "You're my best friend in the world, and when I'm ready to share, you'll be the first to know."

"Promise?"

Maybe he senses that I want to pull him into a hug because he steps back but keeps his hand outstretched.

"Promise," he replies as I take hold of his hand. His shoulders hunch. The action is a reminder of how much he's changed. Old Niki was always up for a hug. "Does this plan involve Ralf."

I nod.

"Fine. I'll listen then. Let me get you a drink first." As he

345

fiddles with something that looks like hand sanitiser and grabs two Cokes from the mini bar, he says over his shoulder, "So you love Senna?"

"Ever since I was seventeen," I reply, waiting for a challenge, but none comes.

With his back to me, I've no clue what he's thinking. Maybe he's preparing to throw the Cokes at my head. "I always thought she was just another game to you."

"I didn't think I had a chance with her, especially after the accident. And I didn't think she loved me back. She's distant with me now, but I keep hoping things will be okay after the end of the season."

Niki hands me the Coke. It chills my hand, but his following words make me shiver. "I had it out with her in Vegas. I reacted so fucking badly because I felt betrayed, and I took it out on her. I'm sorry for being a dick to her and you. I've not been in a great space." I open my mouth, but he cuts me off. "And I'm not telling you about that. Anyway, I've tried apologising to Senna, but she won't speak to me. She loves you, but she's terrified of letting people down. Don't give up on her."

"I couldn't. Are you saying the pact is null and void and giving me your blessing?"

"Only on three conditions."

I raise my eyebrows.

"One: if me and her are arguing, you have to pick my side over hers."

"Not a chance."

"For fuck's sake, Connor."

"Niki, I will always pick her. She is the beginning and the end for me. I still love you, though." I open my arms for a hug, and he shoves me away.

"Fine. Two: if I tell you any secrets, you can't share

346

them with her."

"Nope. If she asks me directly, I'm sharing everything."

"Connor!"

He grabs a stress ball from his pocket and throws it at my head. I manage to duck, and the squidgy lobster sails past. A colourful friendship bracelet falls out of his pocket, and we both stare at it.

I reach for it, and he yanks it away and returns it to his pocket. "What was that about?"

"I can't tell you now because you'll tell her."

He's got me there. "Fine, but we'll get it out of you. What's the third condition?"

"You don't kiss in front of me."

I laugh so hard that I'm bent double. That gets me a punch in the arm.

"Ouch!"

"You deserved it. You broke the pact."

"Whatever. But I'm going to kiss your sister whenever I can."

"La la la," Niki shouts, trying to put his hands in his ears while holding his can. "If you ever hurt her, I will rip your intestines out and strangle you with them."

"Fuck."

"Yeah, I've been working on how I'd hurt you since I saw you kissing her. And yes, you get my blessing, you arsehole. Not that you need it, because she doesn't need protecting, according to some jackass who's a fool in love."

I grin as I square him with my stare. "Senna is the strongest member of your messed up and amazing family. She never needed your protection. All she needed was for you and your dad to believe in her and let her run things her way. Let me tell you the plan."

CHAPTER FIFTY-FIVE – SENNA

Jacs hugs me so hard it knocks the air but not the everlasting anxiety out of me.

"It's the last race of the season, Sen. We've just got to get through today," she says.

"Then watch our hopes and dreams die," I add without emotion.

I close my eyes and squeeze them tightly, smelling the typical garage smells of diesel and rubber. I barely feel anymore, so numb from the last week. I'm praying for the end of the season even as I run away from the prospect of what it means.

"You're doing well, Senna." She grips my shaking hand between hers.

I open my eyes and sigh. "For someone about to lose their team because her family didn't believe in her?"

Jacs laughs half-heartedly before lowering her voice as staff members move around the garage. "No, for someone faking being okay and trying to fix everything alone, even though she has the most supportive team and boyfriend ready to take on the world with her. The same boyfriend who gave her all the orgasms."

"Oi." I pull my hand away and shake my head. "You've got a point, but what a way to throw it in my face."

Her mouth tilts in a smile. "What? I know what you did

in my garage—my sacred space. I'm half annoyed and half jealous. You put a dent in one of my cars, for fuck's sake. How hard did he slam you against it?"

I cock my eyebrow. "Who said he did the slamming?"

We burst into laughter, although it dries up quickly.

"Are you excited for Taylor Swift's concert after the race? You've played her songs on repeat a lot recently," Jacs says, straightening the collar of her overalls.

I wince. "Everyone heard, then?"

"Jimmy hates 'Love Story' after the number of times you've played it this week. If he could burn all the copies, including digital ones, he'd do it in a heartbeat," Jacs explains.

My shoulders hunch as I blush. "I won't be going tonight."

"But it might lift your mood."

I raise my eyebrows.

She holds her hands up and adds, "Okay, okay. I knew it was bullshit as soon as I said it. You're losing your team and everything you've worked for. But Connor is waiting for you to say the word, and he'll be by your side."

My soul drops into an abyss it will never find its way out of. That happens every time I think about him, so every second of every day. "I've thought about what my brother said and he's right. I know Connor was supporting me and not protecting me, and I'm over the whole talking about me behind my back. But how can I be a team boss and be with him?"

She throws her gloves down and grips my shoulders so tightly I can't back away. "One of the reasons we're a family now is because of you two. Yes, you made this happen, but you were extra special together and better as a team than alone. You two have a love for the ages, and do you know

what?"

"What?"

Jacs walks away. "Ignore I said anything."

"Tell me."

She turns around. "You've made some off decisions this week. You were trying to keep him at arm's length, but he's not your liability."

"I know." I sit in my chair and hold my head in my hands. "He's my heart and soul—but a driver and the boss? Everyone will lose their respect for me if they learn what I did. It would be cliché if I weren't the only female boss in this industry. Talk about doing a disservice to the women fighting to be respected and recognised in racing."

She smacks her palm to my forehead, making me squeal. "You're the first boss in years to bring a female driver to race in Formula One. You have female engineers and mechanics, not for the sake of it, but because we're brilliant. You set up a sponsorship for future female drivers so they can join the sport, and you petitioned the FIA regarding the bullying you endured to ensure no one else is pushed out of the sport for that reason." With each point, Jacs points at me.

"You knew about all that?"

My face heats. I was lucky to have a dad who ran a team. Lots of other women wouldn't get the same chances as me. He may have been an arse, but he pushed people to let me be part of things others wouldn't. I love him as much as I want to scream at him.

"You're not great at keeping secrets."

I glare at her and pout, but it quickly becomes a smile. "Yeah, whatever."

She grins back. "And in terms of losing the respect of your team, what makes you think they'd ever stop

START YOUR ENGINES

respecting you? You're proud of Connor."

"He's the most amazing man I've ever met."

"Then don't let your brother's comments get to you." I try to quiet her as she raises her voice. The garage is full of pit crew, engineers and the team members who come to races.

I breathe in the scent of my childhood and everything I'll miss as I scan the faces.

The only person absent is Connor.

His car developed a fault in qualifying yesterday, and he's starting in twelfth. He doesn't stand a chance of getting a podium place, and if Tawny does, we need him to be at least fifth for us to come sixth in the Constructors. As he left yesterday, he hung his head, and his face sagged. I tell myself it was because of the race and not me. It's how I'll get through these last hours without him.

He didn't sleep on our video call last night. I didn't either. I've pretended to sleep all week, hoping he might, too. What if he crashes today because I fucked up? I should have been proud of us. I scratch at my tattoo.

"He's not here yet," Jacs says, and I glare at her. "And in terms of what I was saying: when it comes to losing the team's respect because you're dating your driver, you couldn't be further from the truth."

"What do you mean?" I stutter.

"Hey, everyone, I have a question," she shouts while climbing on one of the boxes.

The team bustles around, although everyone has the same sad face I'm wearing. In this manufactured but authentic self-made family, these are our last hours together, but hope ebbs. Grumbles fill the room.

"Oi, Jacs is speaking to you," I shout.

Everyone shuts up quickly.

351

"The boss has spoken," she says back to me with a wink. "Right. I want you to raise your hand because our boss needs to know something."

Slowly, they raise their hands. I point at those with their hands down, and they raise them, too.

"Right," Jacs continues. "If you didn't know about Connor and Senna's not-as-secret-as-they-think relationship, please lower your hand."

I wait for everyone's hand to go down. I press my knuckles against my mouth. All their hands are still in the air, although everyone avoids eye contact with me.

"Exactly!" Jacs shouts. "Please lower your hand if you've lost respect for the boss because of it?"

Macca slides his hand down before pointing at me with a grin. "Only joking, boss. I'm sorry for all the calls last week. I'm glad you had a night off from us because you needed it. I love that you and Connor are together. You're good for each other. If it had been Antoine, I'd have walked, but Dane the Pain is the only person worthy of you."

"You're an arse, Macca, but I love you," I reply, my eyes watering.

"I love you, too, boss and I love Connor."

"I heard my name. What's going on?" Connor says from the open door of the garage. "Why does everyone look like they got the question right at school?"

Silence descends in the garage as everyone looks between me and Connor.

I stare at him. I've tried to avoid eye contact all week. He's the most beautiful man I've ever seen. His big blue eyes resemble an ocean in a storm or at sunset, depending on his mood. His lips are full and never fail to pull me to him, even when he's back chatting me. He challenged me our entire friendship, and he's always been there for me. Having him

by my side doesn't lessen me; it makes both of us better.

"You're thinking a lot, Senna. Use your words," Jacs whispers.

"I'll fire you tomorrow," I cheek, although we both know I won't be in charge of anything after today.

"Stop being scared and admit you love him in front of us."

I nearly stamp my foot—because she's right.

Connor walks through the garage.

Staring at him in front of my team, I'm certain he's the future I want no matter what happens. Jacs was right. He's helped me be the boss I am now—all of these people have.

"Fine." I push Jacs off the box to stand in her place and hover above everyone, including Connor. She huffs as she steps back.

Connor stands before me. His blue eyes are big enough for me to swim in and lose myself forever.

"I'm scared, Connor." His brow furrows, and he tips his head to the side. "I'm scared of loving a racing driver who could die any race. I'm scared of being in this big public relationship with someone who has the power to hurt me beyond anything I've ever known. I'm scared of losing you again after wanting to be with you all these years. But most of all, I'm scared of letting go of control. I'm used to fighting by myself. People always told me what I can't do, yet you've told me what I am capable of and that you will help me do it. What if I fail both of us?"

Tears slide down my cheeks.

"For someone scared of a public relationship, you're being very public right now," Connor says, and the team murmurs in agreement.

I glare at all of them. "That's because we're Coulter team racing, and we are a family. And they all know,

anyway."

Connor turns to Macca, Jimmy, and Silas. "You all knew?"

As one, the gang nod their heads.

"Shit."

"And they're all okay with it," I add.

"Seriously?" Again, they nod. "Good work, team."

"I love you, Connor. I've always loved you, and I always will. I'm sorry for distancing myself from you when my brother arrived. But it's you. It's always been you, and you know what? If you want to protect me sometimes, I'll let you do it. I'm proud you're all mine. You're breathtaking in every way, and I'm lucky you want to be with me. You're my future, Connor fucking Dane."

Connor joins me on a box that isn't big enough for us both. He wraps his arms tightly around me. "And you're mine. You've never needed me to protect you. I've always been here on your side and by your side." He brushes my lip with his thumb. "But, Coults, I've always needed *your* protection. You helped me when I was in the worst place in my life and career. You were there for me, and that meant everything. You are everything. You can't fail for both of us because, together, we're stronger. We make mistakes, and we come back fighting. I've always loved you. I'm the lucky one. I'll always be here if you let me. Will you let me?"

Every person in the garage holds their breath as he waits for my answer.

"Yes," I gasp as his lips crash into mine.

The garage goes wild with shouts and jeers of joy. I bask in it briefly and hold Connor's hand as I shout, "Right, everyone, back to work. We've got a race to prepare for."

I smile at everyone. I'm drawn to the edge of the garage, where I sense eyes on me.

START YOUR ENGINES

Niki and my dad stare at me. How long have they been there? My dad's pinched glare suggests they've heard everything.

I lift my chin and scowl right back at him.

They're in my garage now, and with my team by my side and my boyfriend next to me, I can take anyone on.

CHAPTER FIFTY-SIX – SENNA

My fingers dance across my tattoo as I side-eye my guests. "What are they doing here?" I ask Jacs under my breath.

We're several hours into race preparation, and Dad and Niki have silently judged everything we've done so far.

"What have they said to you?" Jacs replies. She'd left my side to chat with her team and do checks, but she's back again, and a multitude of lines cover her forehead.

I grip the desk. "Nothing. I nodded at them eventually, but that's it. They're both in my bad books, so I'm not going to them."

"Have they killed Connor? I haven't seen him in a while."

"He scarpered pretty quickly after they caught us in the middle of our dramatic love declaration. It's probably for the best, although I'll tease him about it later."

"Fair. But what are they up to?" she says, pointing towards Dad and Niki, who sit at the side, their gaze flicking around the room at the bustle of engineers discussing strategy and finalising plans. Occasionally, their heads dive together and they whisper something.

They've done that several times in the last hour, and I desperately wanted to stare at where they'd looked before their sneaky chats to decipher which part of my team they

were judging.

"What's this now?" Jacs shouts, drawing my attention to Connor and Uncle Ralf, who stride into the garage and make a beeline for my family.

I swipe lip balm on my chapped lips.

"He did not just do that," I exclaim as Connor shakes hands with Niki and my dad. "Why are they not killing him? *I'm* going to bloody kill him."

"It's probably better that they get on than not," Jacs says, wincing.

"Don't be so damn reasonable." Jacs raises her eyebrows, and her lips squeeze into a cheeky smile. "Fine. You make a lot of sense. Maybe I should go over there and give them time to apologise, but I don't want to."

I pout, and Jacs shakes her head and laughs.

"It's time," Macca shouts, shushing the busy garage. He turns up the music and hollers above it. "And in honour of the last race with the best boss..." He stares sheepishly at my dad.

"Say it, Macca," Jacs demands.

Macca clears his throat loudly. "In honour of our great leader and majestic boss, we have three songs for today's pre-race session, and they're her power tunes and one of Connor's, too."

My eyes snap to Jacs, who holds her hands up. I glance at Connor, who grins at me.

The first bars of "The Chain" by Fleetwood Mac play from the stereo, and the garage cheers. The song used to be on a racing television show. For many of us, it was the soundtrack to the moments we fell in love with racing. Even the younger members of the team smile as it plays.

"It's not the easiest song to dance to, so I'm speaking over some of it," Macca announces.

REBECCA CHASE

"Get on the box," Jacs shouts.

Macca grumbles but concedes once the garage starts chanting, "Box, box, box."

"We don't shout box unless we're in a race!" Macca reaches into his pocket for notes. "I have words of wisdom to impart before we all smash this race and say goodbye to each other because many of us won't stay if we don't have our leader with us."

After a couple of hushes, the garage is silent. I catch Dad's eye but look away immediately. This wouldn't have happened in his day. There were usually shouts and stress up until the last minute.

"As we all know, this year hasn't been easy. First, we dealt with stroppy Dane and his crashes—"

"Hey," Connor interjects. He points at Macca, who laughs.

"And Antoine acted like a misogynistic, arrogant prick." There are murmurs of agreement. "But while this was happening, we had our great lead mechanic, Jacs, and all of you improving cars and making them the beasts we have now."

There are whoops and hollers amongst the team.

"But the glue in all of this was Senna. She worked more hours than most of us knew existed; she kept an eye on everything, ensuring we had the best conditions to excel while schmoozing investors and guaranteeing the cars were as perfect as possible. But she did something else. She respected our knowledge, cared about our lives, and made this a place where it was safe to have issues or mental health concerns, to get scared, and to miss those we leave at home to be part of this bonkers business of car racing. She loves cars and racing as much as us, but she cares about this family, too."

358

START YOUR ENGINES

There are more murmurs of agreement.

A tear brims at Macca's eyes, and I rush over. He steps off the box briefly for a hug before resuming his place.

"And she made us a competitor. I'm not saying we weren't before. But you brought something into the team we hadn't had in a while." Macca grips my hand tightly. "And no matter what happens, we will always have this moment when, against all odds, we brought fire, and we became a team people talked about for our spirit, fight, and ability. We love you, boss."

I press the heels of my hands to my eyes, but the tears slip down regardless.

"Now shut up while we listen to the best bit of the song, and then we dance."

The bridge of the song kicks in. Everyone stills, then cries, from the burliest of engineers to the grumbliest pit crew member to sweet Tawny. Jacs lets out a sob that surprises everyone, and I swear my dad and Niki have tears in their eyes as the song hits hard.

Thankfully, the next one is "The Man," and everyone shimmies. My heart swells as the crew reminds me they've fought to be here in this moment, too.

"No sashaying?" Connor mouths from across the room, and I glare at him. His chuckle makes me shake my head and smile.

"Fine," I shout, and I sashay over to him as everyone shouts along to the line about Leo in Saint-Tropez.

As the last beats of "Rebellion" by Arcade Fire, Connor's race preparation song, play and everyone gathers in some

359

form of calm, I give my last pre-race speech. We can't get in the top six, but I finally believe that's okay, because we'll go off on a high no matter what.

"I wanted to say one last thing."

The team stares at me with heads high and the respect I've earned over the season. This isn't about my dad or Niki. This is for a group who worked hard and came on the journey with me. I moisten my lips and taste the remnants of my mango lip balm.

"As I observe each of you, my team, for the last time, I want you to believe that whatever the future brings, I'm here for you if you need to chat, deal with some shit, or show someone your new baby photos, even if you have an ugly baby no one else wants to look at."

Everyone stares at Silas, whose ugly baby turned into a swan. He laughs with his hands in the air.

"I also want to say thank you. You all gave me a chance to lead you; I will forever be grateful. You impressed me and made me proud every day of this season. No matter what happens, remember you're the best. You are incredible. You are family. And you've given me the best year of my life. No one can take away what we have done this year. Now let's kick ass, Coulter Racing Team."

Everyone cheers.

"A cheer for Tawny," Macca shouts, because that's our tradition now.

Everyone cheers with their hands in the air.

"A cheer for Dane the Pain."

The cheer is gruffer this time, and fists are raised in a fight.

"A cheer for all of us," Macca hollers, and the team shouts loudly and proudly.

"And finally, and let's make this the biggest cheer this

START YOUR ENGINES

track has ever heard, and let's make the other teams jealous, too, because, let's face it, their bosses are shit compared to ours. A cheer for the best boss in the world, a cheer for Senna 'Coults' Coulter."

The garage goes wild. Dad's mouth drops open, and I beam. Niki and Ralf jump up and down with the rest of the group. Connor jumps so much that I press my lips together to stop shouting at him. He'd better not break his legs before the race starts.

Connor whispers in my ear as the group returns to their race preparations, "I have a confession."

"What now?" I grumble, although it still comes with a smile.

"I'm the one that invited your family today. They want to talk to you about a plan Ralf and I devised."

I lower my voice and pin him with my eyes. "What did you do, Dane?"

"Don't Dane me," he replies. He kisses my cheek. "I've got to go, but hopefully, they will speak to you before the end of the race."

"Stay safe, and don't drive stupid. At twelfth, it's hard enough getting into the top ten, let alone anything else." He grins at me. I've no influence on him today. "Love you, baby."

"Love you more." He kisses my cheek again and dashes away.

CHAPTER FIFTY-SEVEN – SENNA

We're ten laps from the end of the race, and Connor has pushed the whole way around. He and Tawny were lucky because three leading drivers had car issues and minor but safe collisions. The pit strategies have worked in our favour. Somehow, we're now third and fourth in the race. I've reapplied my deodorant and touched my tattoo more times than I can remember.

"Just stay consistent, Connor," I say on the radio.

"You need to make those tyres last, too. We can keep third if you don't push too much," Macca adds.

Connor's laugh down the radio makes me shiver.

"Connor," I warn. "If you and Tawny finish in these positions, we'll make the top six constructors."

"And if I come first, boss?"

"You don't need to come first. Keep your position in the race, and we'll be good."

"Or I'll give it everything I've got and win." Connor has an arrogance that makes my toes curl and my fingers dance across my tattoo.

"Don't make me change your pre-race song to 'Ego.'"

"I came to race, boss. And that's what I intend to do. Trust me. Now, tell Tawny to stay close because we're here to show the rest of the racing world what Coulter is capable

of."

I hold my head in my hands. I don't know whether I should be happy that he loves racing again and wants us to be the best or panicked that he's risking everything.

A finger pokes my shoulder. "Senna, can we talk?"

I meet my dad's eyes. They droop, and his mouth turns down. He was always the most powerful man in the world to me, but he's aged. There's still wisdom and experience there, but something else, too.

"Yes, we can. But does it have to be now? It's the last nine laps."

"Please."

Maybe it's the distraction I need.

Niki joins him, and Ralf appears, too. I pull down my headphones so they hang around my neck. "I can't leave this space, but I'll listen. I have nothing more to add since the last time I spoke to you." I nod at Niki, so he knows I mean him, too.

Dad swallows loudly. "I want to give up the team."

"I know," I reply. I glance at the screen, where Connor continues to fly down a straight and risk his tyres with every passing second. That fucking beautiful demon of a man.

Dad clears his throat. "I decided the best way to give up the team was to sell to someone like Antoine and his dad. I was stupid and didn't see what was in front of me all this time. Connor made me come today, as he said I needed to witness what I was giving up regarding my future and the futures of those who have worked for me for years. He also said I was giving up the future you worked for, too."

I smile softly. "Of course he did. He's always believed in me."

"And I didn't, not enough. I thought I needed to protect you and give you a good life. But today was a revelation. This

363

team adores you. I saw how you get the performance out of them that I hadn't in years. I've underestimated you for a long time, not just this year." I nod. I'm not going to make him feel like shit. "I believed I was being a dad, but I wasn't. I was an arsehole."

"Yep," Niki adds, and I shoot him a glare.

"You've been an arsehole, too." I point at him.

"She speaks the truth," Ralf says.

I grin. "Maybe we all need to listen to Uncle Ralf more."

"No. We all need to listen to you more," my dad replies, and I lean back in my chair, my eyes wide. He takes my hand and smiles when he sees my tattoo. "Your fastest lap time at Silverstone. I was so proud of you that day, although I was terrified. Over the last few years, I forgot to be proud of you and your skills. I'm so sorry. I don't deserve your forgiveness, and there is a lot to forgive, but I shall try and earn it over time."

I swallow loudly. "Of course I forgive you, Dad. You make me so pissing angry, but I should've spoken up more. I tried so hard to be the person you wanted that I forgot who I really was. But that doesn't mean you can't still try harder. This is the first step."

"Do I get your forgiveness, too?" Niki pipes up.

I roll my eyes. "You haven't said sorry yet."

"Oh yeah. I'm sorry, Senna," he says as a blond curl drops onto his forehead. Although he sounds blasé, sweat beads his brow as he pushes the curl back under his cap.

"I should have believed in you as Connor did and believed in him, too. He's a good man for you," Niki says. "He told me you never needed our protection but, rather, our belief. He saw what I wouldn't. I shouldn't have needed to hear it from others or have the proof I saw today. You are incredible; in fact, I probably needed your protection more

than you needed mine. I haven't been able to protect myself."

I stare into his eyes. His subtext is lost on me, but I vow to press him later.

I thumb the collar of my blouse as I survey my family. "The next time either of you treat me like that, we're done. I will burn all my bridges and declare I have no family except Mum. Okay?"

They nod sheepishly. I glance at the screen. Connor is in second place, with Tawny behind him in third. Sickness fills my belly, and I kick my shoes off and pace a couple of steps.

"Macca?" I say into my radio mouthpiece.

"You can't argue with him, and you shouldn't, anyway. He knows what he's doing," Macca replies.

I grumble.

"But I'm here for another reason," Dad says. There are five laps to go, my last five as team boss, but I still glance at my dad and return to my chair. "I don't love owning the team, and I want to spend time with your mum and do everything I missed. But Ralf and Connor devised a better plan than selling the team to Antoine and his dad."

My gaze flicks between the drama on screen and the drama in front of me. I rub my forehead with my thumb. "What are you saying?"

"I am giving 51% of the team to you. It's not just that I missed so much of your life, including your graduation." I glance at Niki, who nods. These bloody Coulter men. "But because you can run this team as it should be. It's a family business and needs to stay in the family with a leader beyond all leaders at the helm. It needs you."

"And the other 49%?" I stutter. His words warm my heart, but I need to know who I'll be fighting against when I

make decisions.

"Niki will get 24%, Connor and Ralf 10%, and you can have the remaining five if you want. You might want to invest to ensure it feels fully yours."

I pull him into a hug. "You know me more than you realise, Dad. I love this. But you'd get more money by selling it."

He laughs. "I don't need money. Your mum manages our finances. We're all set for our holidays."

I gulp air into my mouth and squeeze him tighter. "Thank you. This means everything. But what about Antoine and his dad? They won't walk away easily."

"Leave that little bastard to me," Dad snarls.

"Dad," I gasp.

"I'm so sorry for those years I didn't believe you. That shit terrorised you, made you crash, and then I hired him. I can't forgive myself for that." He takes a breath, and I grip his hand between mine. "But you've given Coulter a new name. No longer is this a team that bullies to get results. Coulter Racing celebrates good, honourable people because of you."

"Because of all of them," I reply, referring to my team. "And we do get results. We might finish top six if Connor doesn't do anything else stupid."

Niki points to the screen. "Too late for that."

I spin so fast in my chair that I wobble.

"What the fuck is he doing now?" I shout at Macca.

Macca chuckles. "What he does best, and if he does it well, we'll be top five in the Constructors."

It's the last lap of the race, and Connor drives head-to-head with Billy, the race leader. There's no point shouting at him about tyre wear, the risk to his life, or stupidity, as anything I say will distract him. Instead, I watch with my

fingers on my tattoo and my jaw tight.

My dad grips my shoulder as Ralf and Niki cheer Connor on.

The pit crew are screaming as Connor levels with the race leader. They're metres from the finish line.

"My tyres," Connor shouts down the radio.

I'm shaking, and my dad grips my shoulder tighter.

"He's not going to make it," Niki shouts.

"Yes, he fucking is," I whisper. "Come on, Connor."

Everyone screams their support as Connor flies over the line, a car length in front. Tawny is third.

"That was for you, Senna!" he shouts. Whatever he shouts on the radio today will probably be repeated on sports coverage for the rest of the week. "You're the best boss ever, and now you get to go on the podium, too."

"He adores you, doesn't he?" my dad says.

"He does," I reply, choked with emotion. "And I adore him. I always will."

CHAPTER FIFTY-EIGHT – CONNOR

Five months ago, I'd have given anything never to drive again, and now here I am, in the top spot on the podium, with my palm against my heart as the British National Anthem plays. I stand straighter than I ever have in my life. I've listened to this before from the top of the podium, but this is the sweetest rendition I've ever heard.

Tears sting my cheeks, and I puff my chest. I smile at Tawny, who beams back so broadly that I bet her face will hurt tomorrow. You never forget your first Formula One podium.

I can't see Senna without jumping out of position, but standing next to Billy in second is the love of my life. Today, Senna gets her first podium, too.

Maybe Billy senses my curiosity, because when I look over, he stands back, and there's Senna, her eyes closed and breathing in the moment. She's mouthing along to the anthem. And that's when I start sobbing. We gave each other the best gift in the world.

I drove like an arsehole and risked it all, but it was worth it to get her up here. We haven't been able to speak more than a couple of words to each other, so I don't know if her smile is also because her dad came through with the plan Ralf and I set in motion.

START YOUR ENGINES

I pinch my bottom lip as I imagine what she'd want me to do right now.

It's like her voice is in my head. *Enjoy this moment, baby.* I grasp it with everything I have. I take a deep breath and sing loudly.

As the anthem ends, everyone cheers with me. And that's when I grab the champagne and rush over to Senna. I'm shaking it like I'm back in the garage dancing.

Tawny gets champagne on my face on her way to Billy. "Payback is a bitch," she shouts at him, confirming their past rivalry. He could be her Connor, for all I know.

"Don't you dare, Connor." Senna points at me as I rush over. She's thrown on a coat in preparation. She knows I wouldn't do it if she were just in a white blouse. Although I'd love that sight, it's not for anyone else. She's mine to lust over.

I pop my bottle down and open my hands.

"You're not even giving yourself a fighting chance, Dane?" she chuckles.

I fix her with my stare. "I want everything you give me."

She stands on my step, so she has a bit more height on me.

My hands itch. I want to grab her, but I don't want her to lose an inch of the respect she's earned as team boss.

"But first." I hold my hand up. "Please tell me one thing."

"Stop delaying. It's your turn to get wet."

"Oi, no flirting while we're up here. Tell me this. Will I be calling you boss after today?"

Her face softens, and fuck, I want to kiss her.

"Yes. I own the team, and as I told you on the day I walked into my boardroom and found your cocky face staring back at me: I own you. I've got you now, Connor, and

369

you will do exactly what I say."

It's like my body lights with stars. "And I wouldn't want it any other way. Now, champagne me up, boss."

The crowd laughs as I open my mouth, and she pours the fizzing liquid into it.

We rush to the concert, Senna in those teeny shorts I love and our team hoodie and me in jeans and a Coulter Racing Team T-shirt. In seconds, Taylor Swift will sing to a maximum capacity crowd. Every boss, driver, and person at the race congratulated Senna and me. She reeled off motor racing facts about female drivers as I tried to push us through the crowd.

As we run from another team boss, she shouts in my ear, "They respect me. Me!"

"Of course they do, baby. Now, we need to hurry. Taylor doesn't wait for anyone." Her giddiness infects me like I'm high on her.

A hand flies in front of us, and we stop in front of Filip, the devilishly handsome Vessa team boss. He stands closer than I like, and I fist my hands to stop from moving him away to a respectable distance from my girlfriend. I'm not protecting her; I'm declaring she's mine.

"Well done, Senna," he says in his charming accent. He smells like a Greek god.

She smiles like a fangirl until she catches my raised eyebrows and sour stare. At her sheepish grin, I shake my head and mouth, "I'll spank you when we get home." She presses her lips together with her finger and thumb.

"Today, I congratulate you, Connor, and especially you,

Senna," Filip proclaims, oblivious to our communication. "Miss Coulter, you brought your team back from the brink and made it a contender."

She nods, although I'm sure she's nervous when her fingers brush her tattoo and she tucks her hair behind her ear. He's the boss of the most successful racing team.

"We did it as a team. One team, one family, and a whole lot of fight."

"You'll need that fight for next season. We'll all be watching Coulter."

That kicks her competitive spirit into action, and she tips her head at him. "Enjoy the view as we kick your ass, Filip."

I grab her hand and drag her away. The soreness of my jaw and the speed with which I'm moving as I glare at Filip over my shoulder is driven by jealousy. "Taylor Swift is on in two minutes."

She slows me down with a yank of my hand. "I'm doing a boss walk, baby. I want him to know I'm not scared. We're going to fuck up every team next season."

"Yes, we are," I reply, brushing my lips to her cheek.

When we reach the concert, we get caught up in the crowd. I turn my cap, and she pops up her hoodie so we're a little hidden. As I drag her in front of me, I let out a moan. She may be a badass boss, but she's the sexiest woman I've ever seen in shorts.

"I can't believe this isn't the end," I whisper to her as Taylor Swift starts with "Love Story." "I've got all I've ever wanted here with me right now."

I wrap my arms around her as she hums in agreement.

"Today is the best day of my life, Connor," she says softly. "When I got out of bed this morning, I was certain it would be the worst, but you've made all my dreams come

true." The smell of fuel and her trademark orange blossom perfume fills my soul. "I used to listen to this song as a teenager. I imagined you'd see me one day like I saw you."

Her heart thrums against my chest, and it's like we're beating as one.

"And all along, I did." She sighs, and I hold her tighter. "I don't deserve you, Coults," I whisper in her ear before pulling her hoodie down and dropping kisses on her hair. "Why do you love me?"

She sighs softly. "Because from the first day I met you, you challenged me and made me feel like I could conquer the world." I close my eyes and put my hands in the pocket of her hoodie. "And now, because you let me ride your face like a rodeo queen."

I laugh loudly, and my cock twitches in agreement. "I owe you special treatment when we get home."

"And you're officially moving in?"

"Fuck yes. I'll follow you to the end of the earth if you'll let me."

"Forever and always. Although, no funny business until you get some sleep. You need rest." Of course she noticed I hadn't slept during our video calls. "But after that, I'll show you exactly what you've earned for giving me fifth place and my first podium as a team boss."

"The first of many. I can't wait." My lips brush her ear as I growl, "I'm imagining you on all fours, my lips on your neck, my cock deep inside you as you scream my name, and I pull the greatest orgasm out of you. And you need a spank for earlier. Is that good for you, boss?"

I press against her. She's as horny for it as I am. If we weren't surrounded by strangers with cameras on their phones, I'd be sliding my fingers between her legs to find out how wet she is for me.

START YOUR ENGINES

"Perfect, baby," she murmurs.

"I don't normally do requests," Senna's favourite singer shouts from the stage. "But I heard that a winning team boss and groundbreaking woman listens to one of my songs when she needs power. This song goes out to all the women who've ever felt less. Let's keep making history, ladies. This one is for you, Senna Coulter."

Senna throws her head back and laughs as the first lines of "The Man" surround us.

EPILOGUE – SENNA

"You can't leave the awards ceremony early," my dad hisses as I start backing away from the table. He may have checked out of the team early and is only the owner for the next three hours, but I had to allow him and Mum to attend the FIA Annual Prize Gala.

"I can do what I like," I reply, smoothing my long, off-the-shoulder black dress with a thigh-high split. "I'm still your feisty daughter, Dad."

I scoop the last bit of chocolate and raspberry torte onto my spoon and shove it into my mouth with all the delicacy of a karting driver to make my point.

"Besides," I add with my mouth full, "my team have got their silverware."

I nod to Connor, who stands by the door with his Action of the Year trophy for his trick when he moved from third to second in the last race of the season. Due to Dad's apologies, I missed it, but Connor's made me watch it fifty times since and at every angle. Not that I'd miss the opportunity to witness my man conquering the track. He caught me enjoying it on slow-mo when I was supposed to be sleeping quietly next to him. I got a substantial reward for that over the end of the bed.

Connor waggles his eyebrows at me as Niki jostles him.

"Jacs is out front. I've got to go," I whisper to my dad.

START YOUR ENGINES

"Let her go, honey. She probably won't be able to sneak off again, and she's done enough this year. She deserves some fun. Remember how you were worried work would be too much for her?"

My dad sighs and kisses her on the cheek, reminding us of what I've realised over recent weeks. My mum was always the boss, but now she gets to act like it.

"Fine. Go, but protect your brother and ensure he doesn't do anything stupid. He's been acting out of sorts since he got back, and he won't tell me what's going on," he says with a huff.

"Yes, Dad." Though, Niki still won't tell me anything. Connor and I tried to get his plans out of him or learn what happened while he was away, but he just shrugged. I kiss Dad and Mum on the cheek. "Love you both. Keep an eye on Tawny. She's breaking hearts all over this room."

With her auburn hair swept to the side and a green cocktail dress highlighting her slender figure and sweeping neckline, she's the belle of the ball. Her dazzling countenance has caught everyone's attention. With her slowly emerging sunshine personality and exceptional driving ability, she's in demand personally and professionally. But she's also as loyal as they come. With her and Connor driving for me next season, we're going to cause trouble, and I can't wait.

"She can handle herself," my dad replies. "She reminds me a lot of you."

"Touché," I reply as I sneak out of the room.

At Dunsfold Aerodrome, I pull on a racing suit. It's similar

to the one I wore as a teenager. I smile at my tattoo as I zip up my white and turquoise suit. My racing history isn't a curse around my neck anymore but another chapter in my life that makes me who I am. Connor gave me that feeling back. I make a mental note to tell him. I can imagine his swagger after he hears it.

I bump into Niki as I leave the building. In the gap in the doorway, Jacs walks a giddy Connor around the Hypercars we were gifted for the race earlier this evening.

"It's like the old days," Niki says, smiling at my racing suit.

I grin. "That's why we're here. We three haven't raced each other since I was seventeen. It's time I prove I was and always will be the best."

He elbows me. "Of course you will, sis."

"Tonight is like an honouring of the past and a celebration of the future. And we get to be reckless adults driving Hypercars instead of sitting in a boring awards ceremony," I announce to him.

"Do you ever miss the old days?" Niki asks. His face drops, and he refuses to make eye contact. "Things were easier then."

"I do, but I like this time now. I've found something and someone that gives me joy, and every morning, I wake up knowing I couldn't get luckier." I bite the inside of my mouth. "Have you ever found that someone?" I ask tentatively.

Niki catches my eye. "Maybe for a brief moment."

"Do you want to talk about it?" I hold my breath.

"I might next week. I need advice about my future. Is that okay?" I'm not used to seeing my brother's vulnerability. I dig my nails into my hands to stop from hugging him.

START YOUR ENGINES

"Yes, always. Come over whenever you want. I'll listen and help in any way I can."

He turns away. "Cool, but if I don't turn up, don't worry."

"Whatever works for you." He's recoiled from my hugs since returning so I touch his shoulder briefly. I don't know who he is anymore. "I love you, Niki."

"Backatcha."

"Could you have a word with your boyfriend?" Jacs says when we get outside.

It's so cold that my breath condenses in the air. Christmas is coming, and it will be my first with Connor. I've got several surprises planned for him. There is a tropical island calling our name, for a start.

"What's he doing now?" I say, staring at my man with a grin I can't wipe from my face.

"What?" Connor throws his hands in the air. "I just asked if the seat went far enough back for someone to sit on someone else's lap."

"You're too horny for my liking," Jacs snaps, pointing at him. "I've established this year that I'm never dating again. I will be happy and alone with my car engines and books. All men are arseholes, and all women are players."

I hold my hand up.

"Except you three," Jacs adds. "But I don't want to date any of you."

"I don't want to date you, either," Connor grumbles.

"Agreed," Niki says. "Some of us have busy enough heads as it is."

Connor and I lock eyes.

"Anyway, enough of this shit. Are we driving or what?" Niki huffs.

"Yep. Me and Connor first, then you two, and then Jacs

377

will start the race where I beat you *and* Connor," I reply, walking towards the turquoise Aston and growling. It's the sexiest car I've ever seen. "Start your engines."

Connor and I line up next to each other. Jacs has sourced helmets with radios so the drivers can talk.

"I can't wait to own you on the track as much as I own you off it," I say into the radio, glad Niki and Jacs can't hear us.

I push my hands into my gloves and grip the wheel.

"Baby, you don't own anything. When I win this race, I'm taking you home, flipping you onto your back, and crawling up your body. I'll play with your soaking wet pussy until you're screaming that I'm the boss of you."

"Your dirty talk isn't working, Connor," I lie. I'm wet already at the prospect of being under him while he makes me beg.

"Of course it isn't, Coults. But on a scale of one to ten, where ten is so horny you'll burn up faster than my tyres on this track, what number are you?"

I bite my lip and imagine his mouth between my thighs. "Eleven."

"That's my good girl."

I laugh down the radio. "I love you, Connor."

"I love you, too, Coults. Now, show me exactly what the woman I adore can do when she's in a Hypercar. But don't do it too well, or my hard-on will hit the steering wheel."

I can't stop cackling with laughter. Connor fucking Dane makes me horny and happy all at once. "Challenge accepted. Now, start that engine, because I'm about to give you the

378

START YOUR ENGINES

drive of your life."
"Fuck yes."

THERE'S MORE...

I hope you enjoyed the first novel in my Coulter Racing Team Series.

Sign up to my newsletter to get updates on my book releases, as well as access to giveaways and exclusive bonus content including a bonus scene between Connor and Senna, which is free to everyone who signs up.

You can sign up via: https://tinyurl.com/Rebecca-Chase

Or via my website: www.rebeccahchase.com

In the meantime, keep reading for the Start Your Engines playlist and information about my previous books. There are also hints about the books I'm releasing in the next two years. And here's a peek of Regally Binding, an enemies-to-lovers bodyguard romance and the first book in my Closest Protection Series.

If you like spicy, humorous British romance with a bad boy book boyfriend then you need to give Bear a try.

REGALLY BINDING
CHAPTER ONE

Liss checked her mobile from under the bar as she wiped down the worn wood. Still no message from her latest Tinder match, although there was a breaking news notification about the Royal family. Liss swiped the notification away without reading it. She just wanted a response to the underwear picture it took all her courage to send. She shouldn't have done it, but she wanted to feel attractive and carefree and like her best friend, Isla, who wouldn't hesitate to send something like that.

"Have you heard from Hugo today? He's checking in a lot," Greg, the pub's regular, whose ear hair was longer than his eyelashes, said through a yawn before supping the head of his pint. His dog, Joyce, was propped on his knees, eyeballing Liss.

"Not yet," Liss replied with a shrug. Hugo, the pub's owner, used to be happy with Liss running the place, but now, there were rumours that he was selling the pub to a chain, which would leave Liss without a job.

"You could do better than this place, you know," Greg added, tipping his head in the direction of the two

university students who were sucking face. "You could run a bar where your boss doesn't take credit for your ideas."

"A smile from you is worth the stuff I have to put up with," Liss said, her gaze flicking to her phone, where another breaking news notification flashed up. She swiped it away without reading it as Greg grunted. It was probably about the royal wedding happening later in the year.

Steve, one of Liss's closest friends and the pub's deputy manager, was making the most of the late morning lull, reading a newspaper while occasionally glancing at Liss above it. "Liss won't leave us. She always says this place is her family."

He had a point. It had been like her family since her mum died.

"We all know why you stay, Steve, even though you spend too much time judging the people who drink here," Greg grumbled as he fed Joyce bits of sausage. "Especially when your middle-class parents with upper-class judgements visit."

"I don't know what you mean," Steve retorted with a huff. But he did. Liss and Isla had spoken to him about it before. He grumbled that he could work in any city job.

Liss stared at her phone, willing the guy she'd sent an underwear pic to respond as she rejoined the conversation. "Why do you stay he—"

"No phones while working," Steve mumbled, cutting off Liss.

Liss dropped her grubby cloth onto the bar and glared. "I'm well aware. I was the one who came up with the rule."

START YOUR ENGINES

"Who are you waiting to hear from?" Steve replied, dropping the paper and collecting glasses.

The one thing Liss refused to talk to Steve about was her dating life or, rather, lack thereof. He always got weird about it but never explained why. And besides, it was humiliating telling anyone that she'd messaged a sexy picture to a man she'd not yet met, and he hadn't replied. She tucked her phone in her pocket. "Oh, it's nothing—"

"3BC1! BBC1! Give me the remote, Liss!" Isla ran into the pub, saving Liss from the awkward conversation.

" sla, chill." Liss paused at the till, pushing back strands of her brown hair before surrendering to the frizz and tying it into a ponytail. The humidity wasn't helping the frizz, nor were the hoodie and jeans she'd thrown on that morning.

Isla dived onto the bar and fumbled for the remote they kept near the tills.

"Isla, no." Liss slapped Isla's hand away and popped the remote into the back pocket of her jeans. This pub was her kingdom; not even her best friend controlled the television. "You have no say on the channel the pub is watch ng."

Isla did a dramatic look behind her. "You're the only one of the five people here who cares."

"We're fifteen minutes from the lunch crowd coming in, and they'll want to watch horse racing," Liss countered, hands on the curve of her hips. "Tell me what's so important, and I'll consider changing the channel."

Isla huffed before throwing her arms in the air.

Liss stood on the step behind the bar she used when she needed to meet customers' stares, which was tricky at her five-foot height. She eyeballed her bestie.

"Liss has more attitude than the King's corgi," Greg said with a chuckle.

He was kind of right. If you put her in front of anyone but her friends and punters, she turned into her latest date, running for the door with no intention of returning. But in the bar, she controlled her anxiety.

"The King, the actual King, is doing a live broadcast in two minutes," Isla ranted.

"And that's important because?" Liss wiped the bar with the damp and oddly smelling cloth. Maybe she should consider moving on, but this was the only place she'd worked since dropping out of university five years ago. And her only skills were pulling pints and cleaning toilets.

Joyce walked around the bar and sniffed the spilt beer on Liss's dirty Doc Martens. Even the scents from her mango moisturiser and vanilla and strawberry shower gel weren't strong enough to overwhelm the beer smell. Liss's raised eyebrows were enough to send the pup back to its owner, though not before Liss sneaked her a biscuit from her pocket.

"This never happens." Isla's leg bounced.

Liss moved around the bar and started moving chairs to prepare for the lunchtime rush. Isla followed her around the pub.

"Kings don't do live broadcasts," Isla continued. "Every year, he makes a Christmas speech that's filmed weeks before and has a carefully managed script. He doesn't do anything like this because it's not allowed. My

media colleagues have messaged our networks for the last hour, and it's all over Instagram."

"So I'm asking again, why is this important?" Liss's voice echoed around the pub.

Steve collapsed into a chair and propped his feet up on a table, commentating, "The big fight resumes, Liss Granger in one corner and Isla Redding in the other."

Liss raised her eyebrow, and he dropped his feet to the floor.

"You don't have social media, so you don't get it. But this is massive. No one talks about the royals on social unless they're in court, doing something controversial, or getting married. The royal media team is streaming his announcement everywhere. This is epic. Please, Liss. I'll come to yours and do your washing up for a week," Isla begged.

The teenagers watched the action from their worn wooden chairs before resuming their kissing. Oh, to be that desperate for someone else that you didn't care about the shitty décor and bad furnishings. This pub needed work. If her mum were still around, she'd have helped Liss improve the place herself with little touches. But she wasn't and never would be again.

Liss shook her head and stepped closer to Isla, crossing her arms over her chest. "You don't do your own washing up."

"Fine. I'll cook for you for a week." This broadcast must have been significant. Isla's career, and climbing the ladder in the PR firm she'd joined out of university, were everything to her. Although they were best friends, they were painfully different. While Isla was conquering the PR world, Liss was still trying to find her purpose.

"A month," Steve called out.

REBECCA CHASE

"Shut up, you," Isla called back, swatting his presence away with her hand. "Please, Liss, I need to see this. It might help my career."

"And you can't watch it on your phone because…?" Liss stared at Isla, who was looking anywhere but at her.

Steve jumped in, "She's run out of data watching all those dodgy videos her Tinder dates send her."

"There's nothing dodgy about sexy videos, Steve. Stop being judgemental."

Liss winced. This wasn't the first time they'd had this argument. At least Isla was getting videos. No one sent Liss videos of what they'd want to do with her. But then again, she'd probably freak if they did. She had to focus on finding a good guy; that was what being around her lonely mum as a teenager had taught her.

"Fine." Liss switched to BBC1 and stood with Isla to get a good view of the television—anything to stop Steve and Isla from arguing. Isla hugged her tightly.

Her phone buzzed with a call as the announcer appeared. Surely, the guy she messaged wouldn't call. Still, she glanced at the phone screen with hope.

"I bet it's Nana Bets," Steve said, sidling up to Liss. Only Liss's two friends, work and her grandma called her, although her grandma only called when she wanted something. "Tell her I won employee of the month again."

Liss glared at him as she answered the phone. Hugo awarded Steve that honour every month. Hugo went to school with Steve's parents, although he denied that had anything to do with his choice.

"Hi, Nana. Is everything okay? I can't talk right now. The King is doing a live broadcast, and we're all watching," Liss whispered as Isla snatched the remote

START YOUR ENGINES

and increased the volume with exaggerated presses of the remote control.

"You can't watch that broadcast until you see me. Come outside," her grandma ordered. She had a lot of audacity for a woman who was usually swanning around the world visiting her former dancer friends. "I'm waiting in a Bentley."

"But—"

"No buts. Right now, Felicity," she snapped.

Liss winced before mumbling, "Everyone's so bloody demanding today. I don't like stressy people."

"And yet you're friends with us." Steve chuckled. His skin turned pink when she shot him a look.

Isla grabbed her hand giddily. Liss liked to see her pseudo family happy. They were the only family she had aside from her nana.

"Hello. I am sure this is a surprise for you all." The King stared into the camera, his chin raised in pride. There was that charisma the country loved.

"He looks a bit off. He should be wearing a tie," Steve mumbled.

Isla shushed him.

The way the King slouched slightly in a grey woolly jumper ticked the "break from protocol" boxes.

The King continued, "It's unprecedented for a monarch to speak to his country like this, and I realise you are all waiting to hear what I have to share. But first..."

"Felicity, you'd better not still be listening to the King. My only grandchild is usually so obedient when her poor grandma needs her," Nana Bets whined down the phone. Liss ground her teeth. Her nana's guilt-tripping tactics were legendary.

387

"Don't worry about the lunchtime rush," Greg said, understanding her reluctance. "Mr. Employee of the Month can cover it."

"I'm not doing toilets," Steve grumbled. Liss stared at the two of them. She always cleaned the toilets. Her job used to make her feel valued, but not recently.

Isla gasped. "The King is talking about abdicating in the future because he's unwell."

"And I have something further," the King continued. "I believed this would remain private my entire life, but I'm nearing death due to a complicated illness, and I must share something personal because it has implications for the country."

That one statement stopped the teenagers from kissing. They stared at the screen as people drifted through the doors, instantly drawn to the news.

"Felicity," her nana pressured.

"Fine," Liss grumbled, hanging up and sauntering around the bar, locating her bag and keys.

Liss tiptoed to the door, stalling to catch the King's announcement. Since Liss's mum died four years earlier, she always responded to her demanding grandma when she called, but Isla's enthusiasm about the announcement and her grandma's command she not watch it had piqued her curiosity.

Liss grabbed the edge of the door as the King said, "Nearly forty-five years ago, while I was a prince and learning about my country, I met a woman studying dance at a nearby college, and we fell in love. Our secret relationship was brief, but it broke my heart when I had to choose between her and the throne."

Everyone gawked at the television.

START YOUR ENGINES

"After lengthy discussions," he continued, "we agreed that royal life wasn't for her and that my calling took precedence for me. However, this week, I learned that she gave birth to my child after we split. Elizabeth Mead, the woman I once loved, later became Guinevere Granger."

Isla and Steve gasped in Liss's direction as she speed-dialled her grandma, still gawking in the direction of the King.

He slowly sipped water before continuing, although his voice remained gruff, and his eyes appeared glassy. "She was my sweet Bets."

"Nana, we really have to talk!" Liss shouted down the phone as she bolted through the door.

CHAPTER TWO

A black Bentley sat outside the pub on double yellow lines. It was a joke between Isla and Liss that her grandma had friends in high places, but the King's revelation thrust that into a new light. The spring sunshine glinted off the paintwork, straining Liss's eyes, but she made out the personal number plate that shouted luxury. It was totally out of place in her dog-eared neighbourhood.

One of the back passenger windows lowered, and her nana's pinched face popped out of it. Her make-up was immaculate, as always. The years spent performing in ballet shows enabled her to draw attention to her doll-like eyes and cute button nose. She'd tried to impart her make-up skills to Liss several times, but the information never stuck. The flawless make-up and coiffured hair were the last straw. Her grandma must have spent hours perfecting her look when she should have shared crucial information.

"You have so much explaining to do. What the actual hell, Nana?" Liss cried out.

Her grandma glared at her from the open window.

"We don't have time for one of your tantrums. Get in the car, Felicity," she snapped. Liss learned her brusque manners from her grandma, although she saved them for critical pub situations to avoid offending others.

START YOUR ENGINES

The passenger door flew open. Liss folded her arms with a humph to avoid stamping her foot. Her grandma always brought out the teenager in her. It was lucky they had so little to do with each other. Liss let her nana get away with her behaviour to keep her only family happy in case she was left with no one. The door wasn't closing anytime soon, and arguing with her grandma, who won every battle, was pointless, but Liss took her time climbing into the car.

She pushed up the sleeves of her hoodie as she sat in the backseat. "This is fu—"

Three pairs of eyes whipped her way.

"Get in the middle," her nana demanded with flaring nostrils. "Bear, get out and go around. I don't want to be sandwiched between you two."

The dark-haired stranger with big brown eyes and impressive broad shoulders grunted before getting out and walking around to her side. Liss barely resisted the temptation to touch his arms to check his body wasn't just padding as he climbed in beside her.

Nana Bets smoothed her classically tailored skirt, took a deep breath, and waved to an empty pavement as if she were the queen while the car pulled away from the curb.

Liss's blood boiled. "Who are these guys, and where the bloody hell did you get a Bentley?"

Bear's body pressed against hers. He widened his thighs, forcing hers to close. There wasn't enough space for his hulking body and certainly not enough to mansplay—the audacity of the guy.

Her grandma hissed, "Less attitude from you, young lady. I will explain all later, but for now, be quiet."

Nana Bets lifted her chin and waved again. She curved her hand and smiled demurely at strangers. Liss's phone buzzed with a message from Isla.

Isla: What is going on? Did Nana Bets fuck the King? That makes you a princess or something, right?

Liss: I've no idea. She won't tell me anything. I don't know where we're going, and I've got some hot-suited man next to me.

Isla: Tell me more. Which celeb does he look like?

Typical Isla. There wasn't enough space in the tiny car to hide the phone from him and her nana, but he wasn't paying attention to her anyway. She took a surreptitious look at him from beneath her lashes.

Liss: Maybe Tom Hardy, but when he was younger and without a full beard. He's kinda hot if you like that sort of thing.

Which Liss secretly did even though both her exes were like preppy perfection with button-down shirts and smart jeans. Bear's thighs widened further.

Isla: Would you fuck him?

Liss looked again. The stranger was more likely to feature in her unshareable fantasies than he was to get a right swipe from her. He stared straight ahead, oblivious to what she was typing.

> Liss: God, no. And he's a dickhead. He keeps mansplaying. He probably has a small dick, but he's trying to pretend he has a footlong.

"I'll take that." Bear snatched her phone. His voice was so low it thrummed through the car.

"The hell you will! Give me my phone back." Liss tried to grab it, but Bear slid it into his inside pocket. Had he seen what she'd typed?

"Nana," she implored, "tell the man with a stupid name to give me my phone."

"No, Felicity," her nana said sharply before resuming her wave.

Liss opened her mouth, but Nana silenced her with a pointy finger. Instead, Liss studied Bear with a glare. He was big, the sort of man that little guys wanted to fight to prove something. His suit fitted his body perfectly, gripping every muscle pressing against her. The tailored outfit that displayed a subtle nod to wealth highlighted his biceps and trunk-like thighs. Liss sensed he wasn't comfortable in it but couldn't put her finger on why.

"I want my phone back." She needed to keep Isla updated with her destination. She fixed him with a scowl, but he stared straight ahead. Adrenaline rushed through her limbs, and her fingers tingled. Although she'd never had a sibling, much to her disappointment, she'd learnt via Isla

and Steve how to annoy those close to you. "Are you a naturist, Bear? Is that why they call you Bear, Bear? Is it actually spelt B-A-R-E?"

But her digs hit his vast muscles and pinged off. She was still in fight-or-flight from the stress of the morning. Her nana's attitude and unanswered questions made her jittery, and she poked his thigh with her fingers. Her chipped blue nail varnish was bright against his dark suit. Each prod met resistance. Not only did he have thick muscles, but his mansplaying thighs were taut as if he was tensing. She swallowed the saliva building up in her mouth.

Liss gritted her teeth against a sigh. She was supposed to be getting to him and not vice versa. Was it his muscles, the deep voice that climbed into her body, or her existing annoyance? Damn Isla for making her consider if she'd fuck him. The attraction freaked her out. Her hands were clammy, for goodness sake. She sighed dramatically, making the wisps of her hair falling from her ponytail jump in the air. She'd always crushed on big men with strapping bodies that could throw a woman around a bedroom. Not that she'd experienced it herself, but it was on her fantasy list. Aches pulsed in her belly, and sweat beaded the back of her neck. The guy was pissing her off, and she wanted a reaction from him.

"Is the naturist thing why you're uncomfortable in a suit, Bear?"

Still nothing.

"So that's a yes then, Bear. Do you know where we're going? Give me my phone back, Bear." Every time she said his name, she overemphasised it. The B was like a poke.

Bear's only movement was widening his legs as if hinting at the package in his trousers while squishing her limbs tightly. With broad thighs and taut trousers, she

START YOUR ENGINES

couldn't stop staring, even as he disregarded her space. It turned out her message to Isla was wrong. He did look bigger than she'd suggested. But the size of his package was irrelevant. She shouldn't be attracted to this knobhead. She licked her lips and fisted her hands. Her body was intent on embarrassing her.

She side-eyed her nana, who was busy staring out the window while speaking on her mobile. In her faux upper-class accent, she was giddily telling someone called Sergio about the King's announcement. She was so involved in her conversation that she was unaware of the drama next to her. Why was she allowed her phone?

Liss needed to get her phone back and control her growing lust. If asked, she'd explain her next tactic was because, once, her mum told her after a detention, "You catch more flies with honey than vinegar." But in truth, Bear's widening thighs pressing against hers were doing things to her. She desired a reaction from him and couldn't stop herself.

"Look, Bear. Maybe we can come to a deal." She slid her hand down his thigh. His leg shuddered so subtly that she would have missed it if she hadn't touched it. Liss fought the temptation to squeeze it to get a bigger response. She was supposed to get her phone back, not seduce a stranger.

He cleared his throat, and there was a teeny twitch to his right eye as he picked up her hand and popped it back on her lap. His hand was hot and coarse, like she fantasised a night with him would be.

Liss leaned into his ear. He smelt of aftershave, something with notes of wood and citrus. She was tempted to breathe him in and imagine his scent on her skin after a night of decadence. Fuck. It was too long since she had sex. Maybe that was why she was acting so out of character.

"Okay, so I need my phone. I don't want my grandma to know why." Liss sneaked a look at her nana, but she was still engrossed in her phone call, cackling loudly.

"I'm listening," Bear grunted.

"The thing is, I sent this guy a picture of me in underwear an hour ago, and he hasn't replied," she confessed in a rush of words to the brooding stranger. She wasn't this confident with strangers, yet his impenetrable persona made her want to poke the bear.

"Does the photo include your face?" His voice was gruff, and it made her skin tingle. She added his voice to fantasies she didn't need to be embracing. Her throat dried at the idea of sharing the image with him.

"No," she replied quietly. "I never include my face, and I don't normally send underwear pics, but my potential date asked, and he's really hot, and he probably hasn't replied because—"

"I don't care how hot he is. I was asking for security reasons." He refused to make eye contact, as if she wasn't worth his attention. Seeds of anger threaded through her desire.

"Rude much?" Liss folded her arms and stared at a spot on the windscreen. Her skin heated, and she ran through everything she should say. Usually, with strangers and out of her comfort zone, she'd sink into the seat and hide away.

"And for the record," he whispered in her ear before slowly looking her up and down. Liss clenched her thighs under his inspection. "If he hasn't replied to an underwear picture within five minutes, he doesn't fancy you."

Again, she was reminded that he was too big for the back seat when the driver took a corner too quickly and his entire body pressed into hers. She avoided the need to release the moan tickling her tongue. Liss shifted, which

made his thigh slide against hers. She stilled suddenly, processing his words. How dare he suggest the guy didn't fancy her. But the statement gripped her fears about her Tinder match, who hadn't appeared as keen as she hoped and bruised her further. Bear had no right to say that to her. She hissed, "He's busy, and he's working—"

"I don't care what he's doing." Bear's voice was like thick, sweet honey, and his breath as he leaned in close made the hairs on her skin rise. "Once, my fuck buddy sent me a photo of her in a couple of dresses. They weren't fancy, but she wanted help to decide what to wear before seeing me. I excused myself from a meeting, feigning that it was an urgent work issue. Then I called her immediately and told her what I would do to her in my favourite of her dresses while she played with herself in the changing room. I only returned to my meeting when she came from my words. Her moaning climax made me hard as a rock. And I have a big rock."

Oh shit. He'd seen her messages to Isla.

His dick juddered as if remembering, and Liss fisted her hands, sinking her nails into her palms. The pain from her nails in her skin and the silver ring that dug into her flesh was almost satisfying. Anger and arousal blistered as she imagined his thick London accent telling her to touch him while he stroked between her thighs. Liss shifted awkwardly in her seat. *Don't let him in your head.*

Bear leaned in again, and his scent filled her once more. Her whole body quivered. Her fantasies were suddenly more vivid, filling with colour as she memorised every aspect of him. His full lips parted. "If your date hasn't replied by now, then bin him off, because he doesn't want you. And buy better underwear, because that must have been a shit photo for him not to respond even now."

397

Anger won, and she snapped back, "Fuck off. I looked great. I'll show you."

"No, thanks and you're not getting your phone back. Besides, the last thing I want is to see you like that."

Liss reared away from him, but there wasn't enough space. Her lips were tight, and her face burned.

"I've got to go, Sergio. My granddaughter is being a drama queen." She hung up the phone and handed it to Bear. "Stop wriggling, Felicity," her nana reprimanded, making the fire in Liss's cheeks from Bear's insult grow further. Her nana reached up to touch Liss's hair. "And do something about your hair. You look like you work in a pub."

Liss batted her hands away as her insides flamed. "I do work in a pub."

"Yes, but not as a cleaner."

Bear chuckled, and Liss glowered, but he smirked before mumbling something towards the window.

Liss rallied at Bear. "Is it 'have a go at Liss' day? And you still haven't answered my questions. I don't know where we're going or why you're talking to yourself, Mr. Meathead."

"We're here," the suited stranger in the front passenger seat announced. Camera flashes penetrated the windows from outside the car as they slid through a set of gates, and the driver spoke to someone from his open window.

"Where's h—" But she was cut off by the front passenger getting out and opening the door for her nana. Bear had said earlier that he needed her phone for security reasons, but she'd been too distracted by his body to ask what he meant.

Bear dived out his door before holding it for Liss. She huffed as she slid across the seat and climbed out. He